Blood Beast first published in hardback in Great Britain by
HarperCollins *Children's Books* 2007
Demon Apocalypse first published in hardback in Great Britain by
HarperCollins *Children's Books* 2007
Published together in this two-in-one edition in 2011
HarperCollins *Children's Books* is a division of HarperCollins*Publishers* Ltd,
77-85 Fulham Palace Road, Hammersmith, London W6 8JB

The HarperCollins website address is
www.harpercollins.co.uk

Darren Shan presides over the demon universe at
www.darrenshan.com

1

ISBN: 978-0-00-743644-6

Printed and bound in England by
Clays Ltd, St Ives plc

DARREN SHAN
THE DEMONATA VOL. 5 & 6

Blood Beast & Demon Apocalypse

HarperCollins *Children's Books*

CONTENTS

Blood Beast

PART ONE

LOCH

PART ONE

1968

DAMN THE SANDMAN

→My hands are red with blood. I'm running through a forest. Naked, but I don't care. I'm an animal, not a human. Animals don't need clothes.

Blood on my tongue too. Must have fed recently. Can't remember if it was a wild creature or a person. Not bothered much either way. Still hungry — that's all that matters. Need to find something new to chew. And soon.

I leap a fallen log. As I land, my bare feet hit twigs. They snap and I sink into a pool of mud. I collapse, howling. The twigs bite into me. I catch a glimpse of fiery red eyes peering up out of the mud. They aren't twigs — they're teeth! I lash out with my feet, screaming wordlessly...

... and mud and bits of bark fly everywhere. I stare at the mess suspiciously, my heart rate returning to normal. I was wrong. I haven't fallen victim to a monstrous baby with mouths in the palms of its hands and balls of fire where its eyes should be. It's just a muddy hole, covered with the remains of branches and leaves.

Scowling, I rise and wipe my feet clean on clumps of nearby grass. As I'm using my nails to pick off some splinters, a voice calls, "*Grubbs...*"

The name doesn't register immediately. Then I remember — that's *my* name. Or it used to be, once upon a time. I glance up warily, sniffing the air, but all I can smell is blood.

"*Grubitsch...*" the voice murmurs and I growl angrily. I hate my real name. Grubbs isn't great, but it's better than Grubitsch. Nobody ever called me that except Mum and my sister Gret.

"*You can't find me,*" the voice teases.

I roar into the darkness of the forest, then lurch at the bushes where I think the voice is coming from. I tear through them but there's nothing on the other side.

"*Wrong,*" the voice laughs, coming from a spot behind me.

I whirl and squint, but I can't see anyone.

"*Over here,*" the voice whispers. This time it's coming from my right.

Still squinting, I edge closer, towards the source of the voice. This feels wrong, like it's a trap. But I can't back away from it. I'm drawn on by curiosity, but also something else. It's a girl's voice and I think I know whose it is.

Movement to my left, just as I'm about to round a tree. Eight long, pale arms wave in the light of the moon. Dozens of tiny snakes hiss and slither. I cry out with fear and slam into the tree, shielding my eyes from the horror. Seconds pass but nothing attacks. Lowering my arms, I realise the arms were just branches of a couple of neighbouring trees. The snakes were vines, blowing in the wind.

I feel sick but I force a weak chuckle, then slide around the tree in search of the person who called to me.

I'm at the edge of a pond. I frown at it. I know this forest and there should be no pond here. But there it lies regardless, the full moon reflected in its still surface. I'm thirsty. The blood has dried on my tongue, leaving a nasty copper-like taste. I crouch to drink from the pond, going down on all fours and lowering my head to the water like a wolf.

I see my face in the mirror-like water before I drink. Blood everywhere, caked into my flesh and hair. My eyes widen and fill with fear. Not because of the blood, but because I can see the shadow of somebody behind me.

I start to turn, but it's too late. The girl pushes my head down hard and I go under. Water fills my mouth and I gag. I try to fight but the girl is strong. She holds me down and my lungs fill. The coppery taste is still there and I realise, as I blink with horrified fascination, that the pond is actually a pool of blood.

As my body goes limp, the girl pulls me up by my hair and laughs shrilly as I draw a hasty, terrified breath. "*You always were a useless coward, Grubitsch,*" she sneers.

"Gret?" I moan, staring up at the mocking smile of my sister. "I thought you were dead."

"*No,*" she croaks, eyes narrowing and snout lengthening. "*You are.*"

I weep as her face transforms into that of a mutant wolf. I want to run or hit her, but I can only sit and stare. Then, as the transformation ends, she opens her mouth wide and howls. Her head shoots forward. Her fangs fasten around my throat. She bites.

→I wake choking. I want to scream but in my imagination Gret's teeth are locked around my throat. I lash out at my dead sister, still half in the dream world. When my arm fails to connect, I rub at my eyes and my bedroom swims back into sight around me.

Groaning softly, I sit up and dangle my legs over the edge of the bed. Covering my face with my hands, I recall the worst parts of the dream, then shiver and get up to go to the toilet. No point trying to sleep again tonight. I know from past experience that the nightmares will be even worse if I do.

I pause in the doorway of the bathroom, suddenly certain that demons are lurking in the shadows. If I turn on the light, they'll attack. I know it's ridiculous, a ripple from the nightmare, but despite that my finger trembles in the air by the switch, refusing to press.

"The hell with it," I finally sigh, stepping forward. Letting my fear have its way on this night, as on so many others, I go about my business in the dark.

MISERY

→"Of course I have nightmares — who doesn't?"

"Every night?"

"No."

"Most nights?"

A pause. "No."

"But a lot?"

I shrug and look away. I'm in Mr Mauch's office. Misery Mauch — the school counsellor. He holds court a few times a week. Chats with students who are struggling with homework, peer pressure, pushy parents. Normal kids with normal problems.

And then there's me.

Misery *loves* sitting down for a warts'n'all session with *me*.

Why wouldn't he? Everyone here knows the Grubbs Grady story — parents and sister slaughtered in front of him... long months locked up in a nuthouse ("incarcerated in a facility for the temporarily disturbed," Misery puts it)... came to

Carcery Vale to live in a spooky old house with his uncle Dervish... that uncle lost his marbles soon after... Grubbs played nurse for a year until he recovered... went to a movie set with Dervish and his friend Bill-E Spleen months later... witnessed the tragic deaths of hundreds of people when a disastrous fire burnt the set to the ground.

With a history like that, I'm a dinosaur-sized bone for every psychiatric dog within a hundred kilometre radius!

"Would you like to tell me about your dreams, Grubitsch?" Misery asks.

"No."

"Are you sure?"

I feel like laughing but don't. Misery's harmless. It can't be much fun, trekking around his small cache of schools, dealing with the same boring teenage problems day after day, year after year. If I was in his shoes, I'd be itching to get my hands on a juicily messed-up student like me too.

"Grubitsch?" Misery prods after a few seconds of silence.

"Hmm?"

"Telling me about your dreams might help. A problem shared is a problem halved."

I almost respond with, "What's a cliché shared?" but again I hold my tongue. I'd ruin Misery's day if

I cut him down like that. Might reduce him to tears.

"They're not much of a problem, sir," I say instead, trying to wind the session down. I'm missing physics and I quite like that subject.

"Please, Grubitsch, call me William."

"Sorry, sir — I mean, William."

Misery smiles big, as if he's made a breakthrough. "The nightmares must be a problem if they're not going away," he presses gently. "If you told me, perhaps we could find a way to stop them."

"I don't think so," I respond, a bit sharper than I meant. He's talking about stuff which is way over his head. I don't mind a school counsellor showing interest in me but I dislike the way he's acting like a second-rate mind-sleuth, clumsily trying to draw out my secrets.

"I didn't mean to offend you, Grubitsch," Misery says quickly, realising he's overstepped the mark.

"To be honest, *sir*," I say stiffly, "I don't think you're qualified to discuss matters like this."

"No, no, of course not," Misery agrees, his features sorrowing up. "I don't want to pretend to be something I'm not. I apologise if I gave that impression. I only thought, if you were in the mood to talk, it might help. It might be a beginning. Of course it's not my... I'm under no illusion... as you say, I'm not qualified to..." He mutters to a halt.

"Don't have a breakdown," I laugh, feeling guilty. "It's no biggie. I just don't want to talk about my dreams to anyone. Not right now."

Misery gulps, nods briskly, then says I can go. Tells me he'll be back next week but won't ask to see me. He'll give me some breathing space. Maybe in a month or two he'll call me in again, to "shoot the breeze".

I hesitate at the door, not wanting to leave him on such a down note — his head's bowed over his notes and he looks like he's fighting back sniffles.

"Mr Mau– William." He looks up curiously. "Next time, if you want, you can call me Grubbs."

"*Grubbs?*" he repeats uncertainly.

"It's what my friends call me."

"Oh," he says and his face lights up like he's won the jackpot.

I slip out, masking a smile. School counsellors — child's play!

→Lunch. Loch wants to know what I was talking with Misery about.

"The size of your brain," I tell him. "We wondered how small it was."

"Don't worry about the size of *my* brain," Loch snorts. "My brain's fine. A lot healthier than your pea of a think-tank."

"How big *is* a brain?" Charlie asks. Everyone stares at him. "I mean, does it fill the whole of the head?" He starts poking his skull, searching for soft spots.

"In your case, I doubt it," Loch says. "You've probably got enough empty space in there to hold a football."

Laughter all round. Even Charlie laughs. He's used to being the butt of our jokes. He doesn't mind. They're always light-hearted. Everyone likes Charlie Rall. He's too nice to get vicious on.

Six of us, sheltering from rain in a doorway overlooking the football quad. The usual pack of barbarians are kicking the life out of a tired old ball — and each other — on the quad, oblivious to the rain.

My group — me, Loch, Charlie, Frank, Leon and Mary. Loch and I stand a head or more above any of the others. We're the biggest pair of lunks in our school, which is what drew us to each other in the first place. Loch's a wrestler. He wanted me to be his partner, so he became my friend. I held out for a long time — real wrestling's nothing like the stuff on TV, very calculated and unspectacular — but he eventually persuaded me to give it a go. I'm not much good, and don't get a real kick out of it, but to keep Loch happy I travel to a few meets every month and get down'n'sweaty on the mats.

"I think Misery's sexy in an older-man kind of way," Mary says to a chorus of astonished jeers and catcalls.

"You've got the hots for *Mauch?*" Leon gasps, faking a heart attack.

"No," Mary says coolly. "I just think he's sexy. I bet women are all over him outside school hours."

The laughter dies away and the five testosteronetastic guys in the group look at each other uncertainly. It's not something we'd admit to, but girls our age know a hell of a lot more about the adult world than we do. Adults operate differently. It's easy to tell the winners and losers in school, the cools and geeks. But the world beyond is puzzlesome. Professional sporstmen are obviously cool, as are actors, pop stars, etc. But what about normal guys? What makes an ordinary man attractive to a woman? I don't know. But if Misery Mauch has *it*, we could all be in trouble later on. By their frowns, I know the others are thinking exactly the same.

While we're trying to come to terms with a world where Misery Mauch is a sex god, Reni and Shannon stroll up, arms linked, laughing at some private joke.

"I was just telling the boys," Mary says, "how sexy Mr Mauch is."

"William?" Reni says, nodding thoughtfully. "He's a dish."

"*William?*" Loch barks at his sister.

"That's what he told me to call him."

"I didn't know you'd been going for counselling," Loch growls.

"There's a lot you don't know about me," Reni says sultrily, then raises an eyebrow at Shannon. "William Mauch — dull or dishy?"

"Deep-pan dishy," Shannon says seriously — then laughs. "I'm sorry! Your faces!"

"Swine," Leon snarls as the other girls squeal along with Shannon. "That wasn't funny."

"It was hilarious," Reni counters, crying with laughter. "You lot are so easy to wind up. Imagine Misery Mauch as eye-candy!" She laughs even harder.

"Here," I say, pulling out a handkerchief and handing it to Reni.

Reni smiles sweetly and dabs at her cheeks with the hankie. Four sets of lips immediately purse — wolf whistles galore.

"Grubbs and Reni sitting in a tree…" sings Frank.

"Get stuffed," I grunt and coolly retrieve my handkerchief from Reni — cue more whistles.

→Lunch flies by as it usually does. So much to talk about — friends, teachers, homework, TV, movies, computer games, music, wrestling, the size of brains. Robbie McCarthy joins us midway through. He's not a regular member of the gang but he's been cuddling up to Mary recently so he's had to spend time with the rest of us.

I joke around with Reni a lot. The handkerchief was especially for her. One of Dervish's. I use tissues, like everybody else who isn't living in the Middle Ages. I've been carrying it around for a week, waiting for a chance to present it to her. Corny, and done as a joke — but half serious too. A chance to share a smile and a sweet look.

Reni knows I fancy her. And I think she's hot for the Grubbster. But I've not had much experience in things like this. There's every chance I've read the signals wrong. I won't know for sure until I find the guts to put an arm around her and try for a kiss, but I think the odds are in my favour.

Loch's cool with it. I've seen how he is with other guys who put the moves on Reni — he puffs himself out to look even bigger than he already is and growls like a bear, scaring them away. If Reni was keen on any of them, she'd tell him to back off. But most of the time she lets him play the protective big brother and even encourages it.

It's important to have Loch's approval. He's my best friend. You don't try to date your best friend's sister without his permission. It just isn't done.

*　　*　　*

→Towards the end of lunch, a small, chubby boy with a lazy left eye shuffles over and I feel a stab of guilt, much stronger than the pang I felt in Misery Mauch's office.

"Hi Grubbs," Bill-E says, smiling hopefully.

"Hi," I grunt.

"Hey, Bill-E! How's my man?" Loch exclaims and sticks his hand out. Bill-E extends his own hand automatically, but Loch whips his away, puts his thumb on his nose, sticks his tongue out and wiggles his fingers. "Sucker!"

Bill-E flushes but manages a sick grin and lowers his hand sheepishly.

"Very mature," Reni says drily, rolling her eyes at her brother.

"The shrimp doesn't mind, do you, Spleen?" Loch chortles, grabbing Bill-E's head in a wrestling lock.

"No," Bill-E says, voice muffled. Loch releases Bill-E and ruffles his hair. Bill-E's still smiling but the smile's *very* strained and his face is fire engine red. "How you doing, Grubbs?"

"Not bad. You?"

"OK."

We smile awkwardly at each other. The rest of the group stare at us for a second. Then normal conversation resumes, only we're cut out of it.

"Doing anything this weekend?" Bill-E asks.

"Not a lot. Maybe practising some wrestling moves with Loch."

"Oh. I was thinking of coming over to watch some movies… if that's OK…"

"Hell, you don't have to ask." I laugh uneasily. "You can drop in any time you want. It's your house as much as mine."

"Coolio!" Bill-E's smile resumes its normal shape. "You want to watch a movie with me?"

"Maybe. But I might have to go over to Loch's and practise. You know."

"Yeah," Bill-E says quietly. "I know."

The bell rings and everyone files back to class. Hundreds of kids groaning, shouting, laughing. Bill-E heads off in his own direction. He doesn't say goodbye. I watch him walk alone and lonely in the crowd and I feel twisted and vile, like something a maggot would crawl out of its way to avoid.

Bill-E Spleen was my best friend before Loch Gossel hit the scene. When I moved here after my parents' death and my spell in the nuthouse, he made me feel like I wasn't all by myself in the world. He helped me establish a life again. Settled me in at school, kept me company during lunch when everybody else was wary of me. Fought by my side on the Slawter film set — and it wasn't fire we had to contend with. Tried to help when my nightmares kicked back in hard not long afterwards, even though his own mind was in turmoil.

How do I repay him? By abandoning him for the friendship of Loch, Reni and our little group. Cutting him loose. Being a Judas.

It's wrong but it's the way things go. When an old friend doesn't fit in with your new pals, you cut him loose. It's the law of school. I've dumped other friends in the past, and several have done it to me. The difference here is that Bill-E's my half-brother. Even though he doesn't know it.

→Chemistry. I usually find it interesting but this afternoon I can't concentrate. I keep thinking about Bill-E. I didn't mean to give him the big brush-off. When I first met Loch, I had time for Bill-E. I'd only see Loch occasionally after school. I still hung out with Bill-E a lot.

That gradually changed. Loch began inviting me round to his house and coming over to mine. Through Loch I became friends with Frank Martin, Charlie Rall and Leon Penn. And through them I got to know Shannon Campbell and Mary Hayes — and, of course, Reni.

Reni makes me forget about Bill-E for a few minutes. Daydreaming about her shoulder-length auburn hair, long eyelashes, light brown eyes, her curves... She's not perfect by any means – big and sturdy like her brother, with a ski-slope of a nose – but everybody thinks she's one of the hottest girls in our school.

I shake my head to stop thinking about Reni and my thoughts drift back to Bill-E. All those new friends made demands. It was exciting to be accepted by them, included in their conversation, treated as an equal. It had been a long time since I was part of a crowd. I hadn't realised how much that mattered to me or how much I'd missed it.

I wanted Bill-E to hang out with us but he just didn't fit in. I'm not sure why. He's younger than most of us – he started school a year early – but Leon isn't a lot older than him. He's small, but Frank's no giant either. He uses corny words like "Coolio!" but Robbie's favourite exclamation is the seriously uncool "Radical!" He has a lazy left eye, but Charlie has buck teeth, Shannon has an ugly facial mole, I'm built like the Hulk... We're all a bit odd, one way or another.

Bill-E is clever, funny, a much better talker than me. But he never found a niche at school. I didn't realise it when I first started. Bill-E seemed like the most normal kid around. I knew he didn't have a lot of friends but I was certain he fit in more than I did.

After a while I began to notice things. Like how Bill-E never went to anybody's house after school. How people made jokes about him and aped him when he said things like "Coolio!" How he was bullied by boys like Loch Gossel.

I'm not blind to how Loch treats Bill-E. He teases him all the time, like with the fake hand-shake and head-lock today. It's different to the way he treats Charlie. Nastier. He embarrasses Bill-E in front of others, makes him feel small and unwanted.

I often thought of challenging Loch and the others who pick on Bill-E. If any of them hurt him, I'd have definitely taken them on. But teasing is harder to deal with. You can't punch a guy for being sarcastic to somebody… can you?

I'd have worsened the situation if I'd interfered, made Bill-E look like a weakling who couldn't stand up for himself. Besides, it wasn't so bad. His life wasn't a walking misery. And he always had *me* to cheer him up.

Class ends. English next. I walk to it by myself, quiet, thoughtful.

I feel ashamed. I should go up to Bill-E this afternoon. Invite him back to my place. Free up the weekend to be with him. Watch movies, eat popcorn, go searching for Lord Sheftree's buried treasure. Like we used to.

But I won't. Instead I'll just suffer the guilt, wait for it to pass, then let things go on as they have been.

Lousy, yeah, but that's the way it is. Misery Mauch wouldn't understand if I tried to explain, but I'm sure anyone else in the school — or any school in the world — would.

NIGHTMARES

→"Of course I have nightmares — who doesn't?"

I brushed Misery off with that line, but it followed me home from school like a stray dog. I live a couple of miles outside Carcery Vale, in a massive old house three floors high, filled with antiques and mystical knick-knacks. It was once the property of a tyrant called Lord Sheftree, a charming chap who enjoyed chopping up babies into little pieces and feeding them to his pet piranha. But these days it belongs to my uncle, Dervish Grady — as rich as Lord Sheftree, much more powerful, but without any of the nasty habits.

Dervish is munching a sandwich in the kitchen when I get home. "Good day at school?" he asks, handing me half of the sandwich.

"So-so," I reply, taking a bite. Chicken and bacon. Yum!

Dervish looks much the same as when I first met him. Thin, tall, bald on top, grey around the sides. A tight grey beard which he shaved off a year or so ago but has grown back. Piercing blue eyes. Dressed all in denim. The only real difference is his expression. His face is more lined than it used to be, and he has the look of a man still recovering from a haunting. Which he is.

"Bill-E said he might come over this weekend," I tell him.

Dervish nods and goes on munching. He knows things aren't the same between Bill-E and me but he's never said anything. I guess he doesn't think there's any point — nothing he says could fix the situation. It's best for adults to keep out of things like this. It's widely accepted that we can't solve their problems, so I'll never understand why so many of them think they can solve ours.

I tell Dervish about my session with Misery. He's only mildly interested. "Mauch is a nice guy," he says, "but not much up top. If he gets too inquisitive, let me know and I'll have a word."

"It'll be a cold day in hell when I can't handle the likes of Misery Mauch myself," I snort.

"Oh Grubbs, you're so manly!" Dervish gushes, fluttering his eyelids.

"Get stuffed!" I grunt.

We laugh and finish our sandwich.

→ Of course I have nightmares — who doesn't?"

I can't get the damn line out of my head! All the way through homework, while watching TV, then listening to CDs and flicking through a wrestling magazine of Loch's.

Everyone has nightmares, sure, but I doubt if many have nightmares like mine. Delirious dreams of demons, wholesale slaughter, a universe of webs and comet-sized monsters. All based on first-hand experience.

I get to bed about 11:30, fairly normal for me, but sleep doesn't come easily. And when it does…

I'm in my bedroom at home — my first home. Blood seeps from the eyes of the football players in the posters on my walls, but that doesn't bother me. Gret walks in. She's been split in two down the back. Guts trail behind her. A demon with a dog's body but a crocodile's head is chewing on the entrails.

"Dad wants you," Gret says.

"Am I in trouble?" I ask.

"Not as much as me," she sighs.

Down the corridor to Mum and Dad's room. I've walked this a thousand times in my nightmares, always feeling the heat and fear. A few tears trickle down my cheeks as my hand rests on the doorknob, the way they always do. I know what I'm going to find inside — my parents, dead, and a wickedly smug Lord Loss. I don't want to open the door, but of course I do, and everything happens the way it did that night when my world first collapsed.

The scene shifts and I'm in the insane asylum. Arms bound, howling at the walls, seeing imaginary demons everywhere I look. Then one of the walls fades. It turns into a barrier of webs. Dervish picks his way through them. "I know demons are real," he says. "I can help you."

"Help me escape?" I sob.

"No." He holds up a mirror and I see that I've turned into a werewolf. "Help you die," he snarls and swings at my neck with an axe.

I kick the covers off and roll out of bed. I hit the floor hard and scramble a few metres across it, fleeing my axe-wielding uncle. Then my vision clears and I realise I'm awake. Groaning, I push myself to my feet and check my bedside clock. Nearly one in the morning. Looks like I won't be getting any decent sleep tonight either.

My T-shirt and boxers are soaked through with sweat. I change, pop to the bathroom, splash cold water over my face, then go on a wander of the mansion. I often stroll when I can't sleep, exploring the warren of corridors and rooms, safe here, knowing no harm can befall me. This house is protected by powerful spells.

Creeping through the old restored part of the mansion, feet cold from the stone floors, too lazy to go back and get my slippers. I find myself in the newer section, an eyesore which was tacked on to the original shell when it was uninhabitable. Dervish keeps talking about demolishing the extension but he hasn't got round to it yet.

I return to the ornate, overblown majesty of the older building and wind up in the hall of portraits, as I usually do on sleepless nights like this. Dozens of paintings and photographs, all of dead family members. Many are of young people, cut down long before their natural time — like my sister, Gret.

I study Gret's photo for ages, a lump in my throat, wishing for the millionth time that I could tell her how sorry I am that I wasn't there for her in her hour of need — her hour of lycanthropy.

It's the family curse. Lots of us turn into werewolves. It's been in the bloodline for more generations than anyone can remember. It strikes in adolescence. Loads of us hit twelve, thirteen… maybe even seventeen or eighteen… and *change*. Our bodies alter. We lose our minds. Become savage beasts who live to kill.

We're not werewolves like in the movies, who change when the moon is round then resume our normal forms. When the change hits, it's forever. The victim has a few months before the final fall, when he or she goes a bit nutso each full moon. But then the night of total change sweeps in and there's no way back after that. Except one. The way of Lord Loss and demons.

*   *   *

→Dervish's study. Playing chess against myself on the computer. The study's an enormous room, even by the mansion's grand standards. Unlike the other rooms in the old quarters it's carpeted, the walls covered with leather panels. There are two huge desks, several bookcases, a PC, laptop, typewriter. Swords, axes and other weapons hang from the walls. Dervish removed them when he was prone to sleep-walking and attacking me in his sleep, but he's safe as a baby now so the weapons are back. But he never replaced the five chess boards he once kept here, which is why I'm playing on the computer.

Gret was infected with the family curse. In an attempt to save her, Mum and Dad locked horns with a demon master called Lord Loss. Yeah, this isn't just a world of werewolves — demons also prowl the shadowy corridors of the night. The Demonata, to give them their full title.

Lord Loss is a horrible creature with lumpy, pale red flesh and a snake-filled hole where his heart should be. He's always bleeding from thousands of small cuts and cracks in his skin, and floats around instead of walking. He thrives on pain. Haunts sad, tortured humans, feeding on their misery. Nothing appeals to him more than a person in severe agony — except maybe a cracking game of chess.

My hand moves slowly on the mouse, directing black and white pieces on the screen. A powerful family magician discovered Lord Loss's passion for chess many decades ago. He established a contest wherein two relatives of an affected child could challenge the demon master to a chess match. If Lord Loss was defeated, he'd restore the child's natural form and lift the curse forever. But if he won…

My parents lost. Under Lord Loss's rules, both were killed, along with Gret. I would have died too, but I was able to call upon hidden magical powers and escape.

Months later, under Dervish's care, I learnt the truth about what happened, and that Bill-E was my secret half-brother. I also found out that Bill-E had fallen prey to the lycanthropic curse.

Dervish and I faced Lord Loss. It was the bravest, most terrifying thing I've ever done or hope to do. I managed to out-fox Lord Loss and turn his love of misery against him. He didn't take it lightly. Swore revenge on all three of us.

He almost exacted that revenge months later on the set of a movie called *Slawter*. A horror maestro was making a film about demons. Dervish, Bill-E and I were lured into a trap. Lord Loss set an army of demons loose on the cast and crew. Hundreds of people died horribly, but we managed to escape.

Bill-E was badly shaken by his run-in with demons. With Dervish's help he recovered and is back to his old self, pretty much. But there's a nervousness in his look these days — he's always watching the shadows for flickers of demons.

And me? Apart from the nightmares and sleepless nights, have I got over it? Am I living the good life, getting on with things, making my way in the world? Well, yes, I'm trying. But there are a couple of flies in the ointment of my life, threatening to mess everything up.

First, it'll be a few more years before I know for sure whether or not I carry the lycanthropic gene. There's a strong possibility I could turn into a werewolf.

If I do start to turn, I'm damned. Lord Loss won't intervene. He hates us with an inhuman passion. Nothing in either universe would tempt him to offer me the chance of salvation. Dervish hasn't said as much but we both know the score — if I fall under the spell of the moon and my body changes, an axe to the neck will be the only cure.

As for the second fly... Well, in a way that's even worse than the first.

Back in my bathroom, I splash more water over my face. Letting myself drip-dry, I study the water flowing down the drain. It spirals out of the sink in an anti-clockwise direction, under the control of gravity. I focus and stare hard at the water. An inner force grows at my prompting. The stream of water splutters, then starts to spiral downwards smoothly again — but in a *clockwise* direction.

I watch for a few seconds, then shake my head and break the spell. The flow of water returns to normal. I head back to bed, dejected and scared, to spend the rest of the night awake and miserable beneath the covers.

Magicians are rare. Only one or two are born every century, humans with the magical potential of demons, who can change the world with the flick of a wrist.

There are others called mages. They can perform magic when there's demonic energy in the air, but under everyday conditions they can only manage minor spells. Most mages are part of a group known as the Disciples — they fight demons and try to stop them crossing to our world.

As far as anyone knows, I'm neither a magician nor a mage. I have more magical ability than most people, and tapped into it when I faced Lord Loss and his familiars. But I'm not a true part of the world of magic.

That suits me fine. I don't want to become a demon-battling Disciple. I want to lead an ordinary life. The thought of brushing shoulders with Lord Loss or his kind again terrifies me. And as somebody who isn't naturally magical, there's no reason why I should get involved in any more demonic battles. I can sit on the sidelines with the rest of humanity, ignorant of the wars being fought between the forces of good and evil, free of the curse of magic and the responsibilities it brings.

At least that's what Dervish believes. That's how I'd *like* it to be.

But something changed in Slawter. I discovered a power within myself, and although I masked it from Dervish, it hasn't gone away. The magic is working its way out, keen to break free. It allows me to reverse the flow of water, lift great weights, move objects without touching them. I've awoken several times to find myself levitating above my bed.

I've fought the magic with desperate determination. And for the most part I've been successful. I hope that by focusing and fighting it every step of the way, I can work it out of my system and return to normal.

I'd like to talk with Dervish about it and seek his advice. But I'm afraid. Magic is his life. He's a Disciple first and foremost, dedicated to the task of keeping the world safe from demons. Dervish loves me, but I have no doubt that if he knew about my power he'd press me into learning more spells. He'd say the world needed me. He'd nag, lecture and plead. I'd resist, but my uncle can be extremely persuasive when he puts his mind to it. I'm certain he'd nudge me back into the world of magic… back into the world of demons.

So here I am. I want to be an average teenager whose only worries are puberty, acne, scoring with girls, impressing my friends and getting through school in one piece. But I'm forced to spend the better part of every day brooding about turning into a werewolf or becoming a whizz-kid wizard who has to fight evil, heartless demons.

"Of course I have nightmares…"

PREPARATIONS

→Dervish has to go away for a couple of days. "Meera's heading off for pastures distant, might not be back this way for several months, wants to say goodbye in style."

"'In style'?" I smirk. Meera Flame is one of Dervish's closest friends. Definitely his sexiest. She's hotter than a hot dog that's been cooked extra HOT! "Are you and Meera finally going to get it on?"

"Don't be ridiculous," Dervish snorts. "We're just friends. You know that."

"That's what you always *tell* me…" I tease.

"Well," Dervish huffs, "it's true. I've never made a pass at her and I don't intend to start now."

"Why not?" I ask, genuinely interested.

Dervish pulls a saintly expression. "Grubbs," he says softly. "Remember when I told you that your dad was Bill-E's dad too?"

"Yes…" Warily.

"What I didn't tell you was that your mother… well,

the woman you thought of as your mum only met your dad after you were born. Meera…" He stops.

I gawp at him, head pounding, limbs trembling. My world starts to explode.

Then I catch his grin.

"You son of a jackal!" I roar, swatting him around his balding head. "That wasn't funny."

"Oh, it so was," he laughs, wiping away tears.

Most of the time I get a kick out of Dervish's warped sense of humour. But there are other times when it really gets up my nose.

"Keep it up," I growl. "Maybe I'll tell Misery Mauch about you. I doubt if he'd see the funny side of a sick joke like that. Wouldn't surprise me if he took me out of your custody and put me some place where the people are halfway normal."

"If only," Dervish sighs, then squints at me. "I don't want to lay it on heavy, but I've something to say and I want you to pay attention."

"What now?" I ask with a sulky sneer. "Ma and Pa Spleen are my grandparents? Misery Mauch is your long-lost brother?"

"This house has been wrecked once already," Dervish says. "I don't want it destroyed again. Keep your freakish little friends under as much control as you can. A certain amount of wear-and-tear is unavoidable, I accept that, but they'll only run wild if you let them. Lay down the law and they won't cause too much damage. And for heaven's sake, don't let any of them into my study. Remember that it's guarded by spells, so if anyone wanders in there uninvited…"

"What are you babbling about?" I snap. I hate when he starts on a spiel without making it clear what the subject is.

Dervish frowns. "A bit slow today, aren't you?"

"*What?*" I roar impatiently.

"I'm going away." He raps my head with his knuckles. "You'll have the house to yourself." He raps it again. "It's the weekend."

He goes to rap my head a third time. I catch his hand in mid-air, my face lighting up with a smile as I finally get it. At the exact same moment we exclaim, me excitedly, Dervish sarcastically —

"*Paaarteeeeeee!*"

→"Strip poker," Frank says earnestly. "It's a must."

"Hey!" Loch barks. "My sister will be there."

"So we'll wait till she sneaks off with Grubbs, then… *ba-bumba!*"

Everybody laughs, even Loch.

"Have you told the girls yet?" Charlie asks.

"No. I wanted to discuss it with you lot first, get some ideas, like how many people to invite, should I have a theme, if–"

"*Theme?*" Loch snorts. "This isn't a fancy dress party, fool!"

"I wouldn't invite too many," Leon says, a worried look on his face. "I made that mistake once. Had just about the whole school back to my place while my parents were away skiing. I did what I could to clean up the next day but it was impossible."

"Yeah," Frank nods. "This is your first party. You don't want to blow it by taking on more than you can handle."

"Especially since there's so much opportunity for the future," Loch agrees. "That mansion could be highly valuable over the next few years. Loads of rooms – loads of *bed*rooms – and an uncle who knows the score… It's a goldmine. But we've got to tread carefully. If we trash the house now, Dervish might never leave you alone again."

The discussion continues. Everyone – Loch, Frank, Charlie, Leon and Robbie – chips in with their own ideas. Music, food, drink, the guest list… each is debated at great length. But the guest list is the one we keep coming back to, the topic that creates the most divisions.

"Two girls to each guy," Frank insists. "If not three."

"Nah," Robbie grunts. "Equal numbers or else they'll gang up on us."

"What do you care?" Leon challenges him. "You only have eyes for Mary."

Robbie winks. "A lot can happen at a party."

Out of the blue, Charlie shouts, "Jelly beans. You've got to have jelly beans. Plates of them everywhere."

"*You're* a bloody jelly bean!" Loch roars as we fall apart in tears of laughter.

"What are you hyenas splitting your sides about now?" Reni asks, appearing on the scene without warning, Shannon by her side.

"We're—" Charlie starts.

Loch elbows him and nods sharply at me — my party, my news.

"Dervish is away this weekend," I tell Reni, wishing my heart wouldn't throb so loudly — I'm sure she can hear it. "I'm having a party."

"Great," Reni smiles. "I hope we're invited?"

"Of course," I say miles too quickly. Then, aiming for cool, "But don't tell anyone. I want to keep it exclusive — just a select handful of my more discerning acquaintances."

"Nice," Reni says and strides away, sharing a giggle with Shannon.

"'More discerning acquaintances'," Leon mimics as the others poke me in the ribs and make cat-calls. "You're full of it sometimes, Grady."

→Word spreads quickly about the party. I've never been so popular, surrounded at the start and end of classes, pumped for details, besieged with requests for an invite. I think the location of the party is as much a draw as anything else. Everyone in the Vale knows about the spooky old mansion where I live but most have never been inside.

At lunch I'm faced with a steady stream of party-hungry teens, all in search of a golden ticket. I feel like a king, hearing petitions, flanked by my royal advisors (Loch and co). I play it icy at Loch's advice, saying numbers are limited, I can only invite a select few. I don't say an absolute no to anyone and promise to take all requests into consideration.

So I'm a poser. So sue me.

→Just before the bell rings for class, my last petitioner approaches. Bill-E. He's smiling awkwardly, even more so than usual. "Hi Grubbs."

"Hi."

"How's tricks, Spleenio?" Loch says, putting out his hand. I groan as Bill-E falls for the trick again, makes to shake and is humiliated when Loch whips his hand away. "Sucker!"

I don't wait for Bill-E or Loch to say anything else. "Have you heard about the party?" I ask quickly.

"Yeah," Bill-E says. "I know I was supposed to come over this weekend, but—"

"You're not going to back out, are you?" I cut him short. "C'mon, Bill-E, this is my first party. I need you there for moral support."

A rosy glow of happiness spreads outwards from the centre of the chubby boy's cheeks. "You want me to come?" he asks quietly, half-suspecting a cruel joke.

"Of course," I say firmly. "In fact, if you don't, the party's off."

"Now hold on a minute..." Loch begins, startled.

"I mean it," I silence him, eyes on Bill-E, trying to put right at least some of the wrong things between us.

"Well... I mean... I guess... OK," Bill-E grins. "Sure. Why not?"

"Great." I raise a warning finger. "But don't tell Ma and Pa Spleen it's a party or they'll never let you come."

"No sheet, Sherlock!" Bill-E laughs and heads off, much happier than I've seen him in a long while.

→Dervish is getting ready to leave. In his leathers, pulling the straps out of his helmet. His motorcycle's outside the front door, primed to go. "Is the party tonight or tomorrow?" he asks.

"Tomorrow. Too awkward for people to come tonight. Plus it gives me time to go shopping in the Vale in the morning."

"You know I'll be back early Sunday afternoon," he reminds me.

"I know."

"If I walk in and find pools of puke and mountains of rubbish..."

"You won't," I assure him. "There aren't many coming, and a few are sleeping over to help clean up in the morning. The only thing is, I'm not sure if I'll be able to do all the laundry before you return."

"That's fine," Dervish says, then raises an eyebrow. "Those staying over are all boys, I presume?"

"Of course."

"They'd better be. Because if I find out otherwise…"

"You won't."

"Good."

The pair of massive front doors are already open. Dervish walks out, breathing in fresh spring air. "It's supposed to be cold over the weekend," he says. "Don't leave the windows open or the house will be freezing."

"I have everything in hand," I tell him.

"I doubt it." He climbs on to his bike.

"Say hi to Meera from me."

"Sure."

"Give her a kiss from me too."

"Funny guy." Then without a goodbye he's off, tearing down the driveway, already approaching the speed limit — and he's only warming up. If everyone drove like my maniac of an uncle, the roads would be awash with blood.

→This isn't the first time Dervish has left me alone in the house, but it's the first time he's left me in total control. Before, the understanding was always that I was simply holding the fort. No parties. This time he's as good as said the house is mine for the next forty-odd hours, to do with as I wish.

It feels strange. I find myself thinking of everything that could go wrong — broken windows, smashed vases, someone stumbling into Dervish's study and turning into a frog. I half wish I could cancel. I've been to a couple of wild parties with Loch over the last few months and never worried about what we were doing, the mess we were making, what would happen to the kids who lived there when their parents returned. Now the shoe's on *my* foot, I realise what a risky undertaking it is. Maybe I should pull a sickie and call the whole thing off.

The phone rings. Loch. It's as if he's sensed my wavering mood and is intervening to sway me back into party mode. "Has Dervish gone?" he asks.

"Yes."

"Good. I didn't want to discuss it at school — too many ears — but what about booze? Yay or nay?"

"That might be a bit much," I mutter. "Things will probably be wild enough if everyone's sober."

"Yeah, it'll be wilder if everyone's drunk," Loch laughs, "but a lot more fun! I was thinking about all those bottles of wine in the cellar..."

"No way," I snap. "Most are expensive. *Very* expensive.

Nobody goes near the wine. That's a golden rule. If anyone breaks it, I'll kick you all out."

"Spoilsport," Loch grumbles. "Well, what about beer? I could ask one of my older cousins to get us a crate or two."

"I'd rather you didn't."

"You're not wimping out, are you?" he asks suspiciously.

"Well…" I start.

"Good," Loch says quickly. "Let's forget about the booze then. If anybody brings some, great. If not, we'll just muddle by sober. Fair enough?"

"Yeah," I say unhappily. "I guess."

"Great. See you in the morning. Oh, and I'll be bringing Reni, to help carry the bags. Is that OK?"

"Sure," I say, spirits lifting, instantly forgetting about my reservations. "That'll be… fine. Yeah. Whatever."

A short laugh, then Loch hangs up, leaving me to get on with the planning of the party.

→Loch, Reni and I make three runs to the village. Frank and Leon join us on the last run, when we realise we need more hands. It's brilliant spending so much time with Reni, walking beside her in and out of Carcery Vale, discussing the party, bands, politics… whatever she feels like talking about.

Loch offers to chip in with some money for the drinks and food, but I tell him it's OK. Dervish is rich — there's a family fortune knocking about which will one day be mine and Bill-E's — and he never begrudges me anything. He left a wad of cash for me in his study and told me to make good use of it.

Reni does a lot of the organising. I spent a couple of hours last night drawing up a list of everything we might need and was more than a little pleased with myself. She took one look at the list this morning, laughed and tore it up. "Is Jesus coming?" she asked.

"Uh… no," I replied, astonished.

"Then forget about the loaves and fishes miracle. What you had on that list wouldn't have got us through to nine o'clock. Now, fetch me a fresh pad and pen — this needs a woman's considered touch."

Much as I hate to admit it, she was right. Carrying the supplies back from Carcery Vale, it feels like we've bought far too much — we could feed the starving millions with this lot. But by the time we've divided it out into plates and bowls, and distributed them around the three main party rooms — two big living rooms and the kitchen — there doesn't look to be a whole load.

"Maybe we need to make another run," Frank muses, opening a bag of crisps.

"Maybe you need to stop snacking before anyone arrives," Reni retorts, grabbing the bag from him. "No," she says, casting a professional eye around. "This will do. Any more would be a waste." She checks her watch. "I'm going home to get ready. And you boys…" She wrinkles her nose and pulls a face. "Ever heard of showers?"

She leaves. I look around at Loch, Frank and Leon. They stare back. Then we all raise an arm and sniff.

PARTY ANIMAL

→The party's not set to start until seven, but the first guests begin arriving soon after six. I'm nervous and twitchy, worrying about where their coats should go, if there's enough food and drink, if anyone's smuggled in anything they shouldn't have. But as more arrive and the laughter and buzz of voices increase, I begin to relax as I realise people are having fun.

Not everyone who comes was on the invitation list, but there's nothing I can do about that. If I turned them away, I'd sour the atmosphere. A few blow-ins have to expected at any party.

Loch and Frank help (Leon can't make it until nine), opening the front doors and greeting newcomers while I'm showing others around the mansion. It's cool to be a guide to so many fascinated guests. I love leading them through the corridors, pointing out weapons on the walls, explaining the house's bloody history, showing them the hall of portraits and the faces of the dead.

"How come there are so many young people?" Mary asks, studying the paintings and photos.

"We're an adventuresome lot," I lie. "We don't sit around quietly, waiting to grow old. We embrace life and danger, and as a result a lot of us die young."

"They leave good looking corpses though," Reni says and giggles sweetly when I blush.

→Bill-E arrives at a quarter to eight. I'm coming down the stairs when he enters, admitted by Loch.

"Hey, Bill-E, great to see you, glad you could come," Loch enthuses, offering his hand, which Bill-E predictably – and, I must admit, amusingly – tries to shake. "Sucker!"

But even Loch's teasing can't spoil the mood. Bill-E breezes past him, feathers only mildly ruffled, and makes for the nearest pile of food. Ten minutes of solid munching later, he's by my side, marching after me as I lead the latest group on a tour. By midway he's taken over — he knows much more about the house and its legends than I do and is better at telling the stories. I don't mind. It's nice to see him come out of his shell. I wish he was like this all the time.

→As the night lengthens I start to feel strange. Nauseous, dizzy, the rooms and people around me appearing oddly out of focus. My breath is heavy in my ears and my stomach and chest ache if I move quickly. It's not alcohol – nobody brought booze – but maybe somebody spiked the soft drinks with a spoon of nasty powder or a pill.

"Are you OK?" Reni asks, spotting me staggering towards the kitchen.

"A bit… weird…" I gasp, having to sit on the floor a couple of metres shy of the kitchen door.

Reni squats beside me. "You don't look good," she says and feels my forehead. "You haven't been drinking, have you?" I shake my head. "Drugs?" Her voice is hard.

"Not… that I know… about," I wheeze. "I was going… to the kitchen… to check. Think somebody… might have spiked… the drinks."

"They'd better bloody not," Reni growls, surging to her feet. "I'll have them arrested if they have! You wait here." She storms off to investigate. Five or ten minutes later – hard to keep track of time, my head's throbbing so much – she returns, calmer. "Everyone else is fine. I don't think the drinks have been tampered with."

"Maybe I'm just sick," I mutter.

"That's what it looks like," she says, then grabs my arms and hauls me to my feet. "Let's get you outside. Fresh air will do you a world of good."

She steers me through the kitchen and out the back door, then props me against the wall and stands watch beside me as I take deep breaths and try to focus. After a few minutes my head clears a little and my stomach settles.

"Better?" Reni asks, tilting my chin up, examining my eyes.

"Good as new," I smile.

Reni leans towards me, a serious look in her eyes. I tense. Will this be our first kiss? I hope I don't mess up. How do they do it in the movies — tongue or just lips? But at the last moment her expression crinkles and she kisses me quickly on the nose instead of the mouth.

"Come on, Romeo," she laughs, taking my hands. "It's too cold out here for monkey business."

"What about inside?" I murmur, smiling at myself for getting the line out without stammering.

"Maybe later," Reni grins and heads back in. I follow in high spirits, feeling much better than I did a few minutes ago. It's only when we reach the kitchen door that I stop and feel a stab of real panic.

The light's been switched off inside the kitchen. I can see the reflection of the sky in the dark glass of the door. Letting go of Reni's hand, turning slowly, I look up at the cloudless heavens and fix my sight on the moon — which is round and fat, dangerously near to full.

→Locked inside Dervish's study. Breath coming quickly, raggedly. Trembling wildly. Remembering the night Bill-E changed, the beast he became. Dervish had to cage him up to protect people from him. He would have killed otherwise.

Am I turning into a werewolf?

I don't know. The sickness and dizziness are still there, but they might be more a product of fear than anything else. Maybe it's just worry that's turned me white as a ghost and left me ready to throw up, shaking like a human maraca.

I focus on my hands, willing them steady. After a while they obey me. Then I force myself to breathe normally, evenly. When I feel like I'm in control, I study my reflection in a small hand mirror, looking for telltale signs around the eyes and lips — that's where the marks show first.

Nothing. The same lines and creases. Eyes a bit wilder than normal – which is understandable – but mine. Not clouded over or animalistic.

I wish Dervish was here. I consider calling his mobile. He isn't that far away. The speed he drives, he could be here in a couple of hours. I dig my phone out of my pocket, scroll down to his number, start to bring my thumb down over the dial button… then stop.

"I'm not turning," I grunt, angry at myself for being so scared. "It's after ten." I check my watch. "Hell, nearly eleven. The moon's at the height of its powers. If I was going to change, it would have happened by now."

But maybe it's the start, a voice within me whispers, a voice I last heard in Slawter many months earlier — the voice of magic. *Nobody changes overnight. It's a gradual process, spread out over a few months. This could be the beginning of the end.*

"Maybe," I agree, refusing to panic. "But I'm not going to turn savage tonight. Nobody has anything to fear from me. So there's no point dragging Dervish back."

But if it's the change… If your time as a human is limited…

"All the more reason to party hard while I can," I laugh viciously, then make myself go downstairs, smile and act like everybody else — normal.

→Midnight comes and goes. So do most of the guests, walking or cycling home, a few collected by their parents. By half past, only those who are sleeping over remain — Loch, Frank, Leon, Charlie, Robbie, Bill-E, Reni, Mary and a few others who've begged a bed for the night. (OK, I lied to Dervish about only boys staying, but what he doesn't know can't hurt him, right?)

"Do you want me to show you where you'll be sleeping?" I ask, eager to wind the party down, still feeling sick.

"The hell with sleep," Frank laughs. "Time for spin-the-bottle!"

While there are good-natured groans, nobody objects, so five minutes later we're all in the largest of the party rooms, sitting in a nervous circle around an empty bottle. Lots of giggles, nervous looks, licking of lips. I do a quick head count — nine boys, four girls.

"How are we going to work this?" I ask Frank.

"We each take a turn spinning," he says, rubbing his hands together eagerly. "When it points to a member of the opposite sex — *hoobah!*"

"But there's more of us than them," I object.

"So?" he frowns.

"Well... I mean... at least two of them are going to have to kiss more than one guy." Worried about Reni kissing anyone other than me.

Frank laughs. "That's how it works, moron. We all get plenty of action."

"Only simple kisses," Mary interjects. "No groping or tongues, not unless both want to. Clear?"

"Of course, of course!" Frank says quickly, leering.

"We mean it," Reni says. "If one of you breaks the rules, that's it, end of game, you all miss out."

"OK," Frank sighs, rolling his eyes. "We get the message. Now, who first?"

"It's Grubbs's party," Loch says.

"That's OK," I cough, getting cold feet. "I think Bill-E should have first shot."

"I second the motion," Bill-E laughs, more at ease than I've seen him in a long time. He grabs the bottle and spins it madly. It turns… turns… turns… like it's never going to stop. But finally it does — and it's pointing at Reni.

Bill-E grins. "Sorry, amigo, but the bottle decides."

I feel my temper rise as Bill-E and Reni meet in the middle of the circle to a series of whistles and crude remarks. The bile that's been threatening to bubble over all night forces its way up my throat. But then Reni pecks him on the lips and they both sit down. I relax, swallow the vomit and grin greenly.

The game continues. Great laughs when one of the boys spins and it ends up pointing to another boy. Lewd giggles when that happens to the girls. Most of the kisses are like the first, quick pecks. But a few are stronger, where the pair are attracted to each other — Robbie and Mary, Leon and Nina Duffy.

I get to kiss Mary twice, Nina three times ("This is getting serious," she says jokingly), before Reni finally spins and the bottle ends up pointing at me.

"Whoo-hoo!" Frank chortles.

"Touchdown!" Charlie cries.

"Easy, tiger," Loch grunts, smiling tightly.

Reni and I stand and walk towards each other. Reni nudges the bottle out of the way with her left foot. We smile shakily. Then kiss.

Her lips are drier than I thought they'd be, but nice. My hands slide around her back and I lock my fingers together, careful not to hug too hard in case I crack her ribs. The kiss continues. Her lips move and mine follow — this is easier than I imagined. I don't know why I was so nervous before. I could get used to this very quickly!

Lots of cheers and whistles. I drown them out, eyes closed, feeling so happy I could burst. A warm fire grows within me, burning away the feeling of sickness, spreading rapidly through my body, squeezing out of my pores like steam. I lose myself in the hot, hypnotic kiss, unaware of anything else.

Then gasps of amazement wreck the moment.

"What the–?"

"How the hell–?"

"Oh my god!"

My right eye opens an angry fraction — what's everybody getting so worked up about? Then I spot it. The bottle, spinning again, but not on the ground — about a metre above the floor, suspended in mid-air, floating upwards as it spins.

The bottle rises smoothly. Everyone (with a single exception) is on their feet, backing away, alarmed. Reni realises something's wrong. She breaks off the kiss, takes a step back, sees the bottle. Her expression freezes.

Bill-E's the only one not moving. He's staring at the bottle intently. I think for a second that he's controlling it, using one of Dervish's spells. I huff myself up to roar at him. But then I catch the alarm in his eyes and realise he's trying to stop it. *I'm* the one making it rise.

The bottle reaches a point about half a metre above my head, then levels out. It's spinning faster than ever, making a small whirring sound.

"What's happening?" Robbie shouts. "Grubbs, are you doing this?"

I don't answer. My gaze is on the bottle. Although it's spinning too quickly for the eye to follow, I find that I can slow the action down. The world seems to go into slow-motion around me. People's mouths move infinitely slowly. Words reach me as though dragged through a pipe from a long way away.

"Grrruuuubbbsssss! Whaaaaattttt'sss… gooooiiiinnngggg oooonnnn?"

The bottle explodes and the world speeds up again. Shards of glass shoot at me, Reni, everybody in the room, at our faces and eyes. Instinctively I bark a word of magic. I don't know what the word is or where it comes from. But it freezes the shards in place. They hang in mid-air, dozens of tiny pieces of glass, pointing at us like a flight of mini arrows.

"No way!" somebody shouts, more excited than afraid. My friends start lowering the hands which they'd instinctively raised to protect themselves.

Bill-E stares at the bits of glass — then at me. His eyebrows are furrowed. He knows this is magic but he can't understand how I'm doing it. He saw me do more than this in Slawter, but that enclosed area was crackling with magical energy. Many of us could perform amazing feats there. In the real, normal world, he thought – like Dervish – that I had all the magical ability of a duck.

"Grubbs," Reni says uncertainly, touching my right elbow. "Are you OK?"

"Yes," I whisper.

"Do you know what's happening?" Scared, looking for reassurance, gazing at the shard nearest her face, worried it might shoot forward again.

"Yes," I smile. Without knowing how I'm doing any of this, I wave a hand at the glass and several pieces turn into flower petals, which drop slowly, beautifully to the floor. I wave my other hand and more shards turns into butterflies. They flap away, zoning in on the light overhead. One last wave and the rest of the glass is transformed, a mixture of butterflies and flowers.

I grab one of the falling petals and present it to Reni. "For you, my lady."

Then everybody's cheering, clapping my back, grabbing for petals and butterflies, demanding to know how the trick was performed.

Only Bill-E knows there was no trick. Only he realises this was real magic. And only he can possibly understand and share in my sense of bewilderment and gut-stabbing fear.

→Later. Everyone but Bill-E and me has gone to bed. I'm at the door of my room, still holding a petal. Bill-E's facing me, eyes steady and serious. "How'd you do it?"

"Dervish has been teaching me."

Bill-E shakes his head. "Bull. Dervish told me you don't want to learn magic. He's cool with that. But even if he *was* teaching you, that's way beyond anything I've ever seen him do. Apart from in Slawter." He looks around nervously. "Are demons breaking through? Did you tap into their power?"

"No. We're safe here. Demons can't cross in Carcery Vale."

"Then how did you do it?" he presses. "Where did the magic come from?"

I shake my head miserably. "Forget about it. This doesn't concern you."

"I might be able to help if I—"

"I told you it's none of your business!" Bill-E looks hurt and I feel sorry immediately. "It's no big deal," I lie. "This has been building up for a long time. I haven't spoken with Dervish about it, but after tonight I guess I'll have to."

"This isn't the first time it happened?" Bill-E asks.

"There have been signs but nothing this obvious."

"Do you think…" He can hardly bring himself to say it. "Do you think you might be a magician?"

"No. Dervish would know if I was. But maybe I've got more potential than we thought. I might be a latent mage. If so, Dervish will know what to do."

Bill-E nods, starts to leave, looks back. "You won't be able to turn away from it any more," he says softly. "Magic, I mean. You'll have to learn now, so you can control it. If you hadn't been able to stop that glass tonight… if you hadn't turned it into butterflies and flowers…"

"I know," I sigh.

"You'll really tell Dervish? You won't try to keep it a secret?"

"I'll tell him. I'm not a fool. I know what magic can do if it isn't properly channelled. I don't want to hurt anyone."

Bill-E smiles, says goodnight and leaves.

I slip into my bedroom, lie on top of the covers fully clothed and stare at the ceiling, listening to my heart pound and my blood swoosh through my body, trying to make sense of whatever the hell is happening inside me.

→Later. Slowly coming awake. Sluggishly realising I must have fallen asleep on top of the bed. Then I click to the fact I'm not on the bed any more. I'm standing by

69

the round stained-glass window in my bedroom, listening to howls outside. No, not outside — in here!

My head whips round in panic. Fully awake now. I can't see anything in the room but I can hear the howls of a werewolf! Where is it? It must be close. It's so loud. Where...?

With a jolt, I realise he's in the glass in front of me. At least, his reflection is.

My face is darker than earlier. A wicked glint to my eyes. Lips pulled back over my teeth. Raising a hand, I see that my fingers are curling inwards, claw-like. I start to howl again, stepping into the coloured rays of the moon.

I stop. Focusing on my reflection, I feel the same warmth that I felt when I was kissing Reni, just before the bottle started to rise. I study my face, the sharp lines, the wild eyes. Directing the warmth towards it, I wish the mask away, wanting my normal face back, telling this vision of a man-wolf to go.

And it does. Even though it shouldn't, my skin resumes its ordinary shape and colour. My lips droop back down over my teeth. My fingers unclench. The howl dies in my throat and becomes a dry cough.

Moments later I'm me again, standing by the window, bathed by the tinted light of a moon which for some reason is no longer affecting me. The warmth is still there. I hold on to it like a security blanket, take it to bed with me and sustain it, keeping it alive through the rest of the long, weary night, too terrified to close my eyes, afraid of what I might turn into if I drop my guard and give myself over to unprotected sleep.

TREASURE HUNT

→I sneak a few hours of shut-eye post-dawn, when the sun's chased the moon off and I'm safe. But it's an uneasy sleep, filled with nightmares of werewolves and a body in revolt. I imagine myself doing awful things, causing chaos. Only it's not entirely me. It's a beast with my shape and form, but with a twisted face, fangs instead of teeth, claws instead of nails, blood-soaked hair.

Grubbs Grady — monster extraordinaire.

→When I stumble down the stairs a little after noon, most of the cleaning has been taken care of. Loch tells me Reni had them all up at ten and working like demons. (His choice of phrase is unfortunate.) She had to leave at eleven but left him in charge to make sure nobody slacked off.

"That was some trick you pulled," Leon says, sweeping up petals from the living room floor. "I'd love to know how you did it."

"It was magic," Charlie says, shooing a butterfly out through an open window.

"A magic trick," Leon corrects him.

"No, real magic," Charlie insists. "It was, wasn't it, Grubbs? I've seen the books lying around, about wizards, witches and wotnots. It was real magic, right?"

"No." I force a thin smile. "Just a trick. There's no such thing as real magic."

"But the books—" Charlie exclaims.

"—are just books," I finish tiredly, then go see what state the kitchen's in.

As I'm leaving, I hear Leon mutter, "Magic! You're a real ass sometimes."

"I don't care what he says," Charlie sulks. "I know what I saw. It *was* real magic. I'd bet a million jelly beans on it."

→When everything's as clean as we can get it, my friends say goodbye and make their way home to recover before school on Monday. Bill-E and Loch stay on — they've arranged to spend the day here. Bill-E waits till Loch's in the toilet, then asks how I'm feeling.

"Fine," I lie as my brain throbs with a splitting headache and my stomach gives a sickly rumble.

"I heard howling last night," Bill-E says. "After we'd gone to bed. It woke me. A few others too. There was some talk of it this morning but not much — most people were still trying to figure out how you pulled off the trick with the bottle."

I grunt, saying nothing.

"Grubbs," Bill-E says hesitantly, "I know we've never discussed the family curse. You filled me in on the basics in Slawter, but you've never offered more information and I haven't pushed."

For a long time Bill-E thought Dervish was the one who'd almost changed into a werewolf. I finally told him the truth in Slawter, neglecting only the part about Dervish being his uncle, not his father. I've never told Bill-E that we share the same dad. I want to, but he feels a special bond with Dervish, believing him to be his real father. I've never had the heart to shatter his illusion.

"Well," Bill-E continues after an uncomfortable pause, "I know I almost turned into a werewolf and that you and Dervish saved me. You faced Lord Loss and won back my humanity. But is the cure definitely permanent?"

"Yes."

"I'm safe? For certain?"

"One hundred per cent," I smile.

"What about…?" He hesitates again. "Your magic… the howling… Are *you* safe too?"

I don't answer for a second. Then, quietly, I lie. "Yes."

"I won't have to lock you up in the cage in the secret cellar?"

"No," I laugh edgily. I hate that cellar. I've only been there once since we defeated Lord Loss, when Dervish's nightmares were threatening to destroy his sanity. "I'm fine. That wasn't me howling. Probably just a big dog that got loose. Now stop worrying — you're getting on my nerves."

Loch returns, wiping his hands dry on his trousers, and the questions stop, though I sense Bill-E doesn't fully believe me. He knows something's wrong, that I'm not coming clean. But he doesn't suspect the worst or anything near it. He trusts me. Thinks of me as his closest friend. Doesn't believe I'd lie point-blank to him about something this serious.

How little he knows.

→A long, anticlimactic Sunday. Lounging around the house, all three of us bored, flicking through TV channels in search of something decent to watch, sticking CDs on, turning them off just a few tracks in. Loch makes cutting remarks about Bill-E, winding him up. I worry about lycanthropy and magic.

"This is crap," Loch mutters, switching the TV and CD player to stand-by. He jumps up and rubs his hands together. "Let's wrestle."

"I'm not in the mood."

"C'mon!" he prods, slapping my face lightly, trying to sting me into action.

"No," I yawn.

Loch scowls, then switches his attention to Bill-E. "How about you, Spleenio?" He grabs the shorter boy by the waist and swings him round.

"Let go!" Bill-E shouts, kicking out.

"We've got a live one," Loch laughs. He throws Bill-E to the ground, then falls on him and starts to tickle.

"No!" Bill-E gasps, face red, slapping at Loch like a girl, half-laughing from the tickling, half-crying.

"Leave him alone," I mutter angrily — the noise is worsening my headache.

Loch stops and stands. "Sorry, Bill-E," he says. "Let me help you up." He lowers his right hand. Bill-E reaches for it and Loch whips the hand away. "You're the sultan of suckers, Spleen," he chortles, strolling towards the kitchen, shaking his head with amused disgust.

Bill-E glares daggers at Loch, then at me. "Gossel's scum," he hisses. "I don't care if he is your new best friend. He's the scum of the earth. Shame on you for hanging out with him."

"Don't take it out on me," I snap. "You want to get Loch off your back? Then face him like a man, not a little girl. He bullies you because you let him."

"No, he bullies me because he's a bully," Bill-E retorts, furious tears in his eyes.

I shrug, too exhausted and sore-headed to argue. "Whatever."

Loch returns and Bill-E shuts up, but he glowers like an old man whose pipe's been stolen, then storms off and returns with his coat.

"Going home?" I ask as he buttons it up.

"No," he snarls. "I'm doing what I originally planned to do."

"Huh?"

"You remember. My original plan. If there hadn't been a party." I stare at him blankly and he nods in the direction of the forest.

"Oh," I chuckle. "Lord Sheftree."

"What's that?" Loch asks.

"Nothing," Bill-E says quickly, shooting me a warning look which I ignore, still sore at him for having a go at me. (And sore at myself too, for not being the friend — the brother — he deserves.)

"You know the stories of Lord Sheftree, the guy who used to own this place?" I ask Loch.

"The baby and the piranha, yeah, sure."

"Grubbs…" Bill-E growls, not wanting to share our secret with an outsider.

"There's a legend about his treasure." I take grim satisfaction from Bill-E's enraged expression.

"Treasure?" Loch echoes, interest piqued.

"Apparently he had hoards of gold and jewels which nobody ever found. They say he buried it somewhere around here. That it's still sitting there, underground, waiting…"

Loch squints at me, then at Bill-E. "This true, Spleenio?"

"Get stuffed."

Loch's face stiffens. "I asked if it was true," he says, taking a menacing step forward.

"Yeah, maybe, so what?" Bill-E squeaks, shrinking away from Loch.

"Any idea where the treasure is?" Loch asks.

"Up your butt," I chip in, and both Loch and Bill-E laugh, the tension vanishing in an instant.

"Nah, come on, really," Loch says, facing me again. "Is this on the level or is Spleen-boy paying me back for all those false handshakes?"

"The legend's real," I tell him. "I don't know about the treasure. We've been all over the forest, dug more holes than a pair of rabbits and found nothing. Right, Bill-E?"

"Yeah," Bill-E sighs, resigning himself to sharing our secret with Loch. "But you bury treasure because you want it to be hard to find. There wouldn't have been much point in Lord Sheftree sticking it where any passer-by could find it. It's out there, I'm sure, and one day, if we keep trying..." He trails off into silence, eyes distant.

"I thought you were rich anyway," Loch says to me. "Why are you bothered about a pile of buried treasure?"

"I'm not. But it would be exciting if it did exist and we found it. Bill-E and I used to spend a lot of our weekends searching for it. Even though we never found anything, the searching was fun."

"You've given up?" Loch asks.

I shrug. "Bill-E goes looking every so often, but it's been a while since I bothered."

"He's been too busy wrestling with lunk-heads," Bill-E says sourly, but Loch lets the remark pass.

"I've never searched for treasure," Loch says. "How do you do it — with a metal detector?"

"No," Bill-E says. "We walk around with shovels looking for likely spots. Then we make trial holes. If nothing turns up, we fill in the holes and move on."

"Sounds amateurish," Loch says dubiously.

Bill-E laughs. "Like *Grubitsch* said, the searching is fun. You'd need proper, expensive equipment to go after it seriously. For us it's always been a game."

"What about it?" Loch asks, casting an eye at me.

"You want to go on a treasure hunt?" I groan, wishing I could just go back to bed for a few hours.

"It'd beat sitting around here doing nothing," Loch says.

"But it's raining," I protest.

"A light drizzle. It'll clear soon. C'mon, it's something different."

"Not for Bill-E and me."

"But it is for *me*," Loch presses.

"Why don't you and Bill-E go by yourselves?" I suggest.

"No way!" they both exclaim at the same time, then share a look and laugh, temporary (*very* temporary!) allies.

"I'll let him tag along if you come," Bill-E says. "Otherwise I'll go home. I still have some homework to finish."

"C'mon," Loch huffs again. "Don't be a bloody bore, Grubbs."

"OK," I groan, rising reluctantly. "Give me a few mintues to change. Loch, you and Bill-E go get some shovels. Bill-E knows where to find them."

"Cool!" Loch grins, slapping Bill-E on the back. "You leave it to the Spleenster and me — we know what we're doing."

"Just one thing," Bill-E says stiffly. "On the very off chance that we find any treasure, it's ours. You don't have any rights to it, understand? I don't want you going all *Treasure of the Sierra Madre* on us."

"*Treasure of* where?" Loch frowns.

"It's a black-and-white movie," Bill-E explains as he leads Loch away. "I'll fill you in on the plot while we're fetching the shovels. It's all about treasure hunters and the destructive nature of paranoid greed…"

* * *

→The fresh air clears my head a bit, but after an hour of aimless walking and digging I'd still rather be in bed. Loch's loving it though, digging wildly, *accidentally* hitting Bill-E with clods of earth every so often to break the monotony. Bill-E doesn't mind too much. He's just glad I'm out scouring the forest with him again, even if we do have an extra (unwanted) passenger in tow.

"We've found a few bits and pieces over the years," Bill-E explains as we give up on our third trial dig and refill the hole. "Old coins, scraps of clothes, half a knife."

"Anything worth money?" Loch asks.

"Not really," Bill-E says. "One of the coins would have been valuable if it had been in better condition, but it was very worn and part of it was missing. Dervish let me keep it."

"Why were they buried if they were worthless?" Loch asks.

"They weren't," Bill-E says. "The level of the ground's constantly changing. Things fall or are thrown away. Grass and weeds grow over them. They sink when the ground's wet. New earth blows over them. In no time at all they're half a metre underground... a metre... more. The world's always burying cast-offs and stuff that's been forgotten. Heck, even the giant Sphinx in Egypt was half-buried once and almost lost forever."

"Nonsense," Loch snorts.

"It's true," Bill-E says. "We did it in history. And there are loads of important places in Egypt today — burial chambers and the like — which are covered up. In some towns they know where they are, but people have built houses over them, so they can't excavate."

"I never learnt any of that in history," Loch says suspiciously.

"Well," Bill-E replies smugly, "maybe if you were in the *upper* set…"

→Loch's starting to tire of the wandering and digging. I'm glad. Apart from the fact that I'm weary and grumpy, it's late afternoon and it won't be much longer before the sun starts to set and an even fuller moon than last night's rises over the earth like a plum dipped in cream. Maybe Dervish is back already. If so, I want to sit down with him and have a long talk about what's going on in my life and what we need to do about it.

"This studying," Loch grumbles, studying his hand where he cut it on the last dig.

"One more try," Bill-E says. "We'll quit after that."

"Why not now?" Loch says. "This is stupid. We'll never find anything."

"It's an old superstition of ours. When we decide we've had enough, we always dig one last hole. Right, Grubbs?"

"Yeah," I mutter. "That's the way we've always done it."

"And look where it's got you," Loch snorts, but goes along with the plan, not wanting to be the one who quits first.

Bill-E leads us further into the wild bushes of the forest, trying to pick a good spot for the final dig of the day. Briars catch on my trousers and jacket, and one scratches deep into my neck, drawing a few drops of blood and a loud curse. I'm about to call an end to the farce and demand we go home immediately, regardless of superstitions, when something about the landscape makes me pause.

We're in the middle of a thicket, lots of natural shrubs and bushes. It looks much the same as any other part of the forest to the untrained eye, but when you've spent a few years exploring a particular area, you see things differently. You get to know the various types of trees, flowers and weeds. You make mental pointers so you can find your way around easily and quickly. I've been here before, I'm sure of it, but I can't remember when...

The memory clicks into place. It was shortly before Bill-E turned into a werewolf, before Dervish told me about the Demonata and Lord Loss. Bill-E and I were on one of our treasure hunts. We'd started to dig around here when Bill-E spotted Dervish and went all mysterious. He made me hide, so Dervish didn't see us, then we followed him. That was the day Bill-E hit me with his theory about werewolves. The day my destiny fell into place and I started on a collision course with Lord Loss and his vile familiars.

"Let's dig here."

"I'm not sure," Bill-E frowns, studying the ground. "The earth looks hard."

"No," I say, casting around. "There's a soft patch somewhere, between a couple of stones. At least there used to be…"

I find it and give a grunt of satisfaction. I can still see faint marks from where I began to dig previously, a minute or so before Bill-E went weird on me and the world of werewolves claimed me for its own.

"How'd you know that was there?" Bill-E asks.

"Magic," I reply with a laugh, then drive my shovel into the soil.

→Half an hour later, nobody's laughing. We're surrounded by three fresh mounds of earth and stones, digging deeper by the minute, cutting down at an angle. There's a large rock buried just beneath the briars and grass, under the shelter of which the earth and stones lie. There's rock to either side too. It's too early to tell for certain, but this looks like the entrance to a tunnel or cave.

"What's that?" Loch says suddenly, stooping. He comes up holding something golden. My heart leaps. Bill-E and I crowd in on him, jabbering with excitement. Then he holds it up to the dim light and we see it's just an orangey-yellow stone. "Damn!" Loch hurls it away.

Bill-E pulls a face and resumes digging. He's working on the sides, clearing the rock faces, while Loch and I dig straight down. Bill-E pauses after a while and strokes the rock. "Hard to tell if this fissure is natural or man-made. The sides are smooth, as if they've been ground down. But I guess they'd feel just as smooth if nature had done the grinding."

Loch hits a larger stone and winces. Scrapes around it to find its edges, then inserts the tip of his shovel under one corner and tells me to help him. Together we lever it out, then lift it up on to the bank around us. We're knee-high in the hole (based on my long legs, not Bill-E's stumpy pins) by this stage.

Loch clears the gap left by the removal of the stone, then scowls. "There's another one. Looks even bigger than the first."

"It's getting rockier the further down we dig," I note.

"That's always the way," Bill-E says. "The heavier stones sink deeper than the smaller ones."

"Is it worth carrying on?" Loch asks. "I don't think there's any treasure here."

"How do you figure that?" Bill-E sneers.

"Common sense," Loch says. "This Lord Sheftree miser would have wanted easy access to his treasure so he could dig it up whenever he liked. This ground's too rocky. Too much hard work. It would have been easier for him to do it somewhere else."

"Hey," Bill-E says, "this is a maniac we're talking about — the guy fed a baby to his piranha! Who knows what he might or might not have done? Maybe he hired men to dig this hole, then killed them and left them to rot with the treasure. Maybe he had others dig it up every few years so he could put more treasure down there, then killed them too. Heck, there could be dozens of skeletons down there."

Loch and I share an uneasy glance.

"I don't know if I want to go digging up skeletons," Loch mumbles.

"Afraid of a few old bones, *Gosselio?*" Bill-E cackles.

"No. But if there are corpses, we shouldn't disturb their remains."

"Not even if they're sitting on a chest of gold coins?" Bill-E taunts him. "Five chests? Ten? Not even if we agree to cut you in on a slice of the profits?"

"A while ago you said there was nothing in it for me," Loch snaps.

"You can't expect an equal share," Bill-E drawls, "but if there's a fortune and you help us dig it up, we'll see you right. Won't we, Grubbs?"

"Too much talking," I grunt, stabbing my shovel into the ground, trying to find a crack I can use to pry out the next big stone. "Dig."

→Almost sunset. Without discussing it, we come to a halt and study the fruits of our labours. The hole is thigh-deep now. It's been hard going for the last twenty minutes — one big, awkward stone after another. At least the hole's no wider than when we started, so we've only got to worry about digging down, not out to the sides as well.

"We could be at this forever," Loch gasps, wiping sweat from his forehead. All three of us are sweating badly. "No telling how deep it goes."

"What do you say, Bill-E?" I ask, glancing up at the setting sun, feeling the sickness and headache building within me again. "Time to stop?"

"Yeah," Bill-E agrees. "We can't dig in the dark. But we'll come back, right?" He looks at me, Loch, then me again. "We could be on to the find of the millennium. Metres — maybe centimetres — away from Lord Sheftree's treasure. We can't walk away from that."

"He's right," Loch says. "It's probably just a big old hole, but…"

"What about next weekend?" I suggest.

"I can't wait that long," Bill-E says. "A whole week thinking about it, dreaming of the treasure…"

"Also, what if somebody else comes by, sees the hole and finishes what we've started?" Loch growls. "There aren't any fences around your land, are there?"

"No." I clear my throat. "Actually, this isn't *our* land. We don't own this part of the forest."

Loch stares at me hard, then at Bill-E, who fidgets uncomfortably. "You don't have legal rights to it," he says softly. "You were bluffing, trying to cut me out of any find."

Bill-E shrugs. "You wouldn't have known about the treasure if we hadn't told you. Anyway, it's ours – Grubbs's – by right of birth."

"No it's not," Loch objects. "He isn't any relation to Lord Sheftree. Dervish just bought the house, that's all. If I wanted, I could come back here with others and dig without you."

Bill-E gulps and looks to me for help.

"Thirds," I say steadily. "An equal split. Assuming there's anything down there. And assuming we get to keep it if there is — for all we know, there are laws that won't allow us to keep any of it. But if the treasure's there and we can make a claim, we divide it in three. Agreed?"

"Agreed," Loch says quickly.

Bill-E looks disgusted but nods angrily. "OK."

"And we don't tell anybody, not until we figure out what our rights are," Loch adds. "There's no point doing all the hard work and not being able to reap the rewards. If we find treasure, we keep our mouths shut and check the law. We might have to wait till we're eighteen to declare our find. Or maybe we can never declare it. Maybe we'll have to sell it on the black market." He grins. "The gold and diamond market!"

"I'm not so sure about that," Bill-E says. "Not revealing a find like this could land us in a lot of trouble."

"We can buy our way out of it with the money we make from the treasure," Loch laughs. "Either way, we don't say anything until we know, right?" Bill-E and I share a glance, then nod. "Great. It's settled." He hauls himself out of the hole and lays his shovel aside. "I don't know about you two, but I plan to be back here first thing after school tomorrow and every day this week, and the week after, and the week after that, until we get to the bottom of this damn hole. You with me?"

"I'll come," Bill-E agrees. "Not every day – Gran and Grandad would get suspicious if I was late home every evening – but most of the time it shouldn't be a problem."

"Grubbs?" Loch asks.

"I'll be here," I promise, glad to have something to distract me from my recent fears. I look up at the darkening sky and add a proviso. "But only until dusk. I'm not staying out here nights. Not when the moon's up."

* * *

→Home. Waiting for Dervish. He should have returned by now. I ring his mobile, to check that everything's OK, but only get his answering message. Sitting in the TV room, TV switched off, no lights on. In my guts and bones I can feel the moon rising. Concentrating on my breathing, willing myself not to change, trying to stay human.

→Without any sound of a motorbike, the doors open about 10 o'clock and Dervish stumbles in. "My head," he groans, slumping on the couch next to me, a hand thrown over his eyes.

"What's wrong?" I ask, thinking he's been in a crash. Then I catch the stench of alcohol. "You're drunk!"

"I forgot how much Meera can drink when she sets her mind to it," he mumbles. "And unlike normal people, she doesn't have a hangover the next morning. She was at it again first thing when she woke and she made me join in." He puts his hands over his ears and moans. "The bells, the bells!"

"Tell me you didn't drive home in this state," I snap.

"You think I'm mad?" Dervish huffs. "I cast a sobering spell."

"You're full of it!"

"No, really, it works perfectly. Except it's very short term. It ran out when I was almost to Carcery Vale. I had

to stop and walk the rest of the way. And the worst thing
is, when it wears off, the hangover kicks in with twice as
much venom as before." Dervish doubles over, head
cradled between his hands, whining like a kicked dog.

"Serves you right," I sniff. "You should have more
sense at your age."

"Please, Grubbs, don't play mother," Dervish groans.
He staggers to his feet and heads for the kitchen. "I'm
going to make an absolutely huge cup of hot chocolate,
then retire to my room for the night. I don't want to be
disturbed unless the house is burning." He pauses.
"Strike that. I don't want to be disturbed even then. Let
me burn — I'd be better off."

I think about calling him back, making him sit down
and listen to me. But it wouldn't be fair. Better to let
him get a good night's sleep, then tell him about it
tomorrow. Besides, I don't feel too rough at the
moment, not as bad as I felt last night. I don't want to
jinx myself, but I think I might be over the worst.

→Dervish's snores rock the house to its foundations. I
don't want to sleep. I want to keep a vigil, stay focused
on my breathing, alert to any hint of a change. But I'm
exhausted. All the energy that went into the party…
lack of sleep last night… walking and digging this
afternoon. My eyelids refuse to stay open. Even coffee —
which I hardly ever drink — doesn't work.

I undress and slip into a T-shirt and boxers. Slide beneath the covers. Lying there, I think that maybe I should get a rope, tie it round my ankles and the bedposts, maybe tie up one of my hands too. That should hold me in the event that I change during the night. A good plan, but it comes too late. Even as I'm gearing myself up to get out of bed and fetch a rope, my eyelids slam down and I'm out for the count.

→Harsh breathing. Thumping sounds. Cold night air.

I come to my senses slowly, the same as last night. I see a pair of hands lifting a large rock out of the ground. They throw it overhead casually as if it was a pebble. They stoop, start clearing more earth away… then stop as I realise they're *my* hands. I exert my will and look around.

I'm standing in a hole, dressed only in my T-shirt and boxers. Bare feet. Dirt-encrusted fingers. It takes me a few seconds to realise I'm in the hole where we were digging earlier. The reason I didn't recognise it instantly — it's about four times deeper than when we left it.

I look up. I'm a couple of metres below ground level, surrounded by rock. In a sudden panic, afraid the rocks are going to grind together and crush me, I grab a handhold and haul myself up. A couple of quick thrusts later, I'm standing by the edge of the hole, shivering from cold and fear, staring around with wonder.

There are rocks and dirt everywhere. I don't know how long I was down there but I must have been digging like a madman. The weird thing is, I don't feel the least bit tired. My muscles aren't aching. Apart from some scared gasping, my breath comes normally and my heart beats as regularly as if I'd been out for a gentle stroll.

I walk over to one of the larger stones. Study it silently, warily. I bend, grab it by the sides, give an exploratory lift. I can shift it a few centimetres and that's it, I have to drop it. It weighs a bloody tonne. Under any normal circumstances I doubt I could lift it higher than knee level, not without throwing my back out completely. Yet I must have. And not only picked it up, but lobbed it out of the hole too.

Back to the rim of the mini abyss. Staring down into darkness. What brought me here? I'd like to think I was just sleepwalking, that I came here because I'd been thinking about the hole all evening. But there's more to it than that. My senses are on high alert, animal-sharp (*wolf*-sharp), and I don't think it's any accident that I wound up here, digging as if my life depended on it.

As much as I don't want to, I sit, turn and lower myself into the hole. When I'm on the floor, I allow a few seconds for my eyes to adjust, then take a really good look. The hole isn't any wider than it was earlier — the rocks on the sides run down smoothly, like a mine shaft. The angle which we were following has continued, so although it's a steep slope, it's easy to climb up and down.

I bend and touch the next rock in line for removal. It's jammed firmly in the earth. I tug hard and it barely moves. Yet I'm sure, if I'd tried a few minutes ago, while asleep, I could have ripped it out and...

Whispers.

I frown and cock my head. The sound has been there for a while, maybe since I regained my senses, but I thought it was the wind in the trees. Now that I focus, I realise it's not coming from the trees. It seems to be coming from the rocks.

A jolt of excitement cuts through my confusion and apprehension. Maybe I'm close to a cave and the noise is the wind whistling between earth and rock. I flash on an image of Lord Sheftree's treasure and the glory of being the first to discover it. With renewed enthusiasm I grasp the rock again and pull as hard as I can. I might not be able to toss it out of the hole, but if I can budge it slightly, maybe I can...

A flicker on the rock. A slight bulging. A shadow grows out of it, just for a second, then disappears.

I fall backwards, stifling a scream, heart racing.

Eyes fixed to the rock, waiting for it to change again. A minute passes. Two.

I get to my feet, legs *very* shaky, and climb out of the hole, not looking back. I make for home quickly, head down, striding through the forest, ignoring the twigs, stones and thorns that jab at my bare feet.

Trying hard not to think about what I saw (or thought I saw). But I can't block it out. It keeps coming back, rattling round the inside of my skull like a rabid rat in a cage.

The flicker… the bulging… the shadow…

It might have been a trick of the light or my skittish mind, but it looked to me like a face was trying to force its way up through the rock from the other side. A human face. A *girl's*.

HARD WORK

→No sign of Dervish in the morning. He's normally an early riser so I guess he's still suffering from his binge-drinking at the weekend. I want to wake him, tell him about my inner turmoil, the magic, the howling, what happened at the hole. But instead I decide to let him sleep in and get his head together. We'll discuss it when I come home after school, when he can think and focus clearly.

Scrubbing hard in the bathroom. The dirt doesn't want to come off. Especially bad under my nails. Without wanting to, I think about gravediggers — their hands must be stained like this all the time.

Looking up when I've scraped them as clean as I can. My reflection in the mirror. Remembering the face I saw/imagined in the rock. Something about it niggles at me. It's not just the fact that there shouldn't have been a face in the rock at all. There's something more... something else...

I'm on my way out the front doors when it strikes

me. The face looked ever so slightly like my dead sister Gret.

→The day passes slowly, as if I'm experiencing it second-hand, watching somebody else's body going through the motions of a normal school day. Chatting with Charlie, Leon and Shannon. Greeting Reni with a big smile when she arrives with Loch. Making light of my friends' compliments about the party. Shrugging off the incident with the bottle — "A good magician never reveals his secrets."

Bill-E turns up. I know he's itching to discuss the cave with Loch and me, but we can't speak of it in front of the others, so he slides past silently. Loch yells an insult after him, cruder than usual, perhaps to cover up the fact that he's become Bill-E's secret ally.

Lessons don't interest me. The teachers could be ghosts for all the impression they make. Fading in and out of conversations during break and lunch. The major part of my mind fixed on the twists of the last few nights, the hole I've dug, the face in the rock, the beast I'm apparently becoming.

→Heading back for class after the lunch bell. Loch and me are by ourselves. Bill-E hurries up to us and says quietly, "Still on for this evening?"

"Sure," Loch says.

"No." Both stare at me. "Dervish wants me home," I lie. "Not sure what it's about. Maybe something valuable got smashed at the party."

Loch winces. "Bad luck. Guess it's just me and Spleenio then." He pinches Bill-E's cheek.

"Get off!" Bill-E yelps, pulling away, rubbing his cheek. "That hurt."

"Sue me," Loch laughs.

Bill-E turns his back on him. "Maybe you can come later?" he asks me.

"I doubt it," I sigh.

Bill-E looks worried. "Perhaps I'll cancel too, leave it till tomorrow."

"No you don't," Loch grunts. "If you back out now, you stay out. This is a joint venture. If you don't pull your weight – and I know that's a heavy load to pull, you chubby little freak – get lost. We don't need hangers-on."

Bill-E's fists ball up. The rage inside him froths to the surface. I think he's finally going to go for Loch and I silently will him on. If he fights back, maybe that will be the end of the teasing and Loch will start treating Bill-E as an equal.

But then Bill-E looks Loch over, sizes up his height and muscles, and chickens out. His hands go limp and he turns away with a weak, "See you later then."

Loch leans over and mock-whispers to me, just loud enough for Bill-E to hear, "Do you think anyone would notice if I took Spleeny out to that hole and made him *disappear?*"

"Shut up, you jerk," I snap and march ahead of him, paying no attention to his theatrical gasp.

→Home. No Dervish. A note on the kitchen table. "Gone to fetch my bike. Don't worry about fixing me dinner — still not in the mood for solids."

Hellfire! Of all the times in my life, why does Dervish pick these few days to be Mr Impossible To Pin Down! I wish now I'd hit him with the news as soon as he got home — would have served the old sozzle-head right.

Too itchy-footed to wait for him. Better to be active than hang around here, struggling to kill time with homework and TV. So a quick change of clothes, a hasty sandwich, then it's off to the hole to find out what Loch and Bill-E make of my late-night digging marathon.

→They're gob-smacked. Standing around the pit when I arrive, jaws slack, staring from the rocks and mounds of earth down into the hole, then back again. Both are holding shovels limply and look like you could knock them over with a fart.

"Bloody hell!" I gasp playfully. "You've been working hard."

"We didn't do it," Loch says numbly.

"It was like this when we arrived," Bill-E mutters.

I force a frown. "What are you talking about?"

"We haven't been digging," Loch says, becoming animated. "We only got here a few minutes ago. We found it like this."

"But who... how... what the heck?" Bill-E mumbles.

We spend ten minutes debating the *mystery*. The simplest solution, which I offer shamelessly, is that somebody discovered the hole after we'd left and did some more digging themselves. Bill-E and Loch dismiss it instantly — there are no shovel marks in the newly excavated sections, and no footprints except our own. (I didn't leave any barefooted prints in the night. I must have been extra light on my feet. Padded softly... like a wolf.) Besides, they argue, who the hell would go digging in the middle of the night?

"An earthquake?" I suggest as an alternative.

Snorts of derision. We don't get earthquakes here. Besides, even if we did, that wouldn't explain the earth and rocks piled up around the hole.

Loch wonders if a wild animal is responsible.

"What sort of animal do you think that might be?" Bill-E sneers. "A troll or an ogre? Or maybe it was elves, like in the fairy tale with the shoemaker."

Eventually Bill-E comes up with a theory which satisfies all three of us, at least in the absence of anything more believable. "Lord Sheftree," he says. "If this is where his treasure's buried, maybe he booby-trapped the entrance with explosives. When we were digging, we set them off, but because they'd been buried so long, they didn't ignite straightaway. It took them a few hours to explode, by which time we were safely home, clear of the blast radius."

"I dunno," Loch mutters, examining the rocks around us. "These look like they were pulled out cleanly, not blasted."

"Maybe it was a catapult-type mechanism," Bill-E says, warming to his theory. "He had all these rocks loaded on a platform, which was set to shoot them upwards when the trap was sprung. They'd crush anyone nearby."

We discuss it further, trying to pin down the exact workings of the trap, wondering if there might be more than just one. I advise caution and propose retreat — we should report this and leave it to professionals to mine the dangerous hole. Bill-E and Loch shout me down.

"We'll go slowly," Bill-E says.

"Carefully," Loch agrees.

"If there are other traps, they're probably slow-burners too," Bill-E argues.

"But I doubt if there are more," Loch says. "What would be the point? One's enough. If it was set off, old Sheftree could have simply cleaned up the remains of the bodies, then set the trap again."

In the end, despite the dangers, they decide to proceed. Since they can't be swayed and there's no profit in cutting myself off from them, I reluctantly grab a shovel and all three of us climb down into the hole.

For an hour we work doggedly and fearfully — me fearful of faces appearing in the rocks, Bill-E and Loch fearful of running afoul of the dead Lord Sheftree.

We pause every time there's a rustling in the trees overhead, or when a heavy stream of earth trickles down into the hole, me anticipating whispers, Bill-E and Loch thinking it might be the grinding gears of Lord Sheftree's next weapon of mass destruction. But gradually we adjust to the natural sounds of the forest and stop flinching at every minor disturbance.

Bill-E and Loch are more convinced than ever that we've unearthed the final resting place of Lord Sheftree's buried treasure. Not me. There's something magical about this hole. It drew me to it last night, sang out to the moon-affected beast I'd become and lured it here, turning me into a conspirator, using me to clear the way for... what?

I don't know. I haven't the slightest idea what we might be digging our way down to. But I'm pretty certain it's not a rich miser's hidden treasure.

Loch and I work paired, chipping away at the hard-packed earth around the large rocks, prising them out slowly, often painfully, rolling and dragging them up the slope. Bill-E cleans up after us, removing the smaller rocks, pebbles and dirt. We're an effective team, although as Loch tires from the hard work, he starts cursing and teasing Bill-E, taking out his irritation on him. At first I ignore it, but he keeps on and on, Spleenio this, fat boy that, dodgy eye the other, and eventually I snap.

"Why don't you lay off him?" I snarl after an especially brutal remark about Bill-E's dead mother.

"Make me," Loch retorts.

I square up to him. "Maybe I will."

Loch holds his shovel in both hands and raises it warningly. I grab the handle and we glare at each other. Then Bill-E slips behind me and whispers, "Do him, Grubbs!" It's so flat, so vicious, so un-Bill-E, that I turn around, startled, releasing the shovel.

"What did you say?"

Bill-E looks confused, but angry too. "I meant… I just…"

"I heard him," Loch growls. "He told you to bump me off."

"What if I did?" Bill-E bristles, and now he tries to get round me, so that *he* can go toe-to-toe with Loch.

"Stop," I say firmly. I lay my left palm against the nearest rock wall and concentrate. After a few seconds I feel or sense the vibrations of a very faint throbbing. A non-human throbbing. "We all need to chill."

"Who made you the leader?" Loch barks.

"We're being manipulated." His forehead creases and I start to tell him there's magic at work, affecting our tempers. But then I realise how crazy that would sound. "The soil," I say instead, inventing quickly. "There must be some sort of chemical in it. Put there by Lord Sheftree. It's making us feel and say things we shouldn't. If we don't stop, we'll be at each other's throats soon."

Loch's frown deepens, then clears. "I'll be damned," he sighs.

"The sly old buzzard," Bill-E hoots. "Chemicals to alter our dispositions and turn us against one another. Coolio!"

"I thought you were my enemy," Loch says wonderingly, staring at me. "It came so suddenly, without warning. I believed you were out to kill me. The shovel..." He looks down at the sharp, grey head, then drops it and clambers out of the pit. Bill-E and I follow. We find Loch sitting by the edge of the hole, shivering.

"Are you OK?" I ask.

"I don't think we should carry on," Loch whispers. "You were right. We should turn this over to someone who knows what they're doing. Chemicals... That's out of our league."

"No way!" Bill-E protests. "We're close, I know it. You can't back out now. That would be real madness."

"But—" Loch begins.

"There might be no chemicals," Bill-E interrupts. "Maybe we're just tired and edgy. It's been a long day, we're hungry, we've been working hard, it's late… Combine all those and you get three sore-headed bears."

"It was more than grumpiness," Loch says.

"Probably," Bill-E agrees. "But let's say there *are* chemicals down there. It's been so long since they were planted, their strength must have dwindled by now. I bet, if we'd dug fifty years ago, they would have blinded or killed us. Now all they can do is make our hackles rise. We should take a short break, clear our heads, then get back to work. If we find ourselves getting short-tempered again, we come up for another rest."

"I'm not sure," I mutter. If we were alone, I'd tell Bill-E about my fears — that this place is part of the world of magic. I'm sure he'd take more notice of my warnings then. But I can't speak about such matters in front of Loch. "Why don't we leave it for today. It's getting late. Let's go home and sleep on it."

"Not yet," Bill-E pleads. "Give it until dusk, like we planned. Since we're here, we might as well make the most of the daylight."

"Spleenio's right," Loch says. Now that the influence of the hole has passed, he's his old self again, intent on getting his hands on the treasure, quickly forgetting his fears. "Let's do what we came to, then go home and relax. It might be weeks before we dig all the way to the bottom. We can't get cold feet every time we run into an obstacle."

I don't like it but their minds are set, so after a brief rest, we up tools and edge down the hole again.

→We remove one of the biggest rocks yet and haul it to the top. Standing by the edge of the hole. Sweating, shaking, flexing our fingers. "This is torture," Loch groans.

"Think the treasure will be worth it?" I ask.

"It better be."

"What if there's nothing there, if it's just a hole?"

Loch smiles. "It isn't. We're on to something big. I can feel it in my bones."

"You're just feeling what you want to feel."

Loch scowls. "Stop being such a—"

Bill-E screams.

Loch and I bolt down the hole. We find Bill-E submerged in earth to his waist, clinging to the rocks around him, face bright with terror. "There's nothing underneath!" he shouts. "My legs are dangling! I'm going to fall! I'm going to fall! I'm going to—"

I grab his right hand. Loch grabs his left.

"We won't drop you!" I yell.

"Not unless you give us reason to," Loch jokes.

"I was digging," Bill-E gasps, fingernails gouging my flesh. "Rooting up stones. The floor gave way. My shovel fell. I heard it clanging all the way down — a *long* way. I thought... I dropped this far... I managed to grab the edge. If I hadn't..." He starts to cry.

"Look at the chubster," Loch howls with delight. "Booing like a baba!"

"Can't you shut up just once in your stupid bloody life!" I roar — then catch myself. "The chemicals," I hiss. "Loch... Bill-E... take it easy. No outbursts. No insults. Relax. Think nice thoughts. Tell me when you feel normal."

"How can I be normal when I'm stuck down a—" Bill-E shrieks.

"Nice thoughts," I interrupt sternly, sensing the throbbing again, coming from the rocks around us. "Loch — you thinking nice things?"

"Yeah," Loch grins. "I'm imagining the baby's howls if we let him drop."

"*Loch!*"

"OK," he grouches and shuts his eyes. After a few seconds his expression clears, he opens his eyes and nods to show he's in control. Bill-E's less composed, but that's understandable given the situation he's in.

"You need to talk to us," I tell him. "We're going to pull you out but we don't want to hurt you. Are there any stones jabbing you, sticks, wire… anything that might cut into you if we pull you up quickly?"

"I don't think so," Bill-E sobs. "But it's hard to tell. I don't know."

"Relax," I soothe. "You're safe. We have you. Now concentrate and let us know how we can help you out of this mess with the least amount of discomfort."

Bill-E focuses and moves slightly, exploring the unseen territory around his legs. Finally he gulps and says, "I think it's safe to pull."

"Great." I smile falsely. "Loch — you ready?" He grunts. "We'll take it easy to begin with. Act on my command. Pull softly when I say. Stop if I give the order. Understand?"

"Whatever," he shrugs.

I'd like to wipe my palms dry but I don't think Bill-E would hang there patiently if I released him. So, gripping tighter, glad of the dirt on my skin which counteracts the sweat, I give Loch the nod and we tug. Resistance, but not for very long. Soon Bill-E's sliding out of the hole-within-the-hole, trembling wildly but otherwise unharmed. When his feet are clear, we give one last yank and he sprawls on top of us, knocking us to the earth, where we lie panting and laughing weakly.

After about a minute, without discussing it, we get up and crawl forward, eager to check out the hole that Bill-E has uncovered. It's a black chasm. Impossible to see very far down it. The light's too poor.

"Wait here," Bill-E says, scrabbling up to the surface. He returns swiftly, a baseball cap on his head, two small torches strapped to either side. "Spent half an hour last night fixing this up," he says proudly, then holds up a bigger, stronger torch. "I brought this too. Been lugging it around all day. Just in case."

"Spleen, you're a genius," Loch says and Bill-E smiles. "A fat, deformed simpleton, but also a genius," he adds and Bill-E's smile turns to a scowl.

"Why don't you take one of the lights off the hat?" I suggest. "Then we can all have one."

"No," Bill-E says. "They're not powerful enough by themselves. You need the two together for them to be worth anything." He brushes by us, justifiably smug, taking temporary leadership. He crouches by the edge of the hole he made and flicks on the strong torch. Loch and I crouch by him and stare. The hole continues down as far as we can see, at a slight angle, lots of little stones jutting out of the main rock face, plenty of niches for hands and feet.

"Bloody hell!" Loch gasps. "It's massive."

"There's no way Lord Sheftree could have dug this," Bill-E notes. "He might have widened the entrance to make it easier to get to this point, but the rest of it's natural."

"How far down do you think it runs?" I ask.

"Only one way to find out," Bill-E grins.

"You've got to be joking!" Loch snorts.

"What?" Bill-E frowns. "You're not coming with me?"

"We can't go down there," I mutter, taking Loch's side. "Not without proper climbing boots, ropes, those metal pegs with the loops that climbers use... all that sort of gear."

"It doesn't look so difficult," Bill-E argues. "I say we try it and go as far as we can. If we run into difficulties, we'll come back later with climbing equipment."

"Why risk it?" I press. "Let's wait until the weekend, stock up, then—"

"You ever used any of that stuff before?" Loch asks. "Boots, ropes and so on?"

"Well, no, but—"

"Me neither," he interrupts. "Spleenio?" Bill-E shakes his head. "If we're going to do that, we need to practise," Loch says slowly.

"So we practise. It means a delay, but—"

"What if someone comes along in the meanwhile, finds this and claims it for their own?" Loch cuts in.

I glare at him. "I hate the way you set out on one side of an argument, then talk your way completely round to the other side."

Loch laughs. "You're too conservative, Grubbs. I share your concerns for our safety, but the Spleenster's right. If we take it easy, advance cautiously, stop if we feel it would be dangerous to go on…"

"What if the batteries in the torches die while we're down there?" I ask stiffly, fighting a losing battle but determined not to give in gracefully.

"I replaced them last night," Bill-E says. "They're all fresh."

"Genius," Loch murmurs, then grins at me. "It can't be *that* deep — old Sheftree needed to be able to get up and down with his cases of treasure. The angle's not too steep. And there are loads of toe- and finger-holds."

"Let's try, Grubbs," Bill-E whispers. "We won't do anything foolish. You can call it off if you think things look dicey. We'll follow your lead. Promise."

I hesitate and check the time. Glance up to where the moon will soon be appearing. I place my right hand on the rocky floor, feeling for vibrations, but there aren't any. I think of all the dangers — then of the treasure, if it's there, if I'm wrong, if this isn't a place of magic, if I've been imagining hidden perils.

A deep breath. A snap decision. I grab the big torch from Bill-E. "Let's go."

THE CAVE

→Descending slowly, testing each foothold firmly before settling my weight on it. Coming down three abreast, me in the middle, Loch on the left, Bill-E on the right. Loch complains several times about not having a light of his own, but Bill-E refuses to relinquish either of his torches. I've been to his house. I know that Ma and Pa Spleen keep several torches around the place, ever fearful of power cuts, determined never to be left stranded in the dark. He could have easily brought another torch for Loch. A mistake or intentional oversight? I don't enquire.

It's stuffy down here, warmer than I imagined. The air's not so bad though. I thought it would be stale and thin, but there's a good supply of it. Easy to breathe.

Part of me knows this is madness. It screams from the back of my head, reminding me of what happened last night, the face, the whispers, the throbbing today. It wants me to assert myself, demand we make for the surface, tell Dervish, leave all this for experienced potholers to explore.

But a larger part thinks it's thrilling. We're the first humans to come down here in decades. In fact, if the others are wrong and this wasn't used by Lord Sheftree, maybe we're the first people to *ever* find it. Maybe it will turn out to be an amazing geographical feature and we'll get to name it and be on the news. Reni would really dig being a celebrity's girlfriend.

You're an idiot, the cautious part of me huffs with disgust.

"Put a sock in it," I grunt back.

→I lose track of time pretty quickly. Have we been down here ten minutes? Twenty? The hands of my watch are luminous, so I could check. But I'm not going to start fiddling around in the dark, rolling up my sleeves, leaning forward to squint. I'm keeping both hands on the rock face and all my senses focused on the climb.

I go carefully, one hold at a time. Foot-hand-foot-hand-foot-hand-foot. Bill-E and Loch are the same. We don't speak. My torch hangs from my right wrist by a strap. The light bounces off the rocks. I'd have to stop, turn around, lean back and point the light down to get a clear view of what lies beneath. But I'm not going to do that. I'm taking no chances. The thought of slipping... sliding... tumbling into the unknown...

Foot-hand-foot-hand-foot-hand-foot-ha—

I touch ground. Or a very large overhanging rock. Can't tell yet. "Wait," I call softly to the others, who are slightly higher than me. "Let me feel around a bit. I think…" I extend my foot outwards. More rock. I tap it — solid. Gently lower my other foot, still holding tight to the wall. Gradually letting my full weight shift to my feet, I release my grip and stand unsupported. The ground holds and my stomach settles.

Bringing up my torch, I shine it around and gasp.

A cave. Not the largest I've ever been in, but a reasonable size. Lots of stalactites and stalagmites. A waterfall to my right. I should have heard the noise before now, except my breath and heartbeat were heavy, muffling my hearing.

"Grubbs," Loch hisses. "Are you OK? What is it?"

"I'm fine," I whisper, then raise my voice. "It's a cave." I shine the light on the floor around my feet, making sure I've truly struck bottom. I spot the shovel which Bill-E dropped. "It's OK," I tell my friends. "You can come down."

They detach themselves from the wall and stand beside me. The light from Bill-E's torches mingles and crosses with mine and we gaze around in awed wonder.

The formations are beautiful, some of the most incredible I've ever seen. Water drips slowly from the tips of many stalagtites, so this is an active cave, still growing. I recall lectures from a couple of class trips to caves. It can take thousands of years for spikes to form. Thousands more for them to alter. If I lived to be a hundred and came back here just before my death, this cave would probably look no different than it does right now.

"It's amazing," I sigh, taking a step forward, head tilted back, looking up to where the roof stretches ahead high above us. "How can this have been here all this time... hidden away... nobody knowing?"

"The world's full of places like this," Bill-E answers even though I wasn't really asking him. "We only see a fraction of what's on offer. People find new caves, mountains, rivers, all the time."

"OK," Loch says loudly, shattering the mood. "It's a lovely cave, beautiful, glorious, la-dee-da-dee-dum. But I don't see any treasure."

"Peasant!" Bill-E snarls. "*This* is the treasure. You couldn't buy a cave like this, not with all the gold and diamonds in the world."

"I don't want to," Loch says sourly. "What good's a damp, dirty cave? I'll settle for the gold and jewels." He looks around and spits. "If there *are* any."

Bill-E turns, temper fraying. I speak up quickly. "He's right, Bill-E. Not about the cave not being worth anything — it's amazing, beyond any price. But we came looking for a different sort of treasure. We should check to see if it's here. If it isn't, that doesn't matter — we'll still have found the cave. But if there's treasure too, all the better."

Bill-E relaxes. "Yeah, let's look. The cave isn't that big. If there's treasure, it shouldn't be too hard to find."

We move forward, three explorers in wonderland. Even Loch looks impressed, although he isn't blown away by the cave's beauty in the same way as Bill-E and me. We stroke the rising pillars, fingers coming away damp. In certain places the stalactites and stalagmites have grown together to form giant, solid structures which join the floor and ceiling. One is wider than the three of us put together, a monster resembling a couple of massive chimneys.

"I've never been down a cave without a guide, or in such a small group," Bill-E says after a while. "It's strange. Quiet. Peaceful."

"Hey," Loch grins. "You know my favourite bit when I'm down a cave? It's when they turn the lights out so you can see what it looks like pitch black."

"No way!" I say quickly.

"Uh-uh!" Bill-E chimes in.

"What's the matter, ladies?" Loch laughs. "Scared of the dark?"

Bill-E and I share a look. Neither of us wants to switch the torches off. But Loch's smirking goadingly.

If we don't meet his challenge, we'll never hear the end of it.

"Go on," I mutter to Bill-E. "You first."

He gulps and turns one light out, then the other.

The cave feels much smaller now, more threatening. It's probably my imagination but I believe I can sense shapes in the shadows, waiting to form fully in the darkness so they can leap forward and pounce on us unseen. My finger hovers over the switch on my torch. I'm torn between not wanting to look like a coward and not wanting to fall prey to forces of magical malevolence.

Before I can make a decision, Loch does it for me. "What a sissy," he crows, then reaches over, jams my finger down hard and jerks it backwards, quenching the light.

My heart races. My breath stops. The walls seem to grind shut around me. In a panic I try to turn the torch on, but my finger's numb from where Loch pressed down on it. I can't find the switch! I can't turn the light on! The shapes are coming! In a second or two they'll be upon us, all claws, sharp teeth and...

Bill-E switches one of his torches on. He's chuckling weakly. "That was cool."

I look around — nothing. The cave looks exactly the same as it did before. I was imagining the danger. I force a short laugh and switch my torch on, then press ahead with Bill-E and Loch. We continue exploring.

→After half an hour I don't feel too hot. It's nothing to do with the temperature of the cave – it's warmer down here than it was on the surface – but with the time. I check my watch to confirm what I already know — it's night. High above, hidden from sight by the layers of rock and earth, the moon's rising, and tonight it's as full as it's ever going to be.

I get the same sick feeling as last night and the night before, only stronger, relentless. In horror movies, people sometimes don't change into werewolves unless they sight the moon — if it's hidden by clouds, or they're locked away, it doesn't affect them. But that's rot. The moon's a powerful mistress. She can reach through any wall or covering and work her wicked charms.

Bill-E and Loch are bickering about the treasure and whether or not it's here. Loch doesn't think it is – we've been around the cave a few times and found nothing – but Bill-E still insists it could be.

"You don't think Lord Sheftree would have left it lying on the floor for anyone to stumble across and walk off with, do you?" he argues. "He'd have thought about somebody finding the cave, either by digging down like we have, or maybe through some other entrance he didn't know about. He'd have hidden the treasure, stuck it out of sight, so that even if a stranger wandered in by accident, they wouldn't find it, not unless they actively searched for it."

"So where do you think it is, geni*ass*?" Loch sneers. "We've looked everywhere. Unless it's invisible treasure, I don't think—"

"We've looked nowhere," Bill-E shouts, and his voice echoes tinnily back at us. "Some of the larger stalagmites might be hollow," he says, quieter this time. "The treasure might be buried in one of them."

"There's an awful lot of stalagmites," Loch says dubiously.

"We have time," Bill-E smiles. "And maybe it's not down here at all." He points up at the walls. "There are ledges, holes and tunnels, maybe smaller caves — or, for all we know, *bigger* caves. This could be nothing more than the entrance to a system of huge, interlinked caverns. We've lots of exploring still to do. We've only scratched the surface."

"Let's do it another time," I mutter, head pounding, feeling as though I'm surrounded by a layer of fire. "It's night. Time to go home."

"Not yet," Loch snaps. "I don't have to be home for a few more hours."

"Bill-E..." I groan.

"Well, Gran and Grandad will be expecting me back soon," he says. "But it's not like I've never been late before. I'll tell them I was with you, that we lost track of time — which isn't a total lie."

I want to scream at them. The fools! Can't they feel it? Even through my sickness, with a brain that's being hammered to a pulp by a searing headache, I can sense danger. The throbbing's back, stronger than ever. We need to get out now, quick, before…

Or am I imagining the danger, like I imagined the monsters in the dark? Maybe it's just my sickness that we have to fear and this is only a beautiful, eerie cave.

Even so, if I turn into a werewolf here, that's more than enough for any pair of humans to worry about. Trapped underground with a supernaturally strong wolfen beast, Bill-E and Loch wouldn't last five minutes.

"Look," I snap, "we have to go. We'll come back tomorrow and explore fully. But it's dark up top — it's night. We said we'd go when the moon rose." I stop, gather my thoughts and try a different approach. "We don't want to draw attention to ourselves. If we come home late, caked in mud and dirt, what will everyone think? If they start asking questions…"

"He's got a point," Bill-E concedes. "Gran and Grandad put Sherlock Holmes and Watson to shame. We should play it safe, act normally, especially if we're going to be coming here a lot."

"OK," Loch sighs. "But one more search before we leave." He points to the top of the waterfall, where it comes gushing out of the sheer rock wall fifteen metres above the cave floor. "Up there, those large holes. We can climb up pretty easily. I want to have a peek at them. Then we can go."

"I dunno," Bill-E says. "They're fairly high and that wall's steeper than the one we climbed down."

"What's a wall to three hardy explorers like us?" Loch laughs. "It won't take long. And if the treasure's there, we can go home on a total, triumphant high."

"Grubbs?" Bill-E asks.

I shake my head violently. I think I'm going to throw up. I'm trembling helplessly. Climbing's the last thing on my mind.

"Are you all right?" Bill-E asks, training his twin lights on me.

"Some kind of bug," I gasp. "I've had it for the last few days."

"Maybe we should get him home," Bill-E says.

"Sure," Loch grunts. "Right after we've explored above the waterfall." He slaps Bill-E hard on the back. "Come on, Spleenario — last one up's an asswipe!"

The ploy works. Bill-E forgets about me. They race to the wall and climb. Loch's laughing, teasing Bill-E, roughly urging him on. I turn my back on the pair, leaving my torch pointing in their direction, to provide some extra light for them. I stumble away and sink to my knees. Lean my head against one of the smaller stalagmites and groan softly. I feel like a corpse that's been stuck in a microwave to defrost — half frozen, half on fire. I try to control my breathing, to think calm thoughts, but my head's full of wild, animalistic images — running, chasing, ripping, fangs, blood.

I stare at my fingers — they're curling inwards. I can't straighten them, no matter how hard I try. I search within for magical warmth, the energy I've drawn upon over the last forty-eight hours, but it doesn't seem to be there for me now. Maybe the cave's got something to do with that. Or maybe I'm just out of fighting spirit. Out of resistance. Plumb out of luck.

"Not… going… to… turn," I snarl. Thinking of Loch and Bill-E, what I could do to them. Cursing myself for being so slack, not going to Dervish when I had the chance, allowing this to happen. I see now that it was fear, plain and simple. It didn't matter what state Dervish was in — I should have told him the minute he got back. I kept the news to myself because I was scared of what he'd do. I was hoping the charms of the moon would pass, that I was just ill, imagining the inner struggle. The same fear which kept me from learning the ways of magic stopped me telling my secret to Dervish. Grubbs Grady — coward of the county. And now Bill-E and Loch are set to pay the price for my cowardice.

I try yelling a warning, telling them to stay up high where I can't reach them. But my throat won't work. The vocal cords are constricting, thickening, cutting off my air supply. I guess since wolves can't talk they don't need all the throat muscles that humans do.

I pull my head back from the stalagmite, meaning to run, get to the surface if I can, before I change. Put space between myself and my friends. *Lots* of space.

But then I see the face again. It's in front of me. Bulging out of the stalagmite, as though carved out of rock. A girl's face. Similar to Gret's, as I noticed before, but not hers. Different. Younger. Darker hair. Smaller. Eyes and lips closed. Like a death mask.

The whispering, stronger than last night, more insistent. Certain words break through, but they're not words I know. A foreign language. Harsh and fast.

I'm staring at the face, listening to the whispers, held firm to the spot, feeling myself change, when suddenly–

A scream. Behind me. At the waterfall.

As I turn towards it, there's another scream. Then a very loud thud.

Then nothing.

I race across the cave, grabbing the torch on the way, lycanthropic fears momentarily forgotten, blocking out thoughts of the face and sounds of the whispers. There's a figure on the ground and it's not moving. That's where all my concerns focus now.

I reach the figure and gently turn it over. It's Loch. Face ashen. Eyelids flickering. Mouth opening and closing softly.

"Loch?" I murmur, holding his head up, trying to see how bad the damage is. I feel something wet and sticky smeared around the back of his head. I don't have to check to know that it's blood.

Scrabbling sounds. Bill-E hits the ground hard, feet first, having jumped from a spot two or three metres above. "Is he OK?" he shouts, panting hard.

"I don't know. What happened?"

Bill-E gulps, kneels, stares at Loch's head and my bloody hands. "He fell," Bill-E croaks. I almost can't hear him — the whispering's louder than ever, the words coming fast and furious. "We were climbing. He slipped. I… I reached for him. He wasn't far away. I grabbed. But he fell. I couldn't catch him. I tried but I couldn't…"

"Just as well you didn't," I comfort him. "He'd have dragged you down with him. Take off your coat." Bill-E gawps at me. "For under his head."

Bill-E shrugs off his jacket and balls it up. While I hold Loch's head, he lays it underneath, then I softly lower Loch down. His eyes haven't opened. He's breathing raggedly. This isn't good.

"I told him not to go up there," Bill-E says hollowly. He's crying. "I warned him. But he wouldn't listen. He thought he knew it all."

"Hush." I'm calmer than my brother. I've seen worse things than this. Blood doesn't alarm me. "One of us has to go for help. The other needs to stay here, sit with Loch, look after him."

"I'll go," Bill-E says quickly. "Please, Grubbs, I don't want to stay. Not in this cave. It's too dark. Please don't make me—"

"OK," I shush him. "You can go. Find Dervish. Tell him what happened. He'll know what to do. But run, Bill-E. Run!"

Bill-E nods, stumbles to his feet, stares at Loch's face, opens his mouth to say something, then races for the exit. I hear him scrambling upwards – but only barely, over the sound of the whispers – then turn my attention on Loch and the dark pool spreading out from beneath his head and Bill-E's blood-soaked jacket.

→Talking to Loch. All sorts of nonsense — school, the treasure, holidays, girls, wrestling. I've put my coat and jumper over him. Have to keep him warm.

His breathing comes jaggedly. His eyelids have stopped twitching. His heartbeat's irregular. I keep on talking, rubbing his arms and chest, but I don't know if I'm doing much good.

The sickness is still in me. My head feels ripe to burst. Sometimes my words come out as growls, and my fingers clench while I'm rubbing Loch, digging into his cold, clammy flesh.

I fight it. Search within for warmth, energy, magic — anything. I can't change, not until Dervish comes, not until Loch's in an ambulance on his way to hospital, safe.

"Won't turn," I snarl, slapping my cheeks one after the other. "I'm not a wolf. I can control myself. Won't let the moon…"

Loch shudders. His breath stops. I thump his chest hard — then remember first aid classes at school. Opening his mouth, I press firmly down on his chest, then release him and count. One, two, three, four. Press and count again. A third time. I place my lips over Loch's. Breathe out, so that his cheeks puff up. Withdraw. Press — two, three, four. Press — two, three, four. Press — two, three, four. Mouth-to-mouth.

Trying to remember if I'm doing it right. Was it three presses on the chest, or four, or five? Should I blow air firmly down Loch's throat or–

Loch coughs and breathes again.

I sink back, whining with relief and fear. That was too close. This can't be happening. We were looking for treasure. Messing about. Loch was teasing Bill-E. Everything was normal. You can't suddenly go from that to a life-or-death situation like this.

Except I know from past experience that you most certainly *can*.

Besides, things weren't normal — the face, the whispers, the throbbing, the sense that we were in danger. I should have been more forceful. Made them leave. Insisted they go home.

The sickness within me grows.

The noise of the whispers increases.

Loch's blood continues to flow.

→Still talking. Telling Loch he's got to stay alive for Reni's sake. "She'll be a mess for years if you die," I sob. "Trust me, I know what losing a sister does to your head. You can't leave her, Loch. She needs you."

It feels like hours since Bill-E left. Loch stopped breathing again a few minutes ago. I resuscitated him, but it took longer than the first time. I was in floods of tears by the end of it — sure I'd lost him.

What's keeping them? Damn it, they should be here by now. Don't they know how perilous this is, how much danger Loch's in? I can't keep him alive forever, not by myself. If they don't—

Loch's breath stops again. Cursing, I start with the chest pressing and mouth-to-mouth. The beast within me wants to suck in air, not breathe it out. It wants to draw the life from Loch, feed on all that blood around his head and shoulders, sip from that terrible pool, dark in the dim light of the torch. If I dropped my guard, just for a few seconds, there's no telling what it — *I* — would do.

The whispers increase. It's like I'm being shouted at now. I want to roar back at them but I need all my breath for Loch.

Press — two, three, four. Press — two, three, four. Mouth-to-mouth.

Nothing's happening. I don't panic. It was like this last time. I just have to keep going, stay calm, stick with it. He'll revive eventually.

Press — two, three, four. Press — two, three, four. Press...

It doesn't work. No matter how much I press and breathe, Loch doesn't respond. His face has shut down. His lungs don't move. His heart is still.

Third time unlucky.

"No," I whisper. "I don't accept this. He can't be... *No!*"

I bring my hands up, meaning to press again, harder than before, wildly. But something about Loch's expression stops me. It's peaceful, calmer than it ever was in life. Staring at him, I know with total, awful certainty — he's lost. I could press and breathe from here till doomsday and it wouldn't make the slightest bit of difference.

Loch Gossel is dead.

→Stumbling around the cave. The whispers deafening. Tears streaming down my cheeks. The wolf within me howling to be set free. Loch dead. Muttering, "This can't be so. This can't be so. This…"

My right foot hits either a large stone or small stalagmite. I fall flat. As I'm picking myself up, the face of the girl forms in the floor in front of me. Her expression is the same as Loch's. I gaze at her in horror. This is what Loch will be like for all eternity, or at least until his body rots. Blank, lifeless, ever still, ever serene, ever—

The girl's eyes snap open. Her lips part. She shouts at me, words I can't understand.

I scream and propel myself backwards. Scream again. Halfway through, it turns into a howl. With an effort, I force the howl down, then fix my eyes on the face in the floor. "No," I snarl, pressing my hands hard against the sides of my head. "*NO!*" I roar.

Something shoots out of me. A force I haven't felt in all its power since I fought Lord Loss and his familiars in Slawter. I shut my eyes, feeling energy zap out of me. The scream rises and rises. I feel as if I'm floating above the ground. I think if I opened my eyes I'd find that I *am* floating. I hold the scream, the cords in my throat feeling like they're going to burst, until…

A sound like cannon fire. Then sudden silence. The scream dies away. My head flops. I collapse. My hands come away from my head, to protect my face from the fall.

When I sit up, I'm breathing hard and crying. But the whispering has stopped. I glance at the spot in the floor. The girl's face has disappeared. And I don't feel sick any more — only small, lonely and scared.

Standing, I shine the torch around, trying to pin down the source of the cannon fire. It only takes a few seconds to spot it — a large crack in one of the walls, close to the waterfall, which wasn't there before. Did I divide the rock with my magical scream, or is the crack coincidence, the result of air flowing into the cave or a change of temperature? I don't know. At this particular moment, I don't really care.

I stagger over to Loch and slump beside his lifeless form. Impossible to believe he'll never move again, or laugh, or wrestle. You think your friends are never going to die, that all the people you know and care for will be with you forever. Then the world makes a fool of you, so quickly, so simply, that you wonder whether any of your family or friends will see out another day intact.

I want to bring him back. I want to shake him, kick him, pump magic into him, make him breathe, make him live. It should be easy, like starting a stalled car or a crashed PC. There should be rules, instructions, things you can do. But there aren't. When it comes to humans, death's death, that's that, and you're a fool if you think any different.

Crying, I lean over Loch to hug his empty shell and tell him how unfair this is, how good a friend he was, how he shouldn't be dead, how much I want him to live, how scared I am. And it's only when I grab his shoulders and haul him up, pulling his head in towards my chest, that I realise — his head, the coat and the area around his shoulders… they're all dry.

At first, I'm so distraught I don't understand why that should be so strange, why it strikes me as being out of place. I'm about to dismiss it, to banish it from my thoughts, when the significance hits and I do a confused, incredulous double-take. Then, because I still can't make sense of it, I cry the question out loud, in case giving it a voice will help me find an answer.

"*Where the hell has all the blood gone?*"

PART TWO
JUNI

THE PROMISE

→Dervish regards the cave with something close to religious awe when he enters. For a long minute he doesn't even glance at where I'm hunched over Loch. His attention is fixed on the walls, the roof, the formations, the waterfall. Then Bill-E nudges him softly and mumbles, "Over there."

Dervish snaps to his senses and advances. "Billy told me what happened," he says, still several metres away. "How is he?"

"Fine—" I say and Dervish smiles "—for a dead man." The smile vanishes. He slows. Behind him, Bill-E covers his mouth with his hands, stifling a sob or a scream.

"You're sure?" Dervish asks softly.

"Check for yourself," I say hollowly. "Prove me wrong." My face crinkles. "*Please.*"

Dervish kneels and gently pushes me away. He examines Loch. Rolls his eyelids up. Puts his ear to the dead wrestler's chest. Goes through all the same resuscitation tricks that I tried. I don't bother telling him that he's wasting his time. Let him find out for himself.

Eventually he draws back, saddened — but worried too. He looks at me. Then at Bill-E. "Tell me again what happened."

"He slipped," Bill-E moans. "I tried to grab him but I couldn't reach."

"There was nobody else in the cave?" Dervish presses sharply. He looks at me and licks his lips. "*Nothing* else?"

"No," Bill-E cries.

"No," I whisper.

"You're sure?" Dervish asks, voice low, directing the question just to me this time. "It's important. You were alone? The three of you? You're *sure*?"

I nod slowly, confused.

"I tried to save him," Bill-E sobs. "But he was too big. Even if I'd caught him, he'd have dragged me down with him, isn't that right, Grubbs? It wasn't my fault. Please, Dervish, don't say it was my fault."

"Of course it wasn't," Dervish sighs. "It was an accident." He rubs his chin, troubled. He stands, looks around, glances at the waterfall and the spot Loch fell from. Doesn't mention the crack — he hadn't seen the wall before I howled and split the rock so he assumes it's a natural feature.

"Is there anything you can do?" I ask. "Any spells…?"

"No," Dervish says plainly. "He's beyond help."

I fight back tears. "Will the ambulance be here soon? Maybe they—"

"Nobody can do anything!" Dervish snaps. "He's dead. You've seen death before. Don't ask the impossible. You're not a child."

I stare at my uncle, stunned by his harsh tone. It sounds like he's criticising me for caring about my friend, as though that's wrong.

Dervish catches my look and his expression softens. "This is bad. And not just because Loch is dead." He looks around again, nervously. "I didn't call for an ambulance."

"What?" I explode. "But—"

"He's dead," Dervish says as if that explains everything. "An ambulance wouldn't have helped."

"But you didn't know that when you came," I shout. "When Bill-E fetched you, Loch was alive. Why didn't you phone for help? Maybe they could have got here before you. Maybe Loch would be alive if—"

"Billy, come here," Dervish interrupts me. Bill-E approaches slowly, fearfully, trying not to look at Loch. Dervish keeps me silent with a fierce frown. I want to scream bloody murder, but I bite my tongue, waiting to hear my uncle out. When Bill-E's a metre or so away from us – the closest he's going to come – Dervish speaks.

"What happened tonight is a tragedy. I feel for you, honestly, even though I'm not showing it. We'll talk about this after. I'll give you all the support I can, make it as easy for you as possible. But right now I have to be hard. And I have to ask something hard of you."

He pauses. Again a nervous glance around. "As far as the official verdict goes, Loch can't have died here," Dervish says. "I'll explain later. Right now you have to trust me. We need to move the body. Make it look like this happened somewhere else. Cover up the entrance to the cave and tell nobody about it. Understand?"

Bill-E and I gawp at him.

"Please," Dervish says. "I wouldn't ask if it wasn't crucial."

"You want to... tamper... with the body?" Bill-E croaks.

"I just want to move it," Dervish says. "We'll take it to the quarry. You can say you were climbing there. We'll call the emergency services once we–"

"Bloody hell, Dervish!" I yell. "Loch is dead and you're playing games? What sort of heartless–"

"You're not listening!" Dervish roars, losing his temper. He glares at me. "Let me say it again — this is *crucial*. This cave has been hidden for hundreds of years for a very good reason. It must be hidden again."

"*Hidden?*" I whisper and Dervish nods. "You mean you knew about it?"

"I didn't know the exact location but I knew it existed." Dervish is white-lipped. "The entrance was deliberately blocked off many centuries ago. We'll have to fill it in again." He stands and offers his left hand to me, his right to Bill-E. I don't want to take it but his eyes tell me I must. Bill-E is even slower to accept the hand but eventually he takes it too.

"You've got to promise," Dervish says. "Promise you'll back me up, lie for me, say this happened in the quarry, tell nobody about the cave. On all that's holy to you... in the name of your dead mothers... promise."

"And if we don't?" I ask stiffly.

Dervish smiles bitterly. "I could force you but I won't." He squeezes our hands tightly. "You both know that we live in a world that's not the exclusive domain of humans. There are other forces. Demonic forces. This cave could be valuable to them. If we don't handle this right, demons will benefit and Loch won't be the only one who dies. *Will you promise?*"

Neither of us says anything.

Dervish sighs wearily. "I'll tell you more about it later. You can retract your promise then, if you feel I didn't have good reason to ask for it. But there isn't time now. We have to work quickly, get Loch to the quarry and phone for the police straightaway. If we delay, it will show on an autopsy. It'll be risky, no matter how we play it, but if we don't act now, while we have the advantage of time, it will be a lot harder. For all of us."

Bill-E and I share a look. Neither of us knows what this is about but we trust Dervish. He's saved both our lives in the past.

"You swear you'll explain?" I ask, voice shaking hoarsely.

"I swear."

"Then I promise."

Dervish smiles gratefully and looks to Bill-E.

"OK," Bill-E says weakly.

"In the name of your mother?" Dervish presses, hearing a wavering tone in Bill-E's promise.

Bill-E hesitates, then nods. "In the name of my mother."

Dervish relaxes and lets go of our hands. "Thank you. This is more important than either of you can possibly realise. It's…" He looks down at Loch and gulps, then mutters under his breath, "At least there wasn't any blood."

That reminds me about the mysterious disappearance of Loch's blood. I start to tell Dervish about it… then stop. It isn't important. The blood must have simply seeped through cracks in the ground. I'll only confuse the situation if I speak up now.

Dervish bends beside the body, gently touches Loch's pale forehead, then sighs and tugs at his beard. A moment's pause, during which I see how hard he's having to work to cover up his true feelings. Then his expression firms and he moves into professional mode. "Billy, you bring the torches. I'll take the shoulders. Grubbs, grab his legs. And for hell's sake, don't drop him — that's the last thing we need."

→The next few hours are nightmarish. We carry the body home, load it on to the back of Dervish's motorbike, strap the arms around Dervish and put a helmet on so if anybody sees Loch it'll look like he's a living passenger. I watch them drive away, shivering next to Bill-E, then go indoors and try to drink a mug of hot chocolate in the kitchen. But I'm unable to gulp it down.

Dervish comes back for us. Usually he'd only allow one of us to ride behind him, but there's no time to follow the rules of the road. At the quarry, Dervish throws Loch over the uppermost edge of the cliff. The dull thump as he collides with the hard floor brings tears from Bill-E and me. I don't know why Dervish didn't chuck Loch down when he brought him out here. Maybe he wasn't thinking straight. Or maybe he wanted our tears, to make the rest of the charade seem more realistic.

I make a phone call. Following Dervish's instructions, I dial the emergency number, report the accident breathlessly, give my details and wait. I wonder why Bill-E and I didn't do that before. We both have mobiles. Why didn't one of us climb out of the cave and ring for an ambulance? Did we simply lose our heads and panic? Or did *something* in the cave control our actions?

The police arrive before the ambulance. Dervish debated whether or not he should stay with us or go home and return after the emergency services got here. In the end he chose to stay, instructing us to tell them that we rang him after calling for help. Everybody here knows Dervish. They know how fast he goes on his bike. The police are always trying to catch him but he's too crafty. They'll assume he tore over here at top speed. They won't like it, but given the tragic circumstances, they're hardly going to make a fuss.

Paramedics examine Loch. They do what they can to bring him back to life. But they go about their job sluggishly, without hope, knowing it's too late. They don't cover his face before loading him into the back of the ambulance because they don't want to upset Bill-E and me. But as soon as he's out of our sight, I'm certain the sheet will be pulled up and over.

The officer in charge asks to take our statements. Dervish clears his throat and gently suggests phoning Loch's parents first. The officer blushes — he's young, probably hasn't seen a corpse before, temporarily forgot his training. Dervish offers to make the phone call. The officer accepts the offer with a grateful smile.

Dervish keeps it quick and to the point. There's been an accident. Loch's been taken to hospital. Says it's serious. Doesn't say Loch's dead. Leaves that for the doctors. Not the sort of news you should break over the phone.

Home. The police drive Bill-E and me. Dervish follows on his bike. More hot chocolate. I still can't drink it. Biscuits which I can't eat. Dervish turns on the heating. While the police are talking with us, Dervish rings Ma and Pa Spleen. They arrive before we're finished, splashing out on a taxi for maybe the first time in their lives. Anxious to protect their grandson. Eager to whip him away from the police and their questions. Dervish has to drag them aside and explain that it will be easier if they let the police finish — if we don't do it here, we'll have to go to the police station later. He takes them into the kitchen and plies them with tea and coffee. I imagine them discussing me, Ma and Pa Spleen blaming me for Bill-E being in the quarry after dark, saying I'm responsible for him risking his life on such a dangerous climb — and for Loch's death.

The interrogation goes softly. The police don't suspect foul play. They just want to get the facts straight. We tell them we went for a walk. Wound up at the quarry. Went climbing. Loch fell. Bill-E tried to catch him. Couldn't. The end.

Kids fool around at the quarry all the time. Every few years some local official vows to block it off. Nobody's ever followed up on the promise, though I think they will after this. The police take the attitude that a fatality was bound to happen sooner or later. Just bad luck that it happened to us.

They leave not long after midnight. (How did it get so late so quick?) They say they might return to take follow-up statements, but that shouldn't be necessary. They tell us to take a few days off school, maybe go away for a while. They warn of a possible backlash — parents sometimes overreact in situations like this. Loch's relatives might blame Bill-E and me, hurl insults and accusations at us. The police say we shouldn't be too upset if that happens, to try and understand their position.

Bill-E wants to stay the night, hear Dervish out, learn why we had to lie. But Ma and Pa Spleen are having none of it. They want out and fast. They've never liked Dervish and aren't a lot fonder of me. Bill-E's arguments are shot down before they're out of his mouth. Then it's into the back of the taxi which they've kept waiting and home, where they can pour poison in his ear and remind him of all the times they warned him about the grisly Gradys, how we'd lead him astray.

Then it's just me and my uncle, alone in our old mansion. A foul smell in the air — the stench of lies and deception.

Without discussing it, we retire upstairs to Dervish's study, where we sit on opposite sides of his huge desk, facing each other, me suspicious and wiping away tears, Dervish ashamed and tweaking the hairs of his beard.

Time for explanations.

COMING CLEAN

→"You know about the Demonata," Dervish begins. "You've seen them at work. You know of their powers, their magic, how destructive they are. You know that some, like Lord Loss, can cross between their universe and ours."

"Does this have anything to do with *him?*" I croak.

"No. He doesn't need the cave, and from what I know of him he isn't interested in it." Dervish stops for a moment, thinking about the best way to proceed. "Lord Loss is an exception. Most demons can't cross readily between universes. If they could, this world would be awash with the Demonata and humans would be their playthings and slaves.

"Many demons hunger for that. They spend a large portion of their time trying to open windows between the two universes. They find weak points where crossing is easier and work on them, assisted by power-crazed mages on this side. The Disciples try to stop them. We look for focal points, prevent crossings where we can, deal with the aftermath when we can't."

"Like in Slawter," I nod. "You explained all that to me before. But what about the cave?"

Dervish puffs his cheeks up, then blows out air. "More than a millennium and a half ago, the Demonata invaded. Normally they cross singly or in small groups. The demons hate each other almost as much as they hate humans — infighting is rife. But in this case thousands banded together to launch an all-out assault. They set out to create a large, permanent opening — a tunnel instead of a temporary window. The cave was the focus for their attempt.

"They were helped by a twisted druid. Our world was more magical then. Magic is an energy and like any form of energy it can ebb and flow over the course of time. Back then it flowed strongly through this world. There were many more magicians and mages than there are now, though they called themselves druids and priestesses. It's a source of debate as to why there's so little magic in the world these days. I guess—"

"You're rambling."

Dervish grins sheepishly. "Sorry. Keeping it simple, the Demonata tried to open a tunnel through the cave. They nearly succeeded. From what we know, many did cross over, but only lesser demons. The tunnel was shattered before the masters could cross and the cave entrance was later filled in and hidden from the world, so nobody could make an attempt there again.

"Since that time a watch has been kept on this area. There's always been a watcher here — even before the Disciples were formed — monitoring the situation, making sure the cave isn't reopened. I'm the latest in a long line of watchmen. That's why I don't wander the world like most Disciples. I get away to deal with other matters occasionally but the cave is my main priority."

"But you said you didn't know where it was. How could you keep people away from it if you didn't know its location?"

"Powerful spells were cast when the cave was filled in. As watcher, I would have known instantly if anyone tried to gain access. The spells would have led me straight to the cave."

"Then why didn't you come as soon as we started digging?" I frown.

Dervish's left eye tics. "The spells didn't work."

"But you said—"

"Something went wrong," he snaps. "That's why I was so worried. I thought a powerful mage must be at work, one with the ability to override the protective spells. When you told me Loch was dead, worry turned to outright panic. Before the tunnel can be reopened, a sacrifice must be made. If Loch had been murdered, the magical potential of the cave would have been reactivated, allowing the Demonata to start building a new tunnel."

"That's why you wanted to know if there was anybody else in the cave," I note.

Dervish nods and licks his lips. "I'm still concerned. Those spells were cast by a magician — they *should* have worked. You didn't see Loch slip, did you?"

"No."

"So you can't be certain there wasn't somebody else present, that he wasn't deliberately killed."

"Bill-E was with him. He would have seen if there'd been anyone else up there."

"Maybe," Dervish says dubiously. "But if there *was* somebody, and they were powerful enough to mute the warning spells when the cave was reopened, they might have been invisible, or used magic to wipe their presence from Billy's memory."

I smile weakly. "You're seeing phantoms where there aren't any. We only broke through to the cave today — yesterday, I mean. We went down by ourselves as soon as we dicovered the entrance. There can't have been anybody else."

"You're right," Dervish sighs. "I'm jumping at shadows. But I'm so wired! Back when the tunnel was open, only lesser demons were able to cross. But the core of the tunnel was widening all the time. It had almost got to the point where the masters could cross.

The shell of that core remains intact. If the Demonata ever restored it, thousands could cross in a matter of days, masters and all."

"Couldn't you force them back again, close it like before?" I ask.

Dervish pulls a face. "Humans are far less magical than they were the last time it was open. And back then they only had to deal with weaker demons. We could stop it happening if we caught wind of it in advance, but if they opened it without our knowing…"

He trails off into silence. It's hotter than normal in here. Dervish doesn't usually have the heating on this late. The temperature reminds me of the time we fought Lord Loss in the cellar, the unnatural heat of the Demonata's universe. I feel highly uncomfortable and shift around edgily on my seat.

"What happens now?" I ask quietly.

"The cave will need to be hidden again. Fresh spells will have to be cast and we'll try to find out why those in place before didn't work. But that's a job for a magician. I'll put out the call and we'll wait."

"I thought there weren't magicians any more, only mages."

Dervish shakes his head. "There's one. He's the head of the Disciples, though we don't have much to do with him personally — he fights most of his battles in the Demonata's universe. I fought alongside him once, a long time ago. He set me the task of guarding this area a few years later. I don't know how long it will take him to come, but hopefully it won't be more than a month or two."

"Are we safe while we wait?" I ask edgily. "What if an evil mage finds the cave and makes a sacrifice?"

"It's not that simple," Dervish says. "The tunnel can't be opened instantly. A sacrifice would have to be made to start the process, then over the next few weeks the entrances would fuse with the core. At that point someone would need to conduct a lengthy, complicated ritual in the cave. I'd feel *that* magic at work — it would be impossible to mask — and I'd move heaven and hell to stop it. But I don't think we've anything to fear. Since I wasn't warned by the spells when you broke through to the cave, nobody else can have been. The Demonata don't know the entrance to the cave has been cleared, so they have no reason to move on it."

"Then we're safe?" I watch his face closely in case he tries to lie.

"As safe as we've ever been," Dervish says calmly and there's no hint of deception in his features. I start to relax slightly. He raises a finger. "But regardless of how safe it is, I don't want you going back to the cave."

"As if!" I lick my lips. "What happens when you block it off again?"

Dervish shrugs. "Life will go on as normal. I'll stay here, keeping watch, and another Disciple will replace me when I'm old and grey and of no use any more."

"What about Bill-E? Are you going to tell him what you told me?"

"Yes. As soon as Ma and Pa Spleen let him out of the house — which might not be any time soon." Dervish stands and stretches. "What a night. I'll be glad to see dawn."

"Loch won't ever see dawn again," I mumble. It's not fair, that I'm having to think about the cave, demons and magic, when I should only be thinking about my poor dead friend.

Dervish smiles helplessly and comes around the desk. Lays a comforting hand on my shoulder. "You can talk with me about him if you want. I know what it's like to lose a friend. I can help."

"Yeah. Maybe. Thanks." I take a deep breath and look up. The fear grows in my chest. It tries to grab my tongue and hold it still. It whispers caution. Screams for silence. But I have to tell him. I can't keep it secret any longer.

"There's more than Loch and the cave that we need to discuss."

"Oh?" A puzzled little smile, not expecting anything major.

"I think I have the family curse." His smile freezes. I push the fear down deep and spit out the words I never wanted to voice. "I think I'm turning into a werewolf."

→I tell Dervish everything — the sickness, the party, the bottle, the magic that's been growing within me since Slawter. Waking to find myself at the entrance of the cave, digging as if my life depended on it. The whispers, the face in the rock, splitting the wall with my scream.

Dervish listens silently for the most part, eyes dark, chewing his nails or stroking his beard. Occasionally he'll ask me to elaborate, to describe the sickness and whispers in more detail. But most of the time he just watches me, his expression impossible to read, head cocked slightly, like a priest hearing confession.

A long pause when I finish. Then Dervish tuts like a teacher. "You should have called me back on Saturday or told me as soon as I got home."

"I know what I *should* have done," I snap. "But I didn't. I was afraid you'd make me become a Disciple if you knew about the magic. And I hoped I was wrong about turning into a werewolf. Keeping quiet was dumb, but I never claimed to be an Einstein. So cut me some slack." I glare at him but he only stares back calmly. "*Well?*" I grunt when he doesn't say anything. "Am I turning or not?"

"I don't know. The signs you describe suggest it, but…"

"What?" I hiss.

"Victims don't realise," he says quietly. "Nobody turns into a werewolf overnight. It's a gradual process, spread out over three or four months. The kids often know things aren't right – if they wake covered in blood, or lying naked outdoors – but I've never heard of anyone being conscious of the change or actively fighting it. When they start to turn, their minds blank out. They can't remember changing or do anything to stop it. What you describe is unlike anything any other member of the family has ever reported. And we've been dealing with this for a *long* time."

"You're saying maybe it isn't...?" I feel hope blossom in my chest.

"I don't know," Dervish says again. "The signs all point to lycanthropy — the distorted face, the hands clenching, the howling. If somebody else had seen it happening to you, I'd say you were definitely damned. But you shouldn't be able to note these things yourself. It..."

He goes quiet again. His forehead's a landscape of worry lines. I've thrown him big time. He looks even more perturbed than he did in the cave. At least he knew where he stood with that and what he had to deal with.

"Tell me about the magic again," Dervish says. "Everything you can recall."

I go through the weirdness one chunk at a time. Waking to find myself levitating above the bed. Reversing the flow of water down the sink. Moving things with my mind. Making the bottle rise, explode and transform into flowers and butterflies.

"Everybody saw that?" Dervish asks. "Bill-E will confirm it?"

"Of course." I frown. "Why?"

Dervish grunts. "If we're lucky, you're losing your mind, imagining the magic and the change. You've had a hard few years, been through a lot — more than just about any kid in the world. Maybe it's caught up with you. Maybe you're going…" He twirls a finger around in the air at the side of his head.

"Know what I like most about you, uncle?" I ask waspishly. "Your subtle tact."

"Stuff that! This is no time to be soft. If you were going mad, I'd be delighted, because we could deal with it, seek help, fix what's wrong. Nobody's seen most of this magic you say you've been working. It could all be in your head. But if you really did those tricks with the bottle and there are witnesses…"

"There are," I say stiffly. "And there's the cave. We found it on Sunday. We only dug down a small bit, but when we returned yesterday it had been excavated. Rocks and earth everywhere. Bill-E will confirm that too. *I* did it, Dervish. I went there, not entirely human, and burrowed down."

"Any idea why?" Dervish asks.

"No. Unless it was the whispers… the face…"

Dervish makes a long humming sound. "If you're not mad – and much as I hate to admit it, I don't think you are – I've no idea what the face means. Unless some spell was cast upon the cave long ago, one I don't know about." He scratches his left ear, then the right. "You couldn't recognise anything the girl was saying?"

"No."

"Did the whispers seem to be drawing you to the cave or warning you off?"

I think about it. "Warning me off. But if that was the case, why was I there? What made me return and dig? Could it have been the Demonata? Calling to the beast I'm becoming? Using me to open a tunnel between universes, so they could cross?"

"Possibly," Dervish says. "I wouldn't have thought they had that kind of power, but if it's true that you're turning, and if there's magic involved…" He frowns and trails off into a very troubled silence. I let him brood for five minutes… ten… twelve. Then I can't stand it any longer.

"What are we going to *do?*" I cry. "I don't want to turn into a werewolf. I don't want to hurt anyone. But–"

"Quiet," he shushes me. "Let's not jump to conclusions. There's a lot going on that's queer to us. But I can ask around, seek advice, search for answers. You haven't turned and you haven't hurt anybody, so don't work yourself up into a state. That won't help."

He takes a sheet of paper off a pile on the desk, balls it up and tosses it from one hand to the other, thinking. "First, I mount a watch of you every night. If you feel the sickness returning – or anything that doesn't feel right – you tell me instantly. If you feel magic forming, tell me that too." He hesitates. "Can you do anything now? A small spell?"

I shake my head, scared of even trying.

"If I could see you in action… pinpoint the source you tap into… it might help establish what we're dealing with."

I shudder, then nod and focus. I stare at the ball of paper which Dervish is still throwing from hand to hand. I try using magic to knock it off course, so it falls to the floor. But nothing happens.

"I can't do it," I say after a minute. "It isn't there now. It comes and goes."

"OK," Dervish smiles. "Don't knock yourself out. Now, it's been a long, tiring night. Let's get you to bed and I'll keep an eye on you."

"But the change… the magic… that's it? We're just going to leave it?"

"Sure," Dervish says, then smiles reassuringly. "We're not going to sort this out tonight. There's not much I can do until I see evidence of your transformation or magical prowess. When that happens, I should have a clearer idea of what you're going through and we can take it from there. Right now the best thing you can do is hit the sack and get some sleep. The problems will still be there tomorrow but we'll be in a better state of mind to deal with them."

Since that's all there really is to do, I take Dervish's advice, get ready for bed, then slip beneath the covers. Dervish sits in a chair by the circular window, keeping watch, protecting me, just as he did when I first moved into this house. Maybe it's his calming presence, or maybe it's simple exhaustion, but within minutes, despite everything, my eyes droop and I slip into unconsciousness.

Just before I go under completely, I remember the one thing I didn't tell Dervish about — the blood disappearing from beneath Loch's head. I don't think it's important, but he should be told just in case I'm wrong. I try to rise but it's too late, I'm too far gone.

Dreams.

→I jolt awake. My eyes snap open and I lurch upright in bed. But it's not like waking from a nightmare. No racing heart or after-images of a bad dream. It's more like somebody jabbed me with a blunt knife and stung me out of sleep.

I stare around, confused, not sure why I woke so quickly. Then I see that Dervish is gone. That's probably what disturbed me — he slipped out for a few minutes, to fetch something, go to the toilet, change clothes or whatever, and I sensed him leave. It alarmed me and I jerked awake. Simple.

I start to lean back, half-smiling, then stop. There's more to it than that. Something's wrong. I have the sense of being in danger.

I get out of bed warily and pad to the doorway. There's a light in the corridor at the top of the staircase. I slip out of my room and make for the light. The house is warm — Dervish hasn't turned the heating off.

I think of calling Dervish's name but don't. If we're not alone, if we're under attack, I don't want to tip off our enemies. I don't think the situation is that grave — the sense of danger isn't overbearing — but it pays to be cautious.

I reach the wide, ornate staircase which links the three floors of the mansion. Darkness below. A dim light above, coming from the direction of Dervish's study. I home in on it.

Moments later I'm standing outside the study door, which is ajar. Dervish normally shuts the door, but tonight he left it open, probably because of the heat. He's talking on the phone. If the door had been shut, I couldn't have heard what he was saying. Open like this, I can hear him perfectly.

"Yeah," he grunts softly, "I know." A pause. "I don't think so. I didn't explore it fully, but…" Another pause. "That's why I said I don't *think* so. I'll go back tomorrow, check it properly and… Yes. No. No. They said there was definitely no one else there." A pause. "Of course I can't be certain. I wasn't there. But I trust them. We're safe. I'm as sure as I can be, without being one hundred per cent."

Dervish fidgets on his chair. I think he's maybe heard a sound and is coming to check. I start to back away but then he speaks again.

"Just let him know what happened." A pause. "Yes, I know the consequences if… Yes!" Snappish now. "I'm not a fool and I'm not new to this. In my opinion we're safe. But only one person can confirm that. And he will when he comes. But he can only do that once you get off the phone to me and pass on the message." A pause. "I know he's not easy to get in touch with. I know I'll have to wait. But the sooner you start, the…"

Silence. A long pause this time. I hear Dervish tapping the desk with his fingers. Finally, softly, he says, "He's like my son." I stiffen and move forward a few centimetres. "Of course, if the worst comes to… Yes, I know. I *know*. But I'm hoping…" Dervish sighs. Another long silence.

If I lean forward I can see him. There's a black folder on the desk close to his hand.

"I have the numbers," he says quietly. He stops tapping and draws the black folder closer to him. Doesn't open it. "Yes, I can do it. I have the strength. If there's no other… if it comes to it."

Another silence, which Dervish breaks curtly with, "Just tell him. You do your job, leave me to worry about mine."

He slams the phone down and gets up.

I race back to my room. Dive under the covers. Pull them up over my chest. Try to look like I'm sleeping.

Dervish returns. Checks that I'm OK. Sits in the chair again. I lie very still, eyes closed, listening intently. Finally, after several long minutes, there's the sound of light snoring.

I sneak out of bed. Tiptoe past the dozing Dervish. Head back upstairs in the dark, not turning any lights on. I think I know what was in that black folder and why I woke with the sense of danger. But I want to make sure. I couldn't see clearly. There's a slim chance it was something else.

The study. The door's still open. I slip inside, gently shut the door, find the desk in the dark and turn on one of the smaller lamps. The desktop lights up. The folder's still there, close to the phone, black as the cave was.

I pick it up and cradle it in my hands, staring at the blank cover, knowing what I'll find when I open it, praying to whatever gods there are that I'm wrong.

Then, with a snap, I flick the cover back. I find several pages, a handful of names, addresses, phone numbers and e-mail addresses on each. And at the top of the first page, not in large letters, bold print or underlined, but standing out anyway, as if they'd been burnt into the paper and were still aflame, the two words which confirm all that I feared.

The Lambs.

MISERY MARK II

→I spend the rest of the week off school. Strangely enough, I'd rather go in. It's dull as hell hanging out at the house all the time, brooding, only Dervish for company. I want something to take my mind off Loch's death and all the other stuff. I want to be with my friends, talk about the tragedy, put it behind me, get on with life. But it's expected that I take the week off to recover, so I do.

→I try hard not to think about the folder or the Lambs. Like Dervish said, the curse has been in our family a *long* time. Some parents kill their own children if they turn, but many can't bring themselves to be executioners. Generations ago, the Lambs were formed to deal with that problem. The wealthier members of our clan founded and continue to fund them. It's their job to kill teenagers who've turned into werewolves. They also experiment on some of the beasts, in the hope of unlocking the genetic secrets of the family curse and curing it.

Dervish doesn't have much to do with the Lambs. He mistrusts them. He always planned to kill Bill-E or me himself if the worst came to pass — there's nothing like the personal touch. But my uncle's been through a lot these last few years. He looks as strong as ever, but looks can be deceiving. Maybe he doesn't feel he has the strength to deal with me if I turn.

I don't like the Lambs either. I've only met one of them, but she was a cold, creepy woman, and the whole idea of letting strangers put me down like a wild dog fills me with distaste. Dervish has made it clear in the past that he would put me out of my misery if such a drastic step was ever called for. I can understand why he might want to retract that promise now, but understanding doesn't make it any easier to accept. As childish as it might seem, I feel like he's betrayed me.

→Bill-E manages to come over on Thursday, after Dervish argued hard on the phone for a couple of days to persuade Ma and Pa Spleen to let him out of the house. He looks shell-shocked. Pale and sickly. His lazy left eyelid flutters so much it looks like worms are wriggling beneath the flesh. He doesn't say much, which is unusual for Bill-E. Listens numbly while Dervish explains about the cave and why we had to move the body. Doesn't seem too bothered by the threat of a demon invasion.

"I rang Loch's house," Bill-E says when we're alone in the TV room. I stare at him, not sure how to respond. I wanted to ring Reni all week but didn't dare. "His father answered," Bill-E continues. "I could tell he'd been crying. I wanted to say sorry, ask how they were, if there was anything I could do. But I couldn't speak. My mouth dried up. In the end he put the phone down. He didn't get angry. He just sounded sad."

Bill-E's staring off into space. The way this has hit him, you'd think it was his best friend who'd died, not a bully he didn't like. But maybe that's why it's harder for him than me. Guilt's mixed up with grief. I think he's sorry for all the bad thoughts he had about Loch, the foul names he no doubt called him behind his back, the times he probably wished his tormentor was dead.

"I'm going back to school on Monday," I tell Bill-E. "What about you?"

He shakes his head. "I don't know."

"You should. It might help."

"Gran and Grandad don't want me to. They said I could stay at home as long as I want. Said they'd hire a private tutor."

The meddlesome, selfish old buzzards! I probably shouldn't be too hard on them. They're old and lonely. Bill-E's all they have. I can understand why they want him to themselves, locked up safe where they can fuss over him twenty-four seven. But they should know better. He needs to be out in the real world, getting back to normal as soon as possible.

"I remember you telling me about when your mum died," I say softly. Bill-E looks at me, eyes coming into focus. "Your gran and grandad kept you indoors for a year. You didn't speak to anybody else. You fought with other kids who tried to talk to you."

"Then I got whacked in the jaw by a boy in a shop," Bill-E laughs jerkily.

"And that put you straight." I sit beside him. I think for a moment of putting an arm around him but decide against it — no need to go overboard. "Don't cut yourself off from your friends, Bill-E."

"Do I have any?" he asks sadly.

"You know you do," I snap. "Maybe not as many as you wish, but there are plenty of people who like you and feel sorry for you, who'll help you through this. But they can't if you shut yourself off, if you let your gran and grandad smother you. Come back to school. Move on. You know it makes sense."

"Loch can't move on," Bill-E sighs.

"No," I agree stiffly. "He can't. But *we* didn't die in that cave. We're alive. Loch isn't and that's a wretched shame. But life goes on. Loch goes to a grave, we go back to school. That's how it has to be."

Bill-E nods slowly. "Are you going to the funeral?"

"I don't want to but I think I need to."

"I can't," Bill-E whispers. "I can go back to school but not…"

"That's OK," I smile. "School will be torture enough."

Bill-E returns the smile briefly, then stares off into space. "I can still hear his scream," he mutters. "And I can see his face. His eyes… He didn't know he was going to die. There wasn't terror in his expression, just worry. And a bit of anger. He should have looked more terrified. If he'd known…"

We sit there for hours after that, TV off, sniffling occasionally, but otherwise as silent as Loch must be.

→Friday. The funeral. It's horrible. And that's all I'm saying about it.

→Monday. School. Everyone staring and whispering. Kids scurry out of my way. It's like the Grim Reaper's walking alongside me.

I spot the gang in one of our usual hangouts behind the cafeteria, sheltering from the rain. Talk dries up as I approach. When I stop, they stare at me, I stare at them, and for a few long seconds nothing is said. Then Charlie breaks the silence with, "Loch must have been mad as hell, looking down on his funeral — he hated flowers. And having to wear a suit as well!"

Everybody laughs.

"You're an ass, Charlie," Frank giggles.

"Don't say anything like that in front of Reni," Shannon warns him.

"Please," he huffs. "I'm not a *total* screwball."

The laughter fades. Frank clears his throat. "Was it really bad?"

"Crapville," I say tightly.

"Did he say anything before he… you know?" Mary asks.

I nod soberly. "His last words… I had to strain to hear them… he…" I cough and everyone leans in close to listen. "He said… his voice a painful croak… fighting for breath… eyes locked on mine… 'Mary Hayes has a face like a cow's dirty rear.'"

Mary roars with fury and clubs me with her bag. The others laugh. Then the bell goes and we march into class. Back to normal — or as much as it can be.

→A rumour at lunchtime. Misery Mauch has gone on sick leave. A mental breakdown. Some say he was overcome with grief when he heard about Loch, but that's rubbish — Loch never went to see Misery. Apparently he's been replaced by a woman. They say she's quite young, though nobody's had a good look at her yet — she's been in Misery's office most of the day.

I don't see Bill-E during lunch. He's with the new counsellor. I hope she's got more of a clue than old Misery. Bill-E needs professional help, not some over-eager do-gooder. I'll have to check her out, make sure she's not going to mess him up even further. Grubbs Grady — rooter-out of frauds!

→Halfway through geography, a kid from a lower year delivers a note to my teacher. The new counsellor wants to see me. Guess I'll get to give her the once-over a bit sooner than I thought.

I'm kept waiting outside the office for a few minutes before I'm called in. The counsellor is standing by the side of Misery's desk when I enter, her back to me. When she turns round, I almost drop through the floor.

A slender woman of medium height, in her late thirties or early forties. Smartly dressed, more like a businesswoman than a teacher. Pretty but not gorgeous. Very little make-up. Pure white hair tied back in a ponytail. Extremely pale skin. Pinkish eyes. She's an albino. But that's not what knocks the wind out of my sails. It's the fact that I know her and last saw her a year ago in Slawter, frying the brains of a demon collaborator called Chuda Sool.

"Juni Swan!" I cry.

"That's Miss Swan to you, young man," she says with a little smile. Then steps forward and wraps her arms around me, hugging me tight while I stand frozen, stunned, staring down at the top of her pale white orb of a head.

* * *

→Juni was one of film producer Davida Haym's assistants. A psychologist, it was her job to make sure the children on set were being well treated. Dervish fell for her and I think she had a thing for him too. I doubt the pair got beyond fond looks and holding hands, but I bet they would have if life hadn't gone crazy on us all.

When hell hit the fan and the demons ran wild, Juni helped us break a hole through the barrier which Lord Loss had erected around the town. Without that gap, everyone would have perished. She was knocked out during the fighting and only recovered when the barrier had closed again, trapping hundreds of members of the cast and crew inside. Like the rest of us, she was helpless and had to stand by, watching and listening as the demons tortured and killed them.

She lost herself to fury and found that like me she could tap into the magical energy in the air. In a fit of rage she used this power to kill Chuda Sool, a demon collaborator who'd slipped through the gap. She regretted it afterwards. Snuck away in the night, leaving a note for Dervish saying she was confused and filled with sorrow. Said she might contact him one day if she sorted her head out, but not to expect to hear from her again.

Now here she is, filling in for Misery Mauch, looking a bit more strained than when I previously knew her, but otherwise no different.

"Why are you here?" I gasp once I've recovered from my initial shock. "*How?*"

"That's what Billy asked," she chuckles. We're sitting in front of the desk, chairs close together. Juni's holding my hands. "Aren't you pleased to see me?"

"Of course. But it's been so long. I never thought… And how did you wind up here, in our school? You're not a school counsellor. Are you?"

"Not precisely." She sighs and lets go of my hands. "It's not a long story or particularly complicated. My head was in a mess after our experiences on the film set." She pauses. Her eyes make flickering contact with mine and I get the message — don't mention the demons or the slaughter. *Please.* "It took me some months to recover," she continues, "but not as long as I feared. I realised early on that work would help, that I needed to be busy, that by helping others with their problems, I could help myself too.

"A friend offered me a job involving school work. I became an advisor to a network of counsellors. I supervised them, provided them with guidelines, helped out with their problems, organised meetings and conferences. The school network I initially covered was far from here. Then, a couple of months ago, I was given an opportunity to relocate. I knew your school would be part of my new network. To be honest, that's largely what drew me to it."

She smiles weakly. "I've been wanting to get in touch with Dervish since the day I ran off. I haven't because of fear, guilt, shame. This was a way to take a step closer. I meant to ease myself into his life, observe from a distance for a while, work up the courage to face him again. Then William Mauch fell ill at the very time you and Billy most needed a compassionate and understanding ear. As his superior I was expected to step in for him. As your friend I felt compelled to. So..." She shrugs, embarrassed. "Tah-dah!"

"Dervish will be well pleased," I grin. "He's missed you."

Her face creases. "Please don't tell him. Not yet. Not until I'm ready."

"But–"

"Please," she stops me, sharp this time. "I'll see him soon, but not right now. Not until I've had time to settle, get my bearings and finish what I came here to do."

"What do you mean?"

She leans forward, eyes warm but serious, and says, "I want to talk about your friend, Loch Gossel." Puts a small, slim hand on one of my large, knobbly ones. "I want to discuss his death and how that hurt you."

→We talk for almost an hour about my friendship with Loch, what he was like, how he died, what I felt, how

I've coped since then. I feel awkward at first, but Juni listens patiently, asks all the right questions, never pushy, always sensitive. She doesn't pretend we're not old friends, but at the same time she treats me like a patient, the way a professional should. No falseness, no charade, no smarm. I find myself opening up to her, telling her things I haven't even told Dervish, about my pain, my nightmares, my loss.

We talk about Bill-E a lot. She spent most of the morning with him and she's worried. "I can't tell you all that we discussed," she says. "I have to respect his privacy. But I got the feeling there was animosity between him and Loch. Would you say that was an accurate assumption?"

"They didn't get on," I admit.

"Did they ever fight?"

I smile. "No."

"Why the smile?"

"Loch was almost as big as me. A wrestler. It wouldn't have been much of a fight."

"But they argued?" she presses.

"Loch…" I hesitate, not wanting to say anything bad about my dead friend.

"He teased?" Juni guesses.

"Yeah. He picked on Bill-E. Sometimes he was cruel. I didn't like that, but I couldn't do anything about it. It was Bill-E's problem, not mine."

"Was Loch teasing Billy on the day of his death?" Juni asks. She's not afraid to talk about death openly. Doesn't hide behind softer terms like 'incident' or 'mishap'. I like that.

I think back. "A little bit, yeah. But we were tired from di– I mean, from climbing in the quarry. We were all a bit snappish."

"They didn't fight?"

"No."

"You didn't argue with Loch or try to stop him from teasing Billy?"

"Not really."

"You're sure?"

I shrug. "I don't remember everything that was said. The hour or two before he fell is kind of blank. I'm not blocking it out. I just… it's like, when I look back, I'm looking through a mist. Do you know what I mean?"

Juni nods. "I know exactly what you mean. Part of my job will be to help you pierce that mist."

"Does it matter that much?" I frown.

"Absolutely. It could be a mist of guilt. If you said something ugly to Loch which you now regret, you might have buried it. If you don't deal with that, it could lie within you for years, then work its way back to the surface, hurting you, making you feel horrible about yourself."

"Is that what you're doing with Bill-E?" I ask. "Piercing the mist?"

"Yes. Although it will be harder with him than you. You're not the still-waters-run-deep type."

"Huh?"

"You're honest and straight. What one sees is what one gets. Loch's death hurt but I don't think it struck you to the core like Billy. You're made of tougher stuff, Grubbs Grady. Tougher than Billy and tougher than me. I doubt we'll have any serious problems. You're too plain to be complex."

"You might be wrong," I mutter, annoyed at being described that way. "Maybe I just do a good job of covering up my pain and confusion."

"Perhaps," Juni says. "But don't worry, I make no rash assumptions. If you *are* suffering deep inside, I'll find out and help. You have my word on that."

We talk a while longer about Loch's teasing and what I thought of it. Then a bit more about the day he died, how long I held him, my efforts to keep him alive, my feelings when I realised he was dead. I cry at that point. Juni makes no moves to comfort me, just sits, watching, waiting. When I recover, she hands me a tissue to wipe my cheeks dry, then moves on.

At the end of the session she stands and shakes my hand. When I try to pull away, she grips tight, pink eyes seeking mine and holding them. "Billy promised not to tell Dervish about me. If you can't make that promise or feel strange about it, please say so. I want to be the one to tell him I'm here. I'd rather do it later, when I'm ready, but if you feel like I'm putting you in an awkward situation, I'll do it now."

"No," I smile. "I'll keep it quiet. He doesn't take much of an interest in school life. If he asks, I'll tell him some nutty dame replaced Misery Mauch. I bet he won't even ask for your name."

"Thank you." She releases me. "We'll talk again tomorrow if you don't mind."

"I'd like that."

She smiles broadly, then ushers me out, leaving me to wander back to class, head buzzing, lips lifting at the edges, feeling for the first time since Loch's death that there might be a slight silver tinge to what previously seemed to be a bleak, black beast of a future.

HOME VISIT

→Bill-E improves over the next few days. He starts talking again, loses that faraway look in his eyes, stops moping around like a zombie. He sings Juni's praises whenever we meet. Tells me how closely she listens, how she understands him perfectly and says the right things at precisely the right moments.

"I never saw her in action in Slawter," he says as we trundle out of school, Thursday afternoon. "I didn't realise how cool she was. I thought it would be weeks, maybe months, before I could smile again. But look at me!" He grins widely. "She's a miracle worker."

I smile, slightly strained, ridiculously jealous. I've seen Juni every day but our sessions have been brief. She's spending far more time with Bill-E than me, and when we meet, she talks more about Bill-E's feelings than my own.

"I feel like I can say anything to her," Bill-E gushes. "She's like…" He stops. We're about to turn a corner. There's a tramp sitting on the pavement, his back against the wall, head low, face hidden by a bushy beard and straggly hair. Bill-E reaches into his right pocket, then his left. Finds some coins and holds them out. The tramp doesn't respond immediately, then reaches out without looking up. Bill-E drops the coins into the tramp's hand and smiles. The tramp doesn't smile back. Bill-E shrugs and moves on.

"Where was I?" he asks.

"Discussing the miracle worker," I grunt.

"Oh yes!" And he's off again, Juni this, Miss Swan that. I want to snap at him to shut up, he's driving me mad with his fanboy drivel. But that would be cruel and childish of me. And I'd only be saying it because I envy the hours and confidences they share.

→Friday. I try getting Juni to take more of an interest in me. I tell her about my parents and Gret, what my emotions were when they were murdered and how I felt after the widescale killing in Slawter. I run her through a few of my grislier nightmares. I expect her to jump at this fresh information and pump me for all the juicy details. But I expect wrong.

"That's ancient history," she says. "I don't think it's relevant now."

"But I thought it was all linked," I splutter. "The past... the present... that what I felt then influences what I feel now."

"Of course," she says. "But I believe you've dealt with the past adequately. Your nightmares are natural, a healthy way of releasing tension and confronting your fears. I see no reason to reopen old wounds. Don't you agree?" She waits, one eyebrow raised.

I shift awkwardly in my seat, blushing.

"It's not a contest, Grubbs," Juni says quietly. I stare at her uncertainly. "My time isn't something you need to fight with Bill-E for. My relationship with Bill-E in school is the same as with you — purely professional. I spend more time with him because he needs me more. There are others who need me too. I've met with several students over the last week, including Loch's sister, Reni, at her home."

"You've met Reni?" I ask, startled.

Juni nods. "Like I told you on Monday, I'm not an ordinary school counsellor. My work takes me outside the classroom. Reni is suffering dreadfully. But she's coping. She'll be back at school next week. And when she comes, I'll be spending time with her here. Which means I'll have even less time for you. That can't be an issue."

"Of course it isn't. I never... I didn't..."

"It's all right," she smiles. "Jealousy is normal, even in a boy your age."

"I'm not jealous," I huff.

"Maybe not. But if you are, it's OK. We can't help irrational feelings. The important thing is to recognise such feelings and not allow them to fester. I don't want a rift to develop between you and Billy."

"I don't know what you're—"

"Grubbs," she interrupts, "I'm being blunt because I respect you. This is how I'd address an adult. If you want, I can treat you like a child and tiptoe around these issues. But if—"

"OK," I cut in, angry but cool. "It's no big deal. I understand. I can keep a handle on my..." I scowl, then spit it out. "My jealousy."

"I'm glad to hear it," Juni smiles, patting my right hand. "Now we have that out of the way, let's talk some more about Billy and what you, as his best friend, can do to help him manage his pain."

→Marching home, thinking about what Juni said. She saw through me as if I was made of glass and knew exactly how to deal with me. She's in a different league to Misery Mauch. Every school should have a counsellor like Juni Swan, someone who can really connect with—

A man steps out in front of me and I almost crash into him. I have to take a quick step back. It's a tramp. He's standing in the middle of the narrow path that leads from Carcery Vale to my home. He's staring at me with small, dark eyes. Very hairy. Smells bad. Dressed in shabby clothes which are thirty or forty years out of date. Wears a small posy of flowers in one of his upper button holes — they look ridiculously out of place.

"Excuse me," I mutter, trying to nudge my way around him. He doesn't react. I take a more cautious look — we're alone, nobody in sight, flanked by trees. My warning senses kick in. I prepare to run or fight if needs dictate. But the tramp makes no threatening moves. Just stares at me, saying nothing, hands by his sides, eyes steady.

"Could you…?" I make a sign for him to shift slightly. But still he doesn't budge. Sighing, I step off to the side, trampling down a patch of nettles. I wave sarcastically at the clear path. The tramp nods at me slowly, then walks past.

Shaking my head, I get on the path again and head for home. I've taken no more than five or six steps when I remember the tramp from yesterday, the one Bill-E gave money to. I turn to give this tramp the once-over, wondering if it's the same guy. But the path is empty. No sign of him. He must have slipped back into the forest. It's like he disappeared.

→Homework. Struggling with a complicated chemistry formula when somebody knocks at the front doors. I gratefully close my textbook and go see who's there, glad of the excuse for a break.

It's Juni.

"Hello, Grubbs," she says nervously. "Is your uncle in?"

"Yeah. But… um… I thought you didn't want to see him yet."

"I didn't." She laughs thinly. "Then, on my way to my hotel, I found myself taking a left instead of a right and I ended up here." She shrugs. "I guess the part of me that makes the big decisions thinks it's time."

"Do you want me to call him or would you rather go find him yourself?"

"Call him, please. It would be more polite."

"Dervish!" I bellow, then gesture for Juni to enter. "May I take your coat?" I ask as she steps inside.

"Thank you." She takes it off and passes it to me. Her fingers tremble as we touch. I think about taking hold of her hand and giving it a friendly squeeze, but before I can Dervish comes trotting down the stairs from his study.

"There's no need to roar," Dervish grumbles. "I'm not deaf. I can…"

He sees Juni. Comes to a complete halt, left foot in mid-air. His jaw slowly, comically drops.

"Hello, Dervish," Juni says, waving awkwardly. "I'm back."

And they blink at each other like a pair of startled owls.

*   *   *

→Two hours later. Dervish and Juni have spent the time shut inside the TV room. I've been in the kitchen, where I'm still stuck on the same chemistry problem. Not that I've been trying hard. Most of my thoughts have been devoted to Dervish and Juni, and the things they might be discussing.

Part of me wants to creep to the door and eavesdrop, but that would be sneaky and unfair. I'd hate if somebody did that to me, so I'm not going to do it to them.

→About half an hour after that, when Juni's gone to the toilet, Dervish pops into the kitchen. He sticks the kettle on, prepares two mugs, grabs some biscuits, then sits beside me. He's grinning softly. "You should have told me," he says but there's no anger in his tone.

"She asked me not to," I reply.

"I know, but..." He chuckles. "No. It doesn't matter. Maybe it was better this way. The shock was nice. I'm just glad I didn't fall down the stairs and break my neck." He focuses on me. "Juni told me about the counselling — without revealing any of the confidential details. Said you're doing great, all things considered. She thinks you're a marvel. Said if everyone had your powers of recovery, she'd be out of a job."

I shrug like it's no big thing, but the compliment tickles me.

"Billy's not so lucky." He sighs. "I knew Loch's death hit him hard but I didn't realise things were this bad. I thought, after Slawter, he'd be prepared for death. He seemed to handle that OK. But Juni says he bottled up his feelings, that his reaction now reflects a delayed response to what happened then."

"She's the expert, I guess."

Dervish nods slowly, then says, "Billy told her I was his father."

"Oh?" Bill-E doesn't know that his mother had an affair with my father, that I'm his half-brother, that Dervish is his uncle. He thinks Dervish is his dad.

"She normally wouldn't share information like that," Dervish goes on, "but this was one time she felt she had to. She needed to know if it was true."

"What did you tell her?"

"The truth. Well, some of it. I didn't mention Cal or your relationship to Billy. That's our secret. I didn't see the need to reveal that much."

The kettle boils. Dervish pours water into the two mugs. Glances at me as he's dunking tea bags. "I thought you might have told Billy about your dad."

"No," I say softly.

"You know that you can if you want? It's your call, not mine."

"I know. I want to tell him and I will. But I've never found the right moment. It's the sort of news that will turn his world upside down. I've been waiting for a quiet, uneventful period, but we haven't had any over the last few years."

Dervish picks up the mugs and pauses. "I wouldn't wait too long. You know better than most that time is precious. Waiting's a dangerous game. Sometimes you miss the boat and end up regretting it."

I nod thoughtfully. "I'll give it a few months, let Bill-E get over Loch. When I think he's ready, I'll sit him down and spit it all out."

"If you want any help…"

"I'll ask. Thanks."

We smile at each other. Then Dervish heads back to the TV room to continue playing catch-up with Juni.

→Eleven. Juni's still here. At her invitation I've joined her and Dervish in the TV room. They're sitting together on the couch, not touching but *very* close. They're chatting away as if they hadn't seen each other for decades. They hardly ever toss a question or comment my way. I feel like a third wheel but I don't mind. It's fun watching them. I've never seen Dervish so gushy. Didn't think the bald old coot had any romance in him.

They talk about all sorts of things — school, Carcery Vale, motorbikes, bands, films, TV. For a man who's never shown any interest in music, movies or sitcoms, Dervish has become awfully knowledgeable all of a sudden.

"You were at that gig too?" Juni squeals – yes, *squeals!* – when talk turns to a punk band they both liked. "I don't believe it. What a small world. I was in the pit — what about you?"

"Backstage," Dervish says modestly. "I knew one of the roadies. He got me a pass. Actually I used to hang out with the lead singer when we were younger."

Dervish hanging out with punk frontmen? Moshing backstage at concerts? It's official — I've stepped through into an alternate reality.

"I'm off to bed," I mutter, rising and faking a yawn. I normally don't hit the sack before midnight but this is getting too surreal.

"Bed?" Juni blinks and checks her watch. "Goodness. How did it get so late? I have to go. I need to get up early in the morning."

She stands. Dervish is on his feet a split second later. "Not yet," he gasps. "It's only eleven. That's not late."

"It is for me," she laughs.

"But I haven't shown you round the house yet." He throws it out in desperation, as if she must see the house now or self-combust. "You said you wanted to see the upper floors, didn't you?"

"Yes," Juni says hesitantly, looking at her watch again. "Perhaps another time?"

"It won't take long," Dervish smiles. "A quick tour. You can come back for a better look later."

"Perhaps you won't invite me back again," Juni murmurs, lowering her lashes demurely. Yipes! What a line! You can't get much cornier than that.

"You can visit any time you like," Dervish simpers. I stand corrected on the corniness front.

"Well... OK," Juni decides. "But it *will* have to be quick — fifteen or twenty minutes max. Agreed?"

"You can have it in writing if you wish," Dervish smirks.

"No," Juni says and touches his hand. "I trust you."

Talk about love-struck puppies! This is excruciating. Any more slushiness and I might vomit.

→I accompany Dervish and Juni around the mansion, hanging back a few paces, grimacing like an old crone every time one of them makes some lovey-dovey coo or comment.

Dervish is super-animated, whisking her through the maze of corridors and rooms, treating her to brief sound bites about the house's history. She loves the cellar — she's a big wine connoisseur too.

"You'll have to come and uncork a few bottles with me," Dervish insists.

"Wine is made for sharing," Juni agrees.

"I was just about to say that," Dervish says excitedly. "I can't believe how much we have in common."

"I know," Juni smiles. "The same bands, movies, books, wine… It's freaky."

She sounds a lot younger when she says things like that. I've noticed that in adults before. People learn a new way of speaking as they grow up, but words and phrases from their childhood pop out sometimes, taking them back twenty or thirty years in the space of a couple of syllables.

Up the stairs the tour continues, although now they're talking more about bands and books, less about the house. I think of injecting some cutting remark – "Maybe you're really twins who were separated at birth" – but why spoil their fun? Besides, the more I let them babble, the more ammo I'll have to tease Dervish with later.

We come to Dervish's study. The lights and PC are still on from when he was in there earlier. The door's ajar. Juni's slightly ahead of Dervish and starts to go in ahead of him. Dervish doesn't mind. He's smiling serenely. But then he remembers the spells. (I think of them before he does but wickedly choose not to say anything, thinking how much fun it will be if she turns into an elk or a zebra.)

"Juni, no!" he barks. She stops short, surprised. He smiles shakily. "I mean, it's a mess in there. Please let me go in first and…"

He tries to press past her but she puts up a hand and stops him. "Wait." She frowns at the door, then takes another step towards it.

"Juni, I really don't think…"

"It's OK." She looks back at him, calm and composed. "Just give me a minute. I want to try something."

She faces the door again and closes her eyes. Raises her right hand and holds her palm up to the open doorway. I nudge up beside Dervish, wondering what she's doing. He's staring at her uncertainly.

Juni takes a breath. Holds it. Murmurs something softly. The light in the room dims and her fingers glow. Then the lights come back up strong again and the glow in her fingers fades.

She steps forward into the study and nothing happens.

Dervish stands outside, gawping at her as she does a twirl and smiles at him. "You… the magic… the spells… you lifted them!"

Juni snaps her fingers. A book shoots off a shelf and into her hand. "Tah-dah!" she sings, like when I first met her at school. Then she looks at Dervish seriously. "I've had a busier year than I led you to believe," she says.

Then Dervish is through the door, by her side, babbling with excitement, asking about her magical abilities, what she can do, who taught her. A dozen questions a second, Juni laughing and shaking her head, struggling to answer them all.

I linger outside, staring with disbelief at my uncle and Juni Swan, bewildered and, for some reason I can't put my finger on, oddly ill at ease.

A FAMILIAR FACE

→It's official — Dervish Grady luvs Juni Swan!

It's only been a week since she turned up at the mansion, but she's seen more of my uncle in that time than I've seen of him in three months. She spent most of last weekend at our place, four of the nights since, and they're getting together this weekend too.

They talk about magic a lot. Juni is able to channel magical energy when it's in the air around her. She tapped into her power in Slawter. She wanted to discuss it with Dervish and learn how to hone her talents, but she wasn't ready to face him. So she made enquiries, found others who are part of that magical underworld, and studied with them in her spare time while she was putting her professional life back together. She made rapid advances and has blossomed into a powerful mage over the past few months.

Dervish has gone gaga over her. He was attracted to her in Slawter and thought of her a lot since then. But his feelings have gone haywire since she came back and he found out they had so much in common — most importantly, magic. He's so dazzled by her, it's unreal. I think if she asked him to get on his bike and ride to the other side of the world, he would.

I'm a bit dazed by it all. From being a vague friend and temporary school counsellor, Juni's become a central part of my life. I feel like a tornado has struck and nothing will ever be the same again. I was used to just having Dervish about the house. It got to feel natural. Now that's changed faster than I would have believed possible. I can't get my head around it.

But I'll have to, because these two are just warming up. I came down for breakfast this morning and found Dervish and Juni already in the kitchen, kissing passionately, and I swear if he'd had his tongue any further down her throat he'd have been licking her lungs!

→Bill-E thinks the Dervish/Juni match is great. We've been spending more time together since Loch's death, hanging out at lunch, having long chats like in the old days. I thought he might be jealous of all the time Juni spends with Dervish but he's not bothered.

"It's what Dervish needs," he contends. "He's been alone too long."

"He had me," I huff.

"Hardly the same thing," Bill-E laughs. "It'll be good

for him. Maybe he'll get out more and stop moping about the place."

"Dervish doesn't mope."

"Yes he does," Bill-E insists. "At least he did until Juni came along."

→Juni knows I've been thrown by recent developments. She hasn't mentioned her relationship with Dervish or how her moving in might affect me. But she's asked several times, at home and in our sessions, if there's anything I want to talk about apart from Loch's death, if anything else is bothering me. Each time I've said no and glanced away. She hasn't pressed. Giving me time. Leaving me alone until I'm ready to discuss it with her willingly.

→In the middle of all the confusion, Reni starts back at school.

I don't know what to say when we first come face to face. Apart from at the funeral, when we didn't speak, I haven't seen her since Loch's death. My first reaction — a huge bolt of guilt. I covered up the truth about the accident, helped move the body, lied to protect Dervish's secret.

Several seconds of horrible silence. Then, "Hi," Reni whispers.

"Hi," I croak.

She leans towards me and rests her face on my chest. "I miss him, Grubbs," she says, voice cracking.

"Me too," I moan.

Floods of tears. Both of us.

It's easier after that. Not the same as before – it never will be – but it's OK, especially when we're with the others. Now everyone talks openly about Loch, the accident, how hard it's been, not shying away from the subject. We have Juni to thank for that. She's had all of us in her office – or visited us at home – since she came, working doggedly to help us talk about and deal with our grief. Life for us would be a hell of a lot harder without her.

→"What are you doing this weekend?" Shannon asks Reni on Friday.

"Nothing much," Reni says. "Staying in. Studying. I have a lot to catch up on."

"Scratch that," Shannon snorts. "You're coming to the cinema with the rest of us. I won't take no for an answer. Grubbs, you're coming too."

"Yes, boss," I grin, glad for an excuse to get out of the house — Juni's not very big, but the place feels crowded when she's about.

"How will we get there?" Reni asks. There's a small cinema in the Vale but we hardly ever go to it. Much more fun going to a multiplex in one of the bigger towns nearby.

"Frank's Dad will take us," Shannon says. Frank's father is a taxi driver and owns a people carrier. "Won't he, Frank?" Shannon flutters her eyelids at him, buttering him up.

"I'll see what I can do," Frank mutters.

"Can Bill-E come?" I ask, eager to involve him.

"Sure," Shannon says after a moment's hesitation. "The more the merrier."

The gang's been kind about Bill-E since the accident. They don't mind me including him in our lunch-time chats and after-school activities. But I can feel the mood shifting back to the way it used to be. Bill-E's not one of us, and though he was temporarily accepted due to the exceptional circumstances, the natural order of the school world must soon be resumed. The day's fast arriving when I'll have to make a choice — Bill-E or the others.

But that's a bridge to cross another time. This weekend's about friends, films and fun. The more serious stuff can wait.

→Dervish and Juni spend the night practising magic. It seems that Juni has quite a gift. She's learnt a lot over the last several months and can run rings around many of my uncle's spells.

"Have you asked her to join the Disciples?" I enquired earlier this evening, half joking, half serious. "You could head off on demon-bashing weekends together, maybe check out some punk concerts at the same time."

"I don't know," Dervish muttered, not picking up on the joke. "I really don't want to involve her. That life's so dangerous. But I can't stand by and let such power go to waste. We need all the mages we can get. And I think she'll want to join. That might even be why she came looking for me — personal feelings aside, she's seen the Demonata in action, and learnt about the Disicples when they came to Slawter to clear up. She knows what the world's up against, the war that's being fought. Maybe she wants to help. I'll have to broach the subject soon but I'm not looking forward to it."

As wrapped up as he is with Juni, Dervish hasn't forgotten about me. He still checks on me most nights, monitoring me, quizzing me about what I'm feeling, worried about what might lie ahead. We're halfway through the lunar month. I'm just a couple of weeks away from the madness again. Dervish isn't treating it lightly. For all the time he's spent with Juni, and all the excitement and hope he's experiencing, he hasn't neglected his obligations to me. He's been in contact with everyone he can think of, trying to find out more about my situation, if anyone's heard of anything like it before. Working hard for my benefit.

He hasn't mentioned the Lambs, but I'm sure he's thinking about them, just as I am every night, unable to turn away from the thoughts of what must be done if the beast emerges and I change.

→ Heading out to the cinema. I stick my head into the study, to let Dervish and Juni know I'm going. They're sitting together on the floor, facing one another, fingers joined, eyes closed, breathing deeply. Working on a spell. They don't hear me when I call.

I walk in and scribble a note. As I'm sticking it to the front of Dervish's PC, my glance slides to where Juni's sitting. I can see her eyes glowing behind her lids. She looks creepy. I exit quickly and race down the stairs, not sure what it was that freaked me so much, only knowing that I'm glad to be putting some space between us.

→ Eating in a 1950s style hamburger restaurant before the movie. Everyone excited and buzzing, except me. I keep thinking about Juni's eyes, trying to pinpoint what it was about them that unnerved me.

Bill-E's excited to be with us, though he finds it hard to join in all the talk. He'll start to say something, then stop and think about the best way to phrase it. By the time he has the words straight inside his head, the topic's changed. If he'd just be himself he'd be fine. But he thinks he has to be extra witty and cool around us, and by worrying and hesitating, he comes across as dumb and stumbling. I think about saying something to him, but then I fall to thinking about Juni's eyes again.

Reni sits beside me for the film. After a while she takes my hand. I half-turn to smile at her and she smiles back. I thought Loch's death might drive a wedge between us, but it hasn't. She still wants to be my girlfriend. Maybe it's even more important to her now than it was before — the more she focuses on me, the less she'll brood about Loch.

I start to lean over, mouth dry, spinal cord tingling.

But then I think of Juni's eyes again and it finally clicks. The glow reminded me of the fiery, eyeless sockets of one of Lord Loss's familiars — the charmless hell-baby known as Artery.

I draw away from Reni. She stares at me, surprised and slightly hurt. I force a bitter smile. "Later," I whisper. "I'm nervous, you know?" Letting her think I've gone shy. Unable to tell her that thoughts of demons have set my teeth trembling, that I'm afraid I might accidentally bite her tongue if we kiss.

Reni smiles back and gives my hand a squeeze. "I know," she says, finding it sweet. She leans her head on my shoulder and sighs. "When you're ready, give me a shout. I can wait."

I lay my head on hers and close my eyes, drowning out the sounds of the film, trying to listen to her heartbeat, feeling her hair soft against my cheek —

but not able to stop thinking about Juni's eyes and demons.

→As we come out of the cinema I spot a tramp sitting by the side of one of the mall's fountains. We're a long way off but he looks like the same one I ran into on the path home last week. As the others file to the restaurant again, for milkshakes, I halt and fix my gaze on the tramp. I'm certain it's him — same shaggy beard, long hair, old clothes, posy of flowers in a buttonhole. And maybe it's my imagination, but he seems to be looking back at me, returning my stare.

I start towards him, not entirely sure why, but bothered by his being here, wanting to make sure it's the same man. Then Reni notices I'm not with the group. She calls my name. When I don't respond, she calls again, sharply.

"Sorry," I mutter, taking my eyes off the tramp. "Thought I saw someone I knew."

"Who?" Reni asks.

"Nobody." I smile when she frowns at me. "A teacher. But it wasn't. Come on, let's go tuck into our shakes."

"You're in a strange mood tonight," Reni comments, towing me along to catch up with the others.

Just before we turn the corner, I look back at the fountain. But nobody's there now. The tramp has gone.

* * *

→Home. Troubled. Thinking about the tramp. Probably nothing, just coincidence that I've seen him a couple of times. But it might be something more. We're protected here from demons, Dervish has said it dozens of times. But some demons have human assistants. What if the tramp is working for Lord Loss, waiting for the chance to knock me out and cart me away to a spot where the demon master can set his evil hands on me?

I decide to tell Dervish. I might wind up looking like a frightened fool, jumping at shadows, but it's best not to take chances with stuff like this. I go searching for Dervish in his study, then his bedroom, but I only find Juni, sitting on the edge of Dervish's bed, staring out the window, pensive.

"Hi," I say. "Is Dervish about?"

"He's gone for a Chinese."

"Oh." The local Chinese takeaway does home deliveries but Dervish doesn't trust them to send the correct food. He always fetches it himself. "No worries. I'll catch him when he's back." I start to leave.

"Grubbs," Juni stops me. She pats the space on the bed next to her. There's a long silence as I settle beside her. She continues to stare out the window. She's so slender, I feel even bigger than normal sitting next to her.

"I saw you earlier, in the study," Juni says.

"How?" I frown. "Your eyes were closed."

"I could see through the lids — part of the spell. You looked scared. You ran away as if I frightened you." I fidget uncomfortably. "Are you afraid that Dervish is falling in love with me? That I'm going to steal his love for you?"

"No," I laugh. "That wasn't it at all."

"Then why did you look so spooked?"

"Your eyes." I clear my throat. "They were like a demon's that I fought."

Juni tenses when I mention the D word. Then relaxes. "We haven't talked much about that, have we?" she notes softly.

"No."

"I'm still haunted by what happened," she whispers. "I'm dealing with it, but it's hard. Knowing there are demons in the world… or tearing at the edges of it… wanting to grab us and destroy…"

"I know exactly how you feel. I hate them too. They terrify me." I blush at the confession. "That's why I ran. I didn't realise it till later, but your eyes reminded me of a demon's. I panicked. It was silly, but…" I shrug.

"You think I have a demon's eyes?" Juni asks, bemused.

"No," I chuckle. "It was just magic. Dervish told me magic comes from demons, that the energy we tap into has seeped through from the Demonata's universe.

Every time we cast a spell, we use a bit of demonic energy. I guess it makes us look like them sometimes. This was just the first time I noticed it."

Juni nods, understanding. Then, out of nowhere, she says, "Dervish is going to ask me to move in."

"Oh?" I blink.

"I don't know if I should." She looks worried. "This has taken me by complete surprise. Maybe I need to slow things down. Stay away for a while. Give us all some space and time."

I stare at her clumsily. I can't think of anything to say. I know nothing about stuff like this. After a few seconds, Juni laughs and lays a hand on my knee. "Sorry. I don't expect you to decide for me. I just needed to say it out loud."

"I... I think... I mean... Dervish likes you. *Really* likes you. I... I think you should say yes."

"You wouldn't mind?" she asks softly.

"No."

"You're sure?" Her fingers tighten on my knee. "Since I got involved with Dervish, I've noticed a change in your response to me. I wasn't sure you approved of our relationship. I thought you didn't like me, that you didn't want me to—"

"No," I interrupt. "That's crazy. I... No." Smiling now. "It's been strange, having you here, but I'm not against it. Honest. I'd like it if you moved in."

Juni smiles blazingly. "You don't know how glad I am to hear that." She leans over and kisses my cheek. My blush darkens and spreads. She tweaks my nose, then gets up. "Come on," she says, heading for the door. "Dervish will be back soon. We ordered extra in case you wanted any. You can help me prepare some plates."

Following her down the stairs, grinning to myself, delighted to find that I truly don't mind if she comes to live with us. Figuring crowded might not be such a bad thing for this hollow old house.

→Late Sunday. Juni was right. Dervish asked her last night if she'd come live with us. She agreed, but said it would have to be for a trial period. They'll see how they get on and if things don't work, she'll move out again.

She made the big switch today. Didn't have much to bring. She's moved around a lot this year, living out of a suitcase. She had a house once, but sold it when she accepted the movie job with Davida Haym. She's been living in hotels since then. Says she has bits and bobs in storage, which she can fetch later, but there's no urgency.

Dervish is like a child at Christmas. When Juni left to check out of her hotel this morning, he spent the time polishing and cleaning, making sure everything would be shiny and perfect when she returned. He's been dancing around the house like a pantomime fairy, whistling, sometimes singing out loud.

Give me strength!

They're in bed now. It's nearly two in the morning. They've probably been asleep for hours, but I can't nod off. Worrying about lycanthropy. Magic. Juni moving in and how that's going to change things. Loch. Reni. The tramp. (I forgot to tell Dervish about him.)

I get up and dress. Pad downstairs and let myself out. Start walking, then jogging. Soon I'm running, breathing hard, breath turning to mist on the cool night air. I develop a stitch. Ignoring it, I run until it feels as if my stomach is on fire. Finally I stop and bend over, panting like a thirsty dog. When I can breathe normally I set off again, but only jogging this time, pacing myself.

It's hard to jog at night. The forest is dark around me. Have to be careful where I put my feet. But I'm not afraid. The sounds and smells of the night don't scare me. I'm safe here, on home turf.

I jog without direction, simply enjoying the exercise. Letting my feet guide me. Not keeping track of my route, confident I can find my way back.

Then I round a patch of briars and spot scatterings of rocks and earth — I'm at the entrance to the cave. I stop and squint suspiciously. Dervish hasn't had time to fill in the hole. He stuck a crate down it and covered it with soil and small stones so nobody would fall down into the cave, but that's as far as he got.

I approach the hole cautiously, wondering if I've been drawn here by some external force or if it's just coincidence. I listen closely for whispers but I can't hear anything. Can't sense anything either — no magical warmth within, or feeling that I'm being summoned.

I stop at the edge of the hole and stare down into darkness, thinking about Loch. It seems so long ago that we were messing about here, dreaming of Lord Sheftree's buried treasure. Everything was simple then. You don't recognise the good times in life until it all goes bad and you look back and see how lucky you were, how easy you had things.

I wonder where Loch is now, if there's an afterlife, what it's like if there is. Is he sitting on a cloud, plucking at the strings of a harp? Wrestling with angels? Being waited upon by beautiful women? Does he know the answers to all the questions in the universe? Has he come back as somebody else or as an animal? Or is there nothing when you die? I know people have souls, but do they vanish into oblivion when the body shuts down? Is life the start and finish of all that we are? Is Loch—

"You're out late."

A voice behind me. I whirl and spot the tramp, half-hidden by shadows, watching me with a little smile that's hard to distinguish behind the tangled bush of his beard.

"Who are you?" I shout. "Why are you following me?"

The tramp steps forward and I get my first good look at him. Dark skin, but I think the colour's more to do with dirt than flesh pigment. Black hair streaked with patches of grey and white. Small build. Cracked fingernails, but not caked with dirt as you'd expect — clean as a surgeon's. Small eyes, blue or grey.

"You should be asleep," the tramp says. A deep voice. Hard to place the accent.

"Who are you?" I growl again, looking for something to defend myself with.

The tramp walks past me to the edge of the hole. Stares down, the same way I was staring moments before. "A grave fit for a king," he murmurs, then looks at me and smiles crookedly. "Have anyone in mind for it?"

"Who are you?" I ask for the third time but my voice is trembling now. This is no ordinary tramp. There's something powerful and dangerous about him.

The tramp doesn't answer my question. Instead he looks up at the sky — at the *moon*. "Won't be long now," he says casually, then skirts the hole and walks off, not looking back, disappearing into the cover of the forest within seconds.

I stay where I am for a minute, shivering. Then bolt for home, to wake Dervish — the hell with his beauty sleep — and tell him about the mysterious, ominous stranger.

→Almost back at the mansion, ready to scream myself hoarse about the tramp, when I slow, frown and pause.

Maybe Dervish already knows.

The tramp knew who I was. I'm pretty sure he knew about the cave too and what happened there. And he definitely knew about the moon and what it's doing to me — that was clear by his mocking tone. If he was a servant of Lord Loss, that would have been the perfect place to ambush me. I was alone. I didn't know he was there until he spoke. He could have clubbed me over the head or injected me with a sleeping drug. But he didn't. So I doubt he's in league with the demon master. If that's the case, he could only have known all those things if he'd been told. And Dervish is the only one who could have told him.

Flashback. Dervish's study... him on the phone... checking afterwards... finding the black folder with the numbers and names.

Figuring — the tramp must be one of the Lambs. A scout, sent to keep an eye on me. Dervish promised to summon a magician to help, but instead he called in the Lambs, to be safe, in case I turn and he can't handle me alone. The tramp has been shadowing me ever since, ready to move quickly if needs dictate.

I enter the house and creep up the stairs. I don't wake Dervish or ask him about the tramp. Just undress and crawl into bed. Cold. Stiff. Terrified. *Alone*.

A SECRET SHARED

→Everything's a blur. School, chatting with my friends, playing happy families with Dervish and Juni. Life goes on as normal around me, and I take part, the way I always have. But I'm not fully there. Always thinking about the moon, the cave, the tramp, Dervish (*possibly*) scheming behind my back. Waiting for the change to hit. Going to bed tense every night, lying in the dark, wondering if this is when I'll turn. Stiffening whenever one of my fingers twitches or my stomach growls. Terror when my lips lift back over my teeth in a wolf-life snarl — then relief when I realise I'm only yawning.

I discuss some of it with Dervish but I'm reluctant to share everything. The more I think about it, the more positive I am — he called in the Lambs. I resent him for that. There's no real reason to. It's not like he's washing his hands of me. I'm sure he'll be extra careful, that he won't let them act unless I'm beyond saving. But why summon them so soon? He didn't with Bill-E. He kept them in the dark. Dealt with it himself while there was still hope. I was sure he'd act the same way with me.

Of course, I'm different. We can't work the Lord Loss angle any more. Dervish didn't call the Lambs in last time because he planned to fight for Bill-E's humanity. If he won, Lord Loss would have cured Bill-E. If he lost, they'd have both been slaughtered by the demon master. Either way, no need for the Lambs. I'm not that lucky. There's no get-out clause in my case.

Also there's the magic. Dervish can deal with a werewolf, but perhaps not one with magical powers. Maybe he's scared, isn't sure what I'll be capable of when I turn, doesn't feel he can handle me solo, wants the security of back-up. Perfectly logical if he does. I can't blame him for that.

But even so, I feel betrayed and the feeling won't go away. I should talk with him, tell him I know he called in the Lambs, discuss my disappointment, give him the chance to explain.

But I don't. Afraid to bring the subject out into the open, like when I first became aware of the magic inside me and kept it secret. Ludicrously hoping that I'm wrong about the tramp, that things aren't at such an advanced stage, that I can still be saved. Figuring if I don't talk about it, maybe it will go away.

Grubbs Grady — human ostrich!

* * *

→A week to go.

Today, at lunch, when we're alone, Reni asks if anything is wrong. I haven't been paying her the kind of attention she expects. She wants to know if I've lost interest, if I'm seeing or thinking about somebody else. She puts it lightly, tries to make a joke of it, but I can see the suspicion and hurt in her eyes.

I lie. Say things are the same as always. Make excuses. Tell her there's a lot of confusion in my life — Loch dying (not that I put it so bluntly), Juni moving in with Dervish. I even mention exams and the future, pretending I'm worried about the direction I'm taking.

She buys it. Thinks I'm going through a mid-teen crisis, that it's nothing to do with her. Willing to wait for my mood to improve. Confident I'll be back looking to put the moves on her once I sort through my problems. Never guessing that they might be the ripping-her-throat-open-with-my-teeth type of moves — if I turn into a werewolf next weekend.

→Walking home slowly, watching for the tramp. I've caught glimpses of him since that night at the cave, hanging around school, on the streets of Carcery Vale, once in the trees across from my bedroom window. But he's kept at a safe distance. No follow-up contact. Slips away if I try to approach.

I'm surprised he even spoke to me that once. Maybe it was an accident — late at night, standing guard in the forest, at the scene of a tragedy. Perhaps the mood affected him and he spoke without meaning to. I'm sure even the executioners of the Lambs are prone to human slip-ups every now and then.

Thinking about the tramp and the Lambs as I let myself in. Wondering how they kill the werewolves. I imagine it's clinical and undramatic, probably a powerful poison, injected humanely. But I can't help playing out shock-horror scenes — hordes of Lambs dressed as tramps surrounding me, attacking me with machetes and clubs, a slow, humiliating, painful death.

"Grubbs," Dervish calls as I'm heading up the stairs, disrupting my train of morbid thoughts. "Could you come see me when you're ready?"

"Sure." Up to my room. Toss my bag into a corner. Out of my uniform swiftly, into jeans and a baggy sweater seconds later. Jog back down in my socks to find Dervish and Juni sitting on one of the couches in the TV room, looking edgy and stern.

I take a seat, wary. I look at them and they stare at me. A long, ragged silence. Then Dervish speaks quickly. "I've told Juni about you. About *us*. The family curse. What's been happening with you recently."

I blink slowly and glance at Juni. Can't tell what she's thinking. Wearing her most enigmatic counsellor's face.

"I thought long and hard about this," Dervish says, leaning forward. "It would have been easy to ask Juni to go away next weekend and keep her out of the loop. Easy and safe." He looks at her. She smiles briefly and lays a hand on his. "But we need her help. I don't know why, but you've stopped talking to me. This last week or two, you've been withdrawn, moody, sullen. Maybe it's just fear. But I think there's more to it. You've cut me out as if you have issues with me and that's not good. I need to know what you're thinking and feeling. I can't help you if I don't know what's going on inside your head."

"You think Juni can open me up," I say stiffly. "Stick me on a couch, get into my brain, worm out the truth."

"Maybe," Dervish mutters.

"We only have your best interests at heart," Juni says. "This is a troubled time for you. Dervish wants to help. I do too. If you have problems with your uncle – or with me – you should lay them out in the open. Or, if it's something you don't want to discuss with Dervish, perhaps you can tell me in private."

"Patient to counsellor?" I sneer.

"If you like," she says calmly. "I'd rather talk informally as a friend, but if you prefer we can do it professionally, with the guarantee of confidentiality."

"I don't mind," Dervish says. "I just want to help you survive the next week. If I've upset you and you don't want to tell me about it, fine. But you don't have to cut Juni out. Surely you can talk with her if not with me."

"What if there's no problem?" I mumble. "What if I'm just scared to death that I'm going to turn into a werewolf and don't feel like talking about it?"

"That would be entirely understandable," Juni says. "But unless you're sure that's the case, you should discuss it with someone. Talking about your fears can be a highly positive experience. You know that, Grubbs. You're not an innocent child. Going through this alone is a bad call."

"Especially as you might not even be going through it," Dervish says. I look at him with a raised eyebrow. "You mightn't be turning. Juni thinks…" He stops and looks at her.

"Just because people in your family are victims of a disease which alters their bodies – I refuse to refer to them as werewolves, since that's a hysterical term – it doesn't mean *you* are going to change," Juni says. "From what you've described, it sounds as if you're in trouble, but it's by no means certain. This might be a mental problem, not a physical one."

"You think I'm imagining things?" I growl.

"Perhaps," Juni says. "The mind can play tricks on the most ordinary people — and you're far from ordinary! To come through what you have… to see so much of the world – and other worlds – at such a young age… to lose your loved ones in a grisly fashion, then fight for your brother's life… what happened to us in Slawter… Your resilience amazes me. You're one of the strongest people I've ever met and I'm not saying that to stroke your ego. You're incredible, Grubbs."

I smile crookedly, blushing, tears coming to my eyes. Part of me wants to leap up and hug her. Another part wants me to wave her compliment away and act cool. In the end I just carry on smiling, blushing and crying lightly.

"But even the strongest of us has a breaking point," Juni says. "Maybe Loch was yours. Or perhaps there's something else, a small upset you're not even aware of. It's possible you're turning — but it's also possible you're not. I want to try and find out. In a week we'll know for definite. But we can cover a lot of ground in a week. It could make a real difference if you're wrong about the change."

"And if I'm right?" I ask tightly.

Juni beams. "We'll just have to fire a silver bullet through the middle of your forehead."

I laugh loudly. Dervish does too.

"My sense of humour's rubbing off on her," Dervish chuckles proudly.

"You say that like it's a good thing."

"Boys, boys," Juni tuts. "Let's not get sidetracked. Grubbs, will you accept my offer of help? Talk with me privately if you have something you don't want to say to both of us? Accept me as a counsellor if not a friend?"

I almost blurt it out and tell them I know about the Lambs, which is why I've been so surly. But that would mean a confrontation with Dervish, admitting to his face that I feel he betrayed me. I can't do that, not after all the good things he's done for me. If I'm wrong, it would hurt him to hear me speak that way.

So I take Juni up on her offer, lower my head to hide my thoughts, and mutter, "Yeah, talking with you sounds good."

"Thank you," Juni says.

"Nice one," Dervish adds.

And we pretend for a while that everything's fine and all our problems have been solved.

→Long talks with Juni at school in the day and at home in the evenings. Not just about Loch. We cover all kinds of ground — my past, parents, Gret, Lord Loss, the institute, life with Dervish, Bill-E changing into a werewolf, Slawter. All the things we didn't discuss before, when she was only interested in helping me deal with Loch's death.

We spend a lot of time on magic, the buzz of energy I sometimes feel in my gut, what I've done with it, my mind-set when the magic was flowing through me. With

Dervish's permission, Juni runs some tests, trying to tap into my magical core, to find out what's going on inside, what I might be capable of doing. But she comes up blank. If the magic's still there, it's buried too deep for her to find.

She also spends a lot of time researching the Demonata, pumping Dervish for information, finding out all she can about them. She's especially hot on Lord Loss — if he's able to cure our lycanthropic curse, she doesn't see why we shouldn't be able to do it too.

"We're not powerful enough," Dervish tells her.

"Maybe it's just a matter of knowing the right spells," Juni suggests.

"I don't think so," he says. "If that was the case, Bartholomew Garadex would have discovered them. He was dogged in his determination to end the curse but he got nowhere by himself. It takes a demon master to overturn the spell."

"But—"

"No," Dervish insists. "Bartholomew was the world's most powerful magician of the last couple of centuries. If he wasn't able to do it, none of us can. We'd be wasting our time if we went down that avenue."

"What if we tried Lord Loss?" she asks. "Maybe you're wrong about him not accepting the chess challenge again."

"No," Dervish laughs shortly. "That isn't an option."

"But if he's the only one who can turn Grubbs back..." Juni persists.

"It's not an option," Dervish says again. Firmly. End of discussion.

→I'm enjoying my time alone with Juni. She's different than when she was merely counselling me. Magic is her thing, what really interests her. She's more open when we're talking about spells and demons. She lets her guard down and stops treating me like a patient. Sometimes it seems we talk more about her and magic than we do about me and my problems, but that's fine.

She still sees Bill-E and some of my friends in her professional capacity, but not as much as before. She's due to finish at our school at the end of the week. Misery's not returning but he's being replaced by another counsellor. Juni's done what she set out to. Time to move on to another job, another challenge. But she's not thinking about that until after the weekend. First she wants to see what happens to me when the full moon rises.

→Thursday. Testing for magical potential again. In the TV room. Dervish is in the kitchen, keeping out of the way. Juni's trying something new. Up to this point she's probed carefully, gently, just scratching the surface. Tonight she wants to go deeper.

"Relax," she says, standing behind me as I squat on a stool. "Clear your mind." She puts her hands on my head. "I'm going to provoke you." Her fingers slide to my neck and her nails scratch the flesh there, lightly. "I'm going to pick and poke at your flesh while I jab magically at you. It will be more irritating that way. I'm hoping something will stir within you in response, drive me out and stop me hurting you."

"'Hurting'?" I repeat uneasily.

"Don't worry." I sense her smile. "I won't really hurt you. Trust me."

She massages my shoulders. At first it's nice but then she digs her thumbs in. Works her way down my arms, pinching, scratching. Nothing too severe. Just irritating, like she said.

She mutters spells while she works. I feel magic seep into me, a weird sensation beneath my skin. It's like having a dead leg, only I'm itchy all over.

Minutes pass. Juni works. Down my back, my chest, my legs. Very prickly now, twitching and jerking, wishing she'd stop, wondering if I should say something or just grit my teeth and bear it. Finally, when I'm on the point of calling it quits, she releases me.

"Nothing," she says, sounding disappointed. She puts a couple of fingers on my left cheek. "You can open your eyes."

As I blink my eyes open, I catch her looking at me. A strange look. As if she thinks I'm lying and disapproves of me. There's even a shade of hostility in it.

"It was definitely there before," I tell her as she takes her fingers away.

"I'm sure it was," she says, the suspicious look disappearing.

"Maybe it'll come back tomorrow or the next night. When the moon…" I nod towards the window, where the curtains keep out the light of the almost full globe.

"Perhaps," she says. "Magic is certainly affected by lunar movements. Most mages experience a surge of extra energy around the time of a full moon. But it's strange for you not to be showing *any* signs."

She sits beside me. Brings a hand up and ruffles my hair. Smiles fondly, then whispers, "Tell me your secret. The thing you won't talk to Dervish about. I haven't asked before and I won't ask again if you don't answer. But I think you want to reveal it."

Mouth dry. Heart beating hard. I wasn't going to tell her. I meant to keep it secret. But now that she's asked, I realise she's right. I want to share it with her. Hell, I'm suddenly longing to spill the beans.

"He called the Lambs," I croak.

"Lambs?" she frown. "What have sheep to do with this?"

"No. Family executioners. The Lambs. When one of us turns… if the parents can't bear to keep them alive, but can't kill them by themselves, the Lambs do it."

"Ah. I remember. The dream in Slawter. Their laboratory." Her frown deepens. "You think Dervish summoned them? That he's plotting against you?"

"Not plotting," I mutter. "But if I turn and he can't control me, I think he wants them to kill me. He said he was going to ask a magician for help, but he didn't. He called in the Lambs instead. And that's… y'know… not *fine*, but I know why he did it. I just wish he'd waited. Or told me he was summoning them."

"He hasn't told you?"

"No."

"Then how do you know?"

I explain about his conversation on the phone, the black folder, the tramp. She asks me to describe the tramp but I can only give her a very general description.

"You're certain he's a lamb?" she asks dubiously.

"Pretty sure."

"He never said?"

"No. But he's been hounding me. I've seen him outside this house. And at the cave." We've told her about the cave, how Loch really died. Dervish took her there to get a sense of it. One magical whiff of the place and she agreed he'd done the right thing, that it needed to be hidden from the world. "Why would he be following me if he wasn't one of the Lambs?" I ask.

"There are all sorts of people in the world," Juni says. "Some follow boys for dark – but very human – reasons."

"I know." I shift uncomfortably. "But it'd be an awful coincidence, this tramp taking an interest in me at this precise time."

"I sometimes think the world runs on coincidences." Juni pats my hand. "Don't worry about the tramp. I'll keep an eye out for him. And I'll do a bit of work on Dervish and find out if he really contacted the Lambs."

"You won't tell him what I said, will you?" I ask, alarmed, not wanting him to think I've been bad-mouthing him behind his back.

"I'll be discreet," Juni vows and gets up to leave.

"Juni," I stop her. "When you find out… if he *did* call them in… will you tell me the truth?"

A long pause. Then, "Do you really want to know?"

"Yes."

"You can handle it if he did?"

"Yes."

She smiles and touches my cheek again. "You're so brave," she whispers, then draws the fingers away. "I'll tell you what I find out. I promise. No lies. You can trust me always, Grubbs, about everything — even if you can't trust Dervish."

SHAKE DOG SHAKE

→The shakes. *Bad*. Dervish and Juni keep me pressed down on the bed, talking constantly, wiping sweat from my face with a series of fresh towels, Juni muttering calming spells which don't make the slightest difference.

Friday. The night before the full moon. The sickness struck at school, in the middle of physics. I had to rush for the toilet. Didn't make it. Was violently sick against the classroom door. Lots of cheers from the boys, gasps of disgust from the girls. Didn't stop to catch an earful from Mr Clifford. Bolted for the toilet and spent the next ten minutes hugging a hard plastic seat.

Juni drove me home. I threw up twice into a bag along the way. I've had the dry heaves since then, though Juni makes me drink lots of water, so sometimes I vomit clear, acidic liquid.

"You're going to be OK," Dervish lies, grasping my shoulders as I cry out in pain. It feels as if there's a second body growing within mine, forcing its way out.

"I could try a sleeping spell," Juni says.

"Don't be stupid," Dervish barks. "The only reason he hasn't turned is because he's fighting so damn hard. He can't fight if he's asleep."

"Sorry. I wasn't thinking. I just hate to see him in so much agony."

I scream hoarsely, sure my head is about to split down the middle. Dimly aware of a heat in my stomach, the magical heat which was there last month. It's battling the wolfen change, keeping me human, denying the demands of the beast. Unable to tell Dervish and Juni about it. Incapable of speech. Only screams.

→Later. The moon starting to dip. Moments of quiet after hours of madness. The sheets of the bed are ripped in many places. Dervish is cut above his left eye and both his cheeks are bruised.

"Did… I do… that?" I groan.

"No," he deadpans, carefully pouring water down my throat. "I walked into a wardrobe."

"We thought we'd lost you," Juni says, squeezing my hand. I've scratched her forehead but it's not a deep cut.

"The… magic," I gasp. Both of them pause. "Did you… feel it?"

"No," Dervish says.

"It was… there. That's how… I fought. Would have… turned… otherwise."

"Juni?" Dervish asks.

"I sensed *something*," she says hesitantly. "I wasn't sure if it was magic or the energy generated by the... the alteration."

"The werewolf," I grin weakly. "Go on, say it, just once."

"There's no such creature," Juni huffs.

I start to reply but pain strikes again, deep in my gut. I double over. The water comes up almost as quickly as it went down. Hits Dervish hot in the face. He ignores it and pins me to the bed, talking fast again, trying to comfort me, his words only a dim murmur above my endless, wretched screams.

→The beast snarls and claws at my skin from the inside. It can't speak — it's a wild animal — but I can sense its feelings and translate them into words. *Release me,* it would demand if it could. *End the pain. Set me free. Become what you must. We can run as one and take the night.*

"No!" I howl back, clubbing it down with fists of a magic I don't understand.

You can't deny me.

"Get stuffed!" is my eloquent response.

The internal battle rages on but I have the sense that I'm winning. The pull of the moon is fading. The creature has lost the fight. But there's another night to come and it will be stronger then. Perhaps too strong.

You can't deny me, the beast hisses again from somewhere deep inside me, deeper than it should be. *This is what we are. It's our fate.*

"I'll choose my own fate," I mutter, staying on guard, ready to fight again if it launches a last-minute attack. But it doesn't. The sun is rising. The moon's losing its lustre. I've won — for now.

→Wearily sitting up. Dervish and Juni regard me suspiciously. Both exhausted. Cut, bruised and scratched in many places.

"What happened to you two?" I quip.

"Now he gets cocky," Dervish growls. "For the last eight or nine hours it's been screams and agony, hell on Earth. But now, with the sun rising, you feel like you can joke, regardless of the agony you've put us through."

We regard each other coolly — then laugh.

"We survived!" I shout.

"You beat it!" Dervish chortles, hugging me tight.

Juni just smiles tiredly, watching us.

When Dervish releases me, I collapse backwards and stare at the ceiling.

"How do you feel?" Dervish asks. "Or is that a stupid question?"

"No," I sigh. "I don't feel so bad. Tired, but not as beat as you or Juni look. To tell the truth, I'm hungry."

"If you're expecting breakfast in bed, you're in for a nasty surprise," Juni snaps. Dervish and I giggle.

"It was strange," I mumble, recalling my battle, especially the end when I imagined the beast speaking to me. "Like I was wrestling with another person – a thing – inside myself. But *really* wrestling. Like it was there physically. My body was a ring and there were two of us inside the ropes. It was the hardest fight of my life."

"No piece of cake for us on the outside either," Dervish says, touching his bruised cheeks. "You put us through the wringer. I know you're a colossus in the making, but I wouldn't have credited you with that much strength."

"It would have been worse if the beast had won," I tell him quietly. "I could feel it. So strong. Without the magic, it would have walked all over me, burst loose, torn into you. Tonight... when the moon's full..."

"Don't think about that. We'll take this one fight at a time. Focus on the victory now. Deal with the next bout when we're faced with it." He stands, stretches and groans.

"Go to bed," Juni smiles. "You worked hard and took most of the blows. We both need to get a lot of sleep today, but you more than me."

"I'll be fine," Dervish says, then wobbles on his feet and almost falls. Juni steadies him, then says firmly, "Bed!"

"Yes, miss," Dervish sighs. "You coming?"

"Soon. I want to sit with Grubbs a while longer."

Dervish leaves, rubbing the small of his back and groaning. Juni watches him go, then examines her wounds. Murmuring spells, she brushes her fingers over the light cuts on her arms. They heal swiftly, the flesh closing neatly, only the slightest lines of red giving away the fact that she'd been scratched at all.

"Neat trick."

"A useful spell." She works on her neck and face. "It's no good on deep gashes but it's perfect for little rips like these. Better than plasters or bandages. I'll tidy Dervish up later."

Finishing, she turns her attention to me. Wipes hair back from my eyes. Heals the scratch on my forehead. Rubs the flesh to make sure it's OK, then says softly, "He was terrified. I was too, but not as much as Dervish. He really loves you."

"I know."

"He'd give his life for you if it would change anything."

I stare at her silently. There are tears in her eyes. I instinctively know why she's saying this, defending him when there's no apparent need. "He called the Lambs," I whisper.

She nods miserably. "I got him to admit it. He didn't want to involve them. But if you turn, you have to be killed. He can't do that, not kill his own nephew. So, as much as he hates them…"

"It's OK," I tell her, forcing a weak smile. "He didn't have a choice."

"I suppose." She sighs, lowering her gaze. "I had a son once." I blink, not sure how to respond to this startling, unexpected confession. "A darling boy. He was my world. Died in his sleep a few months before his second birthday. A brain defect. There were no warning signs. Nothing anybody could have done about it."

She breaks down in tears. I pat her back clumsily, wishing I could wash her hurt away with words, feeling as useless as I've ever felt. Finally she regains control and wipes her cheeks dry.

"It almost destroyed me," she croaks. "I survived, but only just. Became a child psychologist so I could be close to other children, ease my pain by helping them with theirs." She laughs hoarsely. "I once said you were psychologically plain. Well, I'm an open book too. Whenever anything goes wrong in my life, I hide behind work, use it to haul myself out of whatever dark hole I've fallen into."

She takes hold of both my hands and squeezes, stronger than I imagined. "When Dervish asked me to move in, I was delighted, not just because I love him, but because it meant I could become a mother to *you*." She lets go of my left hand and strokes my cheek, smiling warmly. "I've always wanted another son to mother but it never quite worked out until now."

The smile fades. She lets go of my other hand and stands. "I won't abandon you," she says, her voice throbbing with surprising menace. "I won't give you over to the Lambs, not unless there's no hope at all. I'll stand by you until the very, *very* end. Even if Dervish doesn't."

Then she's gone, leaving me to stare after her, jaw slack, senses whirring, not quite sure what to make of her fiercely supportive vow.

→A day of rest. We all sleep until early afternoon and lounge around after that. Juni's oddly distant, withdrawn and quiet. Doesn't look at me straight. Or Dervish. Almost as if she's ashamed of what she said. Or is planning something and doesn't want us to know.

→Evening. The shakes again. Throwing up everything I've eaten. I fight my vomitous body, sitting on the grass out back, taking the warm evening sun, determined to enjoy what might be my final sunset. Dervish and Juni are close by. Dervish asks if I want to go in. I shake my head. Don't want to abandon the outside world. Afraid that once I do, that's it, game on... game over... doomed.

Bill-E rang earlier. Wanted to come and hang out. Dervish made my excuses. Said I'd caught a nasty bug. Told Bill-E to stay away in case it was contagious. Bill-E wasn't suspicious. Why should he be?

Thinking about my brother. Wishing I'd told him about us. Dervish was right — I waited too long. I wanted to spare him the emotional roller-coaster ride of the truth, but I was wrong to stall. If I change tonight and the Lambs exterminate me, he'll only think he lost a friend. He'll never know how close we really were.

I consider phoning him, telling him the truth while I'm still capable of speech. But that would be lunacy. If I survive, beat this thing or at least delay my transformation for a month, I can tell him then. Phoning now would be pointless. Worse — dangerous. He might come over. Get in the way. Fall victim to the blood-crazed beast I might by that stage have become.

"Do you still have the cage?" I ask suddenly. Dervish stops talking to Juni and stares at me. "The cage in the secret cellar. Is it still there?"

He nods slowly.

"Put me in it." I thought my voice might quaver but it holds firm. I stare at him unflinchingly.

"If you start to change, we can–" he begins.

"No," I interrupt. "Do it now. Before I turn. I made a mess of you last night. I hurt Juni too. She was able to fix us up, but I'll be stronger tonight. Wilder. Maybe I'll inflict damage she can't cure."

Dervish is silent. He exchanges a look with Juni.

"That could be detrimental," Juni says softly. "You believed in yourself last night. That belief gave you the strength to fight. If you allow yourself to be caged like an animal, perhaps you'll start thinking of yourself as one. You might stop believing... stop fighting."

"I won't."

"It might be for the best," Dervish mutters. "If he does turn, I'm not sure we can control him."

"You have drugs," Juni says. "You can subdue him if you have to."

"Remember Meera?" I say before Dervish can answer. "When Bill-E changed, he got to her. Knocked her out before you could inject him. Almost killed her. If that happens to Juni..."

Dervish's jaw stiffens. "You're right. It has to be the cage." He takes Juni's hand. "It doesn't mean we're giving up. We're just being safe."

She nods reluctantly and looks at me. Her expression communicates the same thing that she promised earlier — "Trust me. I'll stand by you. Even if Dervish doesn't."

I rise quickly. "Best do it now." I take one last look at the sun. "The moon will be up soon." I put my hands on my growling stomach. "I can feel it."

→The cage. Howling. Screaming. Battering the bars. Dervish and Juni on the other side, roaring encouragement, telling me I'm winning, calling to the human within, the one who's rapidly disappearing, giving way to something new, deadly, beastly.

I fight but it's much harder than last night. The beast is stronger. It assaults me without pause, snapping and growling, hurling itself against the ball of magic that is my only protection, ripping into it, howling bloody murder, hellbent on breaking free to run wild and kill.

I grip my head between my hands and scream, veins in my neck stretched, fingers curling inward into claws. I keep shouting my name, trying to hold on to my voice, but all that comes out is a jumbled snarl. And the light around me is changing, becoming darker, the shades more limited, colours fading to grey.

"Not… going… to… turn!" I bellow, having to fight for each word. I let go of my head. Clutch the bars of the cage. Lock gazes with Dervish, then Juni. "Not… going… to…" The last word becomes an inhuman shriek.

"That's right," Dervish shouts desperately. "You won't turn. You're Grubbs Grady. You'll win this fight. Gradys never lose."

"Keep fighting," Juni pleads. She puts her hands over mine. "You can do it. I know you can."

I fall away from the bars, shaking my head, roaring with pain. The beast cackles. The battle continues. Torment claims me whole.

→I've been fighting for hours. At least I think it's hours. Maybe it's just been minutes. Maybe I'm so far gone that I've lost track of time. Perhaps, for me, this night will last an age, neverending, an eternal fight between humanity and a force of wolfen evil.

I slump on the floor, leaning against the bars of the cage, staring around with wide, wild eyes, seeing the main desk, the key to this cage, candles, books, a chess piece in one corner, left over from my last fight here. My skin feels like it's rippling. I want to let it. I'm tired. I can't go on.

You must.

A new voice. Not my own and not the imagined voice of the beast. The voice of magic. It speaks quickly, softly, telling me we can beat this thing if we work together. It starts to explain how I can use it, the spells I need to cast, the words I must chant — but the beast picks that moment to yowl violently, filling my head with white noise, causing me to jam my hands over my ears and scream.

When the noise passes and I lower my hands, the voice of the magic is gone, or is so quiet I can't hear it. I'm not alone. I still sense it there. But I no longer feel like it can help me. I'm losing this battle. Maybe I've already lost and just don't know it yet.

→More fighting. Pain. Terror.

Another rare moment of rest and understanding. On the opposite side of the cage this time, but in the same slumped position as before. Dervish and Juni are crouched close by, telling me how well I'm doing, how proud they are, I'm going to win, I just have to ride it out.

I turn my head a fraction and smile sadly at Dervish. "Sorry," I croak.

"No," he snaps. "You can't give up. You have to beat this thing."

"Sorry," I mutter again, head dropping, panting hard, crying, tears hot on my cheeks, not feeling like they're mine.

"He's slipping from us," Juni says. She sounds much calmer than my uncle.

"No!" Dervish barks. "I won't let him. We have to–"

"Quiet," Juni commands.

"But we can't–"

"We won't." She reaches in and tilts my head back. It takes a few seconds but my eyes finally focus. She's studying me coolly. "He's losing concentration. We have to help him regain it. Jolt him back into action and spur him on to fight."

"How?" Dervish asks tightly.

"A spell. One to act on the magic within him. It will be like injecting him with adrenaline — only it's magic we'll inject into, not flesh."

"What spell?" Dervish growls. "I don't know any—"

"I've been preparing one," Juni cuts in. "Just in case." She looks away from me and trades gazes with Dervish. "It's dangerous. If it doesn't cure him, it will kill him. I didn't want to use it unless absolutely necessary. I still won't, not unless he slips further and concedes more ground to the... *werewolf*." She smiles fleetingly as she says it. Then her expression firms again. "I won't do it if you object, but I want you to know it's there if we need it. And I have to know if you'll consider letting me use it, so I can finish preparing."

Dervish looks lost, like he wants to cry. For a moment I don't think he's going to respond. But then, with a wrenching effort, he nods stiffly. "But only if there's no other choice," he wheezes.

"Of course." Juni touches his cheek lovingly. "You'll need to go to the house. If I proceed with the spell, there are things I'll need."

"What?"

Juni closes her eyes. A couple of seconds pass. She opens them again. "Got it?"

"Yes." Dervish laughs crazily. "You'll have to teach me how to do that." Then he stumbles for the door leading to the wine cellar.

Juni waits till he's gone, then hurries to the desk, grabs the key to the cage and inserts it in the lock.

"What are you doing?" I mumble, backing away from her as she opens the door and enters my lair. "Get out. It's not safe. I could—"

"The Lambs are outside," Juni says, stooping beside me, taking my hands, helping me to my feet. "Dervish was in contact with them earlier. They have the house surrounded. Ready to finish you off when Dervish gives the word."

I shrug wearily. "Maybe it's for the best. I can't be helped. They—"

"No!" Juni hisses and slaps my face. "I won't let you sacrifice yourself. I don't believe you're lost. We can get through this but only by thinking positively, only if you fight. Dervish doesn't understand. He called this wrong. He loves you but he underestimates you. He doesn't know how strong you are."

"No. I'm weak. I can't fight any more. I just want to let it happen. Simpler that way. I'm sick of all the pain."

"I don't care how sick you are!" Juni snaps. Then her voice changes. "I'm not doing this just for you. I want you to live for *me* too."

She grabs me by the front of my jumper, pulls me in close and kisses me. It starts innocently, the way my Mum used to kiss me when I was little and woke up scared in the middle of the night. But then it changes into something deeper and I kiss her back, the way I kissed Reni when we played spin the bottle.

The beast within me howls as we kiss. The magic surges and seethes. Around us the bars of the cage turn red, then crack and melt, tumbling away. The roof of the cage falls upon us. I swat it aside with a single powerful hand.

Juni releases me. She's breathing hard. "Run, Grubbs," she says, eyes bright, cheeks flushed. "Get away from the Lambs. Go the cave. Wait for me there."

"The cave? But… if I turn…"

"You won't," she vows and kisses me again, quickly this time. "*Go!*"

Without thinking, I bolt. Leaping over the bubbling bars of the cage, I race to the other exit, the one that leads away from the house. I tear the door open and flee up the stairs. Juni cheers encouragingly behind me, then laughs, her laughter trailing me, staying with me, comforting me, urging me on.

* * *

→The top of the stairs. The way ahead blocked by a pair of doors, locked from the other side by chains, covered by a sheet of corrugated iron. I pause for the briefest of seconds, then set my right shoulder to the doors and thrust sharply. The chains snap. The doors explode open. The sheet of iron flies clear.

I emerge into moonlight.

Standing in the open, chest rising and falling rapidly, staring around, seeing the world with eyes one third human, one third animal, one third magic. Picking out shapes, even if they're hidden from direct sight by trees or the house. Nine… ten… eleven… twelve. The dirty dozen. But not dirty enough to hold Grubbs Grady — über-escapee!

The beast in me wants to attack, rip them open, teach them not to mess with the Grubbster. But tempting as that thought is, I push it away and break for the forest instead.

There are three members of the Lambs back here. The unexpected shattering of the doors stunned them. But they recover quickly. Their training kicks in and they move to intercept me. Large men with clubs, stun guns, nets, rifles.

"Halt!" one of them shouts, aiming a rifle. I snarl at his gun and it turns bright red. He screams and tries to throw it away. Fails, because it's burnt into his flesh and welded itself to the bones in his hand.

The second Lamb rushes me, tries to bring me down with a rugby tackle. I grab him as he leaps, spin him round in the air, then slam him down hard, knocking him out — a perfect wrestling move. Loch would be proud. If I had time, I'd pin him for a three count. But as powerful and playful as I feel, I can't linger. If the rest of the Lambs converge, things might not go so smoothly. I think I could take them all on and beat them but it would be stupid to put myself to the test.

The third of the rearguard has fumbled out a walkie-talkie and is barking into it. I growl in his direction. Metallic claws sprout from the hard plastic and dig into the flesh and bones of the Lamb's face. Roaring with shock and pain, he tries jerking the walkie-talkie loose but the claws have dug in too deep, wiring the device to his jaw.

I leave the Lamb stumbling around, screaming, tugging at the walkie-talkie, blood pouring from his ear and cheek. I race for the cover of the trees, moving swiftly, surely, feeling more alive than ever before.

As I reach the forest I spot the tramp standing nearby, watching me. I laugh at him — he saw what happened to the others and is too scared to tackle me. I think about turning his legs to jelly or setting his clothes on fire, but since he's not interfering with my escape, why bother? The spineless creep isn't worth the effort.

I want to shout, "So long, sucker!" but my vocal cords are twisted and words won't form. I settle for a mock salute instead. He stares back silently, face impassive.

Then I'm gone, sheltered from the moon and hidden from the remaining Lambs by the trees. Running with the ease of a wolf. Fast and slick, leaving no trail for anyone to follow. Heading for the cave and my reunion with Juni.

SAVAGE

→For a couple of minutes I feel like a superhuman. Legs of steel, iron lungs, running faster than any normal person ever ran, obliterating records. Where are the Olympic judges when you need them?

But then I slow. Pain sweeps through me. I stumble. The beast snarls. Writhing on the cold, hard forest floor. Sobbing. Trying to fight. I raise my head and try…

→Next thing I know, I'm in the hole that leads to the cave, tugging at the crate which Dervish left there, ripping it to splinters, clambering down into the dark abyss. Part of me hesitates. Grateful to still be human, eager to reach the safety of the cave, happy to wait for Juni, but remembering Dervish's warning — this cave is dangerous, a place of evil magic. Perhaps I should…

→In the cave. I'm howling, the howls echoing eerily. With an effort I make myself stop and the echoes die away. Then all I can hear is the waterfall and the super-fast beating of my over-worked heart.

How long have I been unconscious, howling, the beast thinking it had won, only for me to somehow scrap my way back and regain control? Impossible to tell but it doesn't feel like a lot of time has passed.

The dark is absolute. It scares me. The feeling of invulnerability and supremacy which drove me through the cordon of Lambs has passed. The magic's still there and so is the beast. But mostly it's just me now, human and cold, alone in the dark, thinking with horror how close I came to killing the three Lambs, hoping I didn't hurt them too much, wondering if I did the right thing by running.

I slide to the floor and huddle my knees to my chest, clasping them tight, trying to see something – anything – through the darkness. Remembering Juni's kiss with confusion and shame, wondering what prompted it, or if I just imagined the adult passion. What I definitely didn't imagine — she said she'd stand by me even if Dervish gave up. She set me free and promised to meet me here.

It's wrong. Her intentions were good, but we shouldn't be doing this. I should have stayed and took what I had coming. Let Dervish handle the situation the way he thought best. He knows more about these matters than Juni or me. I've passed a fatal point. Split from Dervish. Crossed swords with the Lambs. Made a pact with Juni that's cut me off from everybody else. What if she doesn't come? What if she changes her mind and leaves me here? What if...

A light. I start to rise, thinking it's Juni. But then I see that it's coming from the wall of the cave, close to where the waterfall flows, just to the left of the crack I created in the rock. A strange, soft light, not of natural origin. It comes from within the wall. Circular but jagged round the rim. And in the centre, forcing its way out of the rock and into shape — the girl's face I saw when Loch died.

The jaw, cheekbones and forehead bulge outwards, illuminated by the light. The face looks like a cross between rock and flesh, neither one nor the other but a splice of the two. When it's jutting out as far as it can – I can see the tips of its ears – the eyes open. A moment later the lips move.

She speaks with urgency, words tripping off her tongue. I can tell it's important – her need to communicate something vital is clear – but I can't understand what she's saying. The language isn't like any I've ever heard.

"I don't know what you're saying," I moan, shaking my head helplessly. In response she raises her voice and speaks even quicker than before — as if *that* will help! "I can't understand you," I shout, losing my temper.

Then the pain hits again. The beast howls. Magic flares. I sink to my knees, moaning. The girl's voice rises. She yells, harassing me, repeating the same sharp phrases over and over. But I couldn't make sense of her words the first time and I can't make sense of them now. I want her to leave me alone.

"Stop," I groan, but she doesn't. "Stop." Firmer this time, glaring at her, letting her see the anger in my eyes. I need peace and quiet if I'm to fight the beast and drive it back into its den. Doesn't she realise how hard this is and that she's only making it harder?

No, she doesn't. Or if she does, she doesn't care. She keeps on jabbering, voice rising, words coming faster and faster. Then a pair of hands grow out of the rock and she points at me accusingly, at the cave in general, at the crack in the rock.

"Shut up," I hiss, feeling the beast scrape the inside of my skull with its claws. "I can't take any more. Stop it. Stop it! *STOP!*"

With the final cry I lunge to my feet, throw my hands wide and scream.

A sharp snapping sound — the crack beside the waterfall widens and lengthens. The girl's face and hands disappear. And the waterfall freezes. It turns to ice. A solid stretch of crystal from top to bottom, glistening beautifully, caught in full motion, an image no artist could ever hope to replicate.

I stare at the ice, mesmerised. How the hell did I do that?

Then the light where the girl's face was fades. I'm plunged into darkness again. Moments later, while my head's still spinning, I notice the glow of another light behind me. I turn, expecting the face again. But this is the flickering of a torch. And it's coming from overhead, from the shaft to the forest above.

"Grubbs?" someone calls — the most welcome voice in the world.

"Juni!" I cry, stumbling towards the spot where she'll enter the cave. "Come quick. You'll never believe—"

Agony. A flash of total torment. The beast, closer to the surface than ever. Incredibly powerful. The magic flares in response. The pair wrestle, spitting flames, fighting for possession of my body and soul.

I collapse, screaming. Juni shouts my name again. The world dims around me. My thoughts go thin. I try to call and warn her to stay away. But it's too late. I go under. The beast drives me down. I vanish.

→Returning to my senses. Indescribable relief. When I felt myself lose control that last time, I thought I was finished. No more Grubbs Grady. Lost forever. Werewolf in command from this night till doomsday. It's good – delicious! – to be back.

But relief fades as quickly as it swelled. I'm no longer in the cave. I'm in a house and there's blood everywhere. A couple of mauled, gutted bodies on the floor. Juni stands across from me, beaten and bruised, bleeding freely from her arms, head, neck. She's facing me, talking rapidly, hands outstretched and making frantic gestures, trying to calm me down.

I'm growling at her, my bloodstained fingers curled into fists, keeping her away from the corpses — apparently the beast wanted them all for himself.

I manage to stop growling and lower my hands.

"Grubbs?" Juni croaks nervously. "Is that you?"

"*Uhrs*." I cough. Clear my throat and try again. "Yes."

"Thank god," she weeps, collapsing. "I thought you were going to kill me."

"I'd never..." I stop and look around. I know this house. And now that I look past the layers of blood, I know the people.

Ma and Pa Spleen!

"No!" I cry. "Not Bill-E! Tell me I didn't—"

"Behind you," Juni says through her tears.

I turn slowly, expecting the worst, ready to rip my own heart out if I've killed my brother. But he's alive. Lying on his stomach, unconscious, bleeding from a blow to his head. But his body's moving with his breath. I go to him quickly, turn him over on to his back, make him comfortable, check that the cut to his head isn't serious.

"You changed," Juni moans. "I couldn't stop it. I thought I could tap into the magic of the cave and help. But you became a monster and tried to kill me. I managed to ward you off. Quenched the light. Hid in the darkness. Masked my smell using magic.

"Then you left. I tracked you here. You burst in before I arrived. Killed the old pair. You would have killed Billy too, but I fought and stalled you. I don't think I could have held you off much longer. If you hadn't turned back when you did…"

She breaks down. I stare at her, then at Bill-E. Then at the butchered Ma and Pa Spleen. I never liked them. They were cranky, selfish busybodies. Always interfering, trying to keep Bill-E and me apart. But they didn't deserve this — ripped to pieces in their own home by a savage animal of the night.

"What have I done?" I cry, sinking to the floor, burying my head in my hands. "I killed them. I'm a murderer."

"No," Juni sobs, crawling across, trying to prise my hands away. "It was the beast… the werewolf. You didn't do this, Grubbs. It wasn't your fault."

"Of course it was!" I scream, head shooting up. "I knew what was happening. I knew I had to be locked up, what I could do if unleashed. I should have stayed in the cage and let the Lambs slaughter me."

"Don't say that," Juni pleads.

"It's true," I cry. "*I* should be dead now, not the Spleens. It should be..." I stop, frowning. "But why did I come here? Why pick on them and Bill-E?"

"You didn't like them," Juni reminds me.

"But I didn't hate them. And Bill-E's my best friend. Why...?"

"Does it matter?" she interrupts sharply. "You were jealous of Billy, or you wanted to kill his grandparents, or the beast just came to somewhere it knew, to a familiar place it stole from your memories. It could have been your home, school, another friend's house. It happened to be here. What of it? Just be glad you regained consciousness before... before..." She can't continue.

I pat Juni's head as she cries. The tears have dried in my own eyes. I'm staring at the dead bodies again, but calmly, detached, knowing what must be done.

"Phone Dervish," I tell Juni. "Give him our position. Ask him to bring the Lambs. I won't fight. They can have me. I'll surrender."

"No!" Juni gasps. "They'll kill you."

"They'll exterminate me," I correct her. "And that's what I need. This can't go on. I was wrong to run. I..." A thought. "Dervish doesn't know you helped me, does he?"

She shakes her head. "I told him you broke out, that I tried to stop you but couldn't. He took off with the

Lambs to track you down. I stayed behind, then sneaked out once they'd gone. He doesn't know anything."

"Good. Forget about ringing him. I'll do it. Go home and clean yourself up. Say nothing about this to him. You don't have to be involved."

"You don't know what you're saying."

"Yes I do. This has gone far enough. Too far. I killed tonight. Whether it was me or the beast doesn't matter. We both know that, if I carry on, I'll kill again. That can't happen. I won't allow it. So go. Thanks for everything, but I'm past helping." I reach for my phone and start tapping in numbers.

Juni gently takes the phone from me. "Come away with me," she whispers. "We'll go where nobody can find us, where you can't hurt anybody."

"What are you talking about?" I frown, trying to get the phone back.

"We'll run," she hisses, holding the phone out of reach. She's stopped crying. Sounds more like her old self. I can imagine her brain whirring behind her eyes. "Head for somewhere secluded and remote. When the next full moon comes, we'll go up a mountain or into a cave. I'll tie you up and sedate you with magic and drugs to make sure you can't kill anyone. I'll only set you free when the moon has passed. We'll stay in that place and carve out new lives for ourselves. Keep the world safe from you… from the beast."

"You're fantasising," I sigh. "It wouldn't work. You saw what I did to the cage. I'd escape and kill again."

"No," she insists. "I can control you. I'm sure I can."

"And if I change forever the next time?" I ask. "If the beast takes over?"

"Then I'll do what the Lambs tried to do tonight," she vows. Takes my hands and squeezes. "Don't doubt my conviction. If I have to kill you, I will, regardless of how much that would hurt me. But I don't want to harm you if I don't have to. I still believe you can be saved. The werewolf should have taken you over tonight, but it didn't. You fought it and won. You can win again, I'm sure you can. If I'm wrong... if you lose..." Her jaw goes firm. "So be it. But we have to try. Life's too precious to throw away needlessly."

"I don't know." I look at the bodies again, at Bill-E. "The risks..."

"There'll be none," she promises, standing and pulling me up. "We'll leave immediately and find a place where you can't hurt anyone."

I hesitate, torn between knowing the right thing to do and wanting to live.

"If not for yourself," Juni says softly, "do it for me. I love you, Grubbs. Please. Stay alive. For me."

I don't know what to say. I want to go with her. But the beast... the magic... the murders. I open my mouth, meaning to ask for the phone again, making up my mind to act bravely, selflessly, for the welfare of those I care about.

But what comes out is a weak, "OK. But you have to promise to keep me away from people. And, if necessary, you'll stop me the next time, any way you can."

Juni crosses her heart and smiles. "I promise."

She goes to the back door and opens it, then pushes me ahead of her, out into the night. I stumble through the doorway meekly, silently cursing myself for my cowardice, head low, crying again. Once I'm out, Juni quietly closes the door on the bloodshed and carnage, leaving Bill-E sleeping, to awaken later in the morning to horror and chaos.

FLY ME TO THE MOON

→Juni finds a car parked close by. She mutters a quick spell and the doors open. Another spell and the engine fires. She smiles at me through the window and nods for me to get in.

Sitting numbly beside her as she drives. Thinking about the last twelve hours. Studying the blood caked to my hands. Wondering if Bill-E saw me kill his grandparents, if he recognised me behind the mask of the beast. If not, will Dervish tell him? Will he hate me or understand? I think hate. If I was in his shoes, I'd despise the monster who let this happen. No excuses. No forgiving.

Running away is wrong. I've killed Bill-E's grandparents, let Juni wreck her relationship with Dervish, and now... what? Drive off into the sunrise, find a sweet little cottage where we can settle down and live happily ever after? Play a warped mother and son game? Let Juni tie me up like a rabid animal every time the moon grows round? Madness. I should call an end to it now, make Juni stop, hand myself over to Dervish, accept what I have coming.

But instead I sit quietly, staring at the blood or out the window. I try to tell myself I'm doing it because of Juni, that I don't want to hurt her. But that's a lie. I'm running because I'm terrified of being killed. I don't want to let myself be executed. Even though I know, for the safety of everyone I love, that I should.

→The car comes to a stop. Juni leans back and sighs, massaging her temples, eyes closed. I look around. We're in a car park. Hundreds of cars. A roaring overhead. My gaze lifts and I see a plane come in to land. It clicks — we're at an airport.

"Juni?" I ask quietly.

"Yes," she says, not opening her eyes.

"What are we doing here?"

"We have to get out. They'd find us if we stayed. We need to go somewhere they can't track us. Fly far, far away. It might take three or four flights before we're really safe."

"But I don't have a passport. Luggage. Clothes. Money."

Juni lowers her hands, opens her eyes and smiles twistedly. "You want to go back to pack a suitcase?"

"Of course not. But how…?"

She rubs her fingers together. "Magic."

* * *

→Inside the airport. Nobody pays us any attention, even though we're bruised and cut all over, covered in blood. A masking spell. Not that difficult to perform. Even Bill-E's able to cast a lesser masking spell. One of the first tricks any wannabe mage learns.

Juni sends me to the bathroom to get cleaned up. Says she'll meet me by the main departures board in fifteen minutes. Tells me to be careful, not to talk to anyone.

Staring at my reflection in the mirror, eyes dark and ravaged. The hopeless expression of the lost, the damned. Dervish has often said I'm a natural survivor, able to wriggle out of any sticky situation. But sometimes it's not worth wriggling free. What's the point of being alive if you have to live with memories and guilt as crushing as this?

I run hot water and splash it over my face, washing away the worst of the blood. The sink's soon a streaky, pinkish mess. I squirt liquid soap into my hands, clean around the sink, then set to work on myself, scrubbing my hair, taking off my jumper and T-shirt, throwing them into a bin, washing my upper body and arms. I should get rid of my trousers too but I don't like the idea of wandering around in just my boxers. Crazy, considering all that's happened, but some habits are hard to break.

*　*　*

→Waiting for Juni. Nervous. Shivering, not from cold but shock. Wanting to call this off. Wanting her to take charge, be a responsible adult, talk me into giving myself up. It's strange how she's acting more irrationally than me. I always assumed a mature adult could control themselves better than a child, regardless of the pressures. Juni's proving me wrong with every bad call she makes.

"Sorry I was so long," Juni says, popping up beside me, smelling of soap. She looks rough but not desperate. Her eyes are no match for my wild pits of fear.

"Juni, this is crazy, we should—" I begin, but she puts her fingers to my lips before I can continue. Shakes her head lightly.

"Just go with it," she whispers. "I know it's wrong. I know what we should and would do if things were different. But they're not. So let's give ourselves over to madness and see where it takes us."

Before I can think of a suitable argument, she glances at the departures board, then leads me to one of the sales desks. I stand behind her as she requests two one-way tickets. No money exchanges hands. Instead, a quick spell and the sales assistant is smiling, handing Juni a pair of tickets, telling her where to check-in, wishing her a safe flight and pleasant holiday.

Queueing for check-in. I don't know where we're going — I wasn't paying attention at the sales counter. I think about asking Juni, but can't be bothered. What does it matter? We're probably just going to hop straight on to another plane at the next airport anyway. And another after that. Throw the Lambs off our scent. Keep moving until we're safe.

We nudge forward. Soon we're at the front. Juni handles the practicalities. No passport? No worries! Not when you use a Juni Swan Confusing Spell™!

Just over an hour's wait once we breeze through security. We spend half of it shopping, replacing our ruined clothes and shoes. I suggest buying extra clothes to change into when these are dirty, but Juni says we can restock at the next airport. It'll give us something to do while we're waiting for our connecting flight.

The new clothes feel stiff. The jumper itches, the trousers dig into my stomach, the shoes pinch. But I don't complain. A bit of discomfort is small punishment for the crimes I committed last night.

Sitting on the hard airport chairs. Juni works healing spells, mending the worst of the damage I caused while on the rampage. Her fingers are gentle on my flesh, her voice soft in my ear. Warmth as my cuts stitch themselves closed. Nice.

We're called to board and shuffle on with the rest of the passengers. A large plane. We're twelve rows from the front, seats A and B. When nobody sits in 12C, Juni edges over just before takeoff, so we both have more room. She smiles at me as I stare out the window at the runway, glistening in the early dawn light. I catch her smile in the glass. Turn and smile back. She holds out her hand and I take it.

"All alone now," she says.

"Yes."

"I'm terrified but strangely exhilarated."

"Me too." I give a sickly grin, lying through my back teeth. I'm not the least bit excited, only scared, confused and disgusted with myself for running.

The engines howl. We're pressed back in our seats. *Arrivederci*, terra firma.

→Exhaustion kicks in before we reach cruising altitude. My eyelids flutter shut. My brain and body scream for sleep. I try denying myself the pleasure – I want to stay alert in case Juni needs me – but I'm fighting a losing battle.

"It's OK," Juni says, touching my cheek. "You can sleep. I'll watch over you."

"But what if you…" I mutter groggily.

"I'll be fine," Juni says. "We both will. Nothing can hurt us now. Not here."

She's right. We're thousands of metres above the earth and rising. The Lambs can't touch us, not until we land. And with Juni's cunning, I doubt they'll catch us then either. No need for the unease I'm feeling. Better to give myself over to my body's demands and... sleep... just for a few...

→Dreams of the cave. The girl's face. Screaming at me. Trying to communicate, to warn me. Frustration in her expression as she realises it isn't working. I want to understand her, if only to calm her down. But the words make no sense, even in my dream.

Then her face changes. The voice stays the same, but it's Juni's face now. She leers at me. A look of vile hatred. It frightens me. I turn to run but Ma and Pa Spleen are there. "You stay away from our Billy," Pa Spleen says, blood gushing from the hole where the right side of his face used to be. "We'll come back and haunt you if you don't," Ma Spleen adds, trying to jam some of her guts back into her stomach.

Whirling away from them. Stumbling for safety. I find Dervish sitting on a stalagmite, looking glum. "You're a fool," he says sadly. "I thought I taught you better. Running away never solved anything. Especially when you don't know what you're running into."

His face changes. He becomes a werewolf. Growls wickedly and leaps. I cringe away from him. Before he strikes, Juni appears and slides between us. She knocks Dervish flat. I rise, shaking, to thank her. But when she turns, there's fire in her pink eyes. "Grubbs," she says, and the word comes out garbled, ragged, as though the lips which formed it aren't entirely human.

The ground rumbles beneath my feet.

→I snap awake but the rumbling continues. I sit bolt upright in my seat, not sure if I'm still in the dream, heart racing as it does when I have an especially bad nightmare. I look for Juni, but she's not there. The rumbling again. My seat is trembling as if it's about to snap loose from the floor. My insides clench. I feel like something terrible's about to happen. We're in trouble. Where's Juni? I have to find her, save her, get her away from…

Nervous laughter. "I'm glad I'm not flying on a full stomach," someone jokes.

"I doubt if anyone will have a full stomach if this keeps up," somebody else replies.

I chuckle and relax. It's only turbulence. We hit another blast of rocky air — *bump!* Groans throughout the cabin. People buckle up their seat belts and sit down if they were standing. Another blast and the whole plane shakes roughly, as if a giant has caught it by the tail and is trying to shake the passengers out. Even the air hostesses and stewards make for their seats. That's worrying — it's always a horrible feeling on a plane when you see the professionals acting like there's trouble in store. But it's a normal, human type of worry. No big deal after what I've come through.

I sit back, smiling as kids cry and adults curse. Nervous fliers don't get any sympathy from me. They'll be fine when we pass through this patch of turbulence. Laughing and grinning when we set down. Telling their family and friends about the rough flight, an amusing story in retrospect, fear forgotten by the time they reach home. You're never as safe as when you're in the air. Everybody knows that, even if they temporarily forget at moments like this. I bet not one person on this plane will hesitate to fly again, regardless of how much rattling and shaking—

The door to the cockpit blows off its hinges and slams into the people in the first set of seats. Screams of shock and pain. Passengers further back crane their necks to see what's happening. Some take their belts off and stand, despite the turbulence. Panic is setting in but not taking over. Not yet.

I snap my belt open and slide across to the aisle seat. Where's Juni? Probably in one of the toilets. I have to find her immediately. Something bad is happening. I need to get to her so we can face it together.

I'm halfway to my feet when I freeze. I can see into the cockpit from here. Pillars of smoke fill the cabin. My first thought — fire! That would be terrifying enough. But it's not normal smoke. There are strands running from floor to ceiling, left to right, all sorts of crazy angles. Smoke doesn't form in strands. In fact, now that I focus and my brain catches up with what my gut knew the instant I saw it, I realise the pillars inside the cockpit aren't smoke at all.

They're *webs*.

Something small shoots out of the cockpit and attaches itself to the face of a man in the second row. It's the shape of a very young boy, but with too large a head and pale green skin. His scalp crawls with living lice – or it might be cockroaches, hard to tell from here – instead of hair. Fire in the bare sockets where his eyes should be. Mouths in the palms of his hands.

"*Artery!*" I gasp, taking a few automatic steps towards the hellchild, numb with shock.

People are *really* screaming now. Those close to the front can see the demon, his teeth, the fire in his eye sockets. Artery rips the man's face off. Blood gushes. Chaos erupts. All the passengers around that row leap to their feet at the same moment and pile into the aisle, getting in each other's way, fighting to race clear of the monstrous baby.

Another demon emerges from the cockpit. This one crawls across the ceiling and drops on to a lady's head. It looks like a giant scorpion but has a face that's almost human. It's bigger than the woman's head. Her neck breaks under the weight. The demon hisses, then strikes the person next to it – a man – with the stinger in its tail. The stinger hits the man's eyes and gouges them out. The demon turns and spits spawn-like eggs into the vacant, bloody sockets. As the man pushes to his feet and screams, some twisted breed of demonic insects hatch from the eggs. They quickly set to work on the flesh around his eyes, spreading like wildfire. Moments later there's not much left of his face and the demon is striking again, this time at a child.

Two more demons spill out of the cockpit, the general shape of humans but covered in boils, gaping sores and pus. They roar mutely, arms flapping, horrible beasts. They seem to be threatening even more bloodshed and terror than Artery and the other demon — but then they fall to the floor, moaning and thrashing. And I realise they're not demons at all. They're the pilot and one of his crew.

Something leaps over the stricken humans and those milling around the aisle. It lands on top of the seats of the fourth or fifth row. It looks like a rabbit, except with a huge, ugly bulge on its back and claws that are much bigger than they should be. ("All the better to slice you up with, my dear," a detached part of me giggles hysterically.) The people in the row stare at it, more bewildered than scared. Then it opens its mouth and sprays liquid over them. They fall back gasping and spluttering. Then choked screams as the liquid eats into their flesh, bubbling and boiling, transforming them into mockeries of the human form, just like the pilot and his mate.

I'm standing in the same spot, frozen with fear. Not just fear of what's happened but what I know will happen next. Thinking numbly — *how?* The Demonata shouldn't be able to cross between universes like this. And how did they know I'd be here?

While I'm searching desperately for answers, and the cabin around me fills with bodies and screams, a new demon glides out of the cockpit. This one is worse than all the others put together. Tall and thin. Pale red skin covered in smears of blood which oozes from a system of cracks in his flesh. Eight arms with mangled hands – like something a young child might draw – and strips of flesh where his lower legs end. Bald. Dark red eyes with even darker pupils. No nose. A hole where his heart should be, filled with dozens of small, hissing, constantly slithering snakes.

A year after Slawter, making good on his vow to track me down and wreak revenge, timing it perfectly for maximum impact and shock, Lord Loss has found me.

"Children," the demon master says, his voice exactly as I remember it, slow and miserable, like he's experienced all the pains of the world. Although he doesn't speak loudly, the word echoes through the plane, right back to the last row of seats. Everyone stops rushing, struggling, fighting and screaming. All eyes fix on the terrible spectacle hanging in the air just outside the door of the cockpit.

Lord Loss smiles weakly at us as though we'd come to a funeral, only to discover we're the ones due to be buried. "Such a tragic way to die," he murmurs. "Above the clouds. Cut off from the Earth from which you sprang. Most of you without your loved ones. Although isn't it worse if they *are* with you? The pain of dying alone versus the torment of seeing one you love die too." He sighs. "Such a tragedy."

He drifts forward. People slide back into their seats, clearing the aisle, almost hypnotised by the sight of the demon floating towards them. He stops at the third row. There's a young woman in the aisle seat, no more than five or six years older than me. He reaches out with one of his eight clammy hands and strokes her cheek, then gently clasps her jaw.

"If it is any comfort, in this time of great sorrow, I promise your suffering will be short," Lord Loss says, smiling at the young woman. I can see tears in her eyes. His fingers squeeze together tightly. He rips the lower half of her face away and tosses it to Artery, who catches it with the mouths in his hands, snapping it in two and devouring it, yapping like a dog being thrown a tasty tidbit. "But it will be painful," Lord Loss adds with morbid relish.

A child tries to scream. Its father puts a hand over its mouth and cuts the cry short. Everyone's staring at the demon master, transfixed. This is the calm before the storm. Within seconds this cabin will be a place of riotous abandon. But nobody wants to be the first to break the spell. Maybe they – *we* – think that if we stay this way, motionless, barely breathing, the nightmare will pass. The demons won't go wild. We won't all be slaughtered and bled dry by these creatures of evil.

Then — movement behind Lord Loss. Somebody steps forward and looks down the cabin, leaning sideways to see past the demon master. My stomach tightens another notch but I find my voice at last.

"*Juni!*" I shout. "Get away from him! Quick! Before he–"

"Why, Master Grubitsch," Lord Loss cuts in, unable to mask his delight. "*You? Here?* What a delightful coincidence."

Juni slips around the floating demon. Lord Loss takes no notice of her. He only has eyes for me, leering, puffing up his chest, snakes hissing wilder than ever. For a moment I think Juni's cast another masking spell, that he can't see her. Hope flares within me, just the faintest flicker. Then dies just as quickly when she says, "I summoned him, Grubbs."

A chill which is colder than ice. "You…?" I gasp. "*Why?*"

"He's the only one who can cure you," Juni says. "Remember what I said to Dervish? I told him the challenge should be made again. I said you'd be fools not to try."

"What have you done?" I shriek. "We can't bargain with Lord Loss. He won't help us. He'll kill me. He'll kill you. He'll kill us all!"

"Do you know something?" Juni mutters, frowning and nodding slightly, as if the thought just occurred to her. "I think you're right. With one exception."

There's a man holding a child on Juni's left. Juni reaches across and tries to take the child from the man's arms. He doesn't let go. She tugs, but he holds firm. She shrugs, leans in close and kisses him. I gawp at her, bewildered. But confusion quickly turns to terror when I see the man's skin turn grey, then peel away, revealing the blood vessels and bones beneath. He shakes madly but still doesn't let go of the child, who has started to cry.

Juni kisses him relentlessly until there's a sharp snapping sound. She brings her mouth up and his face is attached to hers, head severed at the neck, the remains of his lips snagged between her teeth.

She turns her head aside and spits. Sends the man's head flying to the floor.

Panic erupts. People go crazy and surge down the aisle. The demons snicker and lay into the humans around them with renewed relish. Carnage flowers.

I stand my ground, frozen, more horrified than ever, staring at Juni. She leers at me and wipes her lips clean. Then Lord Loss drifts up beside her. He wraps four arms around the albino and picks her off the floor. She smiles at him and pecks his cheek, licking a drop of blood clear of the corner of his mouth. Points to me. Grins like a tiger and says, "He's all yours now — *master*."

Demon Apocalypse

For:

Bas — back with a vengeance!

OBEs (Order of the Bloody Entrails) to:

evil Elizabeth Eulberg — mistress of Duke's!

sinister Cynthia Eagan — steer clear of the spoon!

Prophet of doom:

Stella Paskins

Horsemen of the Apocalypse:

the Christopher Little seers

PART ONE
BERANABUS

THE SNATCH

→A demon shaped like a giant scorpion digs its stinger into a woman's eyes. As they pop, it spits eggs into the bloody sockets, then watches with its almost human face as the eggs hatch and wriggling maggots feast on her flesh.

Another demonic beast — it looks like a cute rabbit, though it has an ugly bulge on its back — vomits over a man and his two children. The acidic liquid sizzles and dissolves them down to the bone.

A third footman of the Demonata runs after an air hostess. He has the body of a young boy, but his head is larger than an adult's, he has a wig of living lice instead of hair and fire burns in the holes where his eyes should be. He also has two extra mouths in the palms of his hands. The teeth of both are eagerly snapping open and shut as he chases the screaming air hostess.

All the people on the plane are screaming — except those who've already been killed — and it's music to the ears of the demon master, Lord Loss. He hovers in the aisle, mouth twisted into a sad smile, red eyes distant. A few of his eight arms twitch in rhythm with the screams, like a conductor's at an orchestra. Then his eyes snap back into focus and he turns his gaze on me.

"You should not have humiliated me, Grubitsch," Lord Loss says, still furious about the time I beat him at chess. "You should have fought fairly, faithful to the spirit of the contest, and won or lost on merit alone. You ruined chess for me. For many centuries it was my only other source of joy. Now I have just the agony and torture of humans to keep me amused."

He slowly drifts down the aisle towards me, the strands of flesh that pass for his legs floating a few centimetres above the floor. The tiny snakes in the hole where his heart should be are writhing, hissing hatefully, spitting venom in my direction. Blood is flowing from the many cracks in his pale red skin. The holes above his upper lip – he has no nose – quiver wildly as he gleefully inhales the stench of terror from the doomed passengers. His dark red eyes are dilated with morbid pleasure. All eight arms are extended. Some of his mangled hands brush the heads and cheeks of humans as he passes, as if he is obscenely blessing them. The white-haired, pink-eyed albino traitor, Juni Swan, is behind him, smiling serenely.

A woman clasping a baby falls to her knees in front of Lord Loss, sobbing painfully. "Please!" she cries. "Not my child. Have mercy on my baby. Don't kill him. I beg you!"

"Suffer unto me the little children," Lord Loss murmurs blasphemously, taking the baby with three of his hands. He strokes the boy's face and the baby laughs. Lord Loss passes him to Juni. "For you, my darling swan."

"You are generous to a fault, my lord," she smiles, then kisses the infant.

"No!" I scream. But it's too late. A moment later she tosses the grey remains of the baby aside, having sucked his fragile life from him. The child's mother chokes, eyes wide with disbelief and horror. Lord Loss bends and breathes in her sorrow, sighs contentedly, then moves on, leaving her to the lesser demons.

Sick with fear, I back away from the approaching demon master. There are several empty rows behind me — the other passengers have fled to the tail of the plane. Lord Loss makes a small humming noise. "At last you move. I thought I might wring no sport from you today."

"Leave them alone," I snarl, hands knotted into trembling fists. "It's me you want, so let the others go."

"I cannot do that, Grubitsch," Lord Loss sighs. "My familiars are hungry. I promised them food. You would not ask me to break my word, would you?"

"My master always keeps his promises," Juni chuckles.

I focus on her. The fair-faced but black-hearted cuckoo in the nest. She acted like my mother. I loved her. I let her steal me away from Dervish. And all the time she was plotting against me. "Harpy!" I sob. "What the hell are you — a demon in disguise?"

"I don't have that honour," she replies smoothly. "I'm merely a human like you. In fact I'm from the same family tree, believe it or not. But unlike you and your fool of an uncle, I chose to serve those greater than ourselves, rather than vainly battle with them."

"You sold us out!" I shout. Then confusion kicks in. "But... I don't understand. In Slawter, when we trying to escape from the demons, you helped us."

"No," she smiles. "That was all a pretence. When I first visited your house with Davida Haym, I used magic to convince Dervish to come to Slawter and bring you and Bill-E with him. On the set it was my job to win your confidence. I found out your secrets, so we could use them against you.

"I played you like pawns," she boasts. "I had you thinking I was one of your pathetic group, a trusted ally. I let you make escape plans and even allowed you to act on them — it would have been more delicious if you failed with freedom in sight. At the end, just before you breached the barrier, I meant to reveal my true self and turn you over to my master. And I would have, except..."

"You were knocked unconscious," I gasp, remembering the dying demon who clubbed her in its death throes.

Juni nods bitterly. "By the time I recovered, it was too late. I paused to silence Chuda Sool – he knew the truth about me – then departed to join my master and plot our next approach."

"We had not planned to strike so soon," Lord Loss says. He's come to a stop three metres away, enjoying my growing understanding of how we were betrayed. "I could sense the magic within you, even though you hid it masterfully. I didn't want to move on you until I knew precisely what I'd have to deal with. But then Juni had a vision."

"I catch glimpses of the future," Juni says smugly. "I saw you change into a werewolf a few months before it happened."

"I could not wait any longer," Lord Loss sighs. "I wished to punish you while you were human — there would be no satisfaction in killing a senseless animal. So I set a watch on you. I'm a fine judge of werewolves. I was confident of timing it so that I struck just prior to the final turning — I liked the idea of letting you suffer the agonies of the impending change for as long as possible."

"It all fell neatly into place in the end," Juni smirks. "I was planning to come to Carcery Vale, looking for an excuse to explain my return. When your friend died, I donned my psychologist's disguise, disposed of William Mauch and replaced him. You and Bill-E couldn't have been more welcoming. And Dervish... Well, *he* was positively overjoyed to see me."

"You betrayed us," I snarl, blinking away angry tears.

"You were easy to betray," she murmurs. I can see the wickedness in her eyes. How did I ever miss it? "Dervish fell for my pretty pink eyes and cool white skin. He never looked into my heart. I didn't even have to use magic on him — he fell in love with me of his own accord. The sap."

I feel magic flare within me when she says that. Howling, I bring my fists up. Energy shoots from my knuckles, a ball of pure, invisible power. I direct it at Juni, meaning to blast her into a million fleshy pieces.

Alarm ripples across her eyes. She starts to cast a protective spell, but it's too late. I'm going to destroy her, rip her atoms apart and...

Lord Loss sticks out four of his arms. He blocks Juni from the force of my blow and absorbs the energy. Flinches, staggers back a few metres, then rights himself and smiles.

"You are powerful, Grubitsch, but untrained. Perhaps, if you had spent more time learning the ways of magic, you would be able to control that great force and defend yourself and these other unfortunate

THE SNATCH

victims. But you ran from your responsibility. Therefore you – and all around you – will die."

I scream at him, then unleash a second blast of magic energy, more powerful than the first. It strikes him in the middle of his chest, drives him back several metres. He knocks Juni to the floor and almost loses his balance. But then he straightens and laughs. Brushes away drops of blood as if cleaning fluff from a jacket.

"Have you finished or do you want to try again?" he asks. "Maybe you will be luckier the third time. What do you think, Miss Swan?"

Juni's getting back to her feet, irate at having been knocked down. "I think we should take him now and drop the games," she snaps.

"'Take me'?" I repeat. "Take me where?"

"My realm," Lord Loss says. "You surely didn't think I'd kill you here, along with these meaningless others, quickly and cleanly? Dear me, no. You robbed me of my great joy in life — chess. You must pay properly for that, in the universe of the Demonata, where time passes oh so slowly, where I can torture your soul for a thousand years… maybe more."

"A bit harsher than detention after school, wouldn't you say?" Juni sneers.

"Artery," Lord Loss calls. The child-shaped demon with fire instead of eyes pulls his head out of the air

281

hostess's stomach cavity and looks up, guts dribbling down his chin.

"Spine," Lord Loss says. The giant scorpion sheathes its stinger and regards its master from the ceiling, where it's hanging upside-down.

"Femur," Lord Loss finishes, and the rabbit-like demon hops on to the head of a corpse, acid frothing from its lips.

Lord Loss points beyond me to where the majority of the survivors are huddled, terrified and weeping. "Make quick work of them. We must leave soon, before our window home closes."

The familiars laugh horrifically, then race towards me. I flinch as the monstrous creatures draw level, but they veer around and leave me untouched. Screams behind — then awful ripping, munching, stabbing, sizzling sounds.

I don't look back. Part of me wants to. Maybe my magic would work against the familiars. Perhaps I could kill them. But I dare not turn my back on Lord Loss. The demon master is the greatest threat. If I let him attack me from behind, I'm definitely doomed.

Hell, who am I trying to kid? I'm doomed anyway. He's shown he can take my worst and shrug it off. I might as well surrender and get it over and done with. And if he promised me a quick death, maybe I'd take that way out. But I don't like the sound of a millennium of torture in his webbed, wicked world. I'm not going to willingly sacrifice myself to such a miserable fate. If he wants to turn me into one of his long-term playthings, he'll have to fight for me.

"Come on then, you lumpy, ugly amateur!" I yell, backing away from him. "You think you can take me? You're wrong. You'll fail, just like you failed to beat me at chess and kill me in Slawter. You're pathetic!"

Lord Loss's face twists. His arms extend towards me. Power crackles in the air as fierce magic gathers in his misshapen fingertips. I bid farewell to life and steel myself to die.

Then his expression mellows and his arms drop. "No, Grubitsch," he chuckles. "I won't be provoked. You hope to goad me into killing you swiftly. A clever ploy, but I shall not fall for your trick. I came to take you and take you I will. I'll kill you later, when we are…"

A burst of heat to my left makes him pause. It's coming from the wall of the cabin. I glance at it, expecting another of Lord Loss's familiars to appear. The wall's glowing with a white, hot, magical light.

"Master?" Juni says uncertainly as Lord Loss draws to a halt.

"Quiet," he snaps.

They don't know what it is!

I move closer to the light, ignoring the heat, figuring if this is something Lord Loss isn't controlling, it can only be good news. Maybe the plane is coming apart and this is the start of a giant explosion. If so, I want to be caught square in the blast. That would wipe the smirk from the demon master's wretched mush.

An oval hole appears in the side of the plane. About two metres from bottom to top and a metre wide. I see a man through the hole, outside, clinging to the wing of the plane. It's the tramp! He's been following me for the last few weeks, waiting to see if I turned into a werewolf. He was lurking near my house last night when I burst free of the cellar where Dervish had me caged. I thought he was one of the Lambs — werewolf executioners *par excellence* — but now I'm starting to have doubts.

The tramp half leans into the cabin and stretches out a hand to me, holding on to the wing of the plane with his other hand as a fierce, unearthly wind whips at his hair and clothes. "Boy!" he shouts. "Come with me. *Now!*"

"No!" Lord Loss and Juni scream at the same moment.

Lord Loss's arms snap up and he unleashes a magical shot of energy at the tramp. But the white light around the edges of the hole absorbs the power and disperses it in a shower of crackling sparks.

I'm staring stupidly at the tramp, jaw slack, mind in a spin.

"Boy!" the tramp shouts again. "I can't take another blast like that. Come now or die."

I look from the tramp to Lord Loss and Juni. Their faces are filled with hate. Juni's muttering a spell, lips moving incredibly fast. Lord Loss is readying himself for a second shot at the tramp.

A quick look in the other direction. Artery, Spine and Femur are rushing up the aisle, desperate to pin me down.

I face Lord Loss again, grin and flip him the finger. Then I dive towards the tramp, sticking out my right hand. The tramp grabs it and hurls me through the hole. He shouts a word of magic and the hull of the plane starts to close. I hear Lord Loss bellow with fury. Then the hole seals itself and there's only the roaring howl of the wind.

I realise I'm clinging to a tramp on the wing of an aeroplane, thousands of metres above the face of the earth. I have a split second to marvel at the craziness of that. Then the wind grabs us. We're ripped loose. The plane soars onwards.

We fall.

FLIGHT

→Dropping at a stomach-punching speed towards the earth. Freefall. Surrounded by blue sky, clouds far below but getting closer every second. I glance desperately at the tramp, praying to spot the hump of a parachute pack. But there's nothing. He's falling the same way I am, with only one way of stopping — the *hard* way.

I scream and flap frantically with my arms. Crazily I wish I was back in the plane. At least I stood a glimmer of a chance with the demons. This is death for certain.

"Boy!" the tramp shouts cheerfully. "Are you having fun?"

"We're going to die!" I roar, clothes rippling madly on my limbs, the scream of the wind ice-cold in my ears.

"Not today," the tramp chortles, then angles his body and glides closer towards me. "We can fly."

"You're a lunatic!" I shriek.

"Perhaps," he grins, then arcs his body up, pulls away from me, swoops over and beneath me and draws up on the other side. "Or maybe not."

"Let me hold on to you!" I yell, grabbing for him.

He pulls away. "No. It's time you learnt to fend for yourself. You're a creature of magic. Use your power."

"I can't," I howl.

"Of course you can," he tuts as if he was a teacher and we were debating an argument in class, safe on the ground, instead of hurtling towards it at a speed I don't even want to think about.

"We're going to die," I shout again.

"I'm not," he says. "You won't either if you focus. But you'd better be quick," he adds as we enter a thick bank of cloud, then burst through it a second or two later. "You haven't much time." He points at the earth, which I can see clearly now we've broken through the cloud.

I start to scream senselessly, thoughts wild, gravity pulling me to my high-impact doom. Then the tramp asks casually, "Are you cold?"

The craziness of the question draws a furious response. "What sort of a nut are you? I'm falling to my death and you're discussing the temperature!"

"Answer me," he says calmly. "Are you cold?"

"No. But what the—"

"At this height, don't you think you should be? It was in the region of minus forty Celsius on the wing of the aeroplane. Any normal person would have felt the icy bite immediately. You didn't because magic kept you warm. It can also keep you aloft — *if* you direct it."

"What must I do?" I moan, the landscape filling my vision, surely no more than half a minute away from a bone-crunching collision.

"Visualise a bird," the tramp says. "Think of the way it flies, how it soars out of a dive with the slightest tilt of its wings. Don't picture your arms as wings or anything like that. Just imagine a bird and fix it in your thoughts."

I do as he says. Close my eyes and think of a swallow swooping and soaring. I've seen them fly many times, when walking home from school or looking out of my bedroom window, glimpsed through the uppermost branches of the forest. They make it look simple — nudge out a wing, duck or pull up their head, catch the wind currents, sail them as if it was the most natural thing in the world.

My head rises. The roar of the wind lessens. A new sensation. Not one of falling, but of…

I open my eyes. I'm moving away from the earth, arms by my side, legs straight, head facing the clouds, the tramp by my side. *Flying*.

"There," the tramp says with a wicked little grin. "Simple, aye?"

→Flying high. A creature of the sky. Laughing and hollering with delight. Flying on my front, back, sides — however I please. Somersaulting mid-air, a far greater rush than any roller coaster.

"This is amazing!" I yell at the tramp, who flies nearby. "How am I doing it?"

"Magic," he says.

"But I'm not trying. I'm not casting spells."

"True magicians don't need spells most of the time."

I stare at him, stunned. "But I'm not a magician."

"No?" He nods at the earth far below. "Then how do you explain this?"

"But Dervish said... I've never... Bartholomew Garadex!" I throw the name out desperately.

"You're different to Bartholomew," the tramp says. "Different to every magician I've ever known or heard about. But you're a magician none the less. You draw your power directly from the universe, like the Demonata."

Mention of the demons reminds me of the plane and its doomed passengers. "We have to go back!" I shout, cursing myself for flying around happy and carefree while Lord Loss and his familiars wreak havoc. "We have to save the people on the plane."

The tramp sighs. "Dead, all of them."

"No! They can't be! We have to—"

"They're dead," the tramp says stiffly. "And even if they aren't, what could we do?"

"Fight!" I roar.

"Against Lord Loss?" He shakes his head. "I'm powerful, boy, and so are you, but Lord Loss is a demon master. We wouldn't last long in a battle with him."

"We have to try," I whisper, thinking of all those men, women and children. Picturing the Demonata and Juni Swan at savage work. "If we abandon them…"

"We've already abandoned them," the tramp grunts. "The choice was taken when I pulled you out. Everyone on that aeroplane is dead and it has crashed – or will shortly – destroying the evidence."

"You let them die," I gasp.

The tramp shrugs. "I would have saved them if I could. I've devoted my life to protecting humanity from the Demonata. But some battles you can't win. Some you can't even fight."

Flying in silence. Thinking about what happened and what the tramp said. Cold inside and scared. Unable to get the faces of the people – *the dead* – out of my mind. Yet a big part of me is secretly glad we didn't go back, that the tramp spared me another run-in with the demons.

"This is insane," I mutter, looking at the world beneath. "Who are you? What were you doing on the plane? Why have you been following me? I thought you were one of the Lambs. I know nothing about you. I need—"

"Soon," the tramp hushes me. "I'll answer all your questions once we're safe on the ground. For now, just fly."

And since there's no point arguing, I tuck my arms in tighter, pick up speed, trail the tramp through the air and try — unsuccessfully — to push the faces of the dead from my thoughts.

→We fly for hours, mostly above the clouds where people on the ground can't see us. I spot the occasional plane, but the tramp always steers us clear. A shame — I love the thought of gliding up to one and tapping on the windows, scaring the living daylights out of the passengers and crew.

I've no idea where we are. I didn't ask Juni where we were going when we set off and I don't know how long I was asleep, so I can't judge how far from home we might have been when the demons attacked.

Juni...

Rage seethes up inside me every time I think about her. I trusted her. I thought she was on my side, that she loved me like a mother. And all the time she was playing me for a fool, setting me up for Lord Loss, cutting me off from Dervish.

I want to quiz the tramp about her. Find out where she comes from, how she operates, where I can find her — so I can track her down and burn her for the evil witch she is. But this isn't the right time. I have loads of questions for the tramp. So much I want to know, that I need to find out. Hell, I haven't even asked his name yet!

* * *

→Finally, five or six hours after I bailed out of the plane, the tramp guides me down. The land is barren desert, more rocky than sandy. No signs of human life — it's been the better part of an hour since I saw any kind of house.

"This is the complicated part," the tramp says as we come in to land. "The easiest way is to hover a bit above the ground, then stop thinking about birds. After a few seconds you'll fall."

"Can't we touch down?" I ask.

"I can, but I've had a lot of practice. If you try it, you'll probably hit hard and break a leg or arm."

He spreads his arms and drifts down, landing lightly on his feet. I'm tempted to copy him, to prove I'm nimbler than he gives me credit for. But it's been a *long* day and the last thing I want is to break any bones. So I float to within a metre of the rocky floor, then empty my head of images of birds. For a couple of seconds nothing happens. Then I drop suddenly, stomach lurching.

I hit the ground awkwardly, landing face first in the dust. Sitting up, I splutter and wipe dirt and grit from my cheeks, then get to my feet and look around. We're in the middle of nowhere. Some rocky outcrops and hills, a few rustling cacti, nothing else. "Where are we?"

"Home," the tramp says and starts walking towards one of the hills.

"Whose home?" I ask, hurrying after him.

"Mine."

"And you are…?"

He stops and looks back, surprised. "You don't know?"

"Should I?"

"Surely Dervish told…" He trails off into silence, then laughs. "All that time in the air, you didn't know who you were with?"

"I was going to ask, but it didn't seem like the right moment," I huff.

The tramp shakes his head. "I'm Beranabus." The name sounds familiar, but I can't place it.

"Beranabus what?" I ask.

"Just Beranabus," he says, then starts walking again. "Come. We have much to discuss, but it will hold. I never feel safe in the open."

With a nervous glance around, I hasten after the shabbily dressed man. Several minutes later we come to the mouth of a cave. Not having had the best experience of caves recently, I pause and peer suspiciously into the shadows.

"It's fine," Beranabus assures me. "This is a safe place, protected by its natural position and the strongest spells I could muster. You have nothing to fear."

"That's easily said," I grunt, unconvinced.

Beranabus smiles. He has crooked, stained teeth. This close I can see that his small eyes are grey and his skin is pale beneath a covering of grime and dirt. He's wearing an old, dusty suit. The only fresh thing about him is a small posy of flowers jutting out of one of his buttonholes.

"If I wanted to harm you," he says, "I could have done so already, with far less effort than it would take on the ground. That should be self-evident."

"I know," I mutter. "It's just... I don't like caves."

"With good reason," he says understandingly. "But this isn't like the cave in Carcery Vale. You'll be safe here. I promise."

I hesitate a moment longer, then shrug. "What the hell," I grunt and push ahead of Beranabus, acting like I couldn't care less.

The cave only runs back four or five metres, then stops. I look for a way out, studying the walls and floor, but I can't see any. "Are you like a monk who doesn't believe in material possessions?" I ask.

"No," Beranabus says, squeezing past me. He touches the ground and mutters a few words of magic. A hole appears. There's a rope ladder attached to the wall at one side, leading down into the dark.

I move to the edge of the hole and look down nervously. There are torches set in the walls, so it's not as dark as it seemed at first. But it runs a long way down and I can only vaguely see the bottom.

"I thought you said a magician didn't need to cast spells," I say, delaying the moment when I have to descend.

"*Most* of the time," Beranabus reminds me. "There are occasions when even the strongest of us must focus our magical energy with words." He sits and swings his legs into the hole. Turns, grabs the ladder and starts down. Looks up at me before his head bobs beneath my feet. "This will close in a few minutes. If you're coming, get a move on."

"Just waiting for you to get out of my way," I retort. Then, when his head's clear, I ignore the butterflies in my stomach, sit, turn and climb down the swaying ladder after him.

The hole closes with a small grinding noise before I hit the ground. I try not to think about the fact that I'm shut off from the world. At the base I step clear of the ladder and find myself in a large, bright cave. There are chairs, a sofa, a long table at one end with a vase of flowers on it, a few statues, books, chests of drawers, other bits and pieces. There's also a fire in the middle of the cave, by which a bald, dark-skinned boy sits warming his hands.

"I'm back," Beranabus calls.

"I noticed," the boy replies without looking around.

"I've brought a guest."

The boy's head turns a fraction. He has bright blue eyes and a sour expression. "I thought you were going to kill him."

I stiffen as Beranabus scowls. "I said I *might* have to kill him."

"What do you—" I start to ask angrily.

"Later," Beranabus soothes me, then points to a blanket spread out on the ground close to the wall. "Get some sleep. I will too. Later we can have a long discussion over a hot meal."

"You think I can sleep after all that's happened?" I snort.

"I know you can," Beranabus says. "Magic. All you have to do is imagine it and you'll sleep like a baby."

"What if I don't want to?"

"You're exhausted. You need rest, so you can focus on our conversation and ask all the questions I'm sure are welling up inside you. You wouldn't be able to process my answers in your current state."

I don't want to sleep – I want to tear straight into the explanations – but what he says makes sense. Just keeping my eyelids open is a major effort at the moment.

"One thing first," I mutter. "Dervish and Bill-E — are they OK?"

Beranabus shrugs. "I think so."

"You're not sure?"

"No. But Lord Loss and *Juni*–" For some reason he sneers as he says her name. "– don't know where we went once we left the plane. I doubt Juni would risk going back in case we got there before her."

"You'll warn Dervish?" I ask. "About Juni working with Lord Loss?"

"I can't contact him immediately," Beranabus says, "but I'll get word to him as soon as I can. He'll have to fend for himself until then."

That's not satisfactory, but it's the best he's going to offer. So, since I'm worn out, and there's nothing I could do even if I was on top form, I stumble to the blanket and lie down fully clothed. I doubt I can fall asleep as easily as Beranabus expects, but as soon as I close my eyes and think about it, I find myself going under. Seconds later I'm comatose.

POWER OF THE BEAST

→A loaf of fresh bread is waved underneath my nose. I come out of sleep smiling, the scent of warm goodness filling my nostrils. For a few groggy moments I think I'm at home with Dervish, it's a Sunday morning, no school, no worries, a long, lazy day stretching deliciously ahead of me.

Then my eyes focus. I see the lined fingers clutching the bread and the bearded face beyond. I remember. And all the good thoughts disappear in an instant.

"How long was I asleep?" I yawn, sitting up, wincing from the pain in my back — I'm not used to sleeping on a stone floor.

"Many hours," Beranabus says, handing me the bread.

"Eight? Ten? Twelve?"

He shrugs.

I look for my watch, but the strap must have snapped during the night of my turning. Standing, I rub the sides of my back, stretch and groan. "Haven't you heard of beds?" I complain.

"You'll grow accustomed to the floor after a few months."

I squint at him. *Months?* I've no intention of being here that long. But before I can challenge him, he walks over to the fire where the sour-faced boy is still perched close to the flames. I follow, tearing a chunk out of the loaf, gobbling it. The bread's chewy and I haven't any butter, but I'm so hungry I could happily eat cardboard.

Beranabus sits close to the boy. I stay on my feet, studying the curious couple. Ancient Beranabus and the teenager, not much older than me. The shabby, bearded, hairy, suited magician and the boy — his apprentice or servant? — in drab but clean clothes, completely bald. The boy's dark flesh is laced with small scars and fading bruises. The tips of the two smallest fingers on his left hand are missing. His eyes have a faraway, miserable look. He wears no shoes. Beranabus is barefoot too, his boots discarded.

"Grubitsch Grady meet Kernel Fleck," Beranabus introduces us.

"Grubbs," I correct him, sticking out a hand. The boy only grunts. "What about your name?" I ask, trying to be friendly despite his cold welcome. "Is it Colonel, like in the army?"

"No. Kernel, like in popcorn," Beranabus answers after a few seconds of stony silence. "It's short for something longer, but neither of us can remember what."

Kernel sniffs and faces the fire. There are sausages speared to a stick close by. He picks up the stick and jams the sausages into the flames. Mutters a spell. The heat of the fire increases and the sausages cook in seconds. He takes one off, blows on it and eats it, then takes off another and gives it to Beranabus. After a pause, he removes a third sausage and offers it to me.

"Thanks," I say, biting into it. Too hot, but delicious. I ravenously munch my way through it, then gratefully accept another.

"Kernel does most of the cooking," Beranabus says, holding a sausage in one hand, picking at dirt beneath the nails of his right foot with the other.

"I have to," Kernel says. "He'd eat the food raw if I didn't."

"It's all the same once your stomach processes it," Beranabus snorts. "Hot, cold, cooked, raw… it doesn't make any difference when you're squatting over a hole."

"A hole?" I frown.

"No toilets," Kernel says, looking at Beranabus sourly.

Kernel cooks some chicken legs, again using his spell. (I wonder where they get the food from, but don't ask.) He piles them on a dusty, cracked plate, then cooks some ribs and potatoes. That done, he takes what he wants from the plate and passes it across.

Bernabus bites into his chicken leg, then looks over at me. "Tell me everything about the last few months. I know a lot already, but I want the complete story. When you realised your body was changing, how the magic developed, the way you dealt with it."

"I thought *you* were the one meant to provide answers."

"I will," he promises. "But you first. It will make my job easier."

While we eat, I fill him in on all that happened, discovering my magical ability after Slawter, fighting it, the sickness, using magic to counter the threat of the werewolf.

"Why did you fight the magic in the first place?" he interrupts. "Most people would be thrilled if they found themselves in your position."

"I know what magic entails," I say quietly. "It's linked to the Demonata. I've been part of that crazy universe before. I didn't want to get sucked into it again."

Beranabus and Kernel share a look. Then Beranabus tells me to continue.

I explain about the cave we unearthed in Carcery Vale, going there under the influence of the beast, digging through the rubble blocking the entrance, Loch's accident, Dervish covering up, Juni entering our lives.

"Who's Juni Swan?" Kernel asks Beranabus.

"One of Lord Loss's assistants," Beranabus says, squinting. "Actually she..." He stops and clears his throat. "We can discuss Miss Swan and her background later. Finish, please, Grubitsch."

"It's Grubbs," I correct him again, then cover the last couple of days and nights, the werewolf taking over, killing Bill-E's grandparents, Juni whipping me out of town and betraying me on the plane. I tell the story as quickly as I can, eager to get it out of the way. I don't go into all the details, like the voice and the face in the rock, figuring they're not important. I can tell Beranabus about them later.

Beranabus listens silently, then spends a couple of minutes thinking about what I've said. "The boy who fell," he finally says, echoing Dervish's concerns when he first came to the cave. "Was it definitely an accident? Nobody else was—"

"No," I cut in. "We were alone, just the three of us. He slipped, fell, died. An accident. No demons or evil mages were involved."

"Good," Beranabus grunts. "When I heard the entrance had been excavated and someone had died in the cave, I feared the worst — especially since my spells of warning hadn't worked. I should have been alerted the moment the first rock was lifted out. I assumed a powerful mage had spun a counterspell and was preparing the way for a demon invasion. I've never moved so quickly in my life."

"He ran like his feet were on fire," Kernel says, smiling for the first time — but it's a brief, thin smile.

"Dervish told me about the cave," I say softly. "How it was used as a crossing point for demons. He said the tunnel between universes could be reopened, that the Demonata could come through in their thousands and take over our world. You don't think Juni and Lord Loss...?"

"No." Beranabus smiles wryly, showing his crooked, discoloured teeth. "Lord Loss has no interest in opening tunnels between universes. Most demons want to destroy humanity, but Lord Loss thrives on human misery. He's as keen to keep that tunnel closed as we are."

Beranabus picks at his teeth with a thin chicken bone. His breath stinks. In fact most of him stinks. He obviously isn't concerned about personal hygiene. Finally, laying the bone aside, he speaks again. "The cave brought me to Carcery Vale, but you're why I stayed. I could feel the power in you, bursting to be released. I wanted to be there when it exploded — or when you imploded."

"*Imploded?*"

"You could have burnt up. If the magic hadn't found an outlet, it would have destroyed you from within. There was no way of telling until the full moon, when I knew you'd be pushed to the point where you and the beast had to settle the matter once and for all.

303

"The werewolf is the key," he continues. "The curse of the Gradys. Many centuries ago, your ancestors bred with demons."

"*Bred?*" I yelp. "No way!"

"It doesn't happen often," Beranabus says. "Most demons are physically incompatible with humans. But it's not unheard of. When such unions occur, the offspring are never natural. Humans and demons weren't meant to mix. When they do, their children are freaks of the highest order, neither human nor demon, caught painfully between. Most die at birth. But some survive."

His face is dark, shadows flickering across it from the flames of the fire. "A few grow and thrive, either in the demon's universe or ours. Your ancestor's child was one of those. The magical strand of the Demonata stayed hidden, at least long enough for the child to mature and bear children of its own. When its demonic legacy finally surfaced, the victim turned into a wolf-like creature."

"So the Demonata are to blame," I growl, hating them afresh. "I gathered as much from Dervish, but I was never sure."

"I don't know about *blame*," Beranabus says. "Such couplings are often set in motion by humans. Your ancestor quite possibly made the first approach, and…" He twirls his fingers suggestively.

"Here comes the bride," mutters Kernel.

Beranabus looks into the flames, considering his next words. "You're a unique specimen, even for a Grady. I've never seen or heard of anyone like you. Magic is unpredictable, chaotic. It works differently in each person. But there are general rules which have always applied — until now. You shattered all of them."

"Is that a good or a bad thing?" I ask.

"I don't know. It's the reason I didn't approach you immediately. I wasn't sure how you'd change, what the magic would do when it surfaced. Of course there was Juni to consider too. I didn't know how close you and Dervish were to her, if you knew who she served."

"Of course we didn't!" I bellow. "Lord Loss killed my parents and sister. Do you think—"

"Peace," Beranabus says. "I trust you now, but I couldn't before. For all I knew, you and Dervish were in league with Juni Swan and I was being lured into a trap. Dervish himself might have opened the entrance to the cave to entice me to Carcery Vale."

"Have you been paranoid for long?" I ask cynically.

"I learnt a long time ago not to trust anybody," he replies tightly. "Not until they've proved themselves worthy. And even then I keep a close watch on them."

"I've been with Beranabus for thirty years or more," Kernel says, "and I still wake up sometimes to find him giving me the evil eye."

"Thirty years?" I study the boy again. "You can't be that old."

"We'll come to that soon," Beranabus says before Kernel can respond. "Let's finish with your magic first. Where was I?"

"You were waxing lyrical about how unique he was," Kernel reminds him.

"Aye." Beranabus's face lights up. "In every other magician, the gift of magic is evident from birth. Even if they're unaware of their potential, other magicians can sense it. Dervish should have seen the magic within you, but he didn't. Because you hid it from him. From yourself too."

"No. I knew it was there."

"You knew after Slawter," Beranabus corrects me, "but it didn't start then. This power has been with you since you were born. Some secret part of you knew what you were from the day you came into this world — but it was afraid. It didn't want the power and responsibility. So it pushed the magic down deep where it couldn't work or even be noticed.

"No other magician can do that. They can deny their calling and refuse to hone their talent, but they can't bury it completely. But you were so powerful that even as a child you were instinctively able to hide your magic from the world. If not for the Grady curse, it would have lain hidden for the rest of your life, a great power wasted."

"I wish it had," I mutter angrily.

"You shouldn't," scolds Beranabus. "If not for the magic, you'd be a wild, raging animal now. The barriers you erected between yourself and your magical potential began to crumble when you first faced demons. You had to draw on your inner power when you fought Lord Loss and his familiars. You drove your magic back down afterwards, but cracks had appeared in your armour.

"The magic has been buzzing around inside you ever since, trying to break free. You kept a lid on it for a long time, but then the curse kicked in. The werewolf came to the fore. That should have been the end of Grubitsch Grady. But the magician within you opposed the beast. You said you used magic to fight the change, but you're wrong — magic used you. It stopped you becoming a monster."

"No it didn't," I say guiltily. "I turned for a while. I killed Ma and Pa Spleen. Next time, when the moon's full and the werewolf takes over, I'll kill again."

"Do you really believe that?" Beranabus asks.

"Of course." I stare at him, confused.

He shakes his head. "The moon has exerted as powerful an influence over you as it ever will. The beast dominated for a short time, but you drove it back. It will rise again, but you'll beat it then too. It will be easier next time. The beast will always be within you, snarling and spitting, battling to break free when the moon sings to it. But you're in control. You won."

"I didn't win!" I snap. "I killed Bill-E's grandparents. That's not winning. Even if I never again lose control, I've already killed. How can you say everything's OK? Maybe you don't count the murder of your half-brother's grandparents as a big deal, but I do. So don't—"

"Show him how to remember," Kernel interrupts. "I'm not going to listen to him rant and rage for hours. Teach him the spell — let him see how it really played out. That will shut him up."

"What are you talking about?" I growl.

"A spell to help you recall everything that happened while you were transformed," Beranabus says.

"Why would I want to do that?"

"To learn the truth."

"But I already—"

"Just let him teach you the damn spell," Kernel snaps.

I feel uneasy — I don't want to relive the murders — but they've aroused my curiosity, so I play along. Beranabus tells me to close my eyes and focus on my breathing. I breathe in... hold it for five seconds... then breathe out. When I have the right rhythm, he tells me the words to use. Breaks them down into simple syllables so I can repeat them, even though I don't know what they mean.

As I draw towards the end of the spell, a screen forms within my thoughts. It's the huge TV screen from home. Blank, grey, like it's on standby. I'm about to tell Beranabus there's no signal, but then the screen flickers. Bursts of light. Static. Then…

The cave. Just after I froze the waterfall into ice. I see everything through the eyes of the beast. I'm crouched low, howling, squinting into the light of Juni's torch as she pads hesitantly towards me. It's crazy, but as I'm watching, in spite of all I know about her now, I feel concern for Juni. I want her to flee before the wolf attacks. I almost call a warning to her, but then I remember this is a screened replay, it's not happening live.

In the cave, Juni comes within touching distance and regards me coolly. "The great Grubbs Grady changes at last," she sneers, then spits at me. "You pathetic creature! If you knew how much I've loathed these past weeks, having to be nice to you and your mongrel of an uncle."

The beast roars at her and raises its fists to beat her to a pulp. This time I root for the werewolf, wanting it to kill the deceitful witch. But before it can strike, Juni utters a quick spell and it falls to the ground and rolls around with muffled grunts and yelps, before coming to a quivering halt.

"There," Juni smiles, falsely sweet. "That should hold you."

She puts her torch down and walks around me, checking from all angles, then produces a large knife — one from our kitchen! — and lays it by my head. The beast tries to howl but can't. Juni strolls to the wall of the cave, where the crack I created runs up near the icy waterfall. She stares at the ice, then at me, troubled. Shakes her head and chants a spell. I listen for a few minutes.

When the spell shows no sign of ending, I say without opening my eyes, "Is there a fast-forward button on this thing?"

"What's happening?" Beranabus asks.

"I'm in the cave. I've turned. Juni's crafting some long-winded spell."

"Probably calling Lord Loss," Beranabus notes. "Very well. Try this."

He teaches me some new words. Once I've repeated them, the picture fades out, then, after some static and crackling, tunes back in. Juni's still chanting, but she's standing over me now. No sign of Lord Loss, but the wall is red and yellow around the crack and the ice is melting, becoming a normal waterfall again. The heat in the cave is vicious. The beast I've become is sweating.

Juni's holding up the knife. She bends, presses it to the left side of my throat, makes a quick swipe. Blood spurts, drenching the blade. I go stiff, both as the werewolf in the past and me in the present. But then Juni puts her face to the cut, breathes on it and the wound closes. She moves the blade to the other side of my throat and does the same thing. Then she takes the red blade to the crack in the wall.

"What's happening?" Beranabus asks, and I describe the scene to him. "Strange. I never heard of a demon being summoned that way. But Lord Loss is unique. Nobody knows why he's the only demon master who can cross to our world, or how he does it. This must be a method he taught her."

Juni smears my blood down one side of the rock within the crack, then the other. She steps back and chants more spells, louder, arms thrown wide. Finishes with a triumphant yowl, then leaps away from the crack, covering her eyes.

Nothing happens.

Juni lowers her arm and stares at the crack for a long time, then at the blade, then me. She walks across slowly and looks down, confused.

"Juni…" The word comes from deep within the rock. I place the voice straight away — Lord Loss. "Juni…" he calls again, distant, hungry, anxious.

Juni returns to the crack and talks quickly, softly. I can't hear what she says. But then Lord Loss hisses a name that chills me to the bone. "*Billy Spleen…*"

Juni bows, sets the knife down, looks at me and grins nastily. "Stay where you are, beastie. I'll be back for you soon."

She leaves, not bothering to take the torch.

On the floor the werewolf struggles to tear free of its magical constraints. After a while the beast goes still. Its hands start to glow. The glow spreads and sweeps up its arms, hits its face and chest, then radiates down its body and legs.

The werewolf stands and cocks its head as if listening to someone speak. Then, with a noise that sounds like a growl of agreement, it races for the exit and heads for the surface.

As the beast lurches through the forest, I fill Beranabus and Kernel in on what's happening. Beranabus is unsure what to make of Juni's behaviour. "She seems to have been trying to summon Lord Loss. For some reason the spell didn't work. But I don't see what difference the other boy's blood would make."

"I don't think she wanted Bill-E for the spell," I murmur. "And I don't think it failed. Lord Loss stopped her. He wanted Bill-E to be there when he crossed, so he could kill us both."

"Perhaps," Beranabus says, but he doesn't sound convinced.

The chase concludes. The beast arrives at Bill-E's house. The back door is open. The wolf bolts inside and finds Juni picking up the unconscious Bill-E Spleen. Ma and Pa Spleen are both dead. The werewolf howls at Juni. She drops Bill-E as the beast leaps. They fight, my transformed self ripping at the albino with its teeth and claws, Juni fighting back physically, no time for spells. She screams my name and the beast roars. Juni screams my name again and again, each time adding more distress to the cry.

Finally, after a minute of Juni screaming, the werewolf releases her. She staggers back, bloody and stunned. The beast growls angrily, standing firmly between Juni and Bill-E, protecting the otherwise defenceless boy. Then the view goes blurry. I sense the creature changing. Juni sighs with relief, then spreads her hands and talks quickly, faking concern. "Grubbs?" she gasps. "Is that you?"

I open my eyes and the screen disappears inside my head. I stare at Beranabus, open mouthed. "I didn't kill them," I whisper. "I tried to save them. I protected Bill-E. *I didn't kill them!*" The last sentence comes out as a sob. I bend over and weep with relief, all else forgotten, eternally grateful to be innocent Grubbs Grady again — not the loathsome killer that I mistakenly believed I was.

THE VETERAN

→My first impulse, when I stop crying, is to rush back to Carcery Vale and warn Dervish and Bill-E of the danger they're in.

"We already had this conversation," Beranabus sighs.

"I don't care," I snap. "Juni didn't just target me — she went after Bill-E too. She might not return to the Vale straightaway, but she can easily phone Dervish and ask about me. If she discovers he doesn't know where I am or what really happened, she can return and…" I shake my head viciously, trying not to think of all the terrible things she could do. "We have to go back and warn them."

"No," Beranabus says softly. "Their welfare isn't my concern."

"How can you say that?" I shriek. "Dervish is your friend."

"No — if anything, he's my employee."

"What do you…?" I stop, finally realising where I had heard Beranabus's name before. Dervish mentioned it when he was explaining about his work. I should have put two and two together when he was talking about the warning spells at the cave, but my head's still in a whirl. "You're the boss of the Disciples," I mutter.

"I wouldn't describe myself that way," Beranabus sniffs. "I don't have much to do with them. I use the Disciples where appropriate, but I fight most of my battles in the Demonata's universe, alone."

"Not *quite* alone," Kernel huffs.

Beranabus grunts offhandedly at Kernel, then addresses me again. "I didn't form the Disciples. They came to me looking for leadership and training. I occasionally demand their help, but I've no vested interest in the group."

"But Dervish is one of your people," I argue. "He told me you sent him to Carcery Vale to protect the cave. You're responsible for him."

"No!" Beranabus barks. He brushes his long hair back from his face, glowering at me. "I sent Dervish to Carcery Vale, as I sent others before him, to watch for demons and their human servants, to report to me if any came sniffing in search of the cave. Everything else in his life was secondary to that task. He should have respected my instructions, kept a low profile, not got entangled with a demon master like Lord Loss. He brought this trouble on himself. I don't have time to get involved in personal conflicts. Lord Loss has nothing to do with the cave, so I don't care what he does to Dervish."

"You're a monster," I sneer. "You're no better than the Demonata."

"Perhaps not," Beranabus concedes. "But the Disciples understand that there are forces at work in the universe far more important than anything in their own lives. They accept the need to put human concerns behind them and focus on the nobler cause to which they've been called."

"I don't do noble causes," I retort. "I care about Dervish and Bill-E. That's all. They're more important to me than anything else, even the safety of the bloody world."

"He's arrogant and stupid," Kernel says, staring at me coldly. "He can't see the bigger picture. You made a mistake bringing him here. Send him back. Let him perish at the hands of Lord Loss."

"That isn't your decision to make," Beranabus says, eyes flashing. "Don't forget your place. You're here to serve."

"Well, it's true," Kernel pouts.

Beranabus takes a steadying breath, then faces me again. "What I'm trying to explain," he says, only barely restraining his anger, "is that Dervish wouldn't want us to rush back. He understands the importance of my work and knows I don't get involved in minor skirmishes — which is all this is. He doesn't expect me to ride to his rescue. This quarrel with Lord Loss and Juni Swan is of his own making and he must deal with them himself.

"Having said that," Beranabus continues, raising his voice to stop me interrupting, "I *will* get word to him, as I promised. I can't get in touch with him now — there are no easy means of making contact with the outside world from here — but as soon as I can, I'll warn him of Juni's treachery and the threat he faces. That's the best I can offer. And it's all Dervish would expect."

"Fine," I grunt, getting to my feet. "But I'm not one of your Disciples, so I don't have to obey your rules. I'll go and warn him right now if you'll just point me in the right direction..." I look at him challengingly, expecting an argument.

Beranabus smiles flatly. "Once you leave the cave, the fastest route is east. It's a long, hard walk. The sun is merciless, waterholes are few and far between, and there's little food to be found. An experienced trekker or a magician might make it out alive. But you're not a worldly traveller and you don't know how to make the most of your magical potential. You'll be dead within a week. But if you want to make the attempt regardless, go ahead. I won't detain you."

"Right," I nod sharply. "I will."

I start towards the rope ladder, but Kernel stops me. "Grubitsch... Grubbs. He's telling the truth. You can't make it. You'll die if you try."

"I'd rather die trying than live and let Dervish and Bill-E be butchered."

"It would be pointless," Kernel argues. "Even if you got out alive, it would take weeks to reach civilisation. Dervish will find out quicker through us. Disciples visit here regularly. One might come tomorrow or the next day. You won't achieve anything by sacrificing yourself. Do you want us to tell your uncle you wasted your life on a pointless mission? How do you think that would make him feel?"

I stare at Kernel coldly, then turn slowly to Beranabus. "You swear you'll let him know as soon as you can?"

The magician nods. "As Kernel said, we receive several visitors a year. When the next Disciple comes, I'll give him or her a message to pass on to Dervish."

"What if it's months before anyone visits?"

Beranabus doesn't reply.

I think it over. Weigh up the pros and cons. Try to decide what Dervish would tell me to do. I finally figure it makes no sense to leave.

"OK," I sigh, taking my place by the fire. "I don't like it, and I'll hold you to account if anything happens to

Dervish or Bill-E. But I'm going to trust you. I don't know for sure that I should, but to hell with it. Now I assume you brought me here for a purpose. What is it?"

Beranabus laughs. "Damn it all, I like you! You're blunt and to the point. I'm sure you'll cause me all sorts of aggravation, but I'm looking forward to having you around."

"Never mind the compliments," I growl. "Just tell me why I'm here."

"Very well. As I explained, I don't have much to do with the Disciples. They deal with largely unimportant matters. They stop some demons from crossing and limit the damage caused by those who get through. That doesn't mean much in the universal scheme of things. Hundreds of casualties... a few thousand... even a few million... what of them?"

I gawp at the elderly tramp, then at Kernel. "Is he for real?"

"You'd better believe it," Kernel says in a low voice, looking at Beranabus darkly.

"I can't waste time worrying about a few dead humans," Beranabus defends himself. "I have more important work to tend to."

"What's more important than saving lives?" I challenge him.

"Saving the world," he answers without the least hint of irony. "Most of the demons who hit our universe are weak. It's relatively easy for a sly demon – with human assistance – to create a window between their universe and ours, but the masters can't squeeze through. Occasionally a tunnel can be opened – like at the cave in Carcery Vale – which more powerful demons can access. But most of the time only the lesser Demonata can cross and they can't stay more than a few minutes. A nuisance, aye, but they don't threaten the existence of the human race.

"I focus on combating the threat of the stronger monsters, those who could wipe out mankind. They're always looking for ways to cross. The Disciples act when they uncover evidence on this world of a potential crossing, but I can't allow that to happen with the masters. I have to prevent such threats in their infancy.

"To do that, Kernel and I work in the universe of the Demonata. Unlike the Disciples, we spend little time on this world. We walk among demons, spying on them, uncovering their plans in the formative stages, wrecking them. We divide demons who are working together. Locate and destroy places where tunnels could be built. It's difficult. We have to fight constantly and the battles are savage."

"Savage," Kernel echoes, his voice a whisper.

"It's a horrible undertaking," Beranabus says. "One might even call it a curse. But it has to be done. The

Demonata are a constant threat. Those of us with the power to limit them to their own realm don't have the freedom of choice. Kernel and I know that if we don't fight the monsters on their worlds, the demon masters will cross and fight us on ours — and everyone will perish.

"We went to Carcery Vale as soon as I heard the entrance to the cave had been opened. My warning spells should have been activated instantly, but for whatever reason they didn't work. When Dervish sent word, we rushed to the scene. I feared the handiwork of the Demonata and thought I might be too late to stop them. To my relief I found no evidence of their presence."

"What about Lord Loss?" I cry. "And Juni?"

"They didn't bother me. Lord Loss doesn't want to open a tunnel. He prefers things the way they are. I considered talking with Dervish about Juni, but I didn't know if I could trust him. For all I knew, he'd pledged himself to her dark cause and was working with her to trap me."

"Dervish would never do that," I growl.

"Probably not," Beranabus agrees. "But he might have fallen under her spell. She could have been using him to strike at me. I decided not to reveal my presence. I sent Kernel back here and remained hidden, to ensure no demons came to make use of the cave. I planned to close the entrance again and let Dervish know about Juni before I left. But then I spotted *you*…"

The hairs on the back of my neck stand up. I'm no fool. I can see where this is heading. But I say nothing. I act ignorant, hoping I'm wrong, not wanting to put ideas in his head if they aren't already there — though I'm certain they are.

"You'd hidden your magic masterfully," Beranabus says, "but it had started to spill out by the time I arrived. I could see it shining through."

"Dervish and Juni didn't," I mumble. "Juni tested me, searching for magic. She couldn't find any."

"Of course she could," he barks. "You still haven't seen through all of her deceptions. I don't blame you. It's hard, when you've trusted someone, to see them as they really are. You know Juni was working against you all this time, but you still think of her as a friend.

"Juni's far more powerful than Dervish. She knew the magic was there. Those tests were to check how strong you were, how much of a threat you posed, so she and Lord Loss could plan their assault. I don't think she was able to find out as much about you as she hoped. That's why they decided to confront you in the cave. They chose a place of magic, where Lord Loss would be more powerful. When you escaped, they switched to the aeroplane, figuring that up in the air you couldn't escape — at worst, they could crash the aircraft and kill you that way.

"Juni's been manipulating you at every step. Worming out your secrets, finding weaknesses to use against you. She's a cunning vixen. She artfully drove a wedge between you and Dervish. Even summoned the Lambs to make you believe he'd sacrificed you to the Grady executioners."

"You mean he didn't?" I gawp at Beranabus, ashen-faced.

"Of course not," Beranabus grunts. "You know your uncle. You saw how he fought to save your brother. He would have done the same for you. He's not a man to give up on his loved ones."

I feel cold inside. I thought Dervish had betrayed me, when in fact *I* did the betraying. I should have known he wouldn't call in the Lambs without discussing it first. Dervish always played straight with me, ever since he came to visit me in the asylum and told me that he knew demons were real.

"I've been a fool," I mutter.

"Aye," Beranabus says. "But we all make fools of ourselves one time or another. It's part of being human. But that's beside the point. I was talking about..." He frowns and looks to Kernel for help.

"You'd just spotted the shining beacon of magic that was Grubbs Grady," Kernel says drily, and I realise he's jealous of me.

"Of course. Forgive me, I lose track of my thoughts so easily. Old age and more battles with the Demonata than I care to remember. Yes, I was on the verge of leaving Carcery Vale, satisfied that no demons were lurking in the wings, when *you* caught my eye. I saw your magic, the struggle taking place within you, the power you could wield if you survived. It's not often that I come across such a promising find.

"I stayed to track your development. I staked you out and let you see me from time to time — I hoped your magic would respond to mine. I was trying to load the deck in my favour. I'd apologise, but that would be hypocritical of me."

"Get on with it," I snarl.

"There's not much more to get on with. I spied on Dervish and Juni when I wasn't following you. I knew that witch was up to no good, but I wasn't sure of her exact plans. Then I saw the Lambs arrive. You burst out of the underground cellar. I trailed you to the cave, but didn't follow you down — Juni would have sensed my presence. I waited while she came, dealt with you and left again. Then you burst out of the cave. I pursued you to your brother's house, then the airport. When I realised Juni planned to board an aeroplane with you, I guessed what her plan was and I followed."

"You could have stopped her," I say icily. "You knew she was going to kill the other passengers. You could have attacked. Ripped me from her before we got on."

"No," he says. "I wasn't sure. She might not have struck on the aeroplane. Or perhaps she was taking you somewhere else to meet Lord Loss. Maybe you were in league with her. I weighed up all my options and I decided to wait. It was the right call and if I had to make it again, I'd do exactly the same thing."

He scowls at the disgusted look I give him, then waves the matter away. "And here we are," he says. "The end of the story."

"Not quite," I reply. "You still haven't said what you want me for, why you rescued me and brought me here."

Beranabus frowns. "Isn't that obvious?"

"Yes. But I want you to say it."

"Very well. You're a magician. I want you to become my assistant, like Kernel, cross into the universe of the Demonata with us, and spend the rest of your life by my side, killing demons."

THE MONOLITH

→Sitting on my blanket, legs crossed, hunched over, fingers locked together. Beranabus is at his table, sorting through papers, muttering and whistling. Kernel is exercising, stretching and limbering up. They're setting off to fight demons shortly. They expect me to go with them.

It's crazy. I told Beranabus I wouldn't do it. Leave my own world? Enter the Demonata's realm? Fight monsters like Lord Loss every day? No bloody way, Jo-bloody-sé!

Beranabus didn't argue. Just shrugged and said we all have to make our own decisions in life, then went to get ready. I sat by the fire a while longer, watching him and Kernel prepare. Then came back here, where I've been sitting for the last half-hour, silent, numb.

Kernel finishes stretching. Bends, touches his toes, then rises in the air. Slowly turns head over heels. Lands softly on his feet and lets go of his toes. Spots me watching him and walks over. "Having fun?"

"It's better than a circus." I stare up at him, his scars and bruises, the marks of past battles, the fear in his eyes. "How do you do it?" I whisper. "I've fought demons. I know what it's like. How do you find the courage to…?"

Kernel shrugs like it's no big deal. Licks his lips and glances at Beranabus, then sits beside me. "I never really had a choice," he says. "I had a brother. Well, I thought… No, let's leave it at that — it gets too complicated otherwise. He was kidnapped by a demon. I followed after him. Met Beranabus and some others — your uncle was one of them."

"You know Dervish?" I ask, surprised.

"Yes. I haven't seen him in thirty-odd years, but we were good friends back then. I wouldn't have survived without him. Is he still a punk?"

"What?" I frown.

"He was a punk. Spiked hair, earrings, leather jacket, chains."

"No," I chuckle. "We must be talking about a different guy. Dervish was never…" I hesitate. How many demon-fighting Disciples called Dervish can there be in the world? "I'll quiz you about that later. Finish telling me about yourself first."

Kernel shrugs. "Things didn't work out with my brother. I returned home, but several years had passed — time works differently in the Demonata's universe. I couldn't pick up the pieces of my old life. I no longer belonged to that world. So I came to work for Beranabus. He taught me how to master my powers and slay demons. I've been doing it ever since."

"What's it like? Do you have days off? Weekends? Holidays?"

Kernel laughs. "Sure — two weeks on a beach of fire in the sunny south of Hades, half-price off-season. Of course we don't have holidays! We don't fight *all* the time – we have to rest, and Beranabus occasionally has to do something on this world – but we're at it most days of any given year."

"What do you do when you're not fighting?"

"Recover and relax here."

"You don't get out at all? Not even for a day trip?"

"Day trip to where?" Kernel snorts. "I pop up the ladder every now and then for a breath of fresh air. Maybe go for a walk for an hour or two. But it's boiling by day, freezing by night, and there's nothing to see or do."

"Doesn't Beranabus take you with him when he goes away?"

"Rarely," Kernel says hotly. "He prefers it if one of us is here when we're not battling demons, in case anyone tries to contact him. And even when he does take me, it's only ever on business. We're in and out as quickly as possible, keeping a low profile, hiding in the shadows."

He stops. His fingers are trembling. There are hard tears in his eyes, but he's holding them back. I try thinking of something comforting to say, but can't. I want to change the subject, but don't know what to talk to him about. So I ask about his age — not entirely off-topic, but hopefully less of a sore point.

"You said you'd been with Beranabus thirty years, but that can't be right. You don't look more than sixteen or seventeen."

He smiles tiredly. "Like I said, time works differently in the demon universe. It varies from zone to zone. In some places it passes faster than here or at the same rate, but usually it's slower. We're often gone for what feels like a day or two, only to return to find six months have passed here."

"Bloody hell!" I gasp.

Kernel nods miserably. "In real time I've been with Beranabus for... I don't know... maybe four or five years. But thirty or more have slipped by on Earth while we've been off fighting demons."

"That's what Beranabus wants me to sign up for?" I gulp. "Spend my life facing demons? Live in a cave when I'm not working? And go out one day to find that decades have passed and everyone I knew is old or dead?"

"It sounds bad when you put it that way." Kernel laughs hollowly. "It has its rewards. I'm more powerful than just about any living human. And I save the planet from unimaginable dangers on a regular basis. But that's not much comfort when I'm rotting away here or being pummelled by a four-headed giant."

Kernel stands and smirks, a hint of pity in his otherwise bitter, mocking smile. "Welcome to the firm." Then he goes to get ready.

→Beranabus works on opening a window to the Demonata's universe. It was a big deal for Dervish when he summoned Lord Loss, but Beranabus is more adept. A few spells, some scrawled symbols on the walls, a silly short dance and the world starts to fade around us. Smoke pours from Beranabus's flesh, all sorts of shapes, mostly a mix of animals and demons. The roof of the cave goes momentarily translucent. I spot a red sky full of giant demons streaking across the heavens like meteors. Then the cave firms up again. The smoke clears. And Beranabus is standing in front of a black pillar which is strangely familiar. The word "monolith" pops into my head, but I don't know why.

"Not bad, aye?" Beranabus says. "Kernel is the master of opening windows, but he's at his best in the universe of the Demonata. From here it's as easy for me to do it. But once we cross he's in a league of his own. You'll see what I mean soon enough — if you come with us." He takes a step back from the monolith. "Made up your mind yet?"

"I made it up ages ago," I snap. "I'm not coming."

"Of course you are," Beranabus smiles. "Who could resist a challenge like this? The chance to flex your magical muscles, eliminate scores of demons, save the world. You'll come with us in the end, so why not drop the reluctant act and—"

"I'm not acting!" I shout, flushing angrily. "I've had enough of demons. I don't want to fight them. I don't care how magical I am. I'm not your assistant and I never will be. So just—"

"There are two fields of thought about the granting of magical talent," Beranabus interrupts smoothly. "Some claim it's pure luck, the random lottery of the universe doling out magic without method or purpose. Others — and I'm one of them — believe there's a force which wants humans to triumph. We think magicians are created to keep the world safe from the Demonata, that at times of great peril, heroes are generated, capable of defeating the otherwise unstoppable forces of evil.

"It doesn't matter which is right. You have the power. Whether you gained it by design or accident is irrelevant. You have the ability to kill demons, to stop them crossing. If you don't make the most of that talent — if you hide from your duty — it's because you're a coward, plain and simple."

I tremble with rage at the insult. Part of me wants to call upon all of my newly revealed powers and hit him with the strongest magical blast I can muster, to teach him never to mess with me again. But I don't. Because he's speaking the truth.

Dervish loved me, so he never said it, but he must have thought it. He didn't object when I refused to learn spells and magic. He respected my choice and never made me feel like I was chickening out. I told myself I'd done my bit and now I was entitled to a normal life.

But that was rot. Deep down I knew I didn't want to fight because I was scared. Dervish knew it, I knew it and now Beranabus knows it. The only difference is, Beranabus has called me out.

Beranabus is leaning towards me, eyebrows raised, awaiting my comeback. When I don't respond to the insult, he smiles sadly. "I can't afford to wet-nurse you. This is a serious business, no room for lies or charades. When you were an average child, you could afford to be a coward — nobody suffered. Now you have to be a hero or untold billions might die."

"That's an exaggeration, isn't it?" I mutter.

"No. Those are the stakes we play for. If it was hundreds, it wouldn't matter — I let that many die on the plane. Even millions… the world can afford to lose a few million humans every now and again. You could think of it as judicious pruning. Mankind would continue whether you joined us or not.

"But we deal in *billions* — wholesale slaughter. If the more powerful Demonata make it through, everybody perishes. That's why you can't be a coward any longer. I won't let you deny your calling just because you're a nice boy and I feel sorry for you. We have a duty — me, Kernel, you. Fair or not, that's the way it is. So you're coming through that window with us. Unless the coward within you is stronger than I think…"

He looks at me harshly. Behind him, Kernel keeps his head down. I think he's ashamed of Beranabus, but also of himself and the choices the pair of them must make. The choice *I* must make.

"I can't do it," I sob. "You don't understand. I've replayed those battles with Lord Loss so many times… Vein and Artery… Slawter… the anguish. I did it the first time to save Bill-E, because he's my brother, and in Slawter because we were trapped and it was fight or die. But there was never time to worry about it in advance or make a considered decision to pit myself against demons. This is different. I'd be *choosing* horror and misery. I've seen the nightmarish work of the Demonata in real life and in dreams. I can't face them again. I *can't*."

"You can," Beranabus says, not giving way. "Unless you want to accept that you're a worthless coward. Unless you're prepared to flee like a whipped, shamed cur. Are you, Grubitsch?"

"I…" My voice seizes. I come within a breath of saying yes. I want to. I almost grasp the yellow mantle gratefully. But the shame… the guilt… to live the rest of my life as a branded coward…

"Please," I moan. "Don't do this to me."

"It's already done," Beranabus says. "I'm not pushing you into anything. I'm just the one who has the unpleasant task of breaking the news to you." He steps forward, grabs my shoulder and looks hard into my eyes. "Hero or coward. There's no in-between. Choose now. The Demonata won't wait forever."

Wanting to scream, to run, to tell him to go stuff himself.

Knowing I can't, that I'm gifted, that I'm damned.

"I hope they kill me," I cry, tearing away from him, trembling wildly. "I hope I don't last five minutes."

"I hoped that too when I first crossed," Kernel says softly, then walks to the monolith, puts a hand on the surface, breathes on it and steps through as the dark face shimmers. He vanishes.

"You will fare better than you fear, Grubitsch," Beranabus says encouragingly, following Kernel to the monolith. He puts a hand on it.

"Wait," I stop him and he looks back questioningly. "If we're going to do this, I want to make one thing clear. It's Grubs, understand? I bloody hate *Grubitsch*."

Beranabus smiles crookedly and says with all the charm of Sweeney Todd, "If you can kill demons, I'll call you anything you please. If not, I'll leave your bones lying scattered in their universe, nameless." He faces the monolith again and exhales. It shimmers and he moves forward. Gone.

I don't think about this being my chance to run, to get out of here, lose myself in the desert and die on my own world. Afraid the coward within me will take control if I give it a chance. Without hesitation, I lurch forward, put both hands on the monolith, breathe on it like the others did and step through into madness.

THE STUFF THAT
HEROES ARE MADE OF

→First impression — this place is infinitely different to the webby world of Lord Loss. Light blue in colour, it's like something out of a Picasso painting, all cubes and weird angles. We're in a valley of sorts. Narrow, jagged pillars of a weird blue substance rise high around us. I edge over to the nearest pillar and sniff, expecting the stench of sulphur. But it smells more like a piece of rotten fruit — a peach or pear maybe.

"Don't touch it," Beranabus says. "It's probably not dangerous, but we don't take chances here. The less physical contact we make, the better."

"Where is this?" I ask.

"The Demonata's universe, idiot," Kernel snaps.

"I meant which part? I don't know anything about the set-up here. Are there ten worlds, twenty, a thousand? Do they have names? Which one are we on?"

"Geography doesn't work like that here," Beranabus says, studying the pillars, eyes sharp. "The worlds and zones are constantly changing. There are many self-contained galaxies within the general demon universe. The stronger Demonata have the power to create their own realms or take over another demon's and reshape it. We never know what we're going to find when we cross."

"Then how do you hunt?" I frown.

"We target specific demons. Realms might change, but demons don't, except for the shape-shifters, and even they don't change on the inside, where it counts. If we know a demon's name, Kernel can locate it within minutes. If we don't know, or if the demon doesn't have a name, it's more complicated. Each demon has a unique spiritual vibration."

"Call it a demonic frequency," Kernel chips in when I look blank. "Demons have souls, like humans, and they emit a certain type of wave which we can sense. Each demon's soul is like a radio station, transmitting on an individual frequency. If we think a certain demon's working on a window or tunnel, we can lock on to its signal and track it down."

"It's not easy," Beranabus says, "especially if it's a demon we've had no first-hand experience of, but we usually find what we're looking for."

Kernel points to one of the shorter pillars. "There."

Beranabus squints. "Are you sure?"

"Positive."

"Either you're getting sharper or my eyes are getting worse," Beranabus mutters, then raises a hand and sends a ball of energy shooting at the pillar. There's a gentle glowing. A sound somewhere between a sigh and a moan. Then the *pillar* moves and an angular demon steps out of a crack.

Fear grabs hold and magic flares within me. I bring up my hands defensively, but Beranabus stops me with a high-spirited, "Rein in those horses, boy!" He faces the demon and smiles. "How do you feel about dying today?"

The demon makes a series of choking noises. The sounds don't make sense to me, but Beranabus can decipher them. "No," he says. "We're not going to leave you alone. You know who we are and what we want. Now, do you have something to tell us or do we make life wickedly uncomfortable for you?"

The demon glares at Beranabus through a series of triangular eyes, but it looks more miserable than angry. It's an odd creature, not really frightening in manner or appearance. It mutters something. Beranabus and Kernel share a glance. "You're sure?" Kernel asks and the demon nods stiffly.

"Excellent," Beranabus beams and cocks his head at Kernel. The bald teenager shuffles away a couple of metres, then starts moving his hands about in the air. It's as if he's sliding invisible blocks around.

"What's happening?" I ask Beranabus quietly, not wanting to disturb Kernel.

"I'm opening a window," Kernel answers before Beranabus can, an edge to his voice. "This is my speciality. I can see panels of light which are invisible to all others. When I slide certain panels together, windows form. I can get to anywhere in this universe – or ours – through them."

"Where will this one lead?" I ask.

"You'll find out soon," Kernel says. "We're going in search of prey. You want to kill demons, don't you?"

"No. But let's say I did. What about that one?" I point to the blue demon, which is edging back into the crack, becoming one with the landscape again.

"Not worth killing," Beranabus says dismissively. "There are untold billions of demons. They're all evil, but most can't hurt us or cross to our world. That cretin doesn't even dare leave this valley. It waits, hiding and surviving, doing precious little else."

"What does it feed on?" I ask.

"Who knows," Beranabus sniffs. "Maybe nothing. Most demons don't need to eat and drink. Many do, but out of choice, not necessity."

"Then why did we come here, if not to kill it?" I frown.

"Information," Kernel says, looking around. "We're like detectives with a team of snitches. We know where to find soft demons. We often come to places like this, rough up the locals, find out if anything foul is afoot — something usually is. Demons like that one might not do much, but they know things. Secrets are hard to keep in this universe. Word spreads quickly."

"What's the *word* now?" I ask, caught off guard. I don't know what I expected, but it wasn't something like this.

"There's a demon trying to possess a woman on Earth," Beranabus says. "That happens all the time. It's not a problem for us, though it's bad for those involved. Some demons who can't cross universes can establish a hold on the minds of humans. They manipulate them, send them mad, use them to create as much chaos as possible. We normally wouldn't bother with small-scale melodramatics like this, but I want to break you in gently."

Kernel grunts. "On *my* first mission we fought a pair of demons who had almost broken through to the centre of Moscow. They were two of the toughest I've ever faced. It was bloody and tight. That's when I lost the tips of my fingers." He stares at his left hand, the fingers flinching inwards as he relives the memory.

"Why couldn't you replace them?" I ask. "You can do that with magic, right?"

"Normally. But the loss made little difference. I decided to leave them as they were. They remind me of the dangers we face, the fact that success isn't a guarantee, that we can and will perish in this hell-hole eventually."

"Here we go," Beranabus says briskly. A purplish window has formed in front of Kernel. Beranabus walks up to it and steps through, not bothering to breathe on this one. Kernel curls his fingers into a fist, then relaxes his fingers and follows.

I look back in the direction of the blue demon, but I can't see it now, even though I know the exact spot where it's hiding. Shaking my head, I think, "This isn't so bad. I can handle this." But I know it's a false start, that worse – much worse – is to come.

There's a sound far overhead, from the meteor-sized demons in the sky. Fearful of being attacked while I'm alone, I rush to the window and push through after the others.

→*Fire!* It's all around me, fierce, intense, out of control. I feel the hair on my arms singe and know I have only seconds before I burst into flames. Total panic. I want to look for Beranabus and Kernel or scream for help, but my eyes and mouth shut automatically against the heat.

"Oh, for the love of..." Kernel tuts, taking hold of my arm and shaking it roughly. "This is ridiculous. He's not fit for this. Send him back."

"He'll learn," Beranabus says and then his lips are by my left ear. "Use magic to guide yourself."

"It's hell!" I moan, speaking out of the side of my mouth, keeping my eyes shut.

"One of many thousands of hells," Beranabus grunts. "For every imaginative demon who constructs a terrifyingly original realm, there are scores who draw upon tired old human myths. Stop acting like a fool. You can already feel your magic responding to this, protecting you from the flames. You'd be burning to a crisp right now if not."

I open one eye, then the other. Nothing to see but flames. Beranabus and Kernel are hard to spot among the flickering licks of yellow and red. Still hot, hotter than I should be able to bear. But magic's humming away in the background, cooling me down, guarding my freckled flesh. Beranabus is right — it kicked in as soon as I set foot here, even as the hairs on my arms began to shrivel. I knew that — I could feel it — but fear made me panic.

"Where's the demon?" I ask, trying to peer through the walls of fire. I look down and realise we're truly in the middle of the flames — no floor. Nothing below, above or to the sides except fire.

"The flames *are* the demon," Kernel says. "It's a universal demon."

"Am I supposed to know what that means?" I growl.

"Universal demons don't just inhabit a galaxy of their own — they become it," Beranabus explains. "This demon has a fascination with fire, so it became flames. Its whole zone – the demon itself – is made of fire."

"But where does it start?" I ask. "Where does it end?"

"Nowhere," Beranabus says. "This demon is its own self-contained and at the same time limitless realm. It's like our universe — infinite."

While I'm trying to make sense of that – I've always had problems thinking of a universe being infinite, never mind one single creature – the flames thicken around us. There's a horrible shrieking sound, piercing and destructive. My eardrums and eyeballs should burst, but magic protects me instinctively. (Which is just as well, since I wouldn't know where to start to control it!)

A shape forms amid the flames, gigantic and bulging, like the wizard's fake head in *The Wizard of Oz*, only a hundred times bigger and more frightening, full of leaping shadows, sparks and flames.

The demon shrieks again. A huge, rough, fiery fist forms and smashes down on Beranabus. He waves an arm at the fist and slices through the flames. The edges of his beard singe, but he's otherwise unharmed.

Another fist forms and tries to swat Kernel aside. He leaps high, somersaults over it, opens his mouth mid-leap and sucks in sharply. He inhales flames, face turning a pure, angry, painful white. The demon screams. Kernel lands, coughs, spins and leaps over another quickly formed fist.

Beranabus grabs handfuls of flames and rams them into his stomach. And I mean *into* — his hands pierce his own flesh. He's stuffing his guts full of fire. The hands come out, the wall of his stomach unharmed. He grabs more flames and jams them in. Out — in. Out — in.

And what does the *heroic* Grubbs Grady do? I hang beside them, helpless and shivering, about as much use as a plastic toasting fork. I want to help, but I don't know how. My magic isn't strong enough. I don't want to be here. This isn't my fight.

Then, in the middle of the battle, the demon focuses on me. Two huge fists form on either side and slam towards me, to hammer me lifeless.

I throw myself to the floor. Except there isn't a floor. Just flames. I don't know how I've been hovering, but I'm not any more. I'm falling, like when Beranabus ripped me out of the plane, dropping like a sack of stones, quickly losing sight of the magician and his assistant.

"Help!" I scream.

"Help yourself," Beranabus roars, then curses brutally.

I come to a stop. Relief evaporates moments later when I realise I haven't been helped by Beranabus or Kernel — I'm being held in the middle of a giant hand of fire. The fingers close upon me. The heat's unbearable. I feel my magic struggling, protesting, pleading with me to direct it, use it, fight back. But what can I do? How can I defeat a creature made of flames? It's impossible. At least Lord Loss and his familiars were real targets. I could hit them. This is lunacy. We're all going to perish, burnt to death by a demon the size of a universe.

I scream at the flames. The fingers stop, shudder, then tear apart. I fall again. I'm crying, taking no satisfaction out of destroying the hand because I'm sure another will form any second now, bigger, stronger, hotter.

Then Kernel is by my side. His eyes are sharp bright blue with rage. "Bloody amateur," he sneers. "Bloody coward."

"I can't do it," I babble. "I told you I couldn't. I didn't want to come here. Make me stop falling. Help me get—"

"Shut up, you worm!" Kernel shouts. "I should let you burn." He laughs cruelly. "The hell with it. Your death would serve no purpose." He darts away from me, angling down, moving much quicker than I'm falling. He becomes a speck, then stops. As I hurtle towards him, I see his hands moving, the way they did when he created the window to this universe.

When I'm maybe a hundred metres away, a dark green window forms. Kernel slides away from it and waves at me like a policeman directing traffic. I'm rushing towards the window. The flames peel away from me. The window gets bigger and bigger as I fall upon it. I just have time to worry about what will happen when I flash through and smash into the ground on the other side. Then I hit it and everything goes green.

A FACE FROM THE PAST

→I land hard on the floor of Beranabus's cave, but no bones shatter. Groaning, I pick myself up and look around. The fire has burnt out — only cold ashes remain. But torches glow on the walls, the flames kept alive by magic. Overhead the window hangs flat, two metres or so above me. A few moments later, as I'm edging clear of it on my hands and knees, it shimmers, then breaks apart and disappears.

I crawl to my bed and lie down, panting, heart still racing from my encounter with the fire demon, bones aching from the impact of the fall. I shut my eyes and shiver, then climb beneath the blanket for warmth.

Lying in the gloom and quiet. Thinking about the universe of the Demonata. My eyes open and tears wet my lashes. I'm ashamed. I acted like a gutless coward. What's happened to me? I was braver than this when I faced Lord Loss. Scared, but I fought bravely. Why can't I be that way now? For long hours I lie still, pondering, before falling into a troubled, restless, shame-tinged sleep.

*   *   *

→No sign of Beranabus and Kernel when I wake. I worry about them for a few minutes, but then recall them saying time usually passes quicker here than in the universe of the Demonata. A fight which lasts an hour or two there can equate to days, weeks or even months here.

Rising stiffly, I explore the cave in search of food and water. I find ample supplies stacked in all corners, the food imperishable, the water carefully bottled. So I won't starve or die of thirst. Not unless they're gone for *years*...

The fire next. There are logs and chunks of turf nearby, but no matches or lighters. I try one of the torches, but they're secured tight to the wall and I don't want to break any off. I guess Beranabus and Kernel use magic to start the fire. Reluctant to disturb my inner powers, I attempt to ape cavemen and ignite the fire by rubbing sticks together, banging a couple of stones off each other, in search of an elusive first spark. But I quickly discover that I'm nowhere near as advanced as a caveman.

Sitting back, frowning at the logs. It's not especially cold in the cave, but I want to light a fire regardless, more for the comfort of its crackling, natural flames than anything else. So, cautiously, I reach within myself and look for magic. But it withdraws as I come near. I sense the power, but it darts out of reach. I feel like it's punishing me, annoyed that I didn't use it to fight the demon. *You can go stuff yourself if you think I'll help you now! Make your own fire, coward!*

Giving up, I grab a tin of beans, a fork and a can-opener, and return to my bed, where I eat the beans cold. Staring at the lifeless fire as I eat. Remembering the flames in the other universe and my cowardice. Trying to justify my actions. What was I meant to do? Suck in flames like Kernel? Jam them into my gut like Beranabus? If they'd shown me how, I could have. But they dropped me into it, no warnings or advice. Maybe I wasn't really a coward, just ignorant.

Unable to convince myself. If we'd been fighting a demon master, I could plead inexperience. But Kernel said this was a lesser demon. Beranabus was starting me off lightly, testing me out on one of the meeker monsters. There can be no excuses.

I lurch to my feet. I'm getting out of here. I don't want to be around when they return. I'll hide my shame in the desert. Take off, let the sun roast me or the chill night air freeze me. Die alone and lost. No more worries or cares. Better off out of this mad game of werewolves, magic and demons.

I rush to the rope ladder and haul myself up, muscles pumping. Going so fast, I smack my skull on the roof of the cave when I get to the top. Wincing, I rub my head and retreat a couple of rungs, then look for the opening. I can't find one. The rock appears to be solid. I run my fingers over it, searching for a crack or button, but there's nothing. It must open by magic.

Descending sourly. Hating magic all the more. Why can't I be an ordinary teen with normal problems? I never looked for magic. Wasn't the least bit interested in it. So why did it pick on me? What the hell have I done to deserve this?

Back to my blanket. Glaring at the cold embers of the fire. Waiting impatiently for Beranabus and Kernel's return. Half wishing I'd stayed in the Demonata's universe and fried.

→Time passes slowly, miserably. No way of telling if it's day or night. When I'm not sleeping, I just sit and think, eat mechanically, or walk in circles around the cave. Go to the back and dig a hole when I need the toilet, then fill it in. Disgusted the first few times, but now it's second nature. No biggie.

I often find myself wondering what's happening in the other universe, wishing I could find the courage to go back, rejoin the fight and redeem myself. Playing out all manner of wild scenarios inside my head, in which I'm Grubbs Grady — superhero. I find Beranabus and Kernel in dire straits, backs against a fiery wall, at the mercy of the demon. It's laughing evilly, about to finish them off. Then I lay into it and rip it to pieces. I shout at the startled Beranabus and Kernel, "You didn't think I'd run away, did you? I just had to pop to the toilet." They cheer as I kill the demon, then rush to clap my back, sing my praises, hail me as a saviour.

Nice dreams. But completely unconnected to reality. Because for all the wishing and make-believe, I don't know how to open a window to the demon's universe. And I'm certain, beyond any shadow of a doubt, that even if one materialised in front of me, I wouldn't have the guts to step through. A hero only inside my head. In the real world I remain a coward.

→Snapping out of a typically disturbed sleep. There are heavy, thumping noises. I think it's Beranabus and Kernel returning or a demon breaking through. But when I look around there's nothing in the cave. I frown, wondering if the noises were part of the dream. Listen for ages, sitting up. Silence.

I try to sleep again, but I'm too unsettled. So I walk around the cave for the millionth time. After a while I jog. Twenty laps, followed by push-ups, squats, more jogging. Shadow-punching as I run. Knocking hordes of imaginary monsters for six.

A series of short sprints. In better physical condition than I've been in a long time — maybe ever. Thinking about Loch and how approving he'd be if he could see me now. He was always pushing me to exercise more. Said I was a mountain of muscles which hadn't been honed, that I could be truly ferocious if I pushed myself to my limits. But I never bothered. There was always something better to do with my time.

Not any more. This is how Olympians should train. Shut themselves off from the world in a musky, murky cave, with nothing else to do except exercise. Works wonders when it comes to concentration. If I ever get out of here, maybe that will be my true calling in life — coach to athletic stars. It would certainly beat the hell out of killing demons for a living!

→Still exercising. I've been at it for hours, pausing only for periods of short rest and to eat. Sweating so much, I have to take my clothes off. Keeping only my boxers on, in case Beranabus and Kernel drop in without warning.

Suddenly — I hear the noises again. Three heavy thumps, a pause, three more. Then silence.

I come to a standstill, listening to the echoes of the thumps. They came from overhead — the closed entrance to the cave. With sudden hope in my heart, I race to the ladder and scurry to the top, where I wait a few seconds for more sounds. When there's only silence, I roar, "Hello!" and listen again. Nothing.

Back to the bottom of the ladder. I look for something to strike the roof of the cave with, but there's not much here. I go through the drawers of Beranabus's table — the first time I've examined it — but there's nothing except papers, pens and small knick-knacks. I note absentmindedly that the flowers are still blooming, fresh as ever.

Eventually I grab one of the longer logs from the wood pile and drag it up the ladder, then pound the roof with it, three times, a pause, then three more. I hold it by my side, trying to stifle my heavy breathing, so I can hear clearly, praying for a series of answering knocks. But there aren't any.

I pound the roof again and again without reply. Eventually I give up and drop the log. I hang there a while longer, then climb down, dejected. Halfway to the floor I realise that if the noises were human-made, maybe the person has left. When there was no immediate answer, maybe he or she decided there was nobody home, that they'd try again later.

Back on the ground I drink half a bottle of water, go to the toilet, then return to the base of the ladder, pick up the log and climb again. At the top I settle back, get as comfortable as I can and wait, desperate to make contact with another human being.

→Many hours later. My legs and arms ache from clinging to the ladder. Tired and irritated. Telling myself I'm wasting my time. The noises were probably a rockfall. I should climb down, get some sleep, then fill the hours with more exercise.

On the point of quitting when the noises come again — three resounding thumps, a pause, then three more, just like earlier. In a fit of excitement I raise the log — then drop it! Reacting swiftly, I grab for it, catch it and arc it upwards, slamming it hard into the roof of the cave, once, twice, three times. A short pause, then I hammer the roof again. Then, heart beating hard, I lower it and listen.

Nothing.

For several minutes I hang there, hopeful, awaiting an answer. But as the silence stretches I realise there's not going to be one. Either the thuds are the result of an especially large animal or the rock overhead is too thick for the noises I make to carry to the other side. Perhaps they're using magic to penetrate the rock sheet or maybe they have an especially large hammer.

Dejected, I descend, then make for bed and the escape of sleep. Even my nightmares are more welcome than the monotony of the cave.

→More empty hours follow, the only distraction — apart from exercise — coming in the form of the thumping noises at regular intervals. I'm sure it's a person — no animal could make the same sounds over and over — but with no way of contacting them, I lose interest and soon stop wondering who it might be. After a while I even start to ignore the thumps and barely notice them when they come.

Then, one day – or night – as I'm halfway through a four-minute sprint, a green window forms close to the remains of the fire and Kernel steps through. I come to a halt almost directly in front of him. He stares at me icily, casts a curious eye over my bare chest and legs, then goes to the fire and starts it with a single word.

As I'm pulling my clothes on, Beranabus appears. His beard is badly burnt and his hands are red, but otherwise he's unharmed. "Been keeping the cave warm for us?" he says sneeringly.

"He didn't even manage to get the fire going," Kernel snorts.

"Why doesn't that surprise me?"

"Did you… the demon… is it…?" I mutter.

"All taken care of," Beranabus says. "Quenched forever, its universe now a cold, lifeless expanse of space. Human saved, order restored, tragedy averted."

"No thanks to *you*," Kernel sniffs.

I ignore the insult. "How long were you in there?"

"No idea," Beranabus says as the window behind him vanishes. "It felt like a day. What about here?"

"A couple of weeks. Maybe three."

"That must have been boring."

"Serves him right," Kernel snaps, shooting me a disgusted look. "Running out like that… leaving us to deal with it ourselves…"

"It's not like we had to struggle," Beranabus murmurs, no idea that his kindness makes me feel worse than ever.

"He wasn't to know that," Kernel hisses. "He left us to fight alone. Didn't stop to think if we might need him. Didn't care."

"That's not true," I say sullenly. "Yes, I ran. But I did care. I just couldn't… it was too… I told you!" I cry. "I didn't want to go. You made me."

"Listen to him," Kernel jeers. "He sounds like a five-year-old. I wouldn't have thought someone his age and size could be so gutless. Maybe he—"

"Enough!" Beranabus barks. Sighing, he heads to his table and motions me to follow. He sits on an old wooden chair, stretches his legs out, cracks his knuckles above his head and yawns. Lowering his hands, he fiddles with some of the flowers, shuffles papers around, then takes a drawing out of one of the drawers and stares at it.

"I'm sorry," I say softly.

"No," he sighs. "It was my fault. I thought you were made of stronger stuff. I could see the fear in you and your reluctance to get involved. But given your background, I thought you'd shrug it off once faced with a demon, that you'd rise to the occasion like you did before."

"It was different then," I tell him. "I didn't know what I was getting into the first time, and in Slawter I was trapped. I had no choice but to fight. I've had so many horrible nights since then, so many nightmares. I'm not just scared of demons now— I'm bloody terrified."

"I understand," Beranabus says. "I didn't before, but I do now." He studies the drawing again, then lays it aside. "I'm a poor judge of character. I've made mistakes before, taken children into the universe of the Demonata when they weren't ready, lost them cheaply. But they've always been fighters. This is the first time I've taken someone who lacked the stomach for battle. It was a grave error on my part. I should have known better."

"You're not mad at me?"

"No. I'm sad. You have such ability, it's a shame to see it go to waste. But if the fighting instinct isn't there, there's no point moping. I thought you were a warrior. I was wrong. You don't criticise a pony for not being a horse."

He falls silent and looks around at the flowers on the table. I'm not sure I like his comparison. Never thought of myself as Grubbs Grady — pony! But I guess it's appropriate. I might lack the guts to be a hero, but at least I've pride enough not to whinge when the truth is pointed out.

"What happens now?" I ask.

"Hmm?"

"I can't fight. So what happens? Will you take me back? Set me loose in the desert? What?"

Beranabus frowns. "I can't spare much time. You wouldn't survive outside and it would be cruel to make you wait here indefinitely. I'll take you to the nearest human outpost. You'll have to make your own way from there. Once you get home, tell Dervish what happened. Ask him to help you work on your magic. Even if you can't fight, you can watch for demons. Become a Disciple. I know you'd rather keep out of this completely, but you might make a difference. Do you think you could do that?"

"Sure," I gush, delighted to be told I'm not entirely worthless. "I avoided magic because I thought if I learnt it, I'd have to fight demons. But if I just have to be a watchdog..."

"Good choice of words," Kernel snorts.

"Now, now," Beranabus tuts. "Let's not be ungracious."

Kernel spits into the fire. His spit sizzles, revealing more about his opinion of me than he could ever say with words.

"When do we leave?" I ask, eager to be out of here, free of this confining cave and Kernel's scorn.

"Soon," Beranabus promises. "I need to get some sleep, and eat when I wake, but after that we'll depart."

"Great," I grin, turning away to let the elderly magician go to bed. Then I remember the noises and turn to tell him. "I forgot, somebody's been…"

I come to a halt. Beranabus is leaning over, stroking the leaves of one of the flowers, smiling fondly at it. I can see the drawing he was looking at earlier. It's a pencil sketch of a girl's face. And though the paper is yellow and wrinkled with age, the face is shockingly familiar.

"Who's that?" I croak. Beranabus looks up questioningly. I point a trembling finger at the drawing. "The girl — who is she?"

"Someone who died a very long time ago," Beranabus says, touching the paper. "She sacrificed her life fighting the Demonata, to keep the world safe. An example to us all. Not that I'm trying to make you feel small. I didn't mean—"

"There was a voice," I interrupt, eyes fixed on the drawing. "At the cave in Carcery Vale. I didn't mention it before — it didn't seem to matter and there was so much else to tell you. But when I went to the cave, I heard a voice and saw a face in the rocks. It was alive. Even though it was in the rock, it could open its eyes and move its lips. It spoke to me."

I pick up the drawing and study the girl's face, the curve of her jaw, the eyes and mouth. "This is the girl from the cave. She called to me… warned me, I think, but I don't know what of. She spoke in a different lan–"

"It can't be!" Beranabus snaps, snatching the drawing back. "This girl has been dead for almost sixteen hundred years. You're mistaken."

"No," I say certainly. "It was her. I'm sure of it. Who the hell was she and why did she try so hard to contact me?"

In answer to that, Beranabus only sits and stares at me, shocked — and *afraid*.

THE WARNING

→Impossible!" Beranabus keeps croaking. "Impossible!" He's striding around the cave, hair and eyes even wilder than normal, clutching the drawing of the girl to his chest, muttering away to himself, occasionally bursting out with another round of, "Impossible! Impossible!"

Kernel and I have drawn together by the fire, temporarily united by our uncertainty. "Has he ever gone off like this before?" I whisper.

"No," Kernel replies quietly. "He often talks to himself, but I've never seen him so agitated."

"Do you know who the girl is?"

Kernel shakes his head. "Just some old drawing that he gets out every now and then and moons over."

"Beranabus said she died sixteen hundred years ago."

"I heard."

"Do you think he knew her? Was he alive then?"

"No." Kernel frowns. "He can't have been. We can live a long time, battling the Demonata in their universe, even a few hundred years. But no human can live that long. At least that's what Beranabus taught me..."

Beranabus stops pacing, whirls and fixes his stare on me. "You!" he shouts. "Come here!" I glance at Kernel for support. "Don't dither! Get over here now!"

Since I don't want to enrage him any further, I edge across but keep out of immediate reach. Beranabus holds the drawing up. His hands are shaking. "How sure are you?" he growls.

"It's her," I tell him. "The girl in the cave. I'm certain."

"Would you stake your life on it?" he snarls.

"No," I say hesitantly. "But it *is* her. You don't forget a face like that. It's not every day a person speaks to you from within the heart of a rock."

Beranabus lowers the drawing. Turns it round so he can study the face again. "You say she's alive?" he asks, voice low.

I shrug. "She spoke to me. But it wasn't a real face. It was a cross between flesh and stone. She could have been some sort of ghost, I guess..."

"Of course," Beranabus says. "But a ghost imprisoned *there*... trapped all this time..." His eyes shoot up. "Tell me what she said."

"I can't. I didn't understand her. She spoke a different language."

"Don't be stupid! You can…" He stops and gets his breathing under control. "First things first. Tell me the whole story. Everything this time. About the cave, what you saw and heard. Leave nothing out."

I don't want to go through it again, but he's not going to tell me anything until I do, so I quickly trot out the story, filling in all the details I skipped the first time. Seeing the face in the rock. The eyes opening. Later, when the girl spoke to me. In the cave, the night of my turning, when she screamed at me and seemed to be trying to warn me.

"Warn you of what?" Beranabus asks.

"Maybe that Juni was a traitor. Or of the danger Bill-E was in."

"Perhaps," Beranabus mutters. "There are blood ties between you, which might account for her interest in your predicament, but to break out of the rock and make herself heard must have required a huge amount of energy and effort. Why would she do that just to save your lives?"

He's not expecting an answer, so I don't try to provide one. Instead I pick up on something else he said and ask stiffly, "What blood ties?"

He waves a hand as though it's nothing. "The girl was called Bec. A distant ancestor of yours."

"*Ancestor?*"

"A distant one," he repeats. "She was a priestess… a magician. A brave, true, selfless girl."

"Did you know her?" Kernel asks. He's slightly behind us, listening closely. "Were you alive then?"

"I'd be a real Methuselah if so," Beranabus says. He looks at the drawing again and frowns. "I need to know what she said. She might have simply been trying to help you, but I think there's more to it. We need to study her words."

"But I told you I couldn't understand her. I don't speak her language."

"I do," Beranabus says, then gestures to the chair behind the desk. "I'm going to teach you another remembering spell, like the one we used to prove you didn't kill your brother's grandparents. But with this one you'll repeat everything the girl said. I'll be able to translate."

I sit. Beranabus clears an area of the table, then lays the drawing down gently, so it's facing me. "Look into her eyes," he says softly. "Forget everything that's happened recently. Let your mind drift back." He gives me a minute, then says, "Repeat after me."

I mimic Beranabus's words carefully. As the spell develops, the lines on the paper shimmer. I'm startled, but I've seen a lot more incredible stuff in my time, so I don't lose concentration. The lines begin to move. The face doesn't bulge out of the page the way it projected from the rocks, but it comes alive. The eyes flicker and the lips part. The girl talks. No sounds come, just the motions. But as the spell concludes and Beranabus stops talking, I find my own lips moving in time with the drawing's. Only it's not my voice — it's the girl's.

I speak swiftly, anxiously, the muscles of my throat hurting from having to form such unusual words. I spot Kernel listening with a frown, unable to interpret. But Beranabus understands perfectly. And the more I say, the more his face pales and he trembles.

Before I finish, the elderly magician sinks to the floor and stares at me, appalled. I want to ask him what the girl said, but I can't. My lips continue to move and the dead girl's words spill out. I'm repeating myself from the beginning.

Beranabus groans and covers his ears with his hands. "No," he wheezes. "Gods be damned. *No!*"

"Beranabus?" Kernel says, approaching his master cautiously. "What's wrong?"

"His fault!" Beranabus shrieks, pointing an accusing finger at me. "If he'd told me when he first came here…" He shakes his head and curses. I carry on talking, unable to stop. I'm afraid he's going to leave me this way, that I'll warble on like this forever.

Finally, rising slowly, Beranabus growls something and the words cease. My mouth closes. I rub my aching jaws and throat, staring at the magician, wondering what I've done to incense him.

"Damn you, Grubitsch Grady," he says bitterly, shooing me out of his chair and lowering himself into it, picking up the drawing and cradling it to his chest. There are angry, hopeless tears in his eyes. "Damn the day you came into this world. If I'd known the trouble you'd cause, I'd have killed you at birth, you meddling, cowardly, destructive brat."

"Beranabus!" Kernel gasps as my insides clench tight.

"It's true!" Beranabus shouts. "I stood up for the wretched fool, but I shouldn't have. I should have just… just…" He stops, closes his eyes and moans. "No. You didn't know what you were doing. I can't blame you."

"I don't care what you think of me," I snap, angry and ashamed. "Just tell me what she said, you horrible old buzzard."

Beranabus opens his eyes and smiles faintly. "That's more like it, boy. Spirit." His smile disappears. "Bec *was* trying to warn you, but she wasn't interested in saving your life. The stakes were much higher. She…"

He clears his throat, then continues lifelessly. "I don't know how she wound up where she is, or how she managed to communicate with you, but her soul has been trapped in that cave since she died, torn between life and death, between our universe and the Demonata's. I've never seen that before. Ghosts, aye, but only pale shades of those who died. This is different. She somehow defied the laws of death and her soul remains intact. It shouldn't…" He coughs and shakes his head, then continues.

"Bec is able to peer into the demon universe from where she's trapped. She's been observing the Demonata for centuries. She became aware long ago of a powerful demon master trying to open a tunnel to this world. When she sensed you clearing the entrance to the cave, she was afraid the creature would learn of it and restore the ancient tunnel. That's why she tried to warn you off. Later she learnt of a more direct threat, which is why she appeared so desperate the last time she established contact.

"I made a fatal error. I thought Lord Loss wasn't interested in opening a tunnel between the two universes. But he's changed his views. When Dervish told Juni about the cave, her master decided to kill two birds with one stone. His plan was to slaughter you, Dervish and your brother – or take you back to his own realm to torture – then open the tunnel, clearing the way for the ranks of demons to cross."

Beranabus pauses. Kernel and I are staring at him, struck dumb.

"Juni must have made a sacrifice after Dervish revealed the cave to her," he goes on. "It takes a few

367

weeks for the blood of a sacrificed victim to prime the tunnel walls. The spells of opening can't be cast until then. I was guarding the cave closely, but somehow she got in and killed someone without my knowledge.

"Lord Loss could have opened the tunnel at any time, but he decided to do it on a full moon, when there was more magic in the air. Tapping into the power of the moon, he could complete the spells within a few hours. That way, if I discovered him while he was at work, he'd only have to hold me at bay for that short time.

"Being a lover of neatness, he planned to kill or abduct you three and open the tunnel on the same night. Unfortunately for him, your magic burst to the surface and derailed things. He missed his chance to get even with the Grady clan at the cave. Since settling his score with you before he opened the floodgates was important to him, he pushed his plans back by a month."

"Then we still have time!" I gasp. "It's not too late. We know what he's going to do. We'll return to the cave and fight."

"*We?*" Kernel says sarcastically.

"Yes! I'll fight to save Dervish and Bill-E. I don't care what those monsters throw at us. When it's family, it's different."

"You really think you can choose not to be a coward if and when it suits you?" Kernel jeers.

Beranabus interrupts wearily before I can retort. "It doesn't matter. You're arguing about nothing. The time for heroics has passed."

"What are you talking about?" I say edgily.

"It's difficult to track time here," Beranabus says softly, "but not impossible. I can reach out and make a quick check on the heavens when I wish. I did that while Bec was speaking. You miscalculated, Grubbs. It's been seven weeks since I rescued you from the aeroplane."

I start to shiver. "But... no... maybe Lord Loss delayed again. He wanted to kill me before he opened the tunnel, but I'm still alive. Maybe—"

"No," Beranabus stops me. "Once I'd established the date, I cast my senses further afield. When there's a rip of great magnitude between universes a magician can detect it. If the spells I'd cast at the cave worked, I'd have known earlier. I should have renewed them, but it seemed like there was no rush. I wouldn't have made that mistake a hundred years ago. I'm getting so old..."

Beranabus sighs and his head drops. "The demons crossed as planned. They've had three weeks to stabilise, multiply and spread. Your town is theirs. Probably your country too. Dervish... your brother... everybody else you know in Carcery Vale…" He finishes in an awful whisper which fills me with a dread beyond any I've ever experienced. "The Demonata have had their way with them. They're all dead now — and probably millions more besides."

PART TWO
BEC-E

THE MESSENGER

→Everybody in the Vale — dead. Unable to believe it. I want to scream my head off, call Beranabus a liar, demand he tell the truth. Except… I can *see* the truth in the old magician's eyes. In his stooped shoulders. In his weariness as he sets his papers in order and prepares to leave for Carcery Vale to find out how far the Demonata have spread. He wasn't lying. They really did break through. Dervish and Bill-E are…

I don't complete the thought. Filled with sickness and fear. The last time I felt this empty inside was when I lost my parents and sister. It took me months to recover, and that was only with Dervish's help. Now I'm alone, wracked with guilt and shame as well as grief. I don't know if there's any way back. Madness looms, waiting to consume me. I doubt if I can fight it.

Kernel is sitting by the fire, staring glumly into the flames. Every so often he trembles as he thinks about the battle to come. He's been fighting demons for years, but in their universe, where his powers are far greater than they are here. On Earth his magical talents are vastly diminished. The Demonata are weaker here too, of course, and if it was just a few of them, he and Beranabus would fancy their chances. But if thousands have crossed and are running riot...

A sudden pounding noise. Three blows, a pause, then three more. Beranabus and Kernel jump nervously at the first sound, then relax.

"I forgot," I say quietly, madness receding temporarily, confident of taking me whenever it chooses. "Those noises have been coming for the last week. I went up the ladder to find out what was making them, but I couldn't get out."

"The entrance is protected by spells," Beranabus says. "Only Kernel and I can open it." He nods at Kernel, who heads for the ladder. "Be careful," Beranabus calls after him. "It might not be one of ours."

A short while later, Kernel returns. An elderly Indian woman in a light blue sari comes after him, limping but making good speed. She has a kind face, but it's twisted with worry. At first I don't know where I recognise her from. Then I remember — she was in a dream I had in Slawter last year.

"Sharmila," Beranabus greets her, smiling wanly.

"Master, there has been a tragic–" the woman begins in a rush.

"I know," Beranabus sighs. "The Demonata have crossed. I just found out. I'm going to Carcery Vale shortly, but perhaps you can flesh out the details before I leave."

The woman stares at Beranabus blankly. "You are going there?"

"I think I should," Beranabus says. "A stand must be made, aye?"

"But there are so many of them," the woman wheezes.

Beranabus frowns, then tilts his head at me. "This is Sharmila Mukherji, one of my Disciples. Sharmila, this is Grubitsch Grady — though I believe he prefers the name of Grubbs. He's Dervish's nephew."

Sharmila looks at me with surprising anger. "*Dervish!* He was on watch. He was supposed to make sure the tunnel was never reopened. He failed. He—"

"I don't believe in finger-pointing," Beranabus interrupts curtly, conveniently forgetting that he himself was pointing a finger at me not so long ago. "I trusted Dervish as much as I trust any of you. I'm sure he did all that anyone could. Now tell me how the situation stands. Quickly."

"There is no point," Sharmila snaps. "We have lost. They…" She stops and looks around the cave. Smiles briefly when she spots Kernel. Frowns when she faces Beranabus again. "I have been waiting in the upper cave for many days, incapable of contacting you. I told you years ago that you should share the access spells with us, so we could reach you swiftly in case of an emergency. It was probably too late even then, but if I had been able to find you directly..."

"It's easy to be wise in retrospect," Beranabus sniffs. "I made that call a long time ago and I stick by it, even now. It was essential that I remain protected from..." He trails off into silence, then growls to himself. "This is getting us nowhere. Tell me what's happening. *Please.*"

"I am not up to date with the latest developments," Sharmila replies sourly. "I was in contact with Shark until four days ago, but he broke the lines of communication. I suspect he lost patience and went into battle without you. He was never the most..."

She shrugs, then straightens her shoulders and speaks quickly. "The Demonata crossed three weeks ago in great numbers. They worked like soldiers, coordinated, attacking set targets, establishing control of the area around the cave. They have fractured since then, individuals branching off by themselves, spreading in chaotic directions. But they were organised to begin with. We did not expect that. They have never banded together in that way before. Who could have commanded them? Who has the power to unite so many monsters for even a short period of time?"

"It doesn't matter," Beranabus says. "The investigation can come later. Tell me more about the invasion. They were able to operate by day as well as night?"

"Most of them," Sharmila says. "There were some weaker demons, but most in the first wave were beasts of great strength. The sun meant nothing to them."

"Strange," Beranabus frowns. "They can't have massed in advance — I would have received word of such a build-up long ago. They must have been summoned when the cave was reactivated. But for so many to gather so quickly… You're right. This was no ordinary attack. There was a leader working behind the scenes, establishing contacts, making allies, forging secret links, priming them to await a call, so they could respond immediately."

He shudders. "It's our worst fear come true. The disorderly division between the Demonata has always been our strongest card. But if they've finally found a figurehead to unite and lead them…" He puts the thought aside and nods sharply at Sharmila to continue.

"They established control of Carcery Vale and the nearby regions within a day," Sharmila says. "They expanded steadily over the next few days and nights, conquering neighbouring towns and villages, establishing bases. Most people had fled their homes by then, but the demons did not care. They were more interested in boundaries than victims — again, very undemonlike behaviour."

"Did anyone survive?" I ask, not wanting to interrupt but having to. "In Carcery Vale, were any spared?"

Sharmila laughs brutally. "Do not be ridiculous! It was a bloodbath. They kept a few alive to torture, but most were slaughtered that first day."

"But not all," I whisper, a faint ray of hope forming, forcing the madness back, giving me a ghost of a reason to stay sane. "Lord Loss hates Dervish and Bill-E. He wouldn't want to kill them quickly. Maybe he spared them, so he could torment them at his leisure."

"It doesn't matter," Beranabus says gruffly. "Alive or dead, it makes no difference, not when an army of demons separates us from them. Finish your report, Sharmila."

The Indian lady shrugs. "The rest should be obvious. Public shock, confusion and denial to begin with. We live in scientific, enlightened times. People do not believe in demons. Even when the film crews went in and the first pictures emerged, most refused to accept it. They thought the pictures were computer generated, the work of a prankster, maybe an especially cunning film producer trying to generate interest in their next movie. There was talk of Davida Haym faking her death a year earlier in order to set this up. Quite ironic, no? But as the days went by, realisation sunk in. There were too many confirmed deaths, a never-ending series of reports and no government denials."

"Bless the governments," Kernel snorts. "How did our great leaders respond?"

"Slowly," Sharmila says. "We warned them of the threat of the Demonata many times in the past, even though Beranabus told us not to bother."

"I've never met a politician who didn't deserve to be tossed into a pit full of Kallin," Beranabus grunts.

"Nobody heeded our warnings," Sharmila continues. "Despite all the evidence we presented, and our predictions of what would happen if a prolonged invasion ever came to pass, we were treated as cranks. We have always had a number of supporters in various high-ranking corners of the globe, but not enough to make a difference.

"Most governments spent the initial week in a blind panic. First they had to confirm the reports were genuine — that took a few days. Then they debated the meaning of it, what the demons might want, how they could placate them, what their response should be if the demons refused to negotiate. A few acted quickly and sent troops in — mostly from nearby countries, who could see they were next on the agenda — but it was the second week before the war began for real."

"*War*," Beranabus murmurs, face crinkling. "Most humans know nothing of true warfare. They wage their silly territorial battles, kill each other ruthlessly and freely, and consider themselves experts on war and suffering. But the real war has always been ahead of them, unseen, unimagined. Enemies who can't be killed by normal weapons, who have their base in an alternate universe, who are interested only in slaughtering every living being on the face of the planet."

"They know about it now," Sharmila says grimly. "They have seen the footage on television and the Internet. Hordes of soldiers firing bullets into demons, dropping bombs on them. The demons falling from the force of the bullets, shattered by the bombs. Then rising, piecing themselves back together. Coming on again. Unstoppable. Ripping the soldiers to shreds. They are still trying – or were, the last I heard – to send in more troops, to drop more destructive missiles. But they can see it is pointless. They realise now – too late – the manner of beasts they are dealing with. The human race has learnt a lot about war over the last three weeks. More than I wish they ever had to."

"Have there been any nuclear retaliations?" Beranabus asks calmly.

"*Nuclear?*" Kernel and I shout at the same time.

"The politicians have resorted to nuclear assaults before," Beranabus says. "They say they don't build such bombs to use, but when the pressure builds, the fingers will come down on the buttons. Only a fool thinks otherwise."

"No nuclear strikes yet," Sharmila says. "There has been talk, and if not for the Disciples it might have happened already. But our voice has been heard at last and officials are knocking each other over in their haste to bring us on board as advisors. We said a nuclear attack would not stop the demons, that the tunnel is of magical origin and can only be closed magically. They did not like that. Some wanted to chance a nuclear blast anyway. But for the moment they are holding off. At least they *were...*"

This is crazy. We're standing here, talking about nuclear bombs being dropped on Carcery Vale. It's insane.

"We have to do something!" I shout. Beranabus, Sharmila and Kernel look at me, eyebrows raised. "We have to... to..."

Beranabus smiles cynically when I run out of words. "I wish you'd been able to finish. If you had a plan, I'd have loved to hear it. But of course you don't. I don't either. But let's hear Sharmila out and, who knows, maybe one will fall together." He turns his attention back to the Indian woman. "What have the Disciples been doing aside from advising?"

"Meera Flame led a small team in when we first realised what was happening," Sharmila says.

"*Meera*," I moan. "Is she…?"

Sharmila sighs. "Most of us thought it was too soon. We did not know enough about what was going on. The general consensus was to wait a day or two, gather more information, then hit them hard. Meera rejected that plan. Dervish was her friend. She thought he might still be alive. She asked for volunteers. A few rallied to her side. They went in. Nobody has heard from them since."

"And the rest?" Beranabus asks as I reel from the news of another friend's almost certain death. "What did you do once you'd sized up the situation?"

"Not much more than Meera," Sharmila says miserably. "We pinpointed the opening to the cave, and that was where we struck, but the demons had it guarded. Eight of our best went in, led by Shark, in the light of midday, hoping to take them by surprise. But they were ready and waiting. Two got out alive — Shark was one of them. The others…"

"That's bad," Beranabus grunts. "It would have been better if you'd waited for me. I know you couldn't," he says quickly as Sharmila starts to protest. "You did what would normally be the right thing. It's usually best to strike early. But as you've observed, this is a most unique attack. The demons have been marshalled by a leader who understands the ways of human warfare. Such a leader wouldn't make the mistake of leaving the cave unguarded. In this case…" He stops short of openly criticising Sharmila and the other Disciples.

"It has been damage limitation since then," Sharmila says coldly, concluding her report. "We have done what we can to contain them. Ordered the grounding of all aircraft, the pulling out or destruction of boats. Established a watch to stop the demons spreading any further. But we are fighting a losing battle. Within a couple of weeks – if it has not already happened – the exodus will begin. Once they have complete control of the country, they will move on to the next. And the next. We will defy them. Shoot down the planes and boats they commandeer, as well as those demons capable of flight. Send soldiers to stall them so we are not rushing around madly all the time. But there are already far too many for us to deal with, and more crossing every day. Unless we can stop them at the source…"

Sharmila falls silent. Beranabus is chewing his right thumbnail, frowning.

"We could attack from their side," Kernel suggests. "Cross universes, find the other end of the tunnel, hit them there."

"They'll be expecting that," Beranabus mumbles. "They'll have left a guard. Also, every demon within a million-world radius will be rushing to the tunnel, eager to squeeze through and get their claws on some humans before they're all gone. We wouldn't have a hope. We're too late to do anything from that side. We stop them at Carcery Vale or nowhere."

"Then Carcery Vale it is," Kernel says and stands. "When do we go?"

"Yes," I say, taking my place beside Kernel. "When?" I expect him to say something cutting, but he only looks at me calmly, then nods approvingly.

"Soon," Beranabus mutters. "We'll catch some sleep first, then—"

"*Sleep?*" I explode. "We can't waste time—"

"Let me make this as clear as I can," Beranabus cuts in. "Mankind is in its death throes. The war has come and gone — we lost. We're going to give it one last try, hit Carcery Vale with all we have, go down fighting. But go down we certainly will, bar a miracle. And while I believe in miracles, I don't think we're going to experience one this time. When we go to the Vale, we go to die. And once we're dead, the rest of humanity will soon follow.

"But we have to pretend that we *do* stand a chance. For the sake of our sanity, we must act like we believe we can pull this off. That means going in fresh and feisty, at our physical and mental best. So I'm going to sleep, fully aware that it will probably be my last ever snooze – bar the never-ending slumber – but desperately hoping it will make the blindest bit of difference. I highly recommend that the rest of you follow suit."

With that he stumbles to the rug which serves as his bed, lies down, closes his eyes, mutters a spell and falls asleep.

"He is right," Sharmila says softly. She looks at me and I see nothing except negativity in her eyes. "I hoped he would be able to offer hope, that he knew some secret way to stop this. But I could not believe it. We should sleep. Once we start, there might not be any later opportunities for rest."

"I'll find a blanket for you," Kernel says.

"My thanks."

While Kernel searches for a spare rug, Sharmila studies me. "What I said earlier about your uncle… I did not mean it. I just wanted someone to blame. I am sure it was not his fault. There are some things you cannot stop."

"No worries," I mutter, though part of me doesn't agree with her. Dervish had been hoodwinked by Juni. He was probably frantic with worry about me. His mind was elsewhere. He wouldn't have been focusing, doing his job. Maybe part of this *is* his fault – and mine – for not seeing through Juni Swan in the first place.

Kernel prepares a bed for Sharmila. She lies down as soon as it's ready and repeats Beranabus's sleeping spell.

Her face goes smooth and I can tell she's having pleasant dreams.

"How about you?" Kernel asks. "Want me to teach you the spell?"

"I don't think so. It doesn't feel right, sleeping at a time like this."

Kernel shrugs. "If you don't, you'll only brood about what's happened and what lies ahead."

I think about that, then sigh wearily. "OK. Tell me." Moments later magic sends me under and I tumble gratefully into the arms of a deliberately dreamless sleep.

VALKYRIES

→In Sharmila's personal jet, streaking through the skies. I'd think that was cool any other time, but I'm hard to impress right now. Versatile Sharmila is the pilot. There are six other seats. Beranabus has taken up the rear pair and is making a series of phone calls — we could have used a window to get to Carcery Vale and saved some time, but he wanted to talk with the Disciples first and manoeuvre them into position. Kernel is on the middle left, staring down at the clouds. I'm on the front right, flicking through newspapers.

Tales of mayhem and terror. Splash photos of demons and their victims. An array of monsters never dreamt of by most people until now. Long, sprawling lists of victims. First-hand accounts from survivors. Speculation and theories — where are the Demonata from? What are their motives? How can we kill them?

That's the most burning question — how to destroy the invaders. Mankind's never had to face an unstoppable enemy before. There have been countless movies and books about such encounters, and the aliens or monsters have always had a weak spot, an Achilles' heel which some clean-cut champion has discovered and exploited in the nick of time. But that's not the case here. The reports are from the early days of the invasion and there's a hint of optimism in them. But even in these columns I can sense desperation as the realisation seeps in — *we can't kill them*!

There are a few reports about the Disciples, but they're vague and patchy. Rumours of a group of experts with knowledge and experience of demons, but no mention of magic or names.

Some of the older papers still have ordinary sections, sports coverage and gossip columns, the usual padding. An attempt to maintain normality. But the later editions focus solely on the Demonata. Nothing else, just page after page of horror and catastrophe.

I stop reading after half an hour. I've had enough. Humanity has hit a brick wall. We're facing our end, like the dinosaurs millions of years before us. The only difference is we've got journalists on hand to document every blow and setback, cataloguing our rapid, painful downfall in vibrant, vicious detail. Personally, I think the dinosaurs had the better deal. When it comes to impending, unavoidable extinction, ignorance is bliss.

* * *

→We set down hours later on a private landing strip outside a small town close to the border where humans and demons are locked in battle. There are several other planes and helicopters parked at the sides of the strip. A large, grey, square building occupies one corner. We head for it once we've disembarked, Beranabus leading the way with the stride of a confident, commanding general.

Inside the building are eleven men and women, a mix of races. A couple aren't much older than me, a few look to be in their seventies or eighties, while the others fall into the thirty-to-sixty bracket. Most are neatly dressed, though one or two could compete with Beranabus in the scruffiness stakes. They all looked tired and drained.

"Hail to the chief!" a large man in military fatigues shouts ironically, saluting Beranabus as he enters. There are letters tattooed on his knuckles and a shark's head covers the flesh between knuckles and thumb. Like when Sharmila turned up at the cave, I know his face and name, even though we've never really met.

"Shark?" Beranabus scowls. "Sharmila thought you were dead."

"When you broke contact, I feared the worst," Sharmila says, shuffling around Beranabus.

"Couldn't wait for the Messiah forever," Shark grunts. "There was fighting to be done. I was going to summon you back, but I knew you wouldn't return without our regal leader."

"I had to wait," Sharmila says stiffly. "Beranabus is our best hope."

Shark snorts. "*Hope?* What's that? I heard about it once, in a fairy tale."

"Be quiet," Beranabus says softly and the larger man obeys, though he eyes Beranabus accusingly, as though he blames the magician for our dire predicament. "Any more to join us?" Beranabus asks, addressing the question to the room in general.

"Two, maybe three," a small, dark-skinned woman answers.

"Then I'll start." Beranabus looks around, meeting eveybody's gaze in turn. "I won't offer false hope. We're in deep trouble and I doubt we'll be able to wade out. But the war isn't lost yet. If we can destroy the tunnel linking the two universes, the demons will be sucked back to their own realm."

There are excited mutterings. "Are you sure?" Shark asks suspiciously. "You're not just saying that to rally our spirits?"

"Have I ever lied to any of you?" Beranabus retorts sharply. He waits a moment. When nobody responds, he continues. "One of Lord Loss's human allies killed a person in the cave, to prime the tunnel opening. The killer later joined with the rock where the mouth of the tunnel was originally situated — he or she has become a living part of the opening. If we dismantle the tunnel walls, the killer dies, the demons get sucked back to their own universe and all will be well with the world."

"How do we close the tunnel?" Sharmila asks.

"There's a lodestone set deep within the cave," Beranabus says. "The demons are using its power. If I can reach it, I know the spells to disable it and rid us of our unwelcome guests. I'll need somebody to help me inside the cave — Kernel or Grubbs. The rest of you only have to concern yourselves with getting us there."

"You want us to clear the way for you, even if it costs us our lives," Shark growls.

"Aye," Beranabus says. "This is a suicide mission. We're going to drop into a nest of demons. They'll be waiting for us, expecting an attack. They'll outnumber us and many are probably more powerful than we are. Our chances of making it to the lodestone are slim. Even if the boys and I get through, the rest of you are doomed — you'll need to continue fighting while I cast the spells, to guard our backs. I doubt any of you will survive."

"That's a lot to ask," Shark says icily.

"It's no more than I ask of myself. Sacrifice opened this tunnel and only sacrifice can close it." He glances at Kernel and me, hesitates, then pushes on. "For the spell to work, I must kill Kernel or Grubbs. If they both perish along the way, I'll offer my own life. I think I can make that work. Whatever happens, it's a death trip for me. I have to get deep inside the tunnel to work the spell. Once it's finished, I won't be able to fight my way out. I'm too old and weary."

Beranabus looks straight at Shark and awaits his response. The big man shrugs thoughtfully and Beranabus addresses the room again. "I don't think any of us will make it through this day. But if we succeed, humanity will go on."

"Until another tunnel is opened," Sharmila notes. "If we all perish, who will protect mankind the next time?"

"That's not our problem," Beranabus says. "I believe the universe will spit out more heroes to lead the good fight. But whatever happens, it's out of our hands. This is what we must do to counter the present threat. Are you with me? If any of you aren't, say so now and leave the rest of us to get on with it."

Nobody backs down from the challenge. Most don't look very happy – who the hell would! – but they accept the magician's verdict. Seeing this, Beranabus smiles approvingly, then circulates, chatting with the Disciples individually, making sure they're prepared for the fight, offering advice and strategic tips, raising morale.

Kernel and I are in the middle of the room, looking at each other uncertainly. Beranabus's announcement that one of us must be sacrificed came out of the blue. Neither of us knows what to say. It's one thing to go into a fight knowing you'll probably lose. Quite another to be told that to win, you must offer up your throat to be slit.

Sharmila approaches, smiling thinly. "He did not tell you that you were to be killed?"

"He's a busy man," Kernel snaps. "He doesn't have time to tell us everything."

Sharmila sighs. "You are loyal. That is good. But are you loyal to the point of death? Will you allow yourself to be slaughtered?" She looks at me. "Will *you*?"

"We'll do what we must," Kernel says fiercely. "We're not ignorant children. We know our duty. If we have to die, so be it. We'd rather not, but we'll be killed by the demons anyway if we lose, and probably more painfully and slowly."

Sharmila tilts her head towards us. "I apologise if I seemed critical. But I had to know the nature of the boys I am to fight and die for. Now I am confident that you will not fail if the opportunity presents itself. Thank you for reassuring me."

She wanders off to talk with Beranabus. Kernel looks sideways at me. "I normally wouldn't give another person's word for them, especially when I'm not sure of it, but it seemed like the right thing to say."

"You don't have to worry about me," I reply stiffly. "I won't let us down."

"I wish I could believe that." He doesn't say it to hurt me. Just speaking the truth as he sees it.

"I chickened out in the Demonata's universe," I whisper, blushing. "But this is different. I'll fight. And I'll die if I have to. I'm not afraid of dying, no more than anybody else in this room."

"Really?" Kernel's unconvinced. "If I fall, and you and Beranabus make it to the lodestone, you'll let him drive a knife through your heart or chop off your head?"

"Without a moment's hesitation. Not because I'm incredibly brave, but because I'm terribly afraid." I give a sickly laugh. "If I don't let him kill me, it would mean fighting to survive in a world overrun by demons. The thought of that scares me more than death."

Kernel chuckles. "Know something crazy? I believe you." He offers his hand and I take it. "Good luck, Grubbs."

"Good luck."

"May we both die honourably," he says.

"And take every damn demon down with us," I add with a twisted grin.

→Tooling up. Everybody arms themselves with guns, knives, axes — pretty much anything we can carry.

393

Demons can't be killed by regular weapons, but we can invest the blades and bullets with magical powers.

"How many of the Disciples are capable of killing demons?" I ask Kernel, testing short swords for feel and weight.

"In this universe?" He pulls a face. "If it was a normal crossing... Sharmila, Shark, one or two others. But there's more energy in the air because it's a tunnel, not a window. Others should be able to tap into that and find the ability to kill. If we're lucky."

One more Disciple arrives while we're readying ourselves. An ancient, tiny woman who walks with the aid of a cane. The sight of her picking up a mace and swinging it over her head makes me smile. A few of the others grin too. But then she mutters a quick spell and a crop of seven-centimetre long blades grow out of the mace head, which glows with magical energy. Nobody doubts her after that.

Then it's to the helicopters which Shark has arranged through his contacts in various armies. We're going to fly in and set down as close to the cave entrance as we can. Three helicopters, five of us to each. I'm with Beranabus, Kernel, Shark and Sharmila — the core of the force. The pilot's an ordinary human, as are the other two. Soldiers on loan from the forces currently engaged in hopeless warfare with the Demonata. Shark has told a few commanders of our plan. They've handed him control of their troops and will do whatever else they can to assist.

The helicopter rises smoothly, as if the ground is dropping away. I haven't been in a helicopter before. It's a curious sensation. Not as much of a blast as flying through the sky with Beranabus, but way more interesting than a plane.

"I never thought I'd be doing this," Shark bellows over the noise of the whirring blades. He's smiling. "How often does the chance come along to end a war? You see it all the time in films, but in real life wars are decided over a variety of fronts and battles. It's possible to play an important role in victory, but only a limited part. To actually be charged with the task of going in and saving the world..." He whoops with joy.

"I'm glad you're having fun," Kernel remarks sarcastically.

"Damn straight I am," he hollers. "Might as well — we're going to die regardless."

I turn my attention away from the battle-hungry Shark. He's probably got the right attitude for a fight like this, but I find his gung ho approach tasteless and disturbing. This isn't a game. We're not competing for a trophy. If we lose, we take humanity down with us. I don't see how you can be anything but stone cold miserable when lumbered with a responsibility like that.

Looking down as we whizz along, closing in on Carcery Vale. We're deep into Demonata territory now. This used to be my home. Not any more. It's theirs now. Abandoned cars. Burning buildings. Pools of blood smear the roads and fields. Slaughtered animals and humans everywhere, some cut up into bits and strewn about the place, others arranged in obscene patterns by the demons, either for their own amusement or to scare anyone who ventures into their realm.

I spot a few of the monsters messing with bodies on the ground. I don't look closely enough to determine whether their victims are alive or dead. I turn my gaze away and pray for their sakes that they're corpses.

Others are lounging in trees or in patches of shade, sheltering from the sun. Although stronger demons can move about during the day, they don't like sunlight and aren't as powerful as they are at night. The land would be teeming with lots more of the beasts if we were a few hours later in the day.

The outskirts of Carcery Vale. More of a visible demonic presence. Most of the buildings are ripped to pieces. Bodies scattered everywhere. We fly over my old school — dozens of children and teachers are impaled on spikes, grey and red, covered in feasting flies, slowly rotting.

For the first time I think about my friends. Until now I've been fixed on Dervish and Bill-E. But all the others will have fallen to the Demonata too. Frank, Mary, Leon, Shannon... *Reni*. I rip my gaze away from the bodies in case I spot the face of someone I know. Tears come, but I fight them back. I can't think about my friends, not even my uncle and brother. The best – only – way I can avenge them is by focusing on the demons and the battle. No room for pity, doubt or fear. Mustn't imagine them suffering, the pain they must have gone through, whether any escaped. The demons. The cave. Dying. These should be my only concerns.

The air above the Vale is thick with planes and helicopters. Shark ordered the regular troops in ahead of us. They've been blanket-bombing the area for the past twenty minutes, most of their force aimed at the demons around the entrance to the cave, disrupting them, blowing up the bodies of the lesser demons. The effects are temporary – the demons will piece themselves back together once the shelling stops – but any minor advantage is a bonus.

Zoning in on the cave. I don't recognise the area any more. There used to be a forest here at the back of our house, stretching all the way to Carcery Vale and for many kilometres in other directions. Now it's been firebombed into oblivion. The land is ash and tree stumps. Bare, scarred, dead. It resembles the face of an asteroid. Doesn't belong to this world. Something from outer space or a bad dream.

We fly over the rubbly ruins of a large building. We're several seconds past it before I realise — that wreck used to be my home! The wonderful three storey mansion has been reduced to a skeletal shell. I'm almost glad Dervish isn't here to see it. He loved that house. The sight of it in this sorry state would bring tears to his eyes.

The pilot's in constant contact with the other aircraft, snapping orders and directions, carefully manoeuvring his way through the fleet. If he's scared, he doesn't show it. I wish the fighting could be left to the professionals like him. But I guess ordinary people always get sucked into battles. It's the nature of warfare.

"Like a scene out of hell, isn't it?" Shark notes with relish, stroking the long, gleaming barrel of a machine gun hanging from his neck.

"Let us hope it is hell for the demons when we finish," Sharmila says.

The helicopter stops advancing. Hovers in the air, the pilot waiting for the other two copters to join us. I stare at the ground. Hard to spot the cave entrance.

Bombs are going off all around, throwing up dirt, stones, bits of flesh and bones. I see stronger demons moving about freely, protected from the explosions by magic. They form a large circle, several demons deep. Pinpointing the centre of that circle, I finally locate the mouth of the cave. Just a small hole in the ground. Doesn't look like anything special. Not the sort of place where you expect the future of the planet to be decided.

The second helicopter moves up alongside us, then the third. The Disciples are on their feet or knees by the open sides of the copters, clinging to straps, ready to jump as soon as they're within safe distance of the ground. The elderly woman with the cane is sitting, legs dangling over the side, stroking the blades sticking out of her mace.

Our pilot looks back at Shark for confirmation. The ex-soldier pauses and casts an unusually sad eye around, swallowing hard, looking doubtful for the first time. For a moment I think he's lost his thirst for battle. Bernabus thinks it too and opens his mouth to yell an order at the pilot. Then Shark raises his head, grins grimly and nods savagely. The pilot speaks rapidly into his mouthpiece, issuing urgent orders. The sky clears of planes. Helicopters packed with ground troops cluster around us. I can see the faces of some of the soliders — underlying terror, overlaid by determination, much like the faces of those closer to me.

The rain of bombs lessens, then stops. Dust swirls below, momentarily masking the hordes of demons. Shark roars commandingly at the pilot.

We drop.

SPARTANS

→The demons attack before we touch the ground, screaming hatefully, hurling themselves at us viciously. More pour out of the cave entrance, all manner of foul monsters, multilimbed, fangs the size of scythes, claws galore, spitting venom, breathing fire — the works!

The soldiers bear the brunt of the assault. They spill out of the helicopters and absorb the rush of demons, firing off round after round of bullets which they know will only delay the beasts, buying precious seconds for those of us in the three central helicopters, laying down their lives to help us.

As the bloodshed begins, Beranabus claps me hard on the back. Almost before I know what's happening, I'm out of the helicopter and running, Beranabus slightly ahead of me, Kernel to my right, Shark and Sharmila flanking us. The other ten Disciples fan out. Everyone's focused on protecting Beranabus, Kernel and me. Even Shark, who'd love to mindlessly lay into the demons, sticks close by, acting only when we come under direct threat.

For several seconds we glide through the ranks of Demonata as if they weren't there. A few challenge us, but the Disciples brush them off without slowing, sending them tumbling out of our way, interested only in clearing a path to the cave. The demons are hell-bent on butchering the soldiers – easy targets for the magical monsters – delighted to have so many new victims drop in on them at once.

Then a familiar demon master rises into the air above the cave entrance. My hands clench into fists, nails breaking the flesh of my palms, and the hope that had been forming within me quickly dwindles away.

It's Lord Loss.

"Demonata!" my old enemy cries, the word piercing my skull and those of everyone and everything around me. "Beware the Disciples! Block their path or we'll be returned to our own universe!"

In an instant the battle changes. Every demon shrugs off the attentions of the soldiers and focuses on our small band. Impossible to tell how many there are… a couple of hundred or more. As if breathing in unison, they all snarl at once, then converge.

A wave of demons breaks over us sickeningly fast. One moment they're metres away. The next we're surrounded. Claws flash, jaws snap, at least a dozen demons to each of us. Three Disciples perish immediately, wrestled to the ground, ripped to pieces. The rest are stranded, cut off from one another, reduced to fighting isolated, individual battles.

Shark disappears beneath three lumpy monsters, then reappears a second later, throwing them off with a ball of magical energy, laughing manically.

Sharmila's muttering spells frantically, gently touching the demons around her, setting them on fire.

The woman with the cane is using it like a gun, shooting bursts of magical bullets at the demons, crushing the heads of others with her mace.

Beranabus presses on, ignoring the carnage, intent on making it to the cave. Kernel runs behind him. So do I, legs working automatically, leaping over the struggling demons, Disciples and soldiers, panting hard. I want to flee. The coward inside me wails and pleads with me to retreat. But I think of Dervish and Bill-E, and cling to the belief that they're alive, that I can save them. That gives me the strength to ignore the craven cries and follow Beranabus and Kernel.

A rabbit-shaped demon leaps up in front of Beranabus. I recognise it from the massacre on the plane. It's Femur, one of Lord Loss's familiars. It vomits acid at Beranabus's face. But the magician is prepared and deflects the acid back at Femur. It drenches the demon and eats through its fur and skin. Femur screams and rolls away, tiny paws frantically trying to wipe the burning liquid away from its cheeks and eyes before its head melts down to the bone.

The hell-child known as Artery appears, grabs Beranabus's left leg with his mouth-encrusted hands and bites hard. Beranabus grunts, then kicks Artery as if he was a football, sending him flying over the heads of several other demons.

Beranabus staggers on. The cave entrance is within sight. So is Lord Loss, still hovering in the air, all eight arms extended, smiling sorrowfully.

A tiger-headed demon latches on to my waist and whirls me around, fangs snapping in search of my throat. The magic within me instinctively sends a wave of electricity through the monster. It turns black, then collapses, synapses sizzling, eyes melting in its sockets.

"Nice work!" Shark yells, popping up beside me. He's bleeding from several cuts and one of his ears has been bitten off. "Came to help, but it looks like you don't need me."

"Beranabus!" I shout at him. "You have to help Ber—"

Before I can finish, Shark's gone, ripped away by a gaggle of demons who swarm over him, ant-like. I see a hand... his teeth as he bites... I hear a laugh... then he's on the ground, covered completely, and I see nothing more of him.

I take a stunned step away from where Shark fell and look around, dazed, searching for Beranabus. He's come to a standstill. A dozen or more demons stand between the magician and the hole. He fires magical bolts at them, but they take his best shots, barely blink, then return fire. There's no way around. Soon they'll wear him down and move in to finish him off.

Kernel slides to his master's side and joins the fight. But just as he fires off a few pinkish bolts of his own, the scorpion demon from the plane – Spine – leaps on to his bald, brown head and aims its stinger at his right eye. With a pop the stinger goes in, then comes out wet and glistening. Shrieking with delight, the demon spits out a mouthful of eggs, filling Kernel's pulpy socket.

Kernel screams with agony as the eggs hatch and maggoty insects gnaw at what's left of his eye, before working their way through to his brain. He wheels away from Beranabus, losing all sense of direction. Spine strikes again and Kernel's left eye pops too.

Something hits me hard in my upper back and I slam to the ground. Claws dig into my flesh. I'm momentarily stunned, unable to use my magic. I feel the end coming and a large part of me welcomes it — anything to break clear of this madness. But then the demon's thrown from me by a blast of magical power. I sit up, groggy, expecting to find Sharmila or the lady with the cane. But neither woman is anywhere to be seen. I can only see demons and Beranabus struggling against them desperately, hopelessly. Then who…?

"Nobody touches the boy!" Lord Loss bellows, and I realise I've been rescued by the demon master. He catches my eye and his smile broadens. "I'm saving you for myself, Grubitsch. You escaped on the aeroplane, but you will not wriggle free again."

The fighting clears around me, demons giving me a wide berth, turning aside to finish off the Disciples and the few remaining soldiers. The path to the hole clears — but it's also the path to Lord Loss. For a long second I stare at the demon master, hovering, waiting. I want to run away. No point trying to push on — Lord Loss will kill me before I get anywhere near the cave. The wise thing would be to turn tail and –

"No!" I yell, deciding not to be a coward, to die with everyone else if that's my destiny, to perish slowly and awfully at the hands of Lord Loss if that's the cost of failure. But I'm not going to flee. I'm through running. It's time to fight.

I lurch ahead, summoning all my reserves of energy, speaking quickly to the magic within me, saying I know I've let it down in the past and held it back, but promising it a free rein now. We're in this together and I won't stop until I'm dead or we've won. Will it help me?

The magic screams back its answer – *Hell, yes!* – and I feel power grow in the pit of my stomach, greater than any I've unleashed before. I don't know if I'll prove a match for Lord Loss and his companions, but right now I feel like I can't be beaten, like I'm the most powerful player here.

"Beranabus!" I shout, almost at the hole, risking a look back. He's surrounded by demons. Cursing, I aim a hand at them and let loose the magic. White flames leap from the tips of my fingers. They hit the demons hard and fire streaks through them like lightning. The demons shriek and peel aside, covered by flames they can't quench, some coming apart at the seams and dying instantly.

"Balor's eye!" Beranabus grunts, limping towards me, stooping to pick up the screaming and writhing Kernel, dragging him along. "I knew you were powerful, but not *that* powerful!"

"Oh, yes," Lord Loss says overhead. "Grubitsch is a most remarkable boy. That is why I chose not to fight him in the cave when I first had the opportunity to kill him. I did not care to face him alone in a place of magic."

"You were afraid!" I holler, reaching the mouth of the cave, sneering up at Lord Loss, feeling invincible. For the first time I believe we can do this — we can win!

"Afraid?" Lord Loss murmurs. "An ugly word, Grubitsch. And not entirely accurate. I was not afraid to fight you. I merely preferred to do so when the odds were stacked in my favour. After all, why fight by yourself when you can wait for…?" He smiles wickedly and gestures to the hole.

I look down and my sense of triumph fizzles out like a live match that's been dunked in a bucket of water.

The tunnel leading down to the cave is full of demons. And I mean *full*. There are more of the creatures down there than up here. Thousands of evil eyes glint at me. An army of jaws open hungrily to reveal row after row of sharpened teeth. And in the claws of the beast closest to me — Dervish's severed, lifeless, blood-rimmed head! Another demon holds the hacked-off head of Reni Gossel. Frank Martin. Charlie Rall. Meera Flame. All the people I cared about. Bill-E's the only one missing — or maybe he's further back, where I can't see him.

"I made your friends and family my first priority," Lord Loss says proudly as my world burns at the edges and madness swooshes down upon me. "I told you I would punish you for humiliating me. A dreadful, all-encompassing punishment. This is how I respond to mockery, Grubitsch. Look upon my work and know at last the true, heartless wrath of Lord Loss."

"Grubbs!" Beranabus shouts. "They don't matter! Ignore them! We—"

"Do not disturb the boy," Lord Loss interrupts gloomily. "This is a time for true grief, not false promise and meaningless heroics. Look down, Beranabus. Even an eternal dreamer like you can't believe in hope now. It's over. The war has been decided. Mankind has fallen."

"Grubbs! We can still…"

The rest of Beranabus's words are lost to me. Lord Loss is right. We're finished. There's no way through. Everyone I knew — dead. Everyone I know who hasn't already fallen to the Demonata — soon to be dead. And everybody else, the billions of men, women and children spread across the world, whom I'd never have known, even if I'd lived a thousand lifetimes — they'll all die too.

I sink to my knees, the enormity of the moment overwhelming me. Beranabus grabs my right shoulder with one hand – still holding the wailing, thrashing Kernel with the other – and tries jerking me back to my feet. But I stay where I am, tears flowing, dread consuming me, hoping Lord Loss doesn't drag the torment out too long, praying for him to take pity on me and kill me quickly.

I rock back and forth, moaning, glancing around, seeing demons in the throes of celebration, corpses of soldiers and Disciples being passed around like canapés at a party. Their howls, grunts and chattering start to sound like music to my ears or the chanting of a long, complicated spell. Then I realise — the sound isn't of demonic origin. It's coming from somewhere else… from the rocks beneath me.

I look down, expecting some new torment of Lord Loss's. Instead I find the face of the girl – Bec – bulging out of the rock, eyes open, lips moving swiftly. Beranabus sees it too. His fingers go limp on my shoulder as he stares at the face, lost for words, forgetting all about the demons and our foolish quest.

"What's this?" Lord Loss frowns. "Little Bec, present and alert after all these centuries? Impossible. How can her soul have…?" He smiles. "No matter. She is powerful, Beranabus, even more than you or Grubitsch. But she cannot save you. Trapped in the rocks, she can only mourn your sad passing."

The girl speaks quicker than ever, her lips a blur. I feel the magic inside me pulse in time with her chanting. I can't understand her, but the magic does and it swirls around inside me, excited, trying to reach out to her. Since I've nothing to lose, I let it have its way. I step back mentally and let the magic and the girl communicate freely. As the pair link in some unknowable way, I feel my own lips moving, the girl's words becoming mine, like when I was relaying her previous outburst to Beranabus in his cave.

"Come now," Lord Loss says, descending gracefully, signalling to the demons around us. "Enough of this childishness. Surrender, Grubitsch, and I will go easy on you. Well… easier than I planned to."

"We'll never surrender!" Beranabus roars, coming alive again, releasing me and Kernel, bringing up his hands to engage the demon master in battle.

"Take him," Lord Loss says, yawning mockingly. The nearest demons howl and hurl themselves at the magician — then strike against an invisible boundary and bounce back off it.

"Impressive," Lord Loss murmurs. "But how long do you think you can sustain such a barrier, old man?"

"This isn't my work," Beranabus says, staring at me uncertainly. The girl's hands have formed now and stick stiffly out of the ground, grey and rocky. I take them, my fingers large and chunky in comparison to hers. We continue to babble, her, me and the magic.

Kernel screams as maggots chew their way deeper into his brain. He jerks aside wildly and the demons eagerly grab for him, but he rebounds against the barrier and is hurled to the ground, landing by my knees. Beranabus stoops and puts his fingers to the boy's forehead. Magic flares. Maggots fall out of Kernel's bleeding sockets and shrivel, dead before they hit the ground. Kernel moans and slumps unconscious.

Beranabus faces me, features alive with hope. "Let's go!" He grasps my elbow. "If you can maintain this barrier, they can't stop us getting into the cave. We—"

My head whips towards him and the girl barks something, using my lips. I don't know what she says, but it brings a groan of desperation from Beranabus. "No! You can't tell me that. Not now. Not after all this. Not when we're so close."

I've no time to ponder his words. My eyes refocus on the girl's and lock on her peculiar stony pupils. We're speaking faster, louder, a fierce magical energy building around us, causing all the hairs on my body to stand up, then burn down to their roots. My clothes also burn away. So do Beranabus's and Kernel's. Within seconds we're naked and hairless, and still the energy builds.

Lord Loss senses danger. "Get them!" he bellows. "Destroy that barrier! Kill them all!"

The demons scurry to obey, but their efforts are wasted. The barrier repels them casually. The harder they throw themselves against it, the harder they rebound. Bolts of magic are returned with interest, tearing apart those who fired them. They try to claw it to pieces, rip it apart with their teeth, burrow underneath to attack from within the earth, all to no avail.

The energy is unbearable. It goes beyond all my notions of normal heat. I think this is what it would be like to hover within the heart of the sun. The rock is melting around the girl's face, but she remains, more of her form becoming visible as the stone recedes.

Screams of panic. With an effort I raise my head. The demons are staring at the sky, horrified and bewildered.

Looking up, I see something incomprehensible. The sky is *pulsing*. It's like looking at the underside of a trampoline while somebody leaps up and down on top. In the centre, a funnel has formed, as if the universe is being pulled towards one point. As I watch, it throbs low, then pulls up high... low/high... low/high. And it might be my imagination, but it seems as if the tip of the funnel hangs directly over me, Kernel, Beranabus and the ghost girl, Bec.

Lights flicker across the distorted sky. Clouds burst into flame. The tip of the funnel pushes lower and lower, ever closer to us. The demons scatter, screeching and keening. Stuff like this happens every day in their own universe. They aren't bothered by magical madness there. But they didn't expect it in this universe of order and sanity. They don't know what it means or how to respond.

"This will not save you!" Lord Loss shouts none too convincingly. "Stay, you scum!" he roars at the fleeing demons. "Fight! We can break through this barrier and kill them. You must not..."

I tune him out. My lips are my own again during a brief pause in the spell. "What's happening?" I wheeze, directing the question at Beranabus. But he can only shake his head and stare at Bec and me. Then the spell starts again and I can't ask any more questions. My lips are Bec's. My magic and her magic — one. Our minds join. I get flashes of her life — a simple farming society, demons, a quest, warriors, a magician, closing the tunnel between worlds, sacrificing herself, trapped in a cave, her spirit somehow separating from her body, dying but not moving on, imprisoned, no way out, haunting the centuries, unable to escape the rocky confines of the cave.

Then I'm inside somebody else's head. I see a small, modern village, thousands of patches of light in the sky around me, a baby that looks oddly familiar, a young punk who... no, surely that's not Dervish! Yes, it is, a young and spiky-haired Dervish Grady, fighting alongside Shark, Sharmila, Beranabus, a dark-skinned man and...

Kernel sits up and groans. He shakes his head groggily. His empty sockets turn left and right as if he's looking for something. They fix sightlessly on Bec and me. Trembling, moaning with pain, he reaches over and lays his hands on top of mine. My magic shoots out to him, then blasts back stronger than ever, drawing power from the blind teenager. His lips move along with mine and Bec's, his magic mingling with ours.

Our voices rise. The sky turns black, red, white. Rocks are ripping out of the ground, shooting upwards, burning, turning into birds, cows, cars, people, then back into rocks. Now everything's rising, the ruins of trees and buildings, corpses, the demons. Gravity loses its grip. Lord Loss tries clinging to the invisible barrier around us, but is ripped away and up. He hurls vile curses at us as he shoots off.

The world is coming apart. Everything's being destroyed. I'm afraid now, even more than when I thought the demons had us. Bec must be insane. Sixteen hundred years of captivity have driven her mad. She only wants to ruin, make everybody else suffer as she has suffered, tear the world apart. And she can do it. With my magic and Kernel's, she has the power to wreak a terrible, misdirected revenge.

I try stopping it. I focus on breaking contact, making my lips stop, getting out of here before all is lost. But the magic holds me tight. There's no escaping. Everything in sight shoots skyward, while the sky itself drops ever further, the tip of the funnel pulsing down... down... down.

Beranabus is frightened too. He was exhilarated when he saw the demons get swept away, but this has exploded out of control. He sees what I see — the literal end of the world. He sits on the ground – the only patch left is the bit contained by our bubble of energy – and gawps at the three of us, eyes wide, twin pools of confusion and fear. Maybe he thinks about killing one of us to stop it. But I don't think he could. He doesn't have the power.

The tip of the funnel is almost upon us. I gear myself up for one last effort, one final push to break the unnatural, destructive bond between me, Kernel and Bec. But before I can attempt anything, the tip of the funnel – blue, like the sky used to be – touches the wall of the invisible boundary.

A flash of light which is every colour. My body explodes, or seems to. I have the feeling of being everywhere and nowhere at once, both an entire universe and an insignificant speck. The funnel sucks me into it. Millions of panels of pulsing lights. Flying from one to another, bouncing around, moving so fast I'm creating a vacuum, sucking the tip of the funnel in after me, pulling it along in my wake. Dimly aware of Kernel and Bec's magic working in tandem with mine.

We stop bouncing, but move quicker than ever. A cluster of purple lights flash, then bolt together and become a small window. We shoot through it. Yellow lights flash and join — we fly through. A series of flashing lights and windows, one after the other, faster and faster. Curious, I focus on the magic and realise Kernel's the one creating the windows and directing us through them. I've no idea how or why. I don't think Kernel knows either.

No sense of time or space. Just one window after another, the colours whirring and blurring, a fearsome noise building in the background. Then the lights fade. Unable to see anything now. Total blackness. As blind as Kernel.

The noise continues to build, so loud it could crush a continent. My ears burst. My skull cracks. My brain bubbles away to nothing. But that makes no difference. I still exist. I still hear, think and feel. The noise squeezes my soul. Pain that's indescribable. No way to scream or release the pressure. A universe of agony.

Then, suddenly, the noise stops. I come to rest. The pain disappears. Delicious, soothing silence. Broken abruptly by a girl's delighted laugh.

A SECOND CHANCE

→At first I think the world and universe have been utterly destroyed and I'm just imagining the laughter. But then the blackness clears slightly. I realise I have eyes again. Blinking, I look around, but can't make out much. It's night and I'm in the middle of a cluster of trees. It's not especially dark – the gleam of a full moon seeps through the branches of the trees – but it's hard to adjust or focus. My mind's spinning crazily in a bewildered whir.

"What happened?" Beranabus croaks, rising from a spot nearby. Kernel lies at the magician's feet, groaning, cradling his head in his hands. "Where are we?"

"I don't know," I whisper. My ears are searching for something. I'm not sure what it is, until after a few seconds it sinks in — the girl's voice has gone.

Kernel mutters something, then bolts upright, screaming. "My eyes!" he howls. "The maggots! My eyes! I can't–"

Beranabus covers his assistant's mouth and whispers words of magic, a spell to ease the pain. Kernel thrashes wildly, then regains control and stops struggling, though his chest continues to rise and fall rapidly.

Beranabus removes his hand. "Are you going to be all right?"

"My eyes...?" Kernel moans.

"Gone," Beranabus says bluntly.

"But... we must... there has to be some way..."

"No. They're ruined. But don't worry — magic will compensate. You won't be entirely helpless." Beranabus squeezes the back of Kernel's neck. "We might even be able to knock together a pair of replacements when we return to the demon universe. If the gods are truly with us, you'll still be able to see the patches of light and create windows."

"Like I give a damn about that!" Kernel snaps sourly, but Beranabus ignores the hostility.

"Peace for a few minutes," the magician says. "I need to determine where we are."

He turns in a slow circle, eyes closed, breathing softly, trying to pinpoint our position. I know I should keep silent and wait for him to finish, but I can't. "What did she do to us? The ground breaking apart and rising... the sky and funnel... the lights and windows... the noise and pain. What was all that about?"

"How should I know?" Beranabus growls. "Maybe she was trying to destroy the demons and the spell got out of hand."

"But the sky! Did you see it? How did she do that? What—"

"Quiet!" Beranabus barks, opening an eye to glare at me. "How can I concentrate with you throwing stupid questions at me?"

"But she tore up the ground!" I shout. "She reversed gravity and brought the sky crashing down. And then she sent us… where? Is this Earth? A demon world? Are we dead?"

"I don't know," Beranabus sighs. "I don't know where this is or how she sent us here — teleportation, I suppose, but I've never seen it done that way before. But I know *why* she did it." He hesitates, then opens the other eye and looks at me with a shamed grimace. "I made another mistake. There have been far too many lately. I missed the sacrifice being made in the cave. I was wrong about Lord Loss not wanting to reopen the tunnel. And now I know my plan to close it was flawed.

"I told the Disciples that if we collapsed the walls of the tunnel, victory would be ours. The demons would be sucked back to their own universe. That's how it happened in the past. I assumed the rules would apply the same way in the present.

"Bec told me they wouldn't."

"You mean, even if we'd succeeded, we wouldn't have got rid of the demons?" I ask quietly.

"We'd have stopped others from crossing," he says. "And those here would have lost much of their power. But the world has changed. There's less magic in the air. My spells wouldn't have dislodged the demons. The masters would have remained and even weakened they'd have had enough strength to crush humanity. I don't think all of the Demonata were aware of that – they certainly didn't act like they were – but Bec knew we were doomed. To spare us, she worked a spell with you and Kernel to get us out, so we could regroup and try again."

"What's there to try?" I sob. "If we couldn't send them back this time, with all the Disciples to back us up… if destroying the tunnel won't work…"

"There must be a way," Beranabus mutters. "That's why I have to focus. Time's precious. Bec gave the demons a taste of their own hellish magic, but there's no guarantee that those sucked up into the sky are dead. Even if they are, the tunnel's still open. More can cross. We need to return and block their way. So be quiet and let me get my bearings. You can ask all the questions you want after that."

He closes his eyes and turns again, reaching out with all his senses. Kernel has dragged himself away to sit against a tree. He's exploring the empty sockets of his eyes with trembling fingers, picking out some dead maggots caught in the corners. I hobble over to check on him, to help if I can, to comfort him if he'll let me.

Then I see the rocks.

My eyes have adjusted and the light from the moon is strong, even under the cover of the trees. I can't miss the rocks. They lie scattered everywhere, but a lot are piled up on my left in a large mound. They can't be real. It isn't possible. I must be imagining them. Except I'm not. The magic inside me says they're genuine. It's smug. Confident. Triumphant.

"Beranabus."

"Grubbs!" he yells angrily. "I told you not to—"

"I know where we are."

He opens his eyes a fraction, suspiciously. "Where?"

"You don't need magic. Just look." I point to the rocks.

Beranabus frowns. Then he realises he's seen the mound before and his jaw drops. "No," he croaks. "It can't be. This is a trick. Or somewhere that looks like..."

"No." I walk across, pick up one of the smaller rocks, then lob it down the hole on the other side of the mound — the mouth of an all too familiar cave. "We haven't gone anywhere. We're still in Carcery Vale."

→Beranabus is striding around the hole, squinting at it, studying it from every possible angle. Every so often he stops, mumbles to himself, shuffles towards the hole, then starts marching again.

I'm with Kernel. I've wiped away the worst of the muck from around his eyes, using leaves and forest water. "How are you feeling?" I ask.

"There's not much pain," he says, "but there will be. You can delay it in circumstances like these, but not indefinitely. I'll need hospital treatment when the spell wears off. Assuming any hospitals are left..." His head turns left, then right. "Is it day or night?"

"Night."

"I thought so. But it was day when we attacked. I didn't think I'd been unconscious that long."

"You weren't."

"Then...?" He leaves the question hanging.

"We don't know," I tell him. "Beranabus is trying to figure it out."

Kernel nods slowly. "How do I look?" he asks.

I stare into the vacant pits where his eyes once were. They're peppered with dead maggots. A few are only half visible, their heads and upper bodies buried in the dark flesh and bone of his sockets. "Fine," I lie.

Beranabus begins to laugh. I think he's laughing at my lie and I turn on him angrily. But then I see that he didn't even hear what I said.

"Of course," he chortles. "It's the only answer. There's just one way she could have channelled that much power, to such an effect. You and Bec are the other two pieces. That's the only thing that makes…"

He mumbles his way back into silence. I say nothing, waiting for him to get it clear in his head, so he can explain it to me in simple terms. I study him while I'm waiting. He looks weird minus his beard and hair, naked as the day he was born. I guess I look pretty strange too, as bare and hairless as an egg. I'd feel awkward any other time, but things have gone so crazy within the last hour, I'm not bothered by my ultra-smooth nudity.

Beranabus glances up and waves a hand at the trees. Their branches part, granting him an unobstructed view of the moon and surrounding sky. His eyes dart from the moon to the stars. I can practically hear his brain whirring as he performs silent calculations. Then the branches rustle back together and he laughs again. "I knew it!"

Beranabus bounds over to where Kernel and I are waiting. He crouches beside us, beaming like a proud father whose wife has just given birth. "The prime rule of magic — anything is possible. It's the first thing I teach my assistants, but when you've been doing it as long as I have, it's easy to forget your own advice. Just because something hasn't been done before, and just because the power involved is way beyond that of even the greatest demon master, doesn't mean it *can't* be done. Bec must have realised what she really was. She spent centuries preparing herself, waiting patiently...

"Or maybe she only saw how to do it during the battle. Maybe you were the catalyst, Grubbs. Or Kernel. Though I don't think so — he came last to the union, didn't he? I don't suppose it really matters. Maybe Bec can tell us, assuming she's..." He stops. "Yes, she must be alive — I mean, her ghost must still be here. It has to be. At least, I suppose..." He trails off into silence again.

"In your own time, Beranabus," I mutter impatiently. "Whenever you're ready."

He flashes me a crazy smile. "This is so extraordinary. Every time I think about it, I discover something new. We've taken an immense leap forwards — well, a leap backwards if you want to be pedantic. It's like going from the first stone wheel to the first manned flight in the space of one incredible day, one amazing spell. This requires years of study and analysis. We have to figure out how the three of you did it, how to control the power, what else we can do. That will—"

"I'm going to hit you if you don't stop babbling," I warn him. "Tell us what you know — or what you guess," I add quickly as he opens his mouth to start telling me he doesn't know anything really.

"I know you're in the dark, I know you want answers, just as much as I do. But..." He stops, focuses, takes a deep breath. "You asked me a question once, Kernel. It's a question most Disciples have asked, normally not long after I've told them that with magic anything is possible. Can you remember what it was?"

"I'm in no mood to solve riddles," Kernel sighs. "I just want my eyes back. Can you do that for me?"

"Not now," Beranabus huffs, waving the question away. "Think, boy. You were telling me about your early life, the night you created your first window and stepped into the universe of the Demonata. You said all your troubles started then, that if you could go back and stop yourself, everything would be fine. You asked me if—"

"No!" Kernel grunts. "It can't be."

"That's what I thought at first," Beranabus chuckles.

"But you said we couldn't!" Kernel protests.

"And I was right. Nobody ever had, and I didn't think anyone could. But now we have. You, Bec and Grubbs did it. You broke the final barrier. I never thought it could happen. I gave up on the notion long, long ago. When you've seen as much of—"

"What is it?" I cut in sharply, furious with ignorance. "What's the big secret? What question did Kernel ask?"

"The one they all ask eventually," Beranabus smiles. "The one you would have put to me if you'd been with me a little longer, when you looked back on all the times you went wrong, wondered how things would have

426

turned out if you'd done this or that differently, gone down one path instead of another."

Beranabus stops, glances up at the trees and the moon beyond, as if to reconfirm it before saying it out loud. When he looks at me again, the smile's still there, but shaky, as if he's not sure whether he should be smiling or not. And he says, very softly, "Kernel asked me if it was possible to travel back in time."

→A shocked moment of incredulous silence. Then I laugh. "Good one. You almost had me going. Now quit with the jokes and—"

"This isn't a joke," Beranabus says.

"You're trying to tell me we've returned to the past, like in some bad science-fiction film?"

"No," Kernel giggles, then hits me with the punchline. "Like in some *very good* science-fiction film."

"Don't," I mutter. "Things are mad enough without you two veering off at some ludicrous angle. We need to think about this logically, go through what happened step by step, so we can understand. Wild speculation won't get us anywhere."

"It's not wild," Beranabus says. "And it's not speculation. It's fact."

"I don't accept that. You're wrong."

"How else can you explain this?" He points to the hole, the rocks, the trees.

"It's an illusion. Our minds have conjured it up or Bec fed the image to us to spare us the real, grisly truth. It happened to me before, in Slawter. Maybe we're lying by the cave entrance, unconscious, demons ravaging our bodies, and this is our only way out of the pain. Or we've gone into the universe of the Demonata and created this scene ourselves. Hell, maybe we're dead and this is what we've chosen for the afterlife."

"We're not dead," Kernel says. "And we're not imagining this. I'd have given myself eyes if we were."

"Time travel's impossible," I say slowly, as if explaining something obvious to a young child.

"So is flying," Beranabus says, "but you've soared like a bird."

"That's different," I snap. "What you're talking about..." I shake my head.

"How did it happen?" Kernel asks. "I believe you, Beranabus — at least I think I do — but how? You always said the past was the one thing we could never change."

"It is. I mean, it was. Demons can't do it. Magicians certainly can't. But the *Kah-Gash*..."

Kernel draws his breath in sharply. "Are you sure?"

"It has to be," Beranabus insists. "The ultimate power... the ability to destroy an entire universe... Why not the potential to reverse time too?"

"But if you're right, that means..."

"Grubbs and Bec were the missing pieces. And there must have only been three. It couldn't have worked unless all the pieces were assembled. At least I don't think it could..." He frowns.

"What the hell are you talking about?" I hiss. "What's a *Car Gash?*"

"Kah-Gash," Kernel corrects me. He's trembling, but not from the pain or cold. "It's a mythical weapon. You're meant to be able to destroy a universe with it, ours or the Demonata's. It was split into an unknown number of pieces millions or billions of years ago. Various demons and magicians have searched for it since then, without success. Thirty years ago we discovered one of the pieces. In me."

"You'd been implanted with something?"

"No. I *am* a piece of the Kah-Gash."

"I don't understand. How can you be part of a weapon? You're human."

"I'm magical," he disagrees. "The Kah-Gash is a weapon of magic, not physics. It can take the form of anything it chooses."

I think that through, putting it together with what they were saying a few minutes ago. "You believe Bec and I are part of this weapon too?"

"You have to be," Beranabus says. "The stars don't lie — we've gone back in time, to the night the tunnel was reopened. You three did it. We saw it happening. No force in either universe could have accomplished that, except the Kah-Gash."

"How?" Kernel whispers. "And why? If this is the work of the Kah-Gash, where did it find the energy to alter the flow of time? And why bring us back to this specific moment? Why stop here, not a hundred years ago or a million? Why not shatter the laws of time entirely?"

Beranabus scratches the back of his neck. "What did you feel when it was happening?" he asks.

Kernel shrugs. "Great power flowing into me."

"From where?"

"All around."

"Grubbs? Can you be any more specific?"

"The ground," I mutter. "The power came from the rocks, from beneath."

"And did it flow into you or through you?"

"What's the difference?"

"You'd have exploded if you drew in that much energy and didn't let it out," Beranabus says. "You had to channel the magic. But where to? The demons? The sky? Where?"

"The cave," Kernel answers after several seconds of thoughtful silence. "The power came from the ground, then went through us, back down into the rock, to the cave... the tunnel."

"Yes," I agree, thinking back.

Beranabus smiles. "The Kah-Gash – you, Kernel and Bec – acted as a kind of magnifying lens. You drew energy from the tunnel, then focused it back." He goes to stroke his beard, realises he doesn't have one and taps his chin instead. "I can't be sure – maybe I never will be – but this is how I think it worked.

"Opening a window between the Demonata's universe and ours is like making a hole in a dam — matter flows from their universe to ours, generating energy. Space, time, gravity, the forces which hold our universes together… they seep across every time a demon or one of us makes a rip.

"Windows are small, temporary. The energy generated is minimal. But in this case a tunnel was created, open twenty-four hours a day. A huge river of magic flowed through. You three tapped into that. No… you must have done more than tap into it. You…" He clicks his fingers. "You rode it! It was like a wave of energy. You caught the wave and rode it back to its source, converting and channelling it at the same time."

"Rode it back to its source?" Kernel echoes. "You mean back to the universe of the Demonata?"

"No," Beranabus says. "You followed the wave back in time, transforming it and eradicating it, back to when the tunnel was created." He looks at me, his eyes bright with excitement. "This is the night of the full moon. The night Lord Loss returned to Carcery Vale. The Kah-Gash brought us back in time to the night when the tunnel was reactivated, *so that we could prevent it ever being opened in the first place!*"

He seizes my hands and squeezes tight. "Don't you see? We've been given a second chance. Not just to heal the damage done by the demons, but to stop it happening at all."

"But... no... it can't..." I mutter, head spinning.

"Grubbs," Beranabus says softly. "At this time, Dervish and your brother are still alive. We can help them, but only if we accept this and act fast. Now, are you going to stand there denying what your senses tell you, or are you going to help me save the world and all the people you love?"

And when he puts it like that...

TIMELY INTERVENTION

→Beranabus has entered the hole, but only advanced to the point where it widens into the shaft. He's squatting there, eyes closed, sensing the cave beneath, determining exactly who and what we have to fight.

I wish we'd travelled back another few days. We could have called on the Disciples for support. But Beranabus said we couldn't have come back any further. Because we were riding the wave of energy generated by the opening of the tunnel, we could only follow it back to its origin. He likened it to coming to the end of a train line — when you run out of track, that's it, end of ride.

There's been no sign of Bec. I've kept a close eye on the rocks and listened for her strange whispers, but she hasn't shown. I know Beranabus is concerned for her. He thinks she might have perished to help send us back, sacrificed herself for our sake. I don't see the big deal if she did – she was dead already! – but I don't say that to

Beranabus. That girl seems to be the one person in the world he gives a damn about. I doubt he'd appreciate wisecracks at her expense.

Kernel is walking around, hands by his sides, trying to navigate like a bat. Only instead of emitting radar beams (or whatever bats emit), he sends out magical impulses, which bounce back, letting him know what's around him. At least that's the theory — but with all the trees he's crashed into during the last few minutes, I'm not sure it works.

"Ouch!" Kernel bumps into another low-hanging branch and steps back, rubbing his head.

"Why don't you give it a rest?" I snap. "You'll poke—"

I brake to a halt. I'd been about to say he'd poke an eye out if he wasn't careful, but I guess it's a bit late for warnings like that.

"I have to learn," Kernel mutters. "Beranabus needs me. There are demons to kill."

I walk over to him, take his left arm and gently guide him clear of the trees. His courage fills me with awe and shame. Sure, I found the guts to pitch in when there was no other option, but this is bravery of a different kind. He's just lost his eyes, yet here he is, determined to carry on fighting. In his shoes I'd be moaning like a baby, full of self-pity, seizing the opportunity to take a back seat and keep out of trouble.

"I'll direct you," I promise. "I'll be your eyes in the cave. Focus on your magic. I'll tell you where to aim it when the time's right."

"Thanks," he says, smiling faintly. "But I might as well practise while we're waiting. It can't hurt and it keeps my mind off what's happened. Besides, I think I'm getting the hang of it now." Prising himself free, he starts walking again, arms rigid, face composed, senses alert.

"Ouch!"

→Scrabbling sounds. Beranabus emerges, brushing dirt and small stones off his unprotected skin. He doesn't look too worried — happy even, in a guarded kind of way. "It's better than I dared hope," he says. "Lord Loss and Juni are there, some of his familiars – the three we encountered on the plane – and Dervish and Bill-E. But that's all, unless others are masking their presence, which is unlikely. I think we only have five enemies to deal with." He makes a clicking noise with his tongue. "Or seven."

"Meaning what?" I snap.

"We don't know where Dervish and Bill-E stand."

"Of course we do," I retort. "They're on our side."

"Probably. But we mustn't count on it. We don't know how far into their minds Juni wormed herself. If they've fallen under her spell, they might be acting on the demon master's behalf."

"Never," I growl.

Beranabus shrugs. "I won't argue. Just be aware of the threat. I'm not saying we go down there and blow their heads off. But we might have to knock them about a bit."

"I know Dervish and Bill-E," I say tightly. "They wouldn't betray us, no matter how strong the spell."

"Don't be naïve," Beranabus barks, then calls Kernel in close. "Will you be all right down there or are you just going to get in our way?"

I think it's hugely insensitive of him to speak to his blind assistant like that, but Kernel only smiles. "I'll be fine. Grubbs will give me a helpful shove in the right direction. I can't do much, but I can make a nuisance of myself."

"As long as you're a nuisance for them, not us," Beranabus grunts, then lowers his voice. "Let's not get overly confident. There might be only five of them, but they're a deadly quintet. Lord Loss is more powerful than any of us. Juni's a match for Kernel even with eyes — she's certainly stronger than him now. And the familiars are dangerous too. Let's not forget we're an old man, his blind assistant and a kid who could do anything under pressure."

"You sure know how to steady a guy's nerves before a fight," I note sarcastically.

"I'm not here to make uplifting speeches," Beranabus replies. "We have a good chance to win. The odds are far

3

better than they were before. But we have to be sharp. We can't afford any mistakes. We've been handed a second chance — there won't be a third. We've seen what the consequences are if we lose. So let's stay focused and give it the very best we have. And remember, if we lose, we die, and everybody else in the world will too."

He starts to rise, then stops. "I almost forgot the most important point." He chuckles at himself. "I'm too old and senile to protect the world any longer. If we get through this, it'll be time to invest in a pair of slippers and find some quiet corner of the globe where I can…"

He coughs. "Sorry. Lost my train of thought. What was I saying?"

"The most important point," Kernel reminds him patiently.

"Aye. The key." He taps the ground to signify the importance of his next few words. "I explained earlier how the tunnel was opened. One of Lord Loss's human allies made a sacrifice in the cave and now has to join with the rock, to create the opening. Unless there's somebody down there I don't know about, that person – the key – must be the woman who calls herself Juni Swan."

"Couldn't it be Artery or one of the other familiars?" I ask.

"No. It has to be a human. Those are the rules."

"Rules can change," Kernel says. "According to Bec, you were wrong about the demons being sucked back to their own universe if the tunnel was closed again."

"Aye," Beranabus growls irritably, "but she didn't mention anything about this rule changing. Besides, we saw Lord Loss and his familiars during the fight. Juni's the only one who wasn't present."

"It could be Dervish or the boy," Kernel suggests.

I stiffen, but before I can respond, Beranabus says, "No. If they're under the woman's spell, they only succumbed recently. Lord Loss planned to open the tunnel during the night of the previous full moon. That means the sacrifice had been made some weeks before. Dervish and the boy were definitely in control of their senses then. So it has to be Juni. She's our primary target. If we kill her, we win."

"Can't Lord Loss use another human instead?" I ask.

"No. Only the one who made the sacrifice can serve as the key. He could try again later and get someone else to make another sacrifice. But if we beat him tonight, we'll take steps to ensure he never has that option.

"Juni's the one we go for. Her companions will do everything they can to protect her. We'll have to fight them, but we mustn't let them distract us. Juni is the target. The others don't matter.

"So, you know what we have to do? Are you ready for one more battle, the most important ever? Are you primed to go boldly into the breach and grind these demons into the dirt?" He grabs my right hand and Kernel's left. "Are you with me, boys, all the way to the glorious, victorious end?"

"That's more like it," I grin.

"Exactly what you want to hear before you step into the gladiatorial pit," Kernel agrees.

We enjoy the moment, smiling at one another. (Kernel smiles a little off-centre, at a nearby tree.) Then we face the entrance to the cave and take a decisive step forward.

"Hold it!" I gasp, ruining the mood, but struck by a sudden thought which I can't let pass.

"What's wrong?" Beranabus asks.

"Nothing. I mean… I don't know if you can… it's no big deal, but…" I nod at my naked flesh. "I don't want to face them like this. You couldn't conjure up some clothes, could you?"

Beranabus stares at me in disbelief — then laughs. "The things you worry about! But, in a way, you're right. One should always go into battle suitably clad." He waves a hand regally and the trees rustle overhead. I have the sensation of being wrapped up tight by rough blankets. Looking down, I see that I'm clad from neck to ankles in a suit of green, brown, red and yellow leaves, as are Beranabus and Kernel.

"The best I can do in a pinch," Beranabus says. "The material won't hold for long, but it should see us through the fight."

"Perfect," I smile, shaking my arms to make sure I'm not bound too tightly. Then we face the hole, take a step forward, on to the slope, and down.

→The shaft feels narrower than before. The rock's hot to the touch and it seems to throb with magical energy. I climb silently in the darkness, searching for toeholds and fingerholds, careful not to send any pebbles tumbling in case the noise alerts the demons.

I hate this. No excitement at the thought of the battle to come. Just sheer terror. If there was any way to avoid it, I'd be out of here in a flash. But there are no alternatives. It's fight to the death or surrender this world and everyone I care about to the Demonata. I'd like to think I'm a hero, but the truth is I'm just doing what I have to. There isn't a choice.

Can I kill Juni if the opportunity falls my way? I'm not certain. I despise her, maybe even more than Lord Loss. He's a demon, born to be evil, but she made a conscious decision to betray her people. At the same time, she's human. It wouldn't be like killing a demon. I don't know if I could do it. Hopefully I won't have to. Beranabus is the man for that job, and I imagine he'll relish the task of terminating the treacherous Miss

Swan. But if things don't work out that way… if I come face-to-face with her… if it falls to me to finish her off…

I drive the thoughts away. No point worrying about it. I'll just have to play this out and hope for the best. I've got to go in there focused on the fight, confident of victory, not filled with doubt.

I concentrate on the climb and our crab-like descent, hand by hand, foot by foot, slowly, carefully, edging ever closer to the demons below.

→We reach the bottom and group together on the solid cave floor. I can see light ahead of us. Soft, blue, unnatural. Three distinct, separate sounds —

Someone chanting.

Occasional growls and snapping noises.

Whimpering and moaning.

Beranabus checks that we're ready, then advances. I keep a few steps behind, slightly to his right so I can see ahead of him, guiding Kernel by his leaf-clad arm. I stub my toes on rocks with almost every step I take, but that's a minor pain, easily ignored.

We enter the main cave and the scene unfolds before us. Juni and Lord Loss are in front of the crack close to the waterfall, the crack *I* made. Momentary guilt — have I inadvertently helped the demons? But it doesn't last. Logic tells me not to worry. They could have created a similar opening without much effort.

A few metres behind Juni and her master, Dervish and Bill-E are kneeling, arms bound by ropes, gags in mouths. Artery, Femur and Spine are dancing around them, cackling, making sudden lunges, teeth snapping, claws extended — then pulling away before making contact. Bill-E's the one whimpering and moaning, trying to squirm away from the demons. Dervish is kneeling upright, glaring hatefully at Lord Loss and Juni, beaten but defiant.

Instant relief — Dervish and Bill-E are innocent. They haven't been bewitched by Juni. They're victims, not adversaries. A weight lifts from my heart. Whether or not I can kill Juni, there's no way I could have harmed my uncle or brother, even if they'd been working in league with the demons.

"Good evening, all!" Beranabus booms, startling me almost as much as the others in the cave. Lord Loss, his familiars and Juni whirl round. Dervish and Bill-E's heads twist as far as the ropes allow. "I trust we're not late," Beranabus says, striding forward, saluting Dervish. "Got delayed en route. You'd never believe our story if we told you."

The rabbit-shaped Femur snarls and crouches, meaning to use its powerful hind legs to leap across the cave at Beranabus and splatter him with acid.

"Wait," Lord Loss stops the familiar. He taps Juni's left arm with one of his eight hands and nods at the crack. She shoots us a hateful glance, then faces the rock and resumes her chant. "This is an unexpected pleasure," Lord Loss says icily, drifting past Dervish and Bill-E towards us.

"When we heard about the party, we had to drop in," Beranabus quips, very different to his normal, serious self. "I hope we're not unwelcome?"

"Certainly not," Lord Loss smiles. "I am delighted to see you. Especially young Grubitsch. I thought, when he slipped through our clutches on the aeroplane, that it might be a long time before our paths crossed again. Yet here he is, fresh and wide-eyed, ready to die. And you know you'll die, don't you, Grubitsch? You realise time has run out, that you, your uncle and brother are doomed?"

"Shut up, you ba—"

I stop abruptly. He called Bill-E my brother. Of course Lord Loss knew about that — Bill-E was infected with the family curse — but Bill-E didn't. We never told him. I try looking past the demon master, to catch my half-brother's gaze, but Lord Loss is blocking the view.

"Yes, Grubitsch," the monster purrs. "I told him. We spent quite an amount of time tonight discussing how you kept the truth from him and ran away when the going got tough, leaving him behind for me as an offering."

"That's not true!" I shout. "Don't believe him, Bill-E. I—"

"That's not important now," Beranabus interrupts. "I want to know who's the mastermind behind this? What foul hellspawn are you working for? Who organised the demons and gave them orders to come running when the tunnel opens?"

Lord Loss frowns. "You know about our plan?"

"Obviously. Now tell me who's behind it."

The demon master chuckles. "No, Beranabus. You have been very clever. But if you do not know the full magnitude of the force you've chosen to pit yourself against, I will not enlighten you. It's not my job to explain. Do your own detective work. I am sure you and your capable assistants can…"

He pauses, catching sight of the eyeless Kernel Fleck. "But what is this? What happened to poor Cornelius?"

"Never mind," Beranabus snaps. "I want to know about—"

"I recognise those wounds," Lord Loss continues, raising his voice. "Those are the marks of my familiar, Spine. Such trademark injuries are unmistakable. I can even see some of his maggoty offspring embedded in the bloodied pits. It must have been a recent attack. But Spine has been with me the whole time." He looks back at his familiar. The scorpion with the semi-human face stares at him blankly.

"And your hair," Lord Loss says, facing us again. "You're as hairless as myself. You've been in a fight of great viciousness. Spine seems to have been in it too. But how...?"

"Tell us about the demon who set you up to this and I'll tell you about our fight," Beranabus grins.

"If I thought you were genuine, I'd happily make that deal," Lord Loss replies. "I sense great magic and mystery in this. If I did not know better, I would say..." He trails off into silence, then sneers. "But I know you, Beranabus. You are a rogue. You would renege on your promise and tell me nothing. So I'll hold my tongue and torture the truth out of the boys once I've defeated you."

"Nay," Beranabus snorts. "Secrecy and surprise were the only advantages you had. Now that we've thwarted you, you must face us openly, on our world, where your powers are diminished. You can't beat us. If you abandon the spells and leave, I'll let you walk away and settle for sealing this place off. But if you force us to fight, we'll kill you all. Even those of you who have died before."

"Ah," Lord Loss chuckles. "You've seen through Miss Swan's disguise."

"I knew her for a cuckoo the moment I laid eyes on her," Beranabus says as Juni continues to chant, not

445

glancing round even though she's the subject of their conversation. "It took me a while to pierce the illusion, but I knew of her true face long before she moved against Grubbs."

"What are you talking about?" I mutter.

"Watch," Beranabus says and murmurs the words of a quick spell, waving a hand at Juni. Lord Loss makes no move to defend her. He's loving this. As I stare at Juni, her flesh ripples. She stops chanting and cries out, but with surprise not pain. Her hands dart to her face and she turns sharply, flashing a furious glare at Beranabus. Dervish gives a muffled cry of shock and jerks away from her.

Her face has changed completely. Much plainer. Bad acne scars. Dirty, short blonde hair. Blue eyes. A sullen expression. Quite fat. Pale skin, but not as white as her albino flesh. She appears younger than before, maybe mid- to late-twenties.

"What's happening?" Kernel asks.

Before I can tell him, Juni shrieks in a voice entirely unlike her own, "Give me back my face, you swine!"

Kernel's forehead creases. "*Nadia?*" he gasps.

"You have a good ear," Lord Loss purrs. "Shame about the eyes."

"Nadia Moore," Beranabus snorts. "Another distant relative of yours, Grubbs, and once one of my closest assistants. I thought she died in Lord Loss's kingdom many years ago, but it seems she merely switched allegiances and created a new look for herself."

"Cornelius knew," Lord Loss says with relish. "Not about her rebirth as Juni Swan, but about her survival, the trick she pulled to escape your tyrannical rule. He kept it a secret from you, Beranabus. Perhaps he has other secrets. Are you certain you can trust him?"

Bernabus sniffs away the jibe. "I prefer you this way, Nadia," he says. "Reality's more attractive than façade. You should have kept your original face."

"I'm not Nadia Moore," Juni snarls. "She died, just the way you saw it. I put everything about her behind me — her name, features, loyalties. I'm Juni Swan now and always will be, even if you've disabled my glamour."

"I felt guilty when you were killed," Beranabus says softly. "About as guilty as I've ever felt in my long, wretched life. But I won't feel anything when you die a second time, when I kill you myself." His expression hardens and he addresses Lord Loss. "My offer stands. Walk away now and we won't interfere — I'll even let Nadia leave too. If you stay, you die."

"A generous offer," Lord Loss says. "If you had the backing of your Disciples, perhaps I'd be inclined to accept and slaughter you another time — I prefer to fight when the odds are in my favour. But you come only with a blind boy and a cur who has already proven his cowardice. And though you yourself are a fearsome opponent, you're only one man. And no man, no matter how powerful, has ever got the better of a demon master. So, in answer to your offer…"

Lord Loss smirks vilely, then screeches unintelligibly at his familiars. With ear-piercing howls of delight, the demons attack.

THE HIGH...

→Artery and Lord Loss hurl themselves at Beranabus. The scorpion-shaped Spine targets Kernel, eager to finish the job which it doesn't remember starting. Femur sets its sights on me.

It's almost comical watching the rabbit bound towards me. It's like a sick cartoon, Bugs Bunny gone batty, leaping on people to plant a great smacker of a kiss on them. Except this creature's acidic smooch will melt a person's face and leave them a smouldering, sizzling mess — not the sort of fare you'd usually find in a Looney Tunes flick.

Femur spits acid in mid-air. It spurts towards me, a sheet of liquid death. Directed by the magic inside me, I wave my left hand at the deadly juice. It divides and hisses past my head, hitting a couple of stalagmites behind me, quickly eating into them and eroding the work of thousands of years.

The rabbit's leap brings it within reach. I grab its neck and twist sharply. The neck breaks and I toss the creature away. It gurgles, then heals itself and gets up. I smile, grown bold by the combination of magic and ease with which I shrugged off the demon's attack. I beckon to it. "Try again, lettuce-muncher!"

As Femur tenses its rear legs and works its lips over its gums, Kernel stumbles past me. Spine is on his head, jabbing its stinger at his eye sockets. He's batting it away. "Let me know if you need help!" I shout. Then Femur leaps and spits acid again, and I have to focus on that.

As I fend off the rabbit I spot Beranabus. Lord Loss has the magician within his grasp, all eight arms wrapped around him, a spider devouring a fly. Artery is on Beranabus's back, chewing at his shoulders. One of his hands is under the magician's skin. I see knuckles moving within the flesh.

Maybe it's a trick of the light, but Beranabus's skin appears to be a different colour. There's a purple tinge to it and his eyes seem to have grown and turned a dark grey shade. And the blood streaming from the hole in his shoulder that Artery's chewing at… is it *yellow?*

As I'm studying Beranabus uncertainly, Femur bounces up once more, spraying its corrosive poison. Snapping back to attention, I freeze the acid, then punch through the solid panel of ice and grab the rabbit's ears. "Enough of this crap," I grunt and drive my left fist down the demon's throat.

Femur's eyes bulge alarmingly. It chokes and tries to gnaw through my arm. Cuts the flesh up pretty bad. Pain flares, but I numb myself to it and focus on my hand deep in the rabbit's guts. I fill the fist with magic, then let it explode, incinerating the demon from the inside out. Femur gasps, mouth slackening, blinking furiously. Its legs shake. Acid dribbles over my forearm, but I turn it to mist before it harms me.

The rabbit's ears rip loose and I throw them away. They flop around on the floor of the cave for a few seconds, then fall still as life leaves Femur's body. Its flesh turns a dark red colour, then crumbles away like ash. I pull my arm free and study the mess, lips curled with disgust. I start towards the waterfall to wash clean and sluice out my wounds. Then I have a better idea and direct magic at my arm. Seconds later — spotless, unmarked flesh. Coolio!

My first thought is to go to Beranabus's aid or help Kernel with Spine. But then the magician's warning kicks in. Juni Swan is public enemy number one. She has to be stopped. I'm not sure I can do it — the doubts swim back inside my head — but I have to try.

Skirting Beranabus and Lord Loss, I hurry to where the transformed Juni is chanting into the crack, arms spread wide, words coming fast and furious. For a second I think I glimpse a face in the rock, just within the opening of the crack. But then it's gone and I'm not sure whether it was Bec, the first of the demon hordes or a trick of the light.

I don't want to touch Juni — the thought of physical contact with her repulses me. So I bring my hands together and summon a bolt of magic to fire instead. Nothing happens. I can feel the magic, but it's like there's a barrier between us, blocking the lines of communication. Then I realise what the problem is — the werewolf. There's a full moon. Beranabus told me I'd have no trouble suppressing the wolf now, but it would always be there, scratching away beneath the surface, whining, trying to break free.

"No time for games, wolfie," I mutter, and mentally drive the beast deep down within me, to howl in silent, imprisoned protest for at least another month. The magic burns brightly inside me as soon as the way's been cleared. Once again I tell it what I want and this time I feel energy gather in my hands. Pointing them at Juni, I unleash the power. A huge ball of magic shoots straight at her — then hits an invisible barrier and crackles away into nothing.

Juni glances around, sneers at me, carries on chanting.

"'Ubbs!" Dervish grunts as I prepare a second blast. He's straining to get to his feet. Beside him, Bill-E's staring at me as if he doesn't know who I am. "'Ubbs!" Dervish shouts again, mouth constricted by his gag.

I wave a hand at my uncle and brother. Their gags and the ropes binding them burn away. As soon as he's free, Dervish thrusts himself up and throws his arms around me. "I thought you were dead!" he cries, burying his head in my chest.

"Not me," I grin, hugging back hard, momentarily forgetting the fight and all that's at stake. It's so great to see him again, to have him hold me, to be home and with the closest thing to a father I have left. If the world ended here and now, for me it would be a good end.

"Grubbs?" Bill-E says hesitantly, studying me warily. "Is it really you?"

"Sure is... little brother." I smile at him awkwardly.

"You should have told me," he growls, pointing a finger. "All this time... if I'd known... all my life I thought I was alone. You should have told me!"

"I know," I sigh. "I was a fool. Forgive me?"

"No way, baldy," he smirks. The smile quickly fades when he spots the woman next to the crack. "Her!" he growls, finger swivelling. "Is that Juni?"

"Yes," Dervish snarls. "The face might be different, but the evil stench is the same. She told us you attacked her, Grubbs. That after killing Ma and Pa Spleen, you..." He pauses. "You didn't kill them, did you?"

"Of course not," I huff indignantly, not admitting that I'd thought the same thing myself.

"I told you," Bill-E says proudly. "I knew Grubbs wasn't a murderer."

"I didn't think so either," Dervish mutters. "But she was so convincing. Sobbed hard when she came back. Said she saw you murder them, that you tried to kill Billy, but she lured you away. She was a pillar of strength. Guided us through the burials. Comforted Billy. Helped deal with the police enquiries. I loved her more than ever.

"Then she said we could find you, that she could use the magic of this cave to locate you. Fool that I was, I believed her. Billy had moved in with us. Juni said we should bring him along, that it might help with the spell. I didn't see how, but she was stronger than me. She knew more about magic. I trusted her.

"When we got here, the demons jumped us. Juni clubbed me over the back of my head and they trussed us up. Lord Loss told us he was going to open the tunnel. A sacrifice had been made and the killer would join with the rock and keep the tunnel open. He said he'd let the Demonata cross, then murder me slowly. Said he had something extra special in mind for Billy. He—"

"Dervish," I interrupt softly. "If she finishes that spell, we're in for seventy-seven different types of hell. We need to kill her. *Now.*"

Dervish nods grimly. "OK. You work on bringing down the barrier. I'll handle the rest."

"You're sure?" I ask, grateful that he's offering to take the horrible task out of my hands, but wanting to provide him with an alternative if he feels he can't slaughter the woman he once loved.

"I'd fight anybody who tried to kill her before I had a shot," Dervish says, and the burning hatred in his expression scares me.

One quick glance behind. Kernel's pinned Spine to a stalagmite and wrapped the demon's stinger around the needle of calcium. He's pummelling its face with his right fist, holding the tip of the stinger in place with his left hand.

Beranabus – his flesh an even darker shade of purple than before – is locked in combat with Lord Loss, the demon master howling like a dog, the snakes in his chest cavity lashing the magician with their forked tongues. Artery has worked both hands under Beranabus's skin and is trying to get his head in too, to chew his way through the bones and into the meaty innards. It's not looking good for the old magician, but I know he'd rather we killed Juni and let him perish than go to his rescue and leave her free to open the tunnel.

I let magical energy charge within my fists again — charge *blast!* Charge — *blast!* Charge — *blast!* Dervish is standing a metre or so ahead of me, out of the way of the explosions, fingers twitching, eyes locked on Juni, eager to squeeze his hands around her throat. Bill-E is watching my back, keeping track of the demons, making sure none springs on me unawares.

The barrier starts to give. Each ball of magic crackles louder and lasts longer when it smacks against the energy field. A few more and she'll be at our mercy.

"Master!" Juni screams. "Help me! I need more time!"

"Spine!" Lord Loss roars. "Femur!" I sense him looking for his familiars. Then he curses. "Attack them, Artery. Leave Beranabus to me."

Ripping sounds. Bill-E yells a warning. "Grubbs! Look out! He's—"

Artery lands on my back and I stagger. Before I can turn to deal with the hell-child, Dervish grabs his legs, swings him round and batters his head off a low-hanging stalactite. The skull splits down the middle and brains ooze out. Lice fall from the fiendish baby's crown and scuttle around on the ground. Dervish twirls the demon overhead a couple of times, then throws him far across the cave, where he smashes hard into a wall and collapses. Artery will recover, but it'll take him a minute or two. That should be more than enough time.

"Master!" Juni screams again, spitting the cry out between the words of the spell that she's chanting. Her real face looks far less commanding than the one she wore when she was pretending to be our friend. It carries the scars of fear and low character. "One more minute. That's all I need."

Lord Loss howls louder than any wolf, then reluctantly releases Beranabus and whacks him aside. I hear a whoosh as he propels himself towards me. "Grubbs!" Dervish yells.

"Just a second," I mumble, taking aim, letting off one last blast of energy. It sounds like a gunshot when it hits the barrier — then crashes through and connects with Juni, knocking her to the floor.

I open my mouth to cheer, but Lord Loss is on me before I can, cursing foully, eight arms around my mouth and throat, squeezing, tearing, intent on pulling me to pieces and choking me all at once.

Gasping for air, I grab two of his arms, focus my magic and tug with all my strength. The arms rip free of their sockets. Lord Loss wails and tries to reattach them, but I send fire shooting up the limbs and they burn away to nothing before he can restore them.

Dervish steps in to help. "No!" I yell, feet dangling a few centimetres above the ground as a furious Lord Loss clutches me to his chest, where the snakes fight with each other to bite out my eyes. "Kill Juni! I can deal with—"

The demon master gets a few mangled, lumpy, bloody fingers into my mouth. They lengthen and extend back into my throat. Out of the corner of my eye, I see Dervish wavering. His natural instinct is to help me. But then he sees Juni back on her feet, muttering the spell again. With a wild curse he goes after her.

I bite off the fingers and spit them out. Lord Loss screams obligingly. One of the snakes digs its fangs into my bald skull and rips out a chunk of flesh. I snatch the snake from its heartless home and chew its head off. I'm starting to enjoy this biting business.

Lord Loss's six remaining arms tighten around my body. I feel the bones of my ribcage creak and groan. I know that if the demon maintains this pressure, the bones will snap and pierce my lungs and heart, and that will be the end of me. But it doesn't matter. I'm buying time for Dervish. Stopping Juni is my only reason for being here, for living. If I have to die to thwart her evil plans, that's just bad luck. I'll give my life gladly.

But before I can die nobly, Beranabus stumbles back into action. Picking up a stone, he invests it with magic and hurls it at Lord Loss's head. The stone pierces the demon master's flesh and bone, and ends up sticking half in and half out of the monster's skull, just above his left ear.

Lord Loss shrieks with pain and rage, then twirls and throws me at Beranabus. I collide with the magician and we sprawl across the ground. Lord Loss starts after us, then remembers Juni. Hesitating, he looks over his shoulder. Juni's wrestling with Dervish, shouting the spell even as they battle. Dervish is striking her hard, weeping, hands clenched together to form one mighty club. Juni's pockmarked, pasty face has been smashed to a pulp. Her hair and skin are flecked with blood, and her eyes are almost invisible behind her mashed flesh.

As Lord Loss turns to help, she stops chanting and smiles at Dervish. Her flesh ripples, changes colour, and she looks like the old Juni Swan again, only battered and bleeding. "Dervish, my love," she wheezes. "Please stop. You're hurting poor Juni."

"You betrayed us!" Dervish roars, tears coming harder than ever.

"I made a mistake," Juni murmurs. "I love you, Dervish. Please don't hurt me. I can make this right if you give me the chance."

Dervish stares at her, hands dropping, fury leaving his body, shoulders sagging. He takes a step forward. I think he means to hug her. That scares me, but not as much as what I suddenly spot happening overhead — the rock around the crack has started to pulse! Light is shining from deep within. And it's beginning to split wider apart.

"Dervish!" I yell. "She finished the spell. The demons are coming. You have to kill her!"

Dervish stops moving, but doesn't bring his hands together. Beranabus throws himself forward desperately. Lord Loss grabs him and laughs.

Skittering footsteps behind me. I half turn and spot Artery leaping, three sets of sharp teeth gnashing savagely. I raise my arms — too late. The demon strikes me in the chest with his tiny feet. I fly across the cave and smash into the rock at the back of the waterfall. Come up spluttering and cold, my leaf-suit soaked through and disintegrating, the water cutting out the sounds and sights of the cave.

I drag myself clear of the waterfall as Artery bounds towards me. He leaps to kick me again, but this time I grab him by his childish torso and hold him at arm's length, trying to find the strength to kill him, but too exhausted and dispirited. I glance around wearily, looking for help or inspiration.

Kernel is still out of the main action, unable to kill Spine, struggling to keep the demon pinned to the stalagmite. Lord Loss is bearing down mercilessly on Beranabus, squeezing tightly, snakes more active than ever. The demon master's laughing triumphantly, confident of victory. The opening in the rock is pulsing faster and faster, the colours and shades of light changing with every pulse, the mouth of the crack stretching, widening, extending. A magic-laced wind whistles up out of nowhere. I feel it blowing past me, towards the hole. Soft at first, but growing steadily, sucking up dust and bits of grit, sending them shooting down the crack. Bill-E's scrabbling away from the hole, moaning, sensing disaster.

And just beneath the crack — what will soon be the entry point for hundreds of demons — Juni Swan is kissing Dervish, her luminous white hair billowing out in a fan shape, gusting away from her skull in the ever-increasing breeze.

"My love," Juni gurgles, pulling back from him slightly, pink eyes twinkling maliciously. She strokes his cheeks, smiles seductively, kisses him again. Dervish is motionless, mesmerised, under her spell. Moving her head to his shoulder, she murmurs into his throat, "You could never harm your Juni. You love me, as I love you. What savagery, hitting me like that. But I forgive you. I love you too much to bear a grudge."

Her fake flesh has already healed and is as smooth and white as ever, though a few streaks of blood remain. She looks beautiful. It's strange, but unconcealed evil suits her. She's more stunning now than she ever was when she was pretending to be good.

I try shouting a warning, but I don't have the strength. Holding Artery at bay is all I can manage.

"I'll take you to the universe of the Demonata when this is over," Juni promises Dervish. "You'll have to be killed eventually, but there's no rush. I'll show you such wonders and treat you so sweetly, you won't care about dying. In fact you'll die gladly, to please me. Won't you, my love?"

Dervish stares at her blankly. Then Bill-E screams. "Dervish! I'm afraid!"

Juni laughs. "Don't worry, silly Billy, I haven't forgotten about you. How could I? You're the most important—"

Dervish grabs Juni by the waist and picks her up as if she's weightless. "*No!*" she screams, lashing out at him but unable to connect because of the angle he's holding her at. Dervish lunges away from the pulsing rock, struggling against the wind. Juni's hands stretch upwards, searching for magic. Her lips start on a new spell. Lord Loss shouts with alarm and springs away from Beranabus.

But Dervish is too quick for both of them. He looks around. Takes a couple of steps to his right, holding Juni high above his head. Then slams her down with all his strength on top of a small stalagmite.

The tip pierces Juni's flesh and slices in through the skin of her back — then bursts through her chest a moment later. Dervish cries out and falls away, staring with wonder and disbelief at Juni as blood spurts and her legs and arms thrash, as if he doesn't know how she got there.

"My swan!" Lord Loss howls, flying to her side.

"Master…" Juni groans, her mouth full of blood. "Help… me."

Lord Loss reaches out to her, then stops and studies the wound. He shakes his head softly, sorrowfully. "I cannot," he says.

Juni stares at him incredulously. Then her expression clears. "I understand. Thank you, master. For… everything you showed me… all that you did for me… I offer my everlasting gratitude… and love."

Lord Loss stretches out a single arm and touches Juni's cheek with his clammy fingers. He's smiling sadly, but it's not his usual mocking smile — this one is almost human. "I will miss you," he mutters.

"And I…" Juni shudders and her eyes go wide. "Death!" she wheezes. "It's here. I sense it. I… no! Don't let it take me, master! I want to be free. Don't…"

She stops. Her mouth and eyes freeze. Lord Loss bends, kisses her forehead, then floats back a few paces. "Goodbye, sweet swan," he murmurs, and that's when I know for sure she's dead, though it's not until I hear Beranabus chuckling softly that I realise what that means.

The key has been eliminated… The tunnel can't be opened… *We've won!*

...AND THE LOW

→The sweetness of a hard-won victory lasts all of two seconds. Maybe three. Then it hits me — the rocks within and around the crack are still pulsing. The lights are flashing more vibrantly than at a disco. The wind is growing stronger.

"Beranabus!" I yell. "Why isn't it stopping?"

"It is," he mutters, staring at the crack doubtfully. "It must be. We killed her. But sometimes it can take a minute for a body to properly die, for all the senses to expire. When the last spark of life flickers out in her, this will end."

"But if the demons cross before that..."

Beranabus shrugs, then winces and reaches back to try and heal the wounded flesh between his shoulder blades. His skin and eyes are normal now. He looks like a tired old man, not a mighty magician. "A few might squeeze through, but not many. We'll just have to—"

"Imbeciles," Lord Loss snorts. He glares at Beranabus, then Dervish, who's lying close by Juni. Her face has lost its glamour, changed back to its real appearance, scarred and bloody from the beating she took. Dervish is staring at her with a mix of horror and loss. "You think you have defeated us? You believe we fall that easily? You are arrogant and ignorant, Beranabus, the result of too many soft victories over lesser demons. Killing Juni won't save your pitiful excuse of a world — or your lives. It only makes me more determined to see you and the grotesque Gradys suffer slowly and agonisingly."

"We were wrong!" I roar. "The key wasn't Juni. It's one of the demons." I spin, trying to figure out whether it's Artery or Spine.

"It can't be," Beranabus pants, struggling to his feet. "It doesn't work that way, and we saw them both in the future."

"Then I was right," Lord Loss hisses. "You travelled back in time!" He stares at Beranabus, awestruck. "How did you do it? I thought *that*, of all things, was impossible. How—"

"Beranabus," I interrupt. "We have to kill them now, before the Demonata—"

"But it's not them," he insists. "We *saw* them."

"Then somebody else!" I holler. "Another human assistant, invisible, hidden by magic. We have to find him… her… whatever!"

Beranabus nods and stumbles away, feverishly scouring the cave with magic and his eyes. I start off in the opposite direction.

"Grubbs," Bill-E moans, crawling towards me, wind snapping at him, clothes and hair rippling, the crack threatening to suck him in.

"Not now. Dervish." My uncle doesn't respond. "Dervish!" I yell. He blinks and looks up. "The key's still alive. It wasn't Juni. We have to find the person who made the sacrifice. If we don't, the tunnel will—"

"Grubbs," Bill-E moans again.

"Stop bugging me!" I scream, then stoop to look him in the eyes. "I'm sorry but there isn't time. If we don't find the person who made the sacrifice, they'll merge with the rock and the demons will flood through and kill us all."

I stand. Bill-E clutches the sodden, straggly left leg of my makeshift trousers. I curse and kick his hand away. I'm turning to continue searching when he whispers something, too soft for me to decipher. I almost don't pause, but there's an urgency in the whisper that demands attention.

"What did you say?" I shout without looking down, eyes piercing the shadows of the cave. It's difficult to see. The lights inside the crack are throbbing more brightly, changing colour swiftly. Bill-E repeats himself, but again too softly for the words to carry. "Speak up, damn it. I don't have time for—"

"I think the key might be *me*," Bill-E croaks.

And for the second time within the space of an hour the world appears to stop.

* * *

→Staring at Bill-E. Certain I heard him wrong. Praying that if I heard him right, I misunderstood. "What?" I wheeze.

"I think... it wasn't intentional... I'm not sure... but..."

He wasn't one of the dead, a voice inside my head murmurs. *In the future, when you looked into the hole, you didn't see Bill-E. Dervish was there, Reni, most of the other people you cared about. But not your brother.*

"Oh dear," Lord Loss snickers, floating out of reach, expression twisting with malicious joy. "The penny drops at long, painful last."

"No," I gasp, the syllable whipped from my lips by the wind. "It can't be."

"Grubbs?" Dervish asks, seeing something fearful in my face.

"Grubbs!" Beranabus roars. He's a long way off. Doesn't know what's going on. "Make yourself busy, boy. We have to find the killer. There isn't much time left."

"But you've already found him, haven't you, Grubitsch?" Lord Loss teases.

"You're lying," I snarl.

Lord Loss shakes his head. "I never lie."

Bill-E falls flat on his stomach and slides towards the crack. Dervish grabs him and holds tight. I crouch beside them, ignoring Lord Loss's laughter and the bite of the

467

demonic wind. I can hear the cries and chitterings of other demons, coming from a universe that isn't our own. I tune them out and focus on Bill-E. He's utterly terrified. I smile at him and even though the smile's weak, he finds comfort in it, and in spite of his terror, he speaks.

"It was Loch," he mutters. "I hated the way he teased me, always making me feel small and worthless. He was a bully. You should have stood up to him, Grubbs. You're my big brother."

"I didn't want to fight your battles for you." I sense what he's going to tell me and I feel like crying, but tears won't come. I can't let them.

"Always teasing," Bill-E says sourly. "Making fun of me. Any excuse to take a dig. That day when we discovered the cave... you were sick... me and Loch went climbing in search of Lord Sheftree's treasure..."

It seems a lifetime ago. Did we really engage in such playful, innocent games? Was there truly a time when buried treasure seemed important, when a school bully was our only concern? Or did we dream it all?

"I saw a chance to get my own back," Bill-E continues, voice breaking. "We were near the top of the waterfall. He slipped and grabbed hold of a rock. He was clinging on by his fingertips. I stuck my hand out. He snatched for it. But then I... I... *I whipped my hand away!*"

Bill-E and I lock expressions. We both understand what he means. Dervish doesn't. He never saw Loch doing that very same thing to Bill-E at school, making him look like a fool in front of everybody. He's staring at us as if we're mad.

"I whipped it away," Bill-E says numbly. "Put my thumb on my nose. Said, 'Touché, sucker!' Stuck my tongue out. I didn't mean for him to fall. I just wanted to have a laugh. But he lost his grip. Fell before I could help him. Hit his head on the ground. His skull cracked open. He…"

Bill-E stops. His face is white. He's trembling. The wind pulls strongly at him — more strongly than at me, Dervish or anybody else in the cave.

"No," I say calmly. "You didn't kill him. It wasn't a sacrifice. You aren't the key." But I know it's not true. Even as I deny it, I *know*.

"Grubbs," Dervish wheezes. "What are you saying? What does it mean? Are you mad? You think Billy caused this?"

"No," I lie. "Of course not." But putting the pieces together inside my head. The death — not an accident. Loch's blood vanishing into the floor of the cave. I'd forgotten about that, but I remember now, the bare floor, wondering where all the blood had gone. Now I know — sucked up by magic. Taken as sacrificial blood, even though it wasn't intended to be.

Bill-E guilty. By the strictest letter of the law he killed Loch Gossel and the magic in this cave is holding him accountable. I should have suspected sooner. Beranabus kept a tight watch on the cave when he arrived. He couldn't understand how Juni slipped past him and made a sacrifice. Never suspected Bill-E. Took me at my word when I told him we were alone, that Loch died accidentally.

The demons had it easy. No need to slaughter one of their mages, or even enter the cave and risk alerting Beranabus. A sweet deal. The sacrifice had already been made. All Lord Loss and Juni had to do was turn up a few weeks later, chant the correct spells and make sure the *killer* was present.

Except they didn't know who that was. They thought it was me, that the beast or my magic made me murder. That's why Juni sent me to the cave the night I turned, why she took my blood and smeared the edges of the crack with it. When that failed to produce a reaction, they realised Bill-E must be the guilty one. So Juni hurried over to his house, to haul him in. Nothing personal. It wasn't for revenge. Lord Loss wanted Bill-E solely for business. And he never meant to kill him. He had other plans for the younger Grady brother.

The wind increases. Dervish has to dig his heels in hard to hold Bill-E back. He looks at me, panicking. "Grubbs! What can we do?"

That tells me he knows too and understands what must be done. He just doesn't want to admit it, because that would place the burden on him. He doesn't want the responsibility. Well, too bad — I don't want it either.

"Bill-E's the key," I tell him.

"No," Dervish protests, but weakly, unconvincingly.

"Grubbs!" Beranabus yells. "I hear them coming. What the hell are—"

"Bill-E's the key!" I scream and Beranabus gawps at me. "He made the sacrifice. He didn't mean to. It was an accident. But—"

"You don't know what you're saying," Dervish hisses.

I look at him miserably. "Yes I do."

"What's wrong?" Bill-E mutters, glancing from one of us to the other. "This is good, isn't it? Now that we know, we can cast a spell to stop it, can't we? Or... should I have kept my big mouth... shut?"

"No," I smile. "You did the right thing. Everything will be OK now. We can stop the demons. You're a hero. You've shown us the way to win."

Bill-E beams proudly. Dervish is staring at me awfully, trembling, gripping his chubby nephew tight. I turn hopelessly to Beranabus, maintaining the smile until I'm facing away from Bill-E, so he can't see the anguish in my eyes. "Is there another way?" I cry.

"No," Beranabus says, no pity in his voice, just determination. He starts across the cave, fingers flexing. But he's taken no more than three or four steps when Lord Loss drops into his path and fires a bolt of magic at him, forcing him back.

"No, no, no, Beranabus," the demon master coos. "I won't allow you to spoil such a fascinating scene. This is tremendous sport. Uncle and brother speared on the horns of a most gruelling dilemma. What excruciating entertainment!"

Beranabus tries to respond with a magic bolt of his own, but Lord Loss hits him first. The magician collapses, defences crumbling, all washed up.

The wind is a storm now. Bill-E's feet are rising into the air. Dervish won't be able to hold him much longer. Another minute, maybe less, then Bill-E will be torn into the crack, his flesh will join with the rock and he'll become a living tunnel between this universe and the Demonata's.

"Dervish!" I scream.

"I can't."

"But the demons…"

"I know. But I can't." He pulls Bill-E to his chest and wraps both arms around him, fighting the storm, tears coursing down his cheeks.

"Grubbs," Bill-E grunts, jerking his head clear. "What's happening? What do we have to do?"

"Dervish," I say steadily, ignoring the question. "If you don't, we'll all die. Everybody else too. Including Bill-E. We can't save him."

"You do it then," Dervish challenges me.

"No. He's my brother."

"Do *what?*" Bill-E howls as Dervish and I glare at one another.

Then the fingers of Dervish's right hand creep up Bill-E's back. They stop at his neck and spread, gripping the flesh tight. He hasn't broken eye contact with me. I'm crying, unable to hold back the tears any longer. Bill-E doesn't know what's happening. He looks at me, forehead creased, trying to make sense of this. I hope he doesn't. Better if he never knows, if Dervish does it quickly and it comes as a short, sharp surprise.

His right hand in place, Dervish moves his left hand up. I don't know if he means to choke Bill-E or snap his neck. And I never find out. Because the fingers halt halfway up Bill-E's spine.

"I can't," Dervish says quietly, and this time the words are the confession of a broken man.

"I knew it," Lord Loss laughs. "Humans are so predictable. Even though all else must fall, you cannot bring yourself to harm your beloved nephew. You'll damn yourself, him, the whole world, all because of misplaced love." He sighs happily. "Moments such as these make the long, monotonous millennia worthwhile."

Dervish moans and clutches Bill-E close, planning to hug him as long as he can, to maybe get sucked into the crack with him, so the pair can perish together. Except Bill-E won't die. He'll become something terrible and twisted, inhuman and beastlike.

I think of Bill-E suffering, captive within the rock, alive down here indefinitely, wracked with guilt, a plaything for the Demonata when all the other humans have been slaughtered. They'll torment him. Guilt will eat him whole. Madness will be his only escape, but the demon masters will use magic to restore his senses, to torture him afresh. An eternity of misery, madness and sorrow.

I can't let that happen.

Entering this cave, I realised I couldn't kill Dervish or Bill-E if they were in league with Lord loss, not even to save the world. I still can't. But to save Bill-E from a fate genuinely worse than death… for my brother's sake, as opposed to the sake of billions of others who mean nothing to me…

"Bill-E." I lean forward, smiling. "Want to help me kick the crap out of these demon creeps?"

Bill-E returns the smile. "Now you're talking! What do we have to do?"

"Grubbs," Dervish groans.

"Shut up," I snap, then smile at Bill-E again. "Take my hands, little brother. Close your eyes. Focus on…" I gulp. "Your mum. Think of your mother."

"How can that help?" he asks doubtfully.

"It'll clear your head of bad thoughts and fear," I improvise. "I need your help to stop this. But I can only do it if you're calm. It won't be easy, but you have to try. Think of your mum and every good time you ever shared.

474

That will generate a positive energy which I can channel. I can use that power to stop the demons."

"Brilliant!" Bill-E gasps, face lighting up. He sticks his hands out, shuts his eyes and concentrates, lids twitching, eyeballs rolling behind them as he searches his memories for cherished moments. He trusts me completely.

Lord Loss has drifted closer. He could stop this, kill or delay me, but he's entranced. He's forgotten his mission of all-conquering mayhem. Living only for the bittersweet pain of the moment. Dervish has lowered his face to Bill-E's shoulder, diverting his gaze. I can't see Beranabus, Kernel, Spine or Artery. I don't care. There's only Bill-E and me in the world now. We're all that matters.

I let magic build within me, then reach out to take Bill-E's hands. I stop. A moment of doubt and disbelief. *I can't do this!* Then I look over Bill-E's head. I see claws coming out of the crack. A massive, shadowy cloud of a face, pure evil. Every shade of darkness imaginable. It fills the gap entirely. I'm not sure what it is – no ordinary demon, that's for sure – but I know it exists only to destroy, and will unless it's stopped.

"I love you, Bill-E," I whisper, my heart breaking. And take his hands.

Magic flows from me into my brother. Soft, warm, pleasing energy. His smile spreads slowly from the warmth of the magic or an especially fond memory.

Maybe both. The face of shadows within the crack splits with hatred. It hisses — the sound of a sea boiling dry. Tendrils of darkness dart towards me, a thousand writhing snakes, intent on tearing me away from my brother, separating us forever, using Bill-E for their own evil ends.

"Time to fly, little brother," I sob, and quickly push. The energy touches Bill-E's heart and stops it instantly. No pain. Bill-E's smile freezes in place. The tendrils of darkness blow apart. A furious, hateful bellow as the shadowy face disintegrates. Screams within the crack from scores of cheated demons. The wind stops dead and the howl is replaced by the noise of rocks grinding together as the crack closes. The screams rise sharply, then die away.

It's over.

I lean forward. Put my lips to my dead brother's forehead and kiss him, my tears dropping on to his still warm flesh. Then I hug him and Dervish tight, and pray for Lord Loss to kill me swiftly, before I lose my mind to wretched, soul-destroying grief.

EMPTY VESSEL

→Growls coming nearer, the patter of tiny feet and the snapping of sharp teeth — Artery. I squeeze my eyes shut, silently willing on the demon child.

"No," Lord Loss stops him. "To me."

I reluctantly open my eyes and look up. Lord Loss's face is glowing with sad satisfaction. Artery is making his way to his master's side, glowering. Behind them I spot Beranabus, looking old and frail, but triumphant. Kernel is still locked in combat with Spine.

Dervish puts his ear to Bill-E's chest. Listens a few seconds, then raises his face — his eyes are those of a haunted man. "He's—"

"Shut up," I sob before he finishes the sentence. Then, softer, "I had to. Not to stop the Demonata, but for his sake. He would have suffered worse than any of us. They'd have used him. He couldn't have died. He'd have been stuck down here, tormented by demons, knowing he'd handed our world to them. I couldn't let that happen. If there'd been any other way..."

Dervish finds my left hand and squeezes reassuringly. We both weep fresh tears.

"Delicious," Lord Loss murmurs, savouring our sorrow. "I wish this moment could last an eternity. It was worth having our plans thwarted. My brethren will break through another time. This world cannot stand against the Demonata much longer. There is a force in motion which cannot be repelled. That is why I pledged myself to the cause of destruction, much as I delight in humanity's enduring pain. Things might have gone badly for me if I'd resisted. But this is the best of both universes. You have a done me a great favour tonight. I am almost tempted to let you all live... but there are scores to be settled. A few more minutes to relish your agony, then I shall extract my long overdue retribution."

"Yeah, yeah," I mutter halfheartedly, brushing Bill-E's hair back from his eyes. I don't care about the demon master's threats. I don't care about anything except the fact that I've killed my brother and life can never hold any pleasure for me again. Better to die sooner rather than later.

But part of me cares. It stirs in response to Lord Loss's pledge. Energy slides down my arms to my hands. I call it back, but it doesn't respond. It's a strange type of energy, not like the magic I used to fight the demons (*or kill Bill-E*). This is more like the power I felt when I thought all was lost, when I distorted the laws of time and…

"We can go back!" I gasp, bolting upright. "We can travel into the past again and save Bill-E!"

Lord Loss hisses, not liking the sound of that. His six arms rise and he glides closer. Laughing hysterically, I bring my own hands up, aim at him and unleash the energy which has been buzzing at the tips of my fingers for the last few seconds. I expect a huge ball of magic to knock the demon master back, then shoot us into the past, where I can make things right. But the magic comes out in a stream, not a sudden burst. And it doesn't fly in Lord Loss's direction. Instead it flows into Bill-E.

I try redirecting the energy, but I can't control it. The magic seeps out of me and into my dead brother. Lord Loss is watching uncertainly, frowning, perhaps wondering if this is part of a time-travelling spell. Beranabus is dragging himself towards us, not willing to die without a fight. Dervish is still weeping over Bill-E, oblivious to all that's going on.

And then Bill-E moves.

At first I think it's just Dervish jolting the body, but then I see Bill-E's fingers shake and curl inwards. His lips part. He shudders. His eyes flicker open.

"What is this?" Lord Loss growls. "Regeneration? It cannot be. I felt his soul depart."

"Billy?" Dervish cries, unable to believe it, falling backwards as Bill-E sits up and looks around.

"Bill-E!" I yell with excitement, grasping his arms, squeezing hard, delight taking the place of dread. Somehow I've brought him back. I've used magic to restore his life. Everything's OK. We've beaten the demons *and* saved Bill-E. How's that for a night's work! "I'm so sorry for what I did, but there was no other way. But it doesn't matter now. You're alive. We whupped their ugly hides and…"

I stop. Bill-E's looking at me curiously, as if he doesn't know me. And his face is strange. His skin is bubbling, rippling, shimmering, a bit like Juni's did when her face changed. Then he opens his mouth and speaks, and I can't understand a word he's saying, because he's speaking the language of the girl in the rocks. They're *Bec's* words, not Bill-E's.

Lord Loss gasps. "You! No! I will not let you—"

Bill-E's right hand points at the demon master. He shouts something in Bec's language and Lord Loss screeches, "Artery! Attack!" The hell-child leaps and Bill-E's hand snaps round. A ball of energy surges from his fingers and Artery explodes into a thousand shredded pieces. He'll never recover from that. The hell-child has been finally, savagely, beautifully killed.

Bill-E stands. His flesh is still changing. The bones seem to be altering too. His eyes and ears. His whole

face. Softening. Narrowing. Becoming more...
feminine.

Lord Loss stares at the remains of his dead familiar.
Trembles with a mixture of rage and fear. "You should
not have come back, girl," he snarls. "This is wrong. You
are asking for trouble, and be assured — it will find
you."

Bill-E laughs in a way he never laughed before.
Catches sight of Spine and waves a hand at the demon —
it melts, screaming shrilly, a pool of gristle-speckled
liquid within seconds, leaving Kernel to grapple around
uncertainly and wonder what happened to his foe.

Bill-E faces Lord Loss again. His face is
unrecognisable. His body too — he's smaller and his
clothes are hanging loosely on his frame. I'd think I was
going mad, but Dervish and Beranabus see it too. Their
faces are contorted with bewilderment.

He speaks again and this time I hear the girl's accent
as clearly as I heard it when she spoke to me from within
the heart of the rock. Lord Loss trembles, then scowls.
"So be it. Perhaps you are right — this is not our time.
But it will come, be sure of that. And you won't have to
wait another millennium and a half for it!"

The demon master draws himself up straight, then
glares at me. "Enjoy your victory, Grubitsch. But
remember — the end of the world is coming and there
is nothing you or that apprentice priestess can do to stop

it. Remember this also — you killed your brother. He died by *your* hand. How do you think you will sleep tonight? And all the—"

Bill-E barks a short spell. The strips of flesh at the end of the demon master's legs are suddenly alive with rats. Lord Loss squeals, slaps several of them away, then darts to the stalagmite where the body of Juni Swan is impaled. Ripping her corpse free, he cradles her to his chest, snarls hatefully at all of us in the cave, then launches himself at the crack in the rock — now just a thin line a few centimetres wide. He hits it hard and uses magic to squeeze through. Even so, the walls of the crack scrape much of his and Juni's flesh away, and the rats on Lord Loss's legs are knocked loose. They fall on the floor, turn in puzzled circles for a second or two, then tear away, heading for the surface, back to wherever Bill-E summoned them from.

Except it wasn't Bill-E who made the rats materialise. It was Bec. And I realise, as I watch him looking down at himself, curiously touching his chest and face, that Bill-E's as dead as ever. The girl from the far distant past has taken control of his body and is transforming it into her own.

→A couple of hours later. Home. Sitting in the TV room with Dervish and Kernel. Kernel is asleep, moaning as he dreams, pain coming at last. Beranabus and Bill-E... no, Beranabus and *Bec* are in another room, having a lengthy heart-to-heart. The magician was ecstatic when he understood what was happening. He practically burst with excitement. Hugged her hard, weeping happily, kissing her face. And she stood there, hugging him back, crying too, repeating one word over and over — *"Bran!"*

Dervish and I haven't said anything to each other. He's staring off into space, his face a mess of dried tears. Every so often he shakes his head or makes a soft grunting noise. That's as close as we've come to communication.

I don't know what to feel. I've saved the world from the Demonata, but at what cost? To kill your own brother... Nobody should ever have to suffer such a cruel fate. I'm already wishing I could go back and change it. Maybe Bill-E would be better off alive and suffering than dead and gone. Did I have the right to make that choice for him? I don't know.

And maybe I *can* go back. I haven't discussed it with Beranabus yet, but I will, as soon as he's through talking with Bec. Find a way to travel back in time like we did before. Stop any of it from happening. Snatch Bill-E from Juni's clutches. Never open the entrance to the cave. I don't see why we can't. We did it once. I don't care what Beranabus said about waves and trains reaching the end of the line — there *must* be a way to do it again.

*   *   *

→Eventually, as the sun rises on a normal day, lighting up a world unaware of how close it came to toppling into an abyss of demonic damnation, Beranabus and Bec return. There's almost nothing of Bill-E left. The girl has taken over completely, remoulding his body in her own image. Even his hair has turned a dark red colour. One or two small traces of my brother remain – she walks like he did, and her left eyelid hangs a fraction lower than her right – but I'm sure those traits will vanish too.

"Sorry we were such an age," Beranabus says, sitting opposite Dervish. "Loads to talk about. We've cut it short as it is, only covered the more important issues."

Bec stares at the couch, then sits on the floor close to the magician's legs. She looks at me with worried eyes. "I hope you do not mind that I took this body."

I blink. "You can speak our language now?"

"A spell," she replies. "Beranabus taught me. I'm speaking in my own tongue, but it allows me to be understood by others." She sighs. "If I could have worked such a spell when we first made contact, things would have been much simpler."

"I'd normally say there was no point worrying about the past…" I begin, but Dervish cuts me off.

"Who are you?" he shouts. "What the hell have you done with Billy?"

"Billy's dead," Beranabus says. "This is Bec, an old friend of mine."

"No!" Dervish yells, lurching to his feet. "That's Billy's body. She stole it. I saw her. I want it back." His hands bunch into fists.

"I apologise, but I cannot give it back," Bec says quietly.

"Even if she could, what would be the point?" Beranabus chips in, roughly but typically. "The boy's dead. Bec took his lifeless flesh and filled it with her spirit. If she vacated it again, you'd only have a dead child on your hands."

"I want him back," Dervish snarls, eyes wild.

"I understand," Bec says solemnly. "You wish to bury him."

"No!" Dervish howls. "I want to hold him and tell him how much I love him. I want to…" He breaks down and slumps sideways, sobbing into the cushions. I long to go to my uncle, hold him, help him. But there are too many questions which must be answered. As cruel as it sounds, Dervish will have to wait.

"How did you do it?" I ask quietly.

"Which part?" Bec replies.

"The last bit — taking over Bill-E's body."

She shrugs. "I could see everything that was happening. I came back inside you — when we worked together to bend time, I joined with your flesh and mind. I could have stayed there within you, hidden away, and I meant to. But when I saw what Lord Loss was going to do, and realised you wouldn't defend yourself, I had to act. I wasn't sure if I could use the dead boy's flesh. Even if I could, I only planned to inhabit it temporarily — I thought I could possess it, drive Lord Loss away, then leave it again.

"But, to my shock, the body accepted me. More than that — I was able to transform it and recreate my own form. I needn't have – I could have kept your brother's shape – but I wouldn't have been comfortable that way and I don't think you would have been either."

"So this is *your* body now?" I ask. "You're alive after all that time in the cave? Free to grow and live like any other person?"

The girl shrugs again and glances at Beranabus.

"We don't know," the magician says softly, touching Bec's short red hair. "This body might age and develop naturally — or it might not. We'll have to wait and see. Only time will tell."

"Speaking of time…" I lean forward anxiously. This was what I wanted to ask about first, but it wouldn't have been polite to barge straight in with it. "How did you bring us back from the future?"

Bec shakes her head softly. "I didn't. *We* did it — Kernel, you and I."

"But you started it. You knew the spells. You were in control."

Again she shakes her head. "It was the Kah-Gash. Although we are parts of the weapon, it has a mind of its own. When we joined, our magic became the magic of the Kah-Gash. It told us how to unite minds and forces. It used us. Like you, I didn't know what it was attempting to do. The time travel came as much of a surprise to me as it did to you."

Bec looks around, staring at the chairs, the windows, the TV. This is all new to her. Unimaginable. She comes from a time when the world was much simpler. She's itching to explore, ask questions, make sense of all the weird shapes and objects. But I can't let this pass.

"Do you remember the spells?" I press. "Could we do it again?"

She thinks a moment and frowns. "It's strange. Normally I only have to hear something once — I have a perfect memory and never forget anything. But in this instance I have only the vaguest recollection of the spells. I couldn't repeat them."

"You could try," I insist.

She nods. "If you prompt me, I will do my best. But I cannot start without your help. You would have to show me the way, like you did before."

"Grubbs," Beranabus says, "you can't go back again."

"Why not?" I shout. Dervish looks up, startled by the ferocity of my tone. "Why the hell can't I?"

"The Kah-Gash reversed time because the world faced annihilation and there was no other way," Beranabus says calmly. "But it was a massive, perilous undertaking. If it had gone awry, the result would have been chaos, timelessness, maybe the destruction of both universes. You can't take such a risk again, just for the sake of one boy."

"That *one boy* means more to me than all the others in the world put together," I snarl.

"Maybe," Beranabus replies, "but he means nothing to the Kah-Gash. If he did, you wouldn't be sitting here arguing — you'd be spitting out spells, trying to find the energy to take you back. *You* set events in motion last time. You were the first to act. If you want to do it again, go ahead."

"I don't know how!" I howl.

"Ask the Kah-Gash," Bec says. "It spoke to us before and directed us. It's like a person. You're able to talk to it. Ask and see how it responds."

"I don't think—" Beranabus begins.

"Let him," Bec insists. "If he feels he must do this, and if he can, it's not our place to stand in his way."

I stare at her uncertainly, then close my eyes and focus. I search for the magic and quickly find it, an energy and consciousness. There are no barriers between us now. I'll never have trouble finding it again. It's as much a part of me as the oxygen in my lungs.

I tell the magic – the Kah-Gash – what I want. I beg it for help. But there's no answer. I guessed there wouldn't be. Now that we're one, I've begun to understand that other, mysterious part of myself. Beranabus is right. It won't let me smash the structures of time just to save Bill-E.

"Even if you could phrase the spells," Beranabus says as I open my eyes, tears flooding down my cheeks, "there isn't a source to track back to. In this time, the tunnel hasn't been opened. There's no river of energy to ride back on."

"We could find another place where demons broke through," I moan.

"No," Beranabus says. "You'd need an open tunnel, but there aren't any."

"Maybe it doesn't have to be open," I whisper — one final, desperate attempt. "We could try a tunnel that's been closed. The energy might be trapped there, held in place, like in a battery or power cell."

"Maybe," Beranabus agrees. "But even if the energy was present, and you could unlock it, you'd have to follow the unleashed river of power back to its origin. I doubt it's possible to set limits, to travel back just a day, a week or a month."

"So what?" I sob. "We'll ride it back to the start and wait. I don't care."

Beranabus smiles softly. "The last tunnel that was anything near to this in size was closed more than three hundred years ago."

"Three…" I mutter, feeling the last sliver of hope die within me.

"Let it go, Grubbs," Beranabus says. "Your brother's dead and you can't bring him back. There's no way around it. You'll drive yourself mad if you can't accept that."

"Maybe that wouldn't be so bad," I sigh, then sit there, crying, saying my silent farewells to poor, unfortunate Bill-E Spleen — R.I.-bloody-P.

ONE SMALL STEP FOR MAN

→Dervish's bedroom. He's sitting on the end of his bed, expression blank. He hasn't washed the dirt and blood from his face and hands yet. I haven't either. Too weary for such mundane tasks. Life will go on, I'm sure — it always does. But right now we're a pair of zombies, capable only of the simplest movements.

"See you later," I mumble, turning to go to my own room.

"Wait," Dervish says. "I don't want to be alone, not now. Stay. Please?"

With a weary nod, I start to pull at the leaves of my magical suit. It's hanging off me in shreds and will be simple to remove. But after picking at a few leaves, I lose interest and crawl onto the bed beside Dervish. I put my arms around him and we hold each other tight. He often held me like this when I first came to live with him, whenever I awoke from a particularly brutal nightmare. But this time the nightmare is reality and there's little comfort to be found in the embrace.

"You had to do it," Dervish whispers.

I break into fresh tears. "He was my brother," I moan. "What would Dad have said?"

"The same thing I'm saying," Dervish croaks. "You did what had to be done. It should have been me. I was his guardian — yours too. The responsibility was mine. But I couldn't find the strength. I failed. If you hadn't been so brave, we'd have all died and Billy would have suffered terribly. You did what was best. You should feel proud, not wretched."

I laugh bitterly. "*Proud!* Yeah, sure."

Dervish sighs. "Wrong word. You should feel... I don't know... maybe there isn't a word for it. But you did the right thing. That has to be enough. It has to keep you going. Because if you let this destroy you – if you let the madness take you – I'll lose two nephews, not one."

"But it's so tempting," I mumble. "I want out, Dervish. I know what it's like to be mad. It's easier than this. Anything's easier than *this*."

Dervish is silent a minute. Then he says, "I'll make you a deal. If you fight the temptation... stay sane, no matter how painful it is... so will I."

"You feel it too?" I ask, surprised by his admission.

He nods. By the way he trembles, I know he's not just saying it. "Like you said, anything would be easier than this. But we have each other. If you fight, so will I. I'll stay sane for you if you stay sane for me. Agreed?"

I hug him tighter, lov

before. "Agreed."

Dervish blinks at the ceiling. "I

sad about Juni too. I know she was evi

what she did, but I loved her. I really thou

going to be together for the rest of our lives. Si

die, and I'm glad I killed her, but…"

"I know what you mean. I miss her too. I was

surprised Lord Loss took her body. I guess he plans to

bury or cremate her."

Dervish snorts. "Eat her, more probably!"

We laugh softly, painfully — the first step back

towards something that might one day pass for a normal

life. And then, holding one another, we close our eyes,

listen to the sounds of the mansion and the world

outside, and slowly drift off into a nightmare-laced but

none the less welcome sleep.

→It's dark when I wake. Dervish is snoring lightly. I lie

still for a few minutes, enjoying the nearness of my

uncle, remembering Bill-E and Loch, my lost brother

and friend, trying not to cry, just about managing to

hold back the tears.

I ease myself off the bed, careful not to disturb

Dervish. My suit of leaves has disintegrated entirely. I

brush the last of the flaky patches off, then pad to my

bedroom, shower and kit myself out in more regular

hile I dress,

f, the plane,

back through

bit much for a

ny friends have

r bad breath to

er to spread the

have been stuck

nk with being a

betrayed by Juni, and Robbie recru... ...us? And let's not leave the girls out. Reni did her bit, losing Loch, but Mary could easily have had to kill one of her brothers, and Shannon could have done the whole trip through time stuff.

I chuckle (nice to see I still can). I'm being ridiculous, but there's a nugget of truth there. It's been a heavy burden for a single person to bear, especially one as young, inexperienced and... hell, let's say it... *cowardly* as me. It isn't fair.

But the universe *isn't* fair. Things don't work out neatly, pain, hardship and challenges divided equally among those best equipped to deal with them. Sometimes individuals have to be Atlases and carry the weight of the world alone. It shouldn't happen that way, but it does.

ONE SMALL STEP FOR MAN

g him more than I ever did

sounds crazy, but I'm

and I hate her for

ght we were

he had to

At least I have the crumb of comfort of not having fallen. I stumbled and wished all the time that I could bail out. But I kept going. I did what I had to. I came through. It would have been sweet to do it unscathed, Bill-E and Loch alive and well. But in the grand scheme of things, I don't have too much to complain about. That's how Beranabus would see it. And he's right. But that doesn't make me feel any better. The devastation of having killed Bill-E is all-consuming. I don't think any amount of reasoning will ever ease that pain.

Dressed, I go looking for Beranabus, Kernel and Bec. Trying to focus on their needs, since it helps me not brood about Bill-E. Beranabus was badly wounded in the fight and might need help. Kernel will be in a lot of pain. He said he'd have to go to a hospital. I can arrange that. And Bec…

I'm not sure what I can do for a girl who's been dead for sixteen hundred years, only to find herself slap-bang in the middle of the modern world. Guide her round the house for a start, I guess. Teach her how to open and close doors and windows, explain what TVs, computers and CD players are. No… they can come later. First teach her how to run a bath and use the shower. Give her some clothes to keep her ticking over until she can go shopping in the Vale. Explain where everything is in the kitchen, what a fridge is, how to open a tin, that water comes from a tap and not a well.

I'm padding down the stairs when I hear her. No... not hear, exactly. I sense her. In the hall of portraits. Changing direction, I go to check that she's OK. I find her studying the faces of dead Gradys and our various relations, slowly moving from one painting or photo to the next, eyes steady, head cocked slightly to one side.

"These are not drawings," she says without looking around, sensing my presence the same way I sensed hers.

"They're photographs."

"Are they magic? Are people alive within them, their souls trapped like mine was in the cave?"

"No. It's just their image. We use machines to take them."

"Machines?"

"Special tools."

She turns. "I've seen nothing of this new world. I was limited to the cave. I could peer into the universe of the Demonata, but this world was a blank. I don't know what has changed and what hasn't."

"Most of it's different to what you knew. Probably everything. It'll take a while to get used to, but you'll be OK. Look at it like an adventure — you'll be exploring a brand new planet."

"Yes. I'm excited. Scared but excited." She sighs and looks at the photos again. "Your family?"

"Some of them." I move up beside her. "They all caught the disease, or died trying to help others who were infected. You know that some of us change into wolf-like beasts, don't you?"

"I saw them in my own time," she answers. "I didn't think the curse would last this long. But I'm not surprised. The blood of the Demonata is strong." She looks at me shyly. "*We* are family. Separated by many generations, but family nevertheless."

"I know."

"The evil priestess – Juni Swan, Nadia Moore, whatever you want to call her – was one like us. Bran told me she could see into the future. Perhaps our demonic heritage was the source of her strange power."

I grunt. I don't want to talk about Juni right now.

"The boy… Bill-E… he was family too."

"Yes," I mutter. "My brother."

"I'm sorry…" she starts to say.

"Don't worry about it," I interrupt. "It wasn't your fault. Bill-E wouldn't mind. He was always keen on recycling."

"'Recycling'?" Bec frowns.

"I'll explain later. Where are Beranabus and Kernel?"

"Outside. They…" She casts a look at me and I instantly know what they're doing, what they want of me.

"Already?" I ask stiffly. "They can't wait a while?"

"No." She looks back at the faces. "I'm not going. Bran told me to stay. He said I would be company for Dervish, that he could look after me and I could look after him. He said we would be good for one another."

"*I'll* be looking after Dervish," I snap.

Bec shrugs. "I'm only repeating what Bran said. He also said Dervish could teach me about the new world, while he could teach you more about magic. In his opinion that arrangement will work best for everyone."

"We'll see about that," I huff, storming off. I pause before turning the corner and glance back at her. "If for some reason I don't return... if anything happens to me... you *will* take care of Dervish, won't you?"

"I've comforted people who lost loved ones before. There were many in my rath — my village. I will do my best. I promise."

I nod thankfully, then hurry downstairs to sort out things with Beranabus and put him straight on a couple of issues.

→The magician and Kernel are in front of the house, squatting in the middle of the road, draped in clothes which they're taken from our wardrobes. They've healed the worst of their wounds, though they're covered in cuts and bruises and Kernel's as blind as he was before. A familiar monolith hangs in the air between them.

"Leaving so soon?" I ask Beranabus tightly.

"Work to be done," he says briskly. "You've seen Bec?"

"Yes. She's under the impression that I'm leaving. Said she'd been charged with the task of looking after Dervish."

"Bec's staying?" Kernel asks, surprised.

"I considered bringing her with us," Beranabus says. "We can't test the Kah-Gash properly without her. I've waited so long to find the different pieces. It might be madness to leave her behind. But the weapon unnerves me. It gave us the power to come back in time and stop the Demonata — but before that it led Grubbs to the cave and initiated this whole train of events."

"I don't recall it leading me," I frown.

"The night you went to the cave when you were turning into a werewolf," Beranabus reminds me. "You cleared most of the entrance. Bec didn't summon you and Lord Loss wasn't involved at that stage. It can only have been the work of the Kah-Gash. It wanted you to reopen the cave — which makes me assume it also wanted to reopen the tunnel."

"You're saying we can't trust it?" Kernel barks. "After all this time and effort, the things we've sacrificed, the risks we've taken… it was all in pursuit of a weapon we don't dare use?"

"We'll use it eventually," Beranabus says. "We'll have to. But I want to study the pair of you first and try to

499

form a better idea of what we'll be dealing with when we next unleash its power. I think it's better not to keep the three of you together until we're sure we can control the Kah-Gash."

"Then why not leave me behind and take Bec?" I ask.

Beranabus sighs. "She's suffered greatly and I care about her deeply. I was scatterbrained as a child — I bet you find that hard to believe! Bec helped me make a vital breakthrough. She set me on track and rooted me in reality. I owe her more than I can ever repay. She deserves to live again, to be human. I'd leave her here forever if I could. That's impossible, but since it makes sense to keep one of you out of the way of the others for a while, I'll gladly give her this free time. As the gods surely know, she's earned it."

"That's the most human thing I've ever heard you say," Kernel murmurs. Then he frowns. "If you knew her, that means you were alive sixteen hundred years ago. I didn't think humans could survive that long."

"They can't," Beranabus grunts. He wipes dried blood from his cheeks, but it's yellow, not red. "You saw me changing in the cave, didn't you?" he asks me.

"I saw... something," I answer cagily.

"It surfaces occasionally. Sometimes I need to draw on its powers. It's a dangerous game, involving it so intimately. I run the risk of succumbing to it and losing control. But there are times when we must gamble." He scowls, then says quickly, bluntly, "I'm half-Demonata. My father was a demon. That's where my magic comes from. It's how I've lived so long."

"You never told me," Kernel whispers.

"It's not something I'm proud of," Beranabus says acidly. "My mother fell foul of the beast. She never meant for this to happen. It was a horrible twist of fate — or the universe's way of protecting itself from the Demonata."

"Could you have been one of *them?*" Kernel asks. "You've passed for human all this time. Could you have lived as a demon if you'd wished?"

"Aye. The possibility of becoming a fully fledged demon was always there. It still is. My demon half constantly tempts me, urges me to give myself over to evil, join the Demonata and help them conquer this world. I fight it daily. I've held it in check — so far."

"Which one of them is your father?" I ask. "Lord Loss?"

"Don't be ridiculous," he snorts. "My father was a lesser demon. I tracked him down many centuries ago. I killed the beast and relieved him of his head. Used the skull as a bedpan for a time." He jerks his thumb at the monolith. "Now that we've had the sordid family history, can we move on?"

"I'm not going," I tell him. "I'm staying here with Dervish and Bec."

Beranabus shrugs. "If that's what you want."

"Don't say it like that. I've done my bit. I stopped the demons breaking through. I killed my brother and saved the world. What more do you want from me?" I scream.

Beranabus doesn't blink. "It's not what I want — it's what the universe wants. And what I've learnt from my long years is the universe only ever wants *more*. It doesn't care about sacrifice and best efforts. It needs us to keep fighting. As far as the universe is concerned, there's no rest for either the good or the wicked. I doubt it even understands the concept."

"Well, the universe can go stick its head where the sun don't shine!" I yell. "I'm through. I did what I had to and now I want out, like Bec."

"It's not within my power to let you go or keep you," Beranabus says softly. "Your conscience will guide you. There's no point shrieking at me. It's yourself you should be angry with. If you were selfish, didn't care about the world, or were a tenth of the coward you believe you are, you'd go back inside, return to school, live out a long, happy, simple, human life. Which you're fully entitled to."

He takes a step closer, shaking his head. "But you can't, can you? You saw the shadow monster in the cave, the one that almost broke through — their leader."

"It was huge," I whisper. "Powerful. Evil."

"All demons are evil," Beranabus says. "This was different. I'm not sure how exactly, but I intend to find out. I'll track it down, even if I have to visit a thousand worlds and kill a million demons. Normally Kernel could lead me to it – he's a marvel at finding rogue monsters – but I'm not sure he can pull his weight any more."

"I might not be able to pull my weight," Kernel growls, "but I can punch your lights out, old man." He bares his teeth. "Or should I say old *demon*."

Beranabus laughs shortly. "Whether or not Kernel can work his magic, I'll find and kill that beast before it discovers another way to open a tunnel between universes. And you'll help me. I know it, Kernel knows it — and *you* know it. That's why you're angry. You don't have a choice because your conscience is directing you. Even after all that's happened – the grief you're going through, the guilt, the fear – you have to do this. You couldn't live with yourself if you didn't."

"Can't we wait?" I cry. "Leave it a few days at least, so I can mourn Bill-E and be with Dervish?"

"The Demonata won't wait," Beranabus says, then smiles faintly. "It's hard for all of us. Kernel needs medical aid. We can build a new pair of eyes for him in the universe of magic, but they'll only work in that demonic realm. When he returns to this world, the eyes will soon dissolve. The pain will be awful and will worsen every time he comes back. He can no longer think of Earth as home.

"I want to sit down with Bec, tell her all that's happened in the last thousand and a half years, discuss old times, get to know her again, guide her through the ways of this new and frightening world. Retire and enjoy a few years of peace in her company before my exhausted old spirit passes on.

"But Kernel's ruined eyes don't matter a damn. My pitiful wishes matter even less. We're pawns of the universe. We go where we're needed, do what we must. All else takes second place to that."

"I know," I sigh. "I understand. But Dervish... Bill-E..."

"Look at it this way," Kernel says softly. "You can mourn your brother here and wait for the world to end — or you can mourn him in the Demonata's universe while you kick seven shades of demon arse all the way to hell." He pushes himself up and walks to the monolith, wincing from the pain, hands outstretched. He touches the dark face of the window, pauses, lifts his head as though trying to see the sky one last time, even without his eyes and through the layers of bandages. Then, with a soft groan, he steps forward and vanishes.

"I want to say goodbye to Dervish," I mutter.

"No," Beranabus replies, "you don't. That would mean more pain. Better to slip away while he's asleep. He won't like it, but he'll accept it."

"How's he going to explain Bill-E's disappearance to the police, his teachers, everyone who knew him?"

"He'll cook up a good story. He was always adept at making fiction fit the facts." Beranabus extends a hand towards me.

"What about the cave?" I ask, stalling for time. "We have to block the entrance again or the Demonata might—"

"I've already taken care of that," Beranabus says curtly, losing patience. "I've cast spells of warning again, and Dervish will ensure the entrance is filled in as swiftly as possible."

"Your spells didn't work last time," I remind him.

"Because of the Kah-Gash," he snaps. "That has the power to override any spell of mine or any other's. But with you and Kernel by my side, I won't have to worry about that happening again. If demons make another move on the cave, I'll know. Now, are you coming or not? And before you answer, don't forget the Lambs are still after you."

I sneer. "They frightened me once — not any longer."

"Aye. Because you have a more powerful enemy to face now."

I nod slowly, reluctantly, then take the ancient magician's hand. "I'm scared," I whisper. "More scared than I've ever been, and that's saying a lot."

"I know," he replies quietly. "You probably always will be. If it's any comfort, I'm scared too, even after all these centuries."

"How do you deal with the fear?" I ask.

He shrugs. "I fight."

"Is that enough?"

"It has to be."

And on that dubious, dark note, we walk to the monolith, the magician and his assistant, saviours of the world, slaves of the universe. We lay our hands on the smooth black slab. There's a surge of magic. Our heads tilt back like Kernel's did, for one final look at a beautiful, twinkling, star-studded sky. I think of Dervish, Bill-E, all I have to leave behind. The battles to come, the loneliness and pain. I want to run away from it all and hide. But I can't. No — I *won't*.

Beranabus tugs gently. I take a breath, hold it, then willingly step forward with him to face my destiny in the universe of all things foul and demonic.

Look out for

THE DEMONATA

Volumes 7 and 8

Crawling out of the darkness
August 2011